"I will grind you down," Palmer Reid said.

"You still have Wilmette and the others," Paul Bannerman told him. "Count your blessings."

Paul listened as Reid vented his rage with sputtered threats and dire predictions. At last he interrupted, suggesting that he be allowed to summarize the situation. Paul then patiently listed all the legal and extralegal measures that were available to Reid, explained why each would fail, and how he, Bannerman, would respond even to the failures. Most of his responses, he pointed out, would necessarily involve killing.

"On the other hand, if you give me control over The Greenfield Foundation, you can still pretend that I answer to you. You can say I'm running a new experiment on your behalf."

"What sort of experiment."

"We're all going to stay here."

"For how long?"

"We'll see. If they can function well here, and they're content to stay, there doesn't seem to be much point in uprooting them after a year or so."

Reid was silent for a long moment. Bannerman could almost hear the workings of his mind.

"You intend to establish them permanently?" Reid asked. "In Westport?"

"That's what I said, Palmer."

"How many?"

"I'm afraid that's a secret."

"Paul..." Another long silence. "On the remotest chance that you're serious about this, and that you have no ulterior motive, can you possibly believe that Westport can absorb that wolf pack of yours without getting eaten?"

THE BANNERMAN SOLUTION

THE
BANNERMAN
SOLUTION

John R. Maxim

BANTAM BOOKS
NEW YORK · TORONTO · LONDON · SYDNEY · AUCKLAND

This novel is a work of fiction. Names, characters, places and incidents are either the product of the author's imagination or are used fictitiously. Any resemblance to actual persons, living or dead, events or locales is entire coincidental.

THE BANNERMAN SOLUTION
A Bantam Book / June 1989

ISBN 0-553-27954-8

Published simultaneously in the United States and Canada

Bantam Books are published by Bantam Books, a division of Bantam Doubleday Dell Publishing Group, Inc. Its trademark, consisting of the words "Bantam Books" and the portrayal of a rooster, is Registered in U.S. Patent and Trademark Office and in other countries. Marca Registrada. Bantam Books, 666 Fifth Avenue, New York, New York 10103.

PRINTED IN THE UNITED STATES OF AMERICA

O   0 9 8 7 6 5 4 3

For Calhoun Sterling
. . . and for Billy

CHAPTER 1

Lesko hated four o'clock in the morning.

Lying in bed. Thinking too much. Having those crazy dreams. He didn't mind the regular kind of dreams. He never remembered them anyway. And nightmares never bothered him because with a nightmare, he always figured, you're more or less along for the ride. You're also fully asleep. What he hated were the dreams where you lie there, not quite awake and not quite asleep. You're getting all upset about something, usually something dumb, and you know it probably isn't real but you can't quite wake up enough to shake it off.

He heard a police psychiatrist say something once. About four in the morning. About the thoughts and dreams that come then. He said that four o'clock in the morning is when most people find out what it's like to be insane.

Lesko could believe it.

Up until the time David Katz got killed, most of Lesko's four-in-the-morning dreams were just plain stupid. There was one time he stewed for what must have been an hour over a tree that fell on his car during a hurricane. It would take forever to cut it up because all he had was this little hacksaw out in his kitchen drawer. The thing was, there wasn't any tree and there wasn't any hurricane. He didn't even own a car.

Go figure.

Another time he laid there convinced that his ex-wife had shown up asking to move back in with him. But

1

she didn't want to be a bother so, she said, she'd just sleep on the floor of his hall closet. All he could think of was how she'd crush his shoes if she did that, but he didn't want to hurt her feelings by saying so.

Lying fully awake at four in the morning wasn't any bargain, either. Not that Lesko was what you'd call a worrier. And nothing much scared him anymore. Not after twenty-six years as a street cop. He always figured: Something bothers you, you fix it fast and forget it. But that doesn't work at four in the morning. You lie there, feeling lonely, feeling sad, remembering old hurts. Sometimes you feel afraid. You don't know why or of what.

If anything was going to scare him at that hour, you'd think it would be the ghosts. There were two or three of them over the years. People he knew. At four in the morning you can find yourself talking to dead people and forgetting they're dead. He'd had dreams like that about his father a few times. They'd have conversations. Nothing weird. Ordinary stuff. His father would be sitting in that chair talking about the Knicks or the Yankees. One time, his father was up by the ceiling looking for a short in the light fixture and he asked Lesko to pass him the pliers. Lesko thrashed all over his bed looking for them until he woke himself up. He felt like crying. Like a kid. But he didn't.

The funny thing was, come to think of it, his father died getting shot in the head, just like Katz. But that's where the resemblance ended. He didn't mind the dreams where his father came. Katz was another matter.

Katz started coming the day after he died. Or Lesko started dreaming he did. Katz, who didn't have hardly any face left the last time Lesko saw him in daylight, comes strolling in the next morning, like nothing happened, to pick him up for roll call. He's carrying, like always, a deli bag with either two bagels or two Danish, slamming kitchen cupboards, bitching that he can't ever find a clean cup in this place, you're such a slob, and come on, get your ass out of bed. That happened five mornings straight, in the beginning. At first, Lesko would wake himself up yelling that he was going to take Katz's face off all over again, but by the fifth time Lesko wouldn't even lift his head when Katz walked in. Not that Lesko believed in ghosts, but Katz did stop coming, or Lesko did stop dreaming about him, as soon as Lesko squared things for him. But now lately Katz was starting in again.

Lesko had pretty much learned to ignore him. But it seemed that the longer Katz was dead, the better he learned to be aggravating. This time, this morning, he walks in, already chewing on a buttered bagel, and says the same stuff about let's get down to roll call and this place stinks. Except this time he also walks over to the chair where Lesko tossed his clothes the night before. He picks up the jacket or the pants and holds them out with two fingers and he says it's not bad enough your clothes are ugly but they smell like a zookeeper's shoe. He says if Lesko is going to keep buying his clothes at Goodwill Industries he should at least pick out something from after the Second World War.

This annoyed Lesko because although it was true he got sloppy and careless for a while, he was dressing much better now because his daughter started making him go shopping with her. And not at Bond's, either. At Barney's. It also annoyed him that Katz thought he knew so much about fashion because what Katz dressed like was a Hollywood pimp. Hollywood, as it happened, was where Katz got his ideas about clothes in the first place when they flew out there a few years back to pick up a fugitive. All of a sudden Katz starts wearing these flashy sport jackets, turtleneck shirts, gold chains, loafers with tassels, a tan from a tanning machine, and that damned gold watch of his. Lesko thought he looked stupid. Even if Lesko wasn't what you'd call real up-to-date on men's fashions, there were a couple of things he knew. One was you don't look good in turtlenecks if you have a big double chin because from the front you look like you have two sets of lips and from the side you look like a fucking pelican. Another was you don't wear gold chains outside a turtleneck, he didn't think. The third was if you're a cop you don't show off gold chains at all and you sure as hell don't wear a two thousand dollar Rolex watch unless you can goddamned well prove you hit the lottery. *"Where'd you get the money?"* Lesko heard himself asking. His face was buried in his pillow but he could see David Katz as clearly as if he was sitting up looking at him. He wasn't sure if he was dreaming or remembering.

"I hit this trifecta," Katz said cheerfully as if for the first time. *"I put down five bucks and I walk away with almost three large."*

"Yeah? What track? Tell me the horses."

"It wasn't a track. I went to jai-alai, up in Connecticut."

"Don't bullshit me, David," Lesko warned.

"Come on, Ray. Lighten up. I got witnesses."

Lesko believed him about the witnesses. Smart cops always had witnesses. They'd take some friends to jai-alai or the track, place some bets, then after the race they look up at the parimutuel board, get this shit-eating grin and say they'll be back in five minutes. Then they go back where the cashiers are, reach into their pockets, count out an amount that's the same as the parimutuel payoff on the board, then go back and flash the money. Where'd he get the money? The track. Honest. We all saw him hit.

Lesko must have had that conversation with Katz at least twice while he was alive and a half dozen more times after he was dead. Lesko wanted to know not only about the watch but about Katz's two new jackets, one ultrasuede, and the other cashmere, which must have cost eight hundred bucks between them.

"If you're dirty, David, I'm going to kick the shit out of you. You know that, don't you?"

But Katz maintains his look of wounded innocence. Come on, Lesko, he says. The watch came from the jai-alai hit and the jackets came from overtime. Yeah, overtime. What's wrong with that? Harriet gets the regular paycheck to pay the bills. Overtime is found money, right? It's to enjoy. I buy some nice clothes, Harriet gets a new dress, maybe we go down to Florida once a year, maybe we take a little cruise down to Bermuda. Hey, Lesko. You and Donna never did that? With what you save on clothes you could have gone to Europe. Would I have started giving you shit about being dirty? Give me a break.

"Then how come you're dead, you son of a bitch?"

This was where the dream always changed.

Katz would just stand there. His face would go stupid.

"I asked you a question, you asshole. You're so clean, tell me how come you got your face shot off?"

Lesko could see his confusion without even looking at him. Katz would stare for a long moment at his hands, and he'd touch his arms, and then he'd bring both hands to his face as if to satisfy himself that his face was still there.

"I'm . . . I'm not dead." His voice became small. Childlike.

"Get outta here, David."

"No, wait. Wait."

"Get outta here. Get lost."

"Wait. Just let me think."

"You want to think about something?" Lesko was more awake than asleep now. He could feel his legs moving closer to the edge of the bed and his hand gripping the blanket. *"How about that you're a fucking thief? How about that you're a dead fucking thief? How about that I'm not a cop anymore because of you?"*

"Listen . . ." Katz seemed to remember. *"We can fix this,"* he said miserably. *"It's not so bad we can't fix it."*

Lesko's feet were on the floor, the bedcovers thrown back. He spun to the place where David Katz had been standing and lunged toward that spot before he could blink away the sleep.

He stopped. The room was dark and empty. The only light was a faint glow from a distant street lamp and the cold blue wink of his digital alarm clock. The clock read 4:06. He stood in the darkness for a minute or two until he could no longer hear the sound of his own breathing.

Lesko stepped back toward the clock. On the floor he found the bathrobe he'd dropped there when he went to bed. He put it on. Then for another long moment he stared into the darkness of his room.

"I already fixed it, David." he said finally. "I fixed it good."

Susan, his daughter, had said something to him once. It was from a book she read. He was talking to her, he wasn't sure how it came up, about the crazy things that go on in your head in the middle of the night. She probably brought it up. She saw he looked tired.

Susan knew right away what he was talking about. She said it's the pre-dawn gremlins. Everybody gets them. It's normal.

He'd used the tree blowing down on his car as an example. Susan thought about that for a while. She said maybe it meant something. Maybe the hurricane was his whole life. All the violence of it. And maybe the tree on his car was the way it left him trapped. Pinned down. And maybe the hacksaw meant frustration because it was so hard for him to dig out and start over and yet it was possible to try. Even a hacksaw was a start.

Lesko knew that Susan knew that the tree dream might mean nothing of the sort. Maybe nothing at all. Anyway, she wasn't the type to sit around psyching out other people's dreams. Lesko knew that she was just using the dream as an excuse to say what she wanted to say anyway. That his life wasn't over. That he didn't have to be lonely. That he could get his butt out of that dumb little apartment in Queens and start living again. She said he just wasn't the type to sit around between pension checks. That wasn't quite fair, of course. For the past year, he'd been a special security consultant to the Beckwith Hotels chain. He'd set up a system, trained a lot of people, but now he was losing interest. It wasn't enough.

He didn't mention the dream about her mother moving back. Not that it was a sore subject but enough was enough. It would only get Susan asking whether he wanted her back and the truth was he didn't. He'd be underfoot. Or Donna would. Susan would probably tell him that's what the shoes and the hall closet symbolized.

But having had his pump primed, he did tell Susan about Katz. Not all of it. Just bits and pieces. She didn't press him because she understood there were parts of that whole story they could never talk about. Not even the parts that were in all the newspapers. But he did tell her that her Uncle David, which was what she grew up calling him, had been showing up again lately at four in the morning.

That's when she told him about the thing she remembered from a book. F. Scott Fitzgerald wrote it. He said, "In the real dark night of the soul, it's always four o'clock in the morning."

Something like that.

How long was it now?

Almost two years.

Two years ago next month when the call came from Harriet Katz. She was screeching. Hysterical. It took Lesko a full minute, trying not to yell at her, to make sense of what she was saying. That it had happened, just now, right outside in her driveway.

"Harriet . . . Harriet, listen to me. Did you call an ambulance?"

"My daughter saw it. Oh, God, my daughter saw it."

"Did anyone call the cops? Harriet? . . . Harriet!"

But all she could do was scream over and over that her daughter had seen it. That he, David, had pulled into the driveway and his daughter ran over to give him his kiss, and they did it right in front of her. Right in front of her. Harriet said that over and over. Lesko had to hang up on her. He broke the connection and punched 911 for the police and for the EMS unit. Then he ran two doors down to borrow the keys to Mr. Makowski's car. Ten minutes later he pulled up to David Katz's two-family house in Forest Hills.

Katz's car was in the driveway. Even as he pulled up to the curb, one tire on the sidewalk, Lesko could see it was bad. There was shattered glass all over. And in front of the car, on a white garage door, he saw a crescent-shaped spray that had to be blood. Two squad cars were already there, their blue lights strobing. So was the emergency services ambulance. A neighbor must have called them before he did. One uniformed officer stood near the car to keep the curious away. He kept his own eyes away from it. He looked like he'd already been sick. Another cop stationed himself at the other side of the small front lawn shaking his head at the questions coming from the growing knot of residents and passersby. A third uniform was at his radio. The EMS crew was nowhere in sight. They must have gone inside the house after looking in the car and deciding it was a waste of time. No one had even wanted to shut off the engine. Lesko flashed his badge and walked up the driveway.

David Katz, his partner of ten years, was sitting upright at the wheel. Lesko could see at once why the medics hadn't bothered with him. Half his head was gone from the left ear forward, and nearly all his face. A shotgun had done most of the damage. There was a ragged four-inch hole through the safety glass on the driver's side, then two smaller holes to the right of it. Two gunmen. The second had used a small-caliber pistol. It wasn't needed. He'd just wanted to be in on the hit. The far window and most of the windshield had been blown outward by the blasts. Bits of bone and flesh clung to what was left. Lesko could see a single tooth imbedded in the dashboard.

There was movement at the front door. Lesko looked up. Harriet Katz. Another woman, probably the neighbor, was steadying her and carefully blocking Harriet's view of her husband's car as they crossed the front lawn to the waiting ambulance. Behind them, a uniformed paramedic emerged carrying Harriet's nine-year-old daughter. Her name was Joni. Her eyes were closed and her mouth was slack. Possibly sedated. More likely in deep shock. Lesko took a few steps toward them. He could think of nothing to say. At least Harriet would see that he'd come. He watched the ambulance leave. Then he turned once more to his partner's body.

Katz was wearing one of the two new jackets he'd bought the week before. Cashmere, glen plaid, mostly a light gray. Five hundred dollars. On his wrist, gleaming brightly, even through the congealing blood, was Katz's gold Rolex chronograph. Two thousand dollars.

"You son of a bitch," Lesko said quietly. "You poor, stupid son of a bitch."

Almost two years now. Lesko could still see him. The only good thing about dreaming of Katz was at least he had his face back. Same jacket, though. Same watch. But Lesko was just as mad at him. For being stupid. For going dirty. For being greedy. For thinking that the Bolivians and the Colombians who will slaughter whole families just to teach one guy a lesson wouldn't blow away one Jewish cop who keeps ripping off their couriers.

He was also mad because the first thing Internal Affairs wanted to know was how could Detective Raymond Lesko, who for ten years was closer to Detective David Katz than Katz's wife, know nothing about the house in Sullivan County and the condo in Florida that his partner bought for cash on a gold shield's salary.

The second thing they wanted to know was where was Lesko when two greaseballs with Bolivian passports plus one other unidentified Hispanic male got splattered all over a Brooklyn barbershop five days later.

The barbershop was in Brooklyn's East New York section, not far from Kennedy Airport. It was a street of boarded-up tenements that still housed an occasional squatter. Most of their padlocks had been pried off. Several of the windows showed scars from fires set by junkies and vagrants trying to keep warm. There was one small *bodega* and a candy store but they were long since shuttered. A half-dozen rusting cars had been abandoned and stripped along both sides of a street that was never swept anymore. The city hadn't even bothered to put up alternate-side parking signs. Police never patrolled the street, certainly not on foot.

Lesko had left Mr. Makowski's car three blocks away. In Mr. Makowski's trunk was a Brooklyn wiseguy named Jimmy Splat, which was really a nickname from when he used to fight welterweight and got his nose permanently flattened. Lesko would let him out if his information turned out to be right.

He'd watched the barbershop for an hour from a rooftop down the block. There was no barber pole outside. The only way you'd know it was a barbershop was from the faded Kreml Hair Tonic sign in the window and a small, dusty display of Barbisol products. There was also a man in a green barber smock who stood in the open front door with his arms folded and who didn't look like he could trim his own nostrils. Jimmy Splat was right so far. No one ever went there for a haircut. The man in the smock was a lookout. The smock was for effect. It also covered a cut-down automatic shotgun that he wore slung under his left armpit. Lesko decided it was time to get closer.

He doubled back two blocks and then made his way over another rooftop, working his way down to the basement entrance of a building ten yards from the filthy glass storefront of the barbershop. If Jimmy Splat was telling the truth, the barber would have company soon. Lesko peeked out, then ducked quickly. A late model car that hadn't been there before was parked at the curb. Another was coming down the street. Lesko stayed low and listened. The second car stopped. One door opened and closed. Then he heard a light clicking sound moving across the sidewalk. Heels. A woman's heels. He hadn't expected a woman. Now he heard the dimmer sound of two sets of feet walking on linoleum. The barber had left the door. He was walking the woman back to the rear of the shop. Lesko moved quickly, a throwaway automatic pistol in one hand and an oversized leather truncheon in the other.

The barber, Lesko was betting, would look first to his left when he returned to his post, if only for a second or two. He would scan the street starting at the end where cars would come from. Lesko would only need that second. He waited, pressed tight against the building near the frame of the storefront door.

The barber never knew what killed him. His last sensations were the chill of winter on his face, the sight of the empty street outside, and then a flash of light and a loud popping sound, and suddenly he was drowning in a warm red sea. He felt no pain. Only a certain breathlessness as his shattered larynx filled with blood and the swelling blocked his trachea. He was drowning and yet he was floating. He felt weightless. And tired. If he could only stop floating he could sleep.

Lesko stopped him from falling. He took the man's weight under one arm and dragged him the length of the barbershop to a wooden inner door. Once there, Lesko propped him soundlessly against a wall as he stripped the cut-down shotgun from its sling and counted its load. It was a Remington automatic. Double-O shot. Six shells. Four more in the barber's pocket. Good.

Now he studied the door. It seemed old and brittle.

One kick should do if it isn't dead-bolted on the other side. If it is, he would kick out a panel and then shoot through it at anything that moved.

The barber made a gurgling sound and sighed. Lesko looked at his torso. He was not a big man, but big enough. Lesko eased him off the wall and turned him so his back was against Lesko's chest and his own chest faced the door. The shotgun was now in Lesko's left hand and the automatic in his right. Both hands were extended under the barber's armpits. He took a breath, balanced himself, and smashed the door with a single sideways kick. Lesko and his shield stepped through.

A large back room, a big table, a suitcase on it, two men near the suitcase, facing him, a woman sitting, her back to him. The man to his right had light skin, a dark suit; well dressed. He danced to one side and dropped to a crouch as Lesko entered, his hand darting to a weapon on his belt. The sight of the barber, dangling like a puppet off the chest of a huge man, well armed, made him hesitate. Lesko shot him. Twice. The man staggered backward until he struck a wall. He died standing there, a look of disbelief on a young and handsome face, and then what almost seemed an embarrassed smile. Lesko was no longer watching as this man slid to the floor.

The shotgun had pinioned the second man. He too had dropped into a reflexive crouch but had frozen in that position. His only motion was the sway of a gold crucifix through a shirt unbuttoned halfway down. This one was also young, middle twenties, but homely. Dish-faced, oily skin, crooked teeth. Mixed blood, Lesko knew, mostly Indian. A mestizo. Slowly, he raised his hands, palms outward in a calming gesture toward Lesko. Lesko let the barber fall.

"Be cool now, man." The mestizo forced the words from a mouth without moisture. "It wasn't us hit that cop. You kiddin', man? You think we want da' kind of trouble?"

Lesko slowly lowered the shotgun until its maw pointed at the floor by his side. Relief washed over the man's face. He released his breath and began to straighten. Lesko swung the automatic and fired low.

The man's eyes blinked then went wide. His body

snapped into a crouch deeper than before but somehow he kept his feet. Transfixed, he lowered both hands to his groin and felt for the place where the bullet had entered. Finding it, feeling the blood ooze out between his fingers, he raised one dripping hand to his face and then held it out to Lesko as if in hope that Lesko would be satisfied.

"Don't . . . don't shoot no more," he managed. "We work this out. We still work this out."

Lesko's automatic remained leveled at this man's chest but his eyes had turned to the woman. She was seated in a chair, her back to him, facing the paint-stained table where the open suitcase sat. He knew that the suitcase contained cash or drugs. Perhaps both. Lesko could see no part of the woman's face, only her streaked blond hair, which seemed expensively styled though even the hair was largely hidden by the up-turned collar of a thick mink coat. She had not moved since he entered, save for a violent hitch of her shoulders as each shot was fired. Lesko was sure he knew why.

He'd walked in shooting. No words. So the woman had to know this was no police raid. She'd know it was a hit. If the shooter wanted her as well, she knew she was dead meat anyway. But she had two chances. One was more like a prayer that whoever was behind her would not kill a woman. Her much better chance was that the shooter might be satisfied with the two Bolivians and the suitcase, as long as it was understood that she didn't see his face.

It might have worked that way. Lesko was there to bury two men, boom boom, in and out, the same way they got Katz. Plus one behind the ear of the barber if he wasn't dead already. The problem now was that the woman was a witness, as hard as she was trying not to be. The greaseball holding his guts in had as good as given Lesko's name when he said they didn't hit "that cop." Who the hell else could he be? The Lone Ranger? It was decision time.

Lesko was not at all sure that he could execute a woman. Maybe it depends on who she is. If she's just some bimbo who had the bad luck to be here with her boyfriend, the answer is probably no. But she's not just some bimbo, is she? She came alone and she came last, as if the others were waiting for her. And she's got a cool head. Very controlled. How many people could sit still like that?

"You awake, lady?" he heard himself ask.

A small shudder moved across her shoulders. Then she nodded slowly, still not turning. The wounded man groaned. He was looking at her now, looking hard. His glazed eyes seemed to be begging for help. But she had withdrawn from him. She kept her own eyes on the floor near her feet. No, Lesko decided. This woman was definitely no bimbo. She was part of this. Maybe even the biggest part.

"Nice try, lady." Lesko whispered the words hoarsely. The woman stiffened as she heard them. In his voice she heard reluctance and a certain sorrow. But she also knew that he had made a decision. The woman raised one gloved hand.

"Give me one more minute of life," came a voice softly accented, surprisingly calm, "and I will try to reach an accommodation with you." She paused, then added, "There will be no lies."

Lesko said nothing.

"My name is Elena. Does it have meaning to you?"

It did. On any chart Lesko had ever seen of the South American cocaine hierarchy, the name Elena was near the top. But there was always a question mark next to it, or a box of dotted lines around it, because so far nobody had come up with proof that she even existed.

"And you are Detective Raymond Lesko. You are here to avenge Detective David Katz." A gentle voice. Polite. Respectful. Sympathetic. "Although it may be hard for you to believe, I applaud that. I applaud loyalty even as I insist upon fair play in all affairs. Do you believe in fair play, Mr. Lesko?"

Lesko blinked.

What the hell is this? Now I'm going to talk ethics with coke dealers and killers?

"Turn around slow," he said.

She ignored the order.

"If your late partner had come to make an arrest, Mr. Lesko, that would have been fair enough. We live by our wits and we accept the risks."

It was an educated voice. The accent as much European . . . maybe German . . . as it was Latin. And there was a tremor in it. Fear but not panic.

"But your partner came to steal," she continued. "If he had stolen once, perhaps twice, we would have overlooked it in the interest of peace. But he came to the well once too often, Mr. Lesko. He forced us to protect ourselves."

"Who ordered the hit?"

She cocked her head toward the dead man in the black suit. "My late associate chose the time and place. He shot Detective Katz. This other man assisted him." At that the wounded man gave a deep sigh of despair and dropped to his knees.

"Naturally," Lesko curled his lip. "The dead guy did it." The hell with this, he thought. Lesko swung the automatic and dropped its front sight onto the middle of the mink collar.

"Of course," she added quickly, "I gave the order."

Lesko wavered.

Shit.

"Okay, what's going on here, lady? Are you asking me to shoot you or not shoot you or what?"

"My hope is that you will not." The shoulders trembled and the voice quivered a bit but still, that reasonable tone. "You are, I think, satisfied that Detective Katz was a thief. The fact that he stole from *trafficantes* makes that no less true. I felt the need to protect myself against him and I have done so. You felt the need to avenge him and you have done so. We have both done what was expected of us. I consider that our accounts are even. To save my life, however, I am prepared to make an additional accommodation."

Lesko could only stare. The woman raised one hand and pointed to the table she was facing.

"May I reach into that suitcase?" she asked. When no immediate answer came, she rose from her chair and walked to the table. She was smaller than she seemed while seated. Taking care not to block Lesko's view, she reached past the open lid and extracted two plastic bags filled with white powder. These she placed on the table's edge nearest Lesko. Still, she kept her face from him.

"Cocaine," she pointed. "A less evil substance than some, I think. Mind you, Mr. Lesko, I do not speak of the derivative you call crack. That is a development we deplore for many reasons. But cocaine, in its proper form, creates no armies of addicted street criminals. It is an entertainment for young men who drive BMW's and young ladies who go to discothèques. It allows frightened little people to feel that they are lions."

"Turn around, lady. I mean it."

"I would prefer that you do not see my. . . ."

"Turn around. Now."

The woman called Elena took a long breath. Her shoulders rose, then fell, and she turned to face him. Lesko studied her. She was, he guessed, in her early forties. A handsome woman, finely boned, deep-set eyes that were oddly gentle. Her skin was tanned. Not naturally dark, but tanned. If she was Bolivian she showed no sign of native blood, unlike the mestizo with the crucifix. Lesko could see now that she was much more frightened than she'd seemed. She was holding her jaw tight to keep it from quivering. And the fingers of one gloved hand were dug into the other.

"You were saying, lady?"

Her eyes fell upon the automatic pistol now aimed between her breasts, and then to the shotgun trained on the other man who was now loudly hyperventilating. She seemed afraid of guns. Not just being shot by them. Guns themselves. Lesko gestured toward the two plastic bags.

"By any chance, are you about to offer me that shit?"

She hugged herself as if for warmth. "They are worth approximately two hundred thousand dollars. It is the accommodation I mentioned. It is a fine that I impose upon myself."

"And you figure that'll make us even."

"It is my hope."

"Lady, you're out of your fucking mind, you know that? Why don't I just blow you apart and take it all?"

Her chin came up. "Because there would be no honor in that, Mr. Lesko. My offer was a fair one."

"I don't believe this."

"It is a serious proposal all the same. You will please consider it."

"What if I should just shoot you and then turn this stuff in? Would there be honor in that?"

"Certainly not. Your duty requires that you arrest me. If Mr. Katz had done his duty he would still be alive."

"You had him killed at his house in front of his family. Why?"

"I did not expect that. Specific instructions were given that his family was not to be harmed. These people can be pigs. They have been known to murder babies and to mutilate wives and mothers as an object lesson. I do not permit such things. These two took it upon themselves to make his death terrible in the memory of those who would be left with the money he stole."

"An object lesson." Lesko showed his teeth.

She nodded weakly.

"So is this." The shotgun thundered. By the time he reloaded, Lesko was shooting through a cloud.

Almost two years. Newspaper headlines, a departmental investigation, another one by the Drug Enforcement Administration, microphones stuck in his face everywhere he went, even a segment on *60 Minutes* in which Lesko declined to participate.

Even Hollywood got interested. Some producer showed up along with a retired detective Lesko knew fairly well, one of the French Connection cops who was now an actor, but Lesko didn't want to listen. Then there must have been a hundred working cops who wanted to buy him drinks no matter how much he insisted he was home fixing his toilet at the time of the shootings. Lesko said thanks, but no. Just leave him alone. There were times, though, when he'd like to have heard from Harriet Katz. But what was she going to say to him? I feel much better now, thank you? I don't wake up scared and crying anymore during my own four o'clock-in-the-morning? I no longer need half a fifth of vodka to get through an evening because I know justice has been done?

Lesko didn't even feel that way himself. He did what he did for his own peace of mind as much as he did it for Katz. He couldn't be a cop if he had left those people walking around, but as it turned out he couldn't be a cop afterward, either. It wasn't that he had to retire. Not even after he told them to take their polygraph and stick it up their asses. He could have hung in for maybe another five, no matter how hot the brass made it for him. But for every cop who thought what he did was terrific, there was another cop who was afraid of him for it. And cops, like everyone else, have a way of hating people who make them afraid. It got lonely. Lesko turned in his papers.

For the first couple of months there was hardly a day when he didn't replay that barbershop scene in his mind. What he did, what he should have done. What he did to the phony barber, and to the black suit who moved for a gun, that was okay. Shooting the second guy was a little less okay. What would have been better was if the one with the crucifix had been reaching, too. But what the hell. This wasn't a cowboy movie. What would have been best of all was if Lesko had shot to kill right off. First the two spics and then one in the back of the woman's head, before he could think it over. Instead, he gets into a goddamned conversation with her. Instead, he ends up executing the guy who's now on his knees and then emptying that shotgun into maybe a million bucks' worth of nose candy. And there's the woman, Elena, just standing there with her fur coat turning white like she's in a snowstorm. Every blast makes her wince but she stays standing straight and her chin is high. She's scared to death but there's also this look of amazement that anyone would blow away all that money. That alone tells her that she's finished. This man who will not take her *accommodation* is saving his last load to spray her head all over that table. An object lesson.

Lesko came within a hair of doing it. The thing about shootings is that once they start you just keep shooting until you're on empty, even after everybody's down and dead. It works the same with street fights. You just keep hitting.

But there was something about that lady. She had tried to deal and if it didn't work she was ready to take what came. She could have begged. She could have said she just stopped in for a haircut. She could have said the two Bolivians acted on their own but she promised she wouldn't lie and she didn't.

He left her standing there.

Two years.

Too many four-in-the-mornings.

Lesko tightened the belt of his terry bathrobe and began feeling his way through the darkness to the bathroom. He paused, involuntarily, at the spot where Katz had stood, then he caught himself and moved on.

It seemed he was dreaming a lot lately. Including about Katz, whom he hadn't dreamed about in months. In fact the only time he dreamed about Katz, night after night, especially in the beginning, seemed to be when something was wrong. When something bad was happening.

Lesko flicked on the bathroom light.

Hold it, he said to himself. Don't start that. Don't start looking for dreams to mean anything. Nothing's wrong. You got a terrific daughter, a few friends, a pretty good pension, and a few extra bucks in the bank from the Beckwith Hotels thing. If Elena's friends were going to do anything, especially to Susan, they would have done it a long time ago. Katz is an asshole but he's a dead asshole. Don't let him make you crazy.

Lesko saw himself in the bathroom mirror.

Ugly.

World-class ugly.

That's what Katz had called him. Katz said he had been lucky Donna stayed with him as long as she did, waking up every morning to a face like that.

Lesko looked at his face. He had to bend his knees to see it in the mirror. They must make bathroom mirrors for women. Not for men who weigh two hundred forty pounds and look like bouncers and would be better off not looking in mirrors too much, anyway.

He ran one hand across his hair to smooth it down. It was more gray than brown now. But at least he still had it. Except he also had creases. He used both hands to pull back the flesh in an effort to soften his features. Maybe, now that he can lay his hands on a couple of grand when he needs it, he could go to one of those plastic surgeons who advertise on television. But what

good would it do? They could take away ten years'
worth of lines but not ten years' worth of ugly. It still
wouldn't be the kind of face you could take to a singles'
club cocktail party. But it had been a good face for a
cop. For a cop, sometimes it was a very good face.

David Katz used to say he was the only cop in New
York who looked scarier when he smiled. When you
smile, Katz said, people always think you're going to eat
them. It's better when you don't smile because then
they think you're only going to crush their faces. How
the hell did you get married, anyway? Did you do it all
by mail? I mean, Donna's not a bad-looking lady. And
how did you end up having a daughter like Susan, who is
not only good-looking but is also even smart and nice?
You know what the answer is? The answer is your genes
skipped a generation. That's a trick God pulls to keep
the species going. Otherwise, who would ever take a
chance on having another you? Some day, some poor
stiff is going to marry Susan thinking that because she's
so nice-looking they have at least a chance of getting a
human baby. But then this poor bastard is going to go to
see his baby at the maternity ward and he's going to run
screaming out of the hospital because there's your face
again looking back at him. The nurse probably used
tongs to carry you to the window.

"Yeah, well, fuck you," Lesko muttered.

He turned on the tap and rubbed cold water across
his face. Look at this, he thought. I'm wide awake and
I'm still talking to him. I'm listening to smartass words
of wisdom from the world's only ghost who stops to pick
up bagels first.

Lesko leaned closer to the mirror and grimaced. His
teeth seemed to fill it. Ugly or not, mean face or not, he
had good teeth. Perfect teeth. Not a single filling if you
don't count the one from root canal. Susan inherited his
perfect teeth. Shows how much Katz knows about
genes.

What's today?

Monday.

Susan got back last night from the Bahamas. Today
he's supposed to call her to decide where they'll meet to
go to the Knicks game Wednesday night. Then to dinner afterward at Gallagher's, which was Susan's idea,

which probably means she wants to sit him down and
nag him about not being such a hermit and how he
should go find a nice mature lady for his autumn years.

Right.

But it might be his last chance to spend any time
with Susan before she takes off again next Friday. This
time to go skiing. In Switzerland, no less.

The thought of it pleased Lesko. One thing Katz was
right about was he did okay with Susan. Smart and
pretty. Also a good person. How many cops' kids were
practically straight-A students at a tough Jesuit school
like Fordham. How many had the hustle to get themselves jobs as reporters with a big-league newspaper
like the *New York Post.* Being his daughter didn't hurt,
because he was sort of famous, but mostly she did it
herself. Twenty-four years old, and they're giving her
bylines already. And how many cops' daughters go
spend New Year's in the Bahamas, let alone go skiing in
Switzerland.

That's class.

The kid's got class.

CHAPTER 2

Susan watched with pleasure as her father made his way back from the washroom at Gallagher's Steak House. A man at one table stopped him and pumped his hand. Another looked up as he passed and then whispered something about him to the woman he was with. Whatever he said caused the woman's mouth to drop open as she turned and stared. Susan smiled. It seemed as if half the people in New York had a favorite Raymond Lesko story. Now two more men were calling him over. And one of the owners had sent over a round of drinks as soon as they were seated.

She was glad, for her father's sake, that some things hadn't changed since he turned in his badge. For most cops the glad-hands and the free drinks ended with retirement. But Gallagher's, at least, was different. He was considered family here. So was his father before him. Lieutenant Joe Lesko. When he was killed, it was the year before Susan was born, they clipped his picture from the paper and gave it a permanent place on the wall next to the bar. It was still there. Right next to Mayor Fiorello LaGuardia.

Susan had always heard that her grandfather had died a hero. The people who said that were almost always men. The women, she felt sure, thought that his death was tragic and stupid although they knew better than to say so. The men needed their heroes. The way it happened, a minor hoodlum had been bullying a cab driver just outside the old Toots Shor's on 52nd Street. Slapping his face. The cabbie had refused to take the

21

hoodlum and his girlfriend, both of them drunk, to
Brooklyn that late at night. Joe Lesko came out,
grabbed the hoodlum, slapped him twice as hard, and
was stuffing him into a trash can when the girlfriend
pulled a revolver from her purse and shot him three
times in the back of the head. Her father was twenty-
four at the time. Her age. He was already on the force
himself and beginning to make a reputation of his own.
She once heard one of the old-timers say that her father
would have decked the woman first in order to give his
undivided attention to the man. Susan found that hard
to believe. Her father was really very gallant with
women, in his way. She'd often thought he was afraid of
them. But he wouldn't have turned his back on her. And
he wouldn't have let himself get loaded at Toots Shor's.

"I'm sorry, sweetheart." Raymond Lesko slid heavily
into his chair and took his first sip of Seagram's and
water. He motioned toward another table with his
thumb. "Couple of guys back there I haven't seen since
you were a kid."

"No problem." She raised her wine glass. "It's good
to see you getting out and mixing."

"And Buzz Donovan back there, you remember? He
used to be a big United States Attorney. Anyway, he
didn't recognize you and was giving me a lot of crap
about robbing the cradle."

"Bet he thought I was a hooker."

Her father's face darkened fleetingly. "As a matter
of fact," the expression softened, "he says you look a lot
like your grandmother. She was a beautiful woman in
her day. Men would pass her on the street and they'd
walk into lampposts if they weren't careful." Lesko
paused, pushing the ice around the rim of his glass. "You
shouldn't say things like that, Susan."

"Oh come on, daddy. It was just a harmless dumb
crack."

"Yeah, but you got too much class. You're a lady. And
you're beautiful."

"I am not beautiful. What I am is okay."

She was, she supposed, maybe a notch better than
okay. She did inherit her grandmother's figure, and her
auburn hair and hazel eyes. But most of the compli-

ments she'd received in her life were more like expressions of amazement that she was her father's daughter.

Susan glanced around the restaurant in search of a way to change the subject. She caught a man at the bar staring in her direction. He lowered his face toward his drink, revealing a balding scalp. Something familiar about him. Then her eyes drifted on, over walls crammed with fading photos of old sports heroes.

"How long have you been coming here?" she asked Lesko.

"First time was my fourteenth birthday. My father brought me. Same as I brought you."

"Oh, right." She remembered him talking about it. Except on his birthday he was taken to a Jake LaMotta fight at the Garden, and she had to settle for the Ice Capades. "That's when Jake LaMotta came back here after the fight and your father got him to give you a boxing lesson."

"Yeah." Lesko smiled at the memory. "What made it great was Rocky Graziano was here that night, too. He comes over and says if I listen to LaMotta I'll spend the whole next year getting knocked on my ass, excuse me, because what LaMotta knows about defense he could fit in his jock. LaMotta gets very insulted at this and these two look like they're going to go at it, but it's all an act for my benefit. Then LaMotta shows me how to counter a right lead. I decide not to mention that my father already taught me to either kick the guy in the crotch or come in under it, spin the guy, and put a choke hold on him until his lights go out.

"Anyway, LaMotta and Graziano are still arguing so LaMotta asks the crowd for a vote on which one of them spent the most time on his ass and another one on which one of them is less ugly. LaMotta wins both times." Lesko turned toward the table he'd sat at that night, his eyes darting around as he spoke as if he could see it all happening again. "I still got the menu they both signed for me that night. Also Johnny Mize of the Giants who was in here too. It's probably up in your mother's attic."

"Want me to look next time I see her?"

He hesitated, then shook his head. "It's no big deal."

"I got to meet a skating clown for my fourteenth birthday." She pretended to pout, as if cheated. "It's

one of my treasured memories. Right up there with
museum trips and rides on the Staten Island ferry."

"Yeah, well, they were your mother's idea mostly.
Anyway, it's not like I didn't take you to fights and
ballgames after you got older."

"After you were divorced, you mean."

"Same thing." He waved off the subject with his
hand. "Listen, can you handle a steak or do you want a
veal chop?"

"I'd like us to have a talk first."

"We haven't been talking?"

"Not about you, we haven't. Things like how you are,
what you've been doing, do you have a lady friend . . .
I mean, this is only about the third time we've talked in
almost two years."

"What do you mean? I call you at least a couple of
times a month and we've been to, like, ten ballgames."

"Yes, and about half those calls were to break dates.
It was like pulling teeth even to get you over on Christmas. And I think you deliberately take me to ballgames
because it's hard to sit and talk at them."

Lesko dropped his eyes. "I'm sorry, sweetheart. I
guess I haven't been much of a father."

"Oh, now there's a good move," Susan arched. "Play
to Susan's sympathy and maybe she'll drop the subject
of her father ducking her."

"I have not been ducking you."

"Liar."

Lesko looked around the room as if for help. "What
is it about women?" he asked. "You all ask questions
whose answers you already know in order to get the guy
to answer out loud just so you can stomp all over him."

"It's because of the trouble you were in. All the
newspaper stories. You didn't want it rubbing off on
me."

"Basically, yeah."

"Well, that's ridiculous."

"I rest my case."

She ignored the sarcasm. "Daddy, I work for a newspaper, remember? When you work for a newspaper,
none of the other media try to hound you for inter-
views. And the *Post* has been very good about not press-

ing me for information about you. I get all the protection I need."

Lesko said nothing.

"Secondly, you don't say to your daughter, 'I might be in trouble. Pretend you don't know me until I tell you differently,' and expect me to go merrily on with my life as if you don't exist. Or worse, as if I'm ashamed of you."

"Look, I give up." He raised his hands in surrender. "Anyway, it's old news. Nobody cares anymore."

At least not the newspapers, he thought. Not the TV reporters, not even the cops. And maybe not Elena or her crazy Bolivians, either. If they were going to have him whacked they've had almost two years to do it. They would have done it in the first few months. Probably Susan first, then him. Another object lesson. Not that he really thought Elena would try. In a funny way they understood each other.

But it might not be her choice if she wants to keep doing business with the greaseballs. And Lesko had never known them to let something like this pass. The other greaseballs would call them women. They'd send them ladies' underwear in the mail. Which brings up something else. Little Elena must be one hell of a tough broad for those guys to do business with a woman. Either that or she has a hell of a lot of clout behind her. Big money. New York or Swiss money, which is almost the same thing these days.

The old days were simpler. Twenty-five years ago if you were talking about drugs you were talking about musicians, about the niggers up in Harlem, and about the dago mob everywhere else. Then one day some dago wiseguy says what are we doing laying out our own money? What we do instead is we go see some of these Harvard and Yale guys down on Wall Street who think they're really screwing somebody if they make a lousy 40 percent on their money. We say, how would you like to make 100, maybe 200 percent with no risk? There's no risk because only one shipment out of fifty ever gets busted so all you do is spread your money over several runs and that way the only question is whether you double it or triple it.

The Harvards look at this and they say, Hey, here's a

commodity trade that beats the shit out of pork bellies, and they jump in with both feet. Million-dollar investments double five times over in a month. All of a sudden you see these corporate raiders. Guys with companies that hardly ever did more than break even are out gobbling up other companies twice their size. Whole airlines and oil companies are being taken over with cocaine money. Half the new high rises going up in this country, even half the movies being made, are financed on either coke or smack.

Drugs are better than gold. Better than oil. The Arabs, who don't know from drugs and who'll cut your hand off for smoking a joint, still think it's petrodollars that make the the world go 'round. They don't know what hit them. In another fifteen years they'll be back playing in sandpiles and fucking their goats.

The other ones who don't know from drugs are economists. Economists look at the budget deficit and the balance of payments and the national debt and they say this is crazy, we should be in a depression. All their figures say so. But their figures don't show drug money and it's drug money that keeps this country afloat.

Besides the Arabs, the other ones who don't know what hit them are the dagos. Show me a mob guy who knows as much about skimming and laundering as a Wall Street investment banker. Show me a mob cooker who can mix a batch of quality shit faster and better than any first-year chemical engineer at Dow or du Pont could do practically on his lunch break.

It isn't simple anymore, Lesko thought. And I don't care anymore. I'm out of it.

"I care," Susan said softly.

"What?" Lesko blinked. "About what?"

"You said nobody cares anymore. I care about you. Very much."

"Yeah," he nodded. "Me, too."

He looked at her. Those first few months, after Katz and after the barbershop, he'd spent every spare hour watching her apartment, following her to work on the subway and home again at night. He'd get other cops who owed him favors to spell him while he was being grilled by Internal Affairs, the District Attorney and the federal narcs. All this in case he was wrong about Elena, or he was right about her not being able to control the Bolivians. A couple of times he even listened at Susan's door when a guy took her home and didn't leave right away. He shouldn't have done that. It was when he learned the hard way that Susan was grown-up and had a private life.

"If we care about each other so much," Susan said gently, "you'd think we'd be able to talk."

"You keep saying that," Lesko made a show of holding his fingertips to his temples, "and I keep trying to remember when we've shut up for two minutes all night."

"Right." She twisted her lips, a mannerism she inherited from him. "And it's all been really good father-and-daughter stuff, too. Like, the Knicks haven't had anyone under the boards since Willis Reed retired; like Jerry Cooney could have taken Larry Holmes if he crowded him early and went to the body; and like the beer at Shea Stadium these days tastes like someone pissed in it. Oh, and you also asked your usual twenty questions about who I'm seeing and how serious it is."

"That last part *is* father-and-daughter stuff. And as usual you ducked it."

"That's different."

"What's different? Two minutes ago you asked if I had a lady friend."

"Okay, but if you said yes and told me her name I wouldn't get someone to run a check on her background."

"I only did that once."

"Is that so?"

"Maybe twice."

"But never again. Promise?"

Lesko made an ambiguous gesture that he hoped would pass for agreement. Susan reached for his hand and dug her nails into it.

"Repeat after me. Never again."

Lesko winced. "Never again."

"Show me your other hand. I bet your fingers are crossed."

Lesko pulled free and slid his chair out of reach. "This is a wonderful conversation. If I don't get stomped on, I get stabbed."

* * *

"You know why we're like this, don't you." Susan kept her eyes on her plate as she trimmed the fat off her veal chop.

"Like what?"

"So secretive."

"Are you sure we're so different from any other father and daughter?"

"Fathers who are cops are different. You almost never talked about your job unless something funny happened or you met a celebrity. Never any of the bad things."

"If I worked in a slaughterhouse, you wouldn't expect me to describe my day at the dinner table."

"If it bothered you, yes. If you needed to talk about it."

"Cops who bring their jobs home get divorced a lot quicker than I did."

"I don't believe that. I think sharing more of yourself would have helped."

Lesko laid down his fork. "Susan, listen to me. All a cop sees is people, even decent people, when they're at their worst. We see and sometimes do some very sickening things. Police departments know this. That's why they all have programs set up to help cops deal with the bad side of being cops. But mostly cops talk to each other because there just isn't anyone outside the job who would understand. This is not just true of cops, either. Guys from Vietnam, hospital nurses, they have the same problem."

"I suppose."

"What worked for me was to keep my home and my job as separate as I could. That's why we didn't socialize with other cop families. Not even my own partner."

Susan saw a peculiar pause at the reference to David Katz. She let it pass.

"Daddy?"

"Um?"

"When a policeman shoots somebody . . . kills somebody . . . is it something you ever get over?"

"Sweetheart, what do you say we talk about something nicer."

"Because I want us to learn to be more open. Maybe

that's a bad place to start but I've had a whole lifetime of you never opening up to me. I've also had a whole lifetime of mom telling me never to bother you with my problems and never to say anything that might worry you."

Lesko frowned at her.

"I'm sorry. Forget it."

"Susan, that last part. Is it true?"

"Of course it is."

"I never knew that. I really didn't."

"It's okay."

"It's not okay. What did she say exactly?"

"She would just talk to me about how dangerous your job is and how you had to have your head clear at all times. And how she didn't want you getting hurt because your mind was on a broken washing machine or any of my little schoolgirl problems."

"Little schoolgirl problems. Are those your words or hers?"

"Mom's."

"With due respect, she could be a real jerk at times."

"It's okay, daddy."

"As for your question about shootings . . . it's not so much that I don't want to answer . . . it's just that general questions can lead to specific questions and there are certain things you and I should never ask each other."

"That isn't true. It shouldn't be true."

"Fine. Then let's talk about your sex life. I realize you're a big girl and the recent stuff is none of my business so we'll just talk about whatever happened while you were under my roof. Don't start until I get my pad out."

"You've made your point, thank you very much."

Susan sipped her second glass of Chablis, sent over by Buzz Donovan, the retired U.S. Attorney.

"Daddy, have you seen Harriet Katz?"

"Not for a while. I hear she's moving to Florida. It'll do her good."

"Could I ask you a question about David?"

Lesko waited. She saw that same odd look.

"Would you have turned him in if you knew what he was doing?"

"Most people think I probably had a piece of it."

"Most people don't know you. You're the single most honest man I've ever met."

"Let's not go crazy here."

"You wouldn't take a dime."

"Sweetheart," Lesko tapped his Seagram's glass, "if someone wants to buy me drinks, or dinner, or give me some free tickets, I'm not about to read him his rights."

"That's different."

"And that word is part of the problem. You can find a way to say 'that's different' about anything. David thought that stealing from drug dealers was different from knocking off a payroll."

"What would you have done if you knew? Would you have turned him in?"

"No."

"Because cops don't turn in cops? No matter what he did?"

"Not no matter what. Just not for that."

"What would you have done?"

"What I wish I'd done is ask more questions when I first saw he was spending more money than he should have had. But it wasn't like he was buying Jaguars. It was just things like new clothes and a watch and picking up more than his share of checks. Besides, it didn't go on all that long."

"But if you'd actually known. What then?"

"That's not really a useful question, Susan."

"Please? I want to see . . . please tell me." What she almost said was that she wanted to see how well she knew him. But she did know him. She saw the anger come flowing right through his eyes. She saw the look that made people afraid of him.

"I would have taken him into a quiet room," his voice came softly through his teeth, "and I would have kicked the living shit out of him. He would have told me where every dollar was that could be converted back to cash. I would have stayed on top of him until we had it all and then I would have taken him down to Catholic Charities and stood behind him while he made a large, anonymous donation."

"From David Katz to Catholic Charities?"

"An object lesson."

"It still bothers you. Talking about David Katz, I mean."

"Lately, I guess. I don't know."

"Why lately?"

Lesko hesitated. But what the hell. They'd talked about this before. "Last couple of weeks I can't get through the night without dreaming about him."

"What kind of dreams?"

"Just dreams. Dumb ones."

"Yes, but what about?"

"What is this? We're learning to be open about dreams, too?"

"No, now we're learning how many times I have to ask the same question to get an answer. What kind of dreams?"

"He just shows up with a bag of bagels, like normal. He makes fun of my clothes, like normal. He doesn't realize he's dead until I tell him he is and then I throw him the hell out."

"Are you fast asleep or are these the pre-dawn gremlins?"

"They're the half-awake kind. Four in the morning." Lesko pushed a cold piece of onion ring around his plate. "Listen, you want some cheesecake?"

"I'll have a bite of yours. Are you worried about anything in particular? Dreams like that usually come when you're worried but you don't know exactly what's bothering you."

"Nothing's worrying me," he lied. Something was. He just didn't know what. It was a feeling he'd learned to pay attention to when he was a cop. Half the time it was nothing. Or it went away. But the feeling made him more alert. He'd see things, make connections, that he wouldn't have made otherwise. This time, for example, he was getting a feeling about the guy at the bar who kept looking at them.

"Maybe Uncle David was haunting you." Susan decided to lighten it. "Maybe he found out about Catholic Charities."

"Maybe."

A grin started small and then it spread across her face. "You know, I love this. This is great."

"What's great?"

"I can't believe we're talking about bad dreams and ghosts."

"You sucker me into telling you things and then you laugh at them?"

"Oh, no." She reached for his hand again. "It's just that no one would ever believe it. My father, Raymond the Terrible Lesko, one of New York's all-time toughest cops, talking about seeing a ghost. Were you scared? Tell me you were a little bit scared."

"I got a better idea," Lesko took her hand and squeezed it. "What if Raymond the Terrible Lesko just crushed your fingers for being such a smartass?"

"So," Lesko shook off the subject of David Katz, "what have you been doing at the paper?"

She spooned some whipped cream off her Irish Coffee. "Just the regular news beat. A little City Hall. And I'm always looking for a good, juicy feature article."

"There's not plenty happening every day in this town?"

"Most days," she nodded. "But all the plum assignments go to the senior writers, and half the time the TV reporters beat us to it, anyway. The trick is to dig something up by yourself and don't tell anyone until you've got it written. I thought I had one up in Connecticut but it doesn't seem to be going anywhere."

"Connecticut stories for a New York newspaper?"

"Sure," she told him. "Half of Fairfield County commutes to New York every day and most of them read the *Post* on the way home."

"What kind of story was it?"

"You ever been to Westport?"

Lesko shook his head. "I don't hang around places where they wear pink pants and paint ducks on mailboxes."

"Or put little onions in their drinks. I know." Her father had spent time in Greenwich about a year before, working on some weird case involving the Beckwith Hotels family. He'd said he thought he'd stumbled into a convention of George Bush look-alikes. "Anyway,

you remember my old roommate, Allie McCarthy?
Well, now she's Allie Gregory, and she and her husband
bought a house in Westport, which is a lot more laid-
back than the planet Greenwich. I was up there last fall
helping her fix it up. She and Tom—that's her husband
—had collected a whole pile of literature on places to
live in Connecticut. You know, stuff about tax rates,
schools, quality of life and all that. In the pile there was
this little statistical abstract that gave figures on absolutely everything . . . lottery income by week, water
tables by average season, gypsy-moth infestation by
area . . . you get the idea." Susan kept her eyes on him
as she took a sip of her coffee. "Guess what laid-back
Connecticut town had the highest suicide rate *and* the
highest accidental death rate in the state last year?"

"That's your angle? Pink pants cause stress?"

"Whatever the cause, isn't that a remarkable statis-
tic?"

"How'd it look in past years?"

"For ten years running, both figures were a third to a
half of last year's. No other town in Connecticut, Massachusetts or Rhode Island had that kind of jump. I
checked."

"Figures like those, they're usually based on so many
incidents per hundred thousand population, right?"

"Per ten thousand, in this case."

"Even so, in a small town like Westport you'd only
need . . . what? An extra six or seven cases a year to
double what they had before?"

"There were six more suicides and eleven more accidental deaths. That's seventeen extra people who died
violently last year, a number way beyond the laws of
chance."

Lesko's expression still showed no more than polite
interest. Violent death would not have been his topic of
choice. "What kinds of people died? Was the mix any
different than before?"

"Not really. That's the first thing I checked. My first
hunch was teen suicides because there's been a rash of
them in other communities. But it's almost all ages and
income groups. There were two odd things. Adult suicides tend to be older people, sick people, but these
were much younger. The other thing I found was that

quite a few had records as petty criminals. Two were drunk drivers with multiple convictions. One had a reputation as a wife-beater."

"You can't be serious."

"About what?"

"You're looking for a vigilante story? In Westport, Connecticut?"

"Not really." An embarrassed smile.

"That sounded more like a maybe."

The smile spread. "Wouldn't that have been great, though? Talk about human interest stories."

"I can see it now," Lesko snorted. "A bunch of Westport types are sitting around the patio drinking out of plastic glasses with little dice in their bottoms. A teenager drives by with a loud radio and he throws a beer can on their lawn. They decide to put out a contract on him and they hire some Mad Max–type to run the kid into a light pole. They say, hey, this is even more fun than our investment club. Why don't we knock off that guy who let Japanese beetles into the country? And then I want the guy down the block whose golden retriever shits on the pachysandra. . . ." Lesko heard a gasp from a woman at the next table. He lowered his voice. "You haven't told anyone about this, have you? Like your city editor?"

"I know. He'd take my head off."

"You got it. And before he threw you out of the office he'd explain to you that conspiracy stories almost never pan out because conspiracies never work. Murphy's law. The *Post* wouldn't touch it but you could always write it for one of those newspapers they sell at supermarket checkouts where no one cares whether it's true, and which the Pulitzer Prize committee wouldn't wipe its ass with. Excuse me. The other thing wrong with a vigilante angle is that vigilantes don't try to make an execution look like a suicide or accident unless they totally miss the point of being vigilantes."

"How about a serial killer, then?"

"That's just a hair more likely. Except serial killers almost always concentrate on one type of victim. And they almost always leave some kind of signature."

Susan let out a breath and sat back. "I admitted it

wasn't going anywhere. It's just that those figures were so striking."

"You want to know what I think happened in Westport in the last year or so?"

"Sure."

"You gotta be careful with suicide figures. In towns like Westport, the local cops will play down a suicide especially if it's someone who has money. A citizen decided to take the pipe and all you see in the obituaries is that so-and-so 'died suddenly.' But then all you need is for some new medical examiner or police chief to decide a spade should be called a spade and there, all of a sudden, is your apparent increase in suicides."

"That wouldn't explain the rise in accidental deaths."

Lesko shrugged. "Same kind of problem. Let's say I'm hurt in a car accident and then a few hours later I have a heart attack. Some will call it an accidental death, some will call it natural. An insurance company will fight to have it recorded as natural to avoid paying double indemnity. But how it's listed can still come down to one public official deciding what to call it."

"So," Susan brightened a bit, "all I have to do is find out if Westport has tightened its definitions in the past year or two."

"In which case you wouldn't have much of a story. But you'll probably never find out because chances are you won't find anyone who'll admit it. The admission could invite all kinds of lawsuits, especially by survivors who think they've been screwed out of insurance money."

"Maybe I'll just forget about that one."

"Up to you."

"Want to hear my new idea?"

"What?"

"Dead partner haunts New York's toughest cop. Inquiring minds will eat it up."

Lesko didn't smile.

"I'm kidding, daddy."

"Yeah, I know." He looked off toward the rear of the restaurant. "Listen, Buzz Donovan's giving me the high sign over there. I'll be back in a second."

"I'm sorry. I guess that wasn't very funny."

"No problem. Really." Lesko slid back his chair.

Buzz Donovan, a florid-faced, tousle-haired man of seventy who looked more like an Irish saloon keeper than a former federal prosecutor, said, "Don't look around, Ray, but do you know any reason why you'd have a tail?"

Lesko scratched a stain from the lapel of his blue suit from Barney's. "The guy at the bar, right?"

"You spotted him."

Lesko nodded. "Could be he's just looking at Susan. That happens."

"Maybe. But he's been looking for an hour over one drink. Hasn't taken his topcoat off."

"Yeah. Thanks Buzz."

"What are you going to do?"

"I don't know. We're going to leave pretty soon. I'll see if he tags along."

"You taking Susan home?"

"Now I am."

"You want some backup? You have friends here."

"It's okay, Buzz."

"Come back for a nightcap. Don't let me sit here wondering."

"Okay. Half an hour or so."

Susan thought he looked a little angry when he returned. He tried to hide it with a wink. Angry or not, she decided, she was not sorry she tried to make a joke of the David Katz thing. That whole business, the killings, the headlines. She didn't know how much her father was involved or not involved and she wasn't about to ask him. But she also wasn't about to treat him like he had cancer, tiptoeing around the episode and falling into uncomfortable silences the way most other people did. After this much time it could use a little lightening up. And he could use a trip himself. Out of New York, someplace where people had never heard of him. She almost wished she could take him to Switzerland with her.

"So," he tapped his knuckles on the table to signal a change of subject. "Tell me about this trip you're taking."

Susan smiled. "Sometimes I think you can read my mind."

"What do you mean?"

"I was half-tempted to drag you along. You could use a vacation."

"You could picture me on skis? Maybe I'll also go to ballet camp."

"That's another thing," she scolded. "Quit being so down on the way you look. You happen to be a very impressive man. If you would let another woman, besides me, see how wonderfully gentle you can be. . . ."

"Come on," he rapped again, "tell me about Switzerland."

"I'm counting the hours now. First we fly Friday night to London and then we. . . ."

"Who's this 'we'?"

Susan took a breath. "I'm going with a friend, daddy," she said evenly. "My friend is a man."

"That's nice." It was said without sarcasm.

"You'd like him."

"If you like him, I'm sure I would, too."

"That'd be a switch."

Lesko spread his hands and looked skyward as if asking God to witness that he had not fired the first shot.

"His name is Paul. Paul Bannerman."

Lesko's face softened. "Thank you." He couldn't remember the last time Susan had volunteered a name.

"What would you like to know about him, daddy?"

"How did you meet?"

"How we met? That's your first question?"

Lesko shrugged.

"Paul lives in Westport. Allie Gregory introduced us during one of my weekends up there last fall. Allie, by the way, is just as picky as you are when it comes to who she thinks is good enough for me."

To say that Allie *introduced* them might have been stretching it just a little. They met Paul together. But all her father wanted to know, she felt sure, was that it was a proper meeting and not a pickup at some West Side singles bar.

She was partly right. And the answer did satisfy Lesko. At least it raised no red flags. It didn't sound as if this Paul Bannerman had gone out of his way to get close to her.

"What does Paul Bannerman do?" he asked.

"He runs a travel agency up there. I'd rather tell you what he's like."

"Fine."

"He's kind, and he's gentle, and a little shy, and funny, and very bright. Every now and then he reminds me of you."

"How so?"

"I don't know. I haven't pinned that down yet."

"It must mean he's middle-aged, suspicious, and has a nasty mouth."

She shook her head, grinning. "Not middle-aged, but he is a bit older. Paul's in his thirties." Late thirties.

"Been married before?"

"Never. He's always traveled a lot."

"That wouldn't stop him from meeting women. It sounds like he just brings them with him. I assume you were just down in the Bahamas with this guy, too."

"Yes, I was." Susan curled her lip.

"And you know for a fact he's not married now."

"Come on, daddy. Don't start."

"Okay." Lesko raised his hands.

"He's a good man, daddy. He really is. And he's definitely not married."

"Listen," Lesko waved off the subject and picked up the check. "Fathers worry about their daughters. It comes with the territory. All I can do is try not to be too much of a pain in the ass about it. Excuse me."

"I understand that."

"That'd be another switch."

Susan winced as the dart struck home. "You know something, Lesko?"

"What?"

"I'm dying for you to meet a woman just so I can be as big a pain in the ass as you are. *Excuse* me."

"Don't hold your breath. Anyway, when do I meet Paul Bannerman?"

"Soon. As soon as we get back."

"What about tomorrow night? I can get my hands on three more Knicks tickets."

"We just can't," she shook her head. "We're both working day and night to clear off our desks. Anyway, tomorrow night I'll be packing."

"It's the Celtics. What kind of a creep would pass up a Knicks–Celtics game?"

Susan reached across the table. Lesko pulled his hands away. "This is where you take my hand again, right? It's where you dig in your nails if I don't shut up?"

"As soon as we get back, daddy. Promise."

CHAPTER 3

There was more that Lesko wanted to know about Susan's upcoming trip and about this new man who seemed to have been very much in her life for the past few months. But for the moment, all he wanted to do was get her out of there and see if the guy at the bar tagged along.

He did not look toward the bar as they walked to the coatroom. But once there, and certain that a tail would not be caught watching them leave, he had a moment to study the man in the topcoat as he struggled into his own. The man could have been a lawyer. Middle thirties, thinning hair, conservative clothes and haircut. And he had money in his hand. He was leaving it on the bar to pay for his still-unfinished drink.

"I can't eat like I used to." Lesko rubbed his stomach as they reached the street. "You mind if we walk it off a little?"

"Sure." Susan took his arm.

Lesko led her on an ambling stroll through New York's theater district, stopping under two marquees to read posters until Susan wondered aloud about his sudden interest in the Broadway stage. A block behind them, the man from Gallagher's bar was showing a similar interest in a window display of "I Love New York" souvenirs.

"Come on," Lesko kept his voice casual. "We'll walk over to Eighth Avenue and get the subway."

He was strongly tempted to put her in a cab alone, then walk around the next corner and wait for the man to catch up. On Eighth Avenue, after midnight, it wouldn't matter how many people were around or how much noise he made. People would just walk by. Or they'd hang around to see what might be left in the guy's pockets when Lesko finished with him. Another option was to put her in a cab and keep walking to see if by chance it was Susan who was being followed. But first and last he wanted Susan safely home. And he wanted the man behind them to be on foot when he got her there.

Susan's apartment building, on the Upper West Side, was a block and a half from the subway exit at 79th Street and Broadway. No doorman, but the entrance was well-lit and there were two sets of heavy glass doors. Lesko stopped at the outer doors and offered Susan his cheek. She hugged him, instead.

Lesko hugged back. "I'll give you a call before you go, all right?"

"Daddy, is anything wrong?"

"A little heartburn from the onion rings. I'll walk some more." A hundred yards behind him and across the street there was a panel truck with the name of a plumber on its side. The man had stopped behind it.

"Take care of yourself." Susan gave a final squeeze. "Love you."

"Love you too, sweetheart." Lesko held on to her. "Listen, don't give me any heat about this, okay? I want you to give me a wave from the window after you've checked out your apartment and locked the door."

No use arguing. "Sure, daddy."

"Go on. Go to bed."

"We'll talk."

Lesko watched her through the lobby and then stepped into the quiet street where he waited five minutes for the wave from the seventh floor window. Returning it, he motioned for her to close her curtains, which she did after a mimed gesture of exasperation. Satisfied, Lesko moved off toward Columbus Avenue, staying to the north side of the street to thwart any notion she might have of watching him go. He walked until he was well out of possible view, then, almost abreast of the panel truck, he crossed abruptly to the south side of the street. In his hand was his service revolver, which he pressed against his thigh.

Lesko considered the other man's options. He could try walking away, gambling that Lesko had not spotted him before just now, he could hide behind the truck or even under it, gambling that he hadn't been spotted at all. Either way, Lesko had to assume he was armed and that his hand would be resting on the butt or hilt of a weapon. But the man showed more imagination than that. By the time Lesko reached the far sidewalk his tail from Gallagher's had become a lurching drunk who stood at the panel truck's door fumbling through a set of keys. Lesko smiled harmlessly as he passed. Then he whirled, his left fist whistling as it slammed into the man's kidney.

The man arched and gasped, sucking in a breathless scream as Lesko took his head and rammed it against the lettering of the plumber's name. Lesko raised his .38 and hooked it under the man's jawline, keeping him from falling as his free hand patted down the rigid body. He found a shoulder holster. It was empty. The Smith & Wesson, also a service model, was tucked under his belt, where it could have been drawn more easily. Lesko pocketed the revolver, then patted further for a second weapon. Finding none, he tore loose the man's wallet and pocketed that as well.

"We'll start with your name." Lesko's teeth were bared.

"I can't . . . I can't brea. . . ." The man's chest heaved and his throat made choking sounds.

"Your name," Lesko repeated.

Another gasp. A shudder. Lesko could feel the man's body sagging down against the truck. But he could also feel the muscles in the man's shoulders. They were taut, not flaccid. And Lesko could feel the spring being readied in the younger man's legs. Lesko lowered the gun and shifted it, unseen, into his left hand. Then he pressed his right thumb hard between the man's shoulder blades and backed off a step. "Okay, let's walk," he said.

The man pivoted and sprang, his left hand whipping toward Lesko's thumb. He spun, his knee cocked in the direction of Lesko's groin, the butt of his right hand aimed at where Lesko's nose should have been, his left hand groping for the gun that was no longer there. He froze in mid-motion, realizing first that Lesko had danced out of reach and second that the muzzle of Lesko's gun had now appeared from the wrong direction and stopped three inches from his forehead.

"Don't you feel stupid?" Lesko asked.

The man stared, then sagged.

Lesko knocked him cold.

Robert Loftus, his driver's license read. 21 Mayfield Road, Arlington, Virginia. Credit cards said the same. But no official ID. No business cards.

There was a stone stoop close by. A townhouse, No lights except for the third floor. Lesko dragged him from the curb and propped him in a sitting position on the cold marble steps. He sat close to him, pressing him firmly against one of the twin stone balustrades of the stoop. Finding his penlight, he began a closer examination of the wallet's contents.

Robert Loftus was a cop. Some kind of cop. Lesko was sure of it the moment Loftus tried that disarming maneuver. It's a good maneuver. Hardly ever fails. As long as you know which hand you're disarming. Okay, Robert. What kind of cop are you? Probably federal, if your address means anything.

"Hey, Robert," Lesko whispered. He jabbed his ribs with his elbow.

The younger man coughed, then moaned.

Lesko jabbed him again. "Come on. You're drooling all over that nice coat."

"Wait . . ." Robert Loftus managed. "Wait a second." He lowered his face into his hands.

"You want to tell me who you work for, Robert?"

". . . No one."

"Yeah, well, I'm just going to have to keep your driver's license until I find out. What if you have to cash a check for groceries, meantime?"

". . . Fuck you."

Lesko rammed his upper arm against Loftus's mouth so he couldn't scream. Then he brought the butt of his gun down hard on the other man's kneecap. It made the dull, hollow sound of a brick being crushed. Lesko felt the man's teeth trying to bite through his coat but the jaws had no strength. He waited for the first surge of agony to subside.

"Just so we understand each other," Lesko said almost gently, "you do know that's my daughter I was with tonight, don't you? Just nod if you know."

Loftus's head jerked rapidly, his face contorted in pain.

"Well, I have to tell you, I don't have any patience at all with people who involve her in things like this. On top of that, you almost ruined a very nice evening. Who do you work for, Robert?"

". . . The government."

"You want to be any more specific?"

". . . Your government." He regretted the wise-crack instantly and reached to cover his knee.

But Lesko only sighed and slid his body even closer. "You see, Robert, basically I believe that. Because if I didn't think you were one of the good guys, I would have already snapped your spine and dumped your body over in Central Park somewhere so my daughter shouldn't worry she lives in a high crime neighborhood. Do you in any way doubt that, Robert?"

"No . . . I know about you."

"And yet you're still going to make me ask you again."

He shook his head. "I'm FBI. But it was a mistake. Tonight was a mistake."

"Convince me."

"We got a tip . . . an informant . . . said you were seen at the Garden tonight with a woman we have a Jane Doe warrant on. It was all wrong. I should have ended the surveillance when I saw how young she was."

"Who's the Jane Doe?"

Loftus hesitated, choosing his words. "The only name we have is Elena."

Lesko looked at him. "Elena," he repeated. Then, after a pause, "What makes you think I know this person?"

Loftus twisted the corner of his mouth. "Give me a break, Lesko," he muttered.

"I asked you a question."

"The word is . . . we hear you had her, and you let her walk."

"Whose word is that, Robert?"

"I don't know. Street talk."

"Tell me some."

"The word is she admitted it. The word is you blew away two greaseballs . . . three . . . but not her. Certain people want to know why. And what deal she made with you. Her story is that she tried to buy you off and you said no. But they still want to know how come you left her alive."

"She's still alive now?"

"She dropped out of sight. But she's presumed at large."

A funny answer, Lesko thought. If the greaseballs didn't buy her story it would be just as easy to presume she's dead. Unless Loftus knew better. Lesko hoped he did but didn't ask about it. He was silent for a long moment. Somehow it hadn't occurred to him that she'd have trouble explaining why he didn't kill her. And whether all that powder really ended up on the floor with the stiffs or did she sweep some up for herself. But why should he worry? If she got in trouble she'd probably talk her way out of it again with that crazy logic she uses. Lesko didn't like people like that. Not even when he liked them.

"Robert," he braced a hand against Loftus's shoulder and pushed to his feet, "I'm going to walk back down to the subway now. Your gun will be under the second car from the corner. Your license I'll mail you in a day or two."

"Come on, Lesko. You don't need. . . ."

Lesko ignored the interruption. "In the meanwhile, Robert, I would like you never to set foot on this street again. Do that for me and I won't ever set foot on Mayfield Road in Virginia. You got a family down there, Robert?"

Loftus nodded sullenly.

"And I got one here. We understand each other?"

"Yeah."

"Some day we'll have a beer and we'll have a good laugh about this little mistake you made here." He stepped onto the sidewalk.

"Hey, Lesko."

"Yeah?"

"Why did you let her go?"

"Good night, Robert."

"Can you check him out?" Lesko handed the photo license to Buzz Donovan.

"If he's FBI, it's easy. I'll make a call or two." Donovan stared thoughtfully at the face he'd last seen following Lesko and his daughter out the door. "You say he had no other ID?"

"That bother you?"

The older man made a so-so wave with his hand. "We've all left home without it sometimes."

"But you'll let me know if he's not kosher."

"Of course." Donovan looked up at him. "Ray, you're not involved in anything here, are you?"

"If I am, I don't know it."

"Why would he . . . ?" Now it was Donovan who was choosing his words. "Why would the FBI think you're involved with Elena? Would this have anything to do with that whole Katz thing?"

Lesko understood his discomfort. He knew that Donovan had heard of Elena. Anyone who'd ever been briefed on the cocaine hierarchy knew the name. Donovan also knew perfectly well, though he'd never have mentioned it directly, that it was Ray Lesko who killed three men in a Brooklyn barbershop shortly after the murder of David Katz. But Donovan never had reason to imagine, until now, that Elena might have been involved. And even if she was, Donovan still did not doubt for a moment that Lesko was otherwise straight.

"We might have met once." Lesko held up an index finger for emphasis.

"In a barbershop, by chance?"

Lesko kept the finger up.

"But not before or since." Donovan studied him.

Lesko waggled the finger.

Donovan did something with his hands. The gesture meant either that he was satisfied with Lesko's answer or that he'd already heard more than he wanted to know.

"Listen," Lesko was sorry he had brought up the

name. "I don't even know if Loftus told the truth about why he was tailing me. He could have pulled that Elena business right out of the air."

"But it would suggest that there are stories going around that link the two of you."

"There are always stories. If you listen long enough, you'd even find people who'd try to tell you Rock Hudson was a fag."

"You want me to ask?" Donovan tried not to smile. "What people are saying about you, I mean?"

"I couldn't really give a shit."

Donovan signaled for his waiter. "Give me a day or two. I'll call you about Loftus."

"Hey, Buzz." Lesko looked down at his fingernails. "How about checking one more name while you're at it."

Donovan motioned to the waiter for two more of the same as he reached for his notebook and pen. "Shoot," he said.

"Paul Bannerman. Spelled like it sounds, I guess. He has a travel agency up in Westport, Connecticut."

"Is this connected to the other thing?"

"No. No connection."

"So who's Paul Bannerman. And what are you looking for, exactly?"

Lesko squirmed in his chair. "This is strictly personal, all right? It's a guy Susan's seeing. All I want to know is he's clean."

Donovan stared over his glasses. "If Susan gets wind of this, Ray, she'll have you for breakfast. And me for dessert."

Lesko sat back. "I know. I'll tell you what. Just forget it."

"I'll see what I can do."

CHAPTER 4

Susan had told her father that she had met Paul Bannerman through Allie Gregory. It wasn't precisely true. It wasn't quite a lie, either.

True enough, she was in Westport at the time, still searching for some common cause behind the town's extraordinary suicide and accidental death rates. Still poring over records at the town hall and newspaper accounts at the library. But for want of a single bit of hard information that might turn a statistical oddity into a bylined feature story, Susan was rapidly becoming discouraged.

By autumn, however, Westport itself had become the attraction. The fall colors of New England were reaching their peak. Lawns parched by summer were made lush again by September rains. Roadstands were bursting with potted mums, pumpkins, Indian corn and plastic jugs of fresh apple cider. And because the weather was at last cool enough for people to climb to their attics and clean them out, there was the usual last great rush of garage sales before winter. Allie Gregory loved scouting the garage sales. They'd helped her fill many bare corners of her new home at a fraction of the cost of new furnishings and accent pieces.

It was at one of these, with Allie, that Susan first took notice of Paul Bannerman. It was a perfect Saturday morning and the place was a brown-shingled, nineteenth century farmhouse that had a separate garage at the end of a long, steep driveway. The owners had set up one table full of knickknacks, and another, two-thirds of the way up, for taking money. The larger pieces of furniture were displayed just beyond. There was more in the garage itself. Allie lingered at the knickknack table, too long a time to suit Susan. Newly arriving buyers had already gone past them. And new arrivals had a way of snatching up exactly the things Susan might want to buy, just before she spotted them. She pushed on toward the garage. She was hoping to find an old-fashioned plant stand for her apartment. Or some books. You can find some marvelous books at garage sales.

There was no plant stand, but the books were there. Three cartons of them, plus a great stack of those wonderful hardbound *American Heritage* magazines. And it happened again. A tall, youngish man, one of those who'd passed her in the driveway, had reached them first. He was standing over them, dressed in a blue shirt, jeans and deck shoes, a look of dreamy pleasure on his face as he leafed through the illustrated pages. As she waited her turn, his obvious delight made Susan smile. He looked up at her. A nice face. A gentle face. Maybe not quite so young after all. Eyes somewhere between blue and green. Intelligent eyes. He was the type who always seemed to marry his college sweetheart right after graduation. She'd be blond and she'd still have her figure after having two bright and gorgeous kids who'd be in junior high about now.

He acknowledged Susan's presence with a small, shy smile of his own. She moved her lips in silent apology for having intruded, smiled once more, then moved off to join Allie Gregory who was writing a check for a pewter saltcellar. She did not return to the garage. This was their fourth stop and it was almost time for lunch. Susan glanced back up as they walked to Allie's car. He was looking back at her, watching her go.

The next day, Sunday, Allie and Susan decided to look in on a start-of-season sale at a ski shop called Sundance on Westport's Post Road. Susan was in the market for a new pair of skis, her four-year-old Rossignols being too short for her now, but she ended up concluding that she'd do as well in New York without having to lug them in on the train. They wandered into the other room where ski clothing was displayed. The same man was

there. The same faded blue jeans and well-worn deck
shoes. The day being cooler, he wore an Irish-knit
sweater with a hole at one elbow. He was trying on ski
parkas. Still no sign of a wife or girlfriend. No gold band
on his finger. No rings at all.

She nudged Allie Gregory. "That man was at one of
the garage sales yesterday."

"What man?"

"The good-looking one just putting on that orange
jacket. Do you know him?"

"I think I've seen him around."

"Orange isn't his color."

"Oops. He's looking."

"Rats," Susan whispered. "This is the second time
he's caught me staring at him."

"So? Just go say hello. This is Westport, not New
York."

"I can't just . . . what'll I say to him?"

"Tell him orange isn't his color."

Twenty minutes and five ski jackets later, Susan and
Allie decided that a red Austrian-made parka would be
just about perfect for him. It had wide khaki trim across
the shoulders and lots of zippered pockets. Very handsome. Made him look rugged. The khaki went with his
thick, curly hair. A Navy outfit might have brought out
those marvelous eyes a little better but she was already
getting tired of him in blue.

The man, though he'd never actually been given a
vote in the matter, seemed equally pleased and grateful
for the help. The fact is, he admitted, the only decent-
looking things he owned were bought at the urging of
one female friend or another. He was not much of a
shopper.

"I take it you're not married," Allie said brightly.

"No. I'm not." That shy smile again.

"Where do you ski?" Susan rushed to ask, horrified
that Allie was about to swing into a series of embarrass-
ingly unsubtle questions meant to determine whether
he was divorced, widowed or gay.

"Europe mostly. How about yourself?"

"Just here in the East. But someday Europe. It's one
of my dreams."

"Well, if you decide to go, I'll be glad to recommend a few places."

"That sounds as if you've been to them all."

A modest shrug. "I travel quite a bit. The fact is, I run a travel agency here in Westport."

"Susan loves to travel," Allie Gregory beamed. "Why don't you take her address and put her on your mailing list?"

Susan struggled not to roll back her eyes.

He saw her discomfort. "To be honest, I've been trying to think of a way to learn more about you. I'm Paul Bannerman, by the way."

"Susan Lesko." She held out her hand and, out of habit, watched his face for any sign of recognition.

All through her teens and into her twenties, the name, her father's name, had often been in the news. Years of crime stories on page three of the *Post* and the *Daily News*. But it was a feature article in a Sunday magazine section, entitled "New York's Toughest Cops," that made him something of a celebrity and even led to an occasional mention in the nightlife columns. After that, it seemed as if every other person she'd meet would ask "Are you by any chance related to . . . ?" Not that she minded. Susan enjoyed her father's fame and she especially enjoyed telling strangers that Raymond the Terrible Lesko was a big teddy bear, down deep. But then, at the beginning of last year, the newspaper stories turned ugly. 'TOUGHEST COP' PARTNER A SUICIDE. . . . LESKO PARTNER A CROOK? . . . LESKO QUESTIONED IN DRUG SLAYINGS. And finally, 'TOUGHEST COP' QUITS.

If the name meant anything to Paul Bannerman, however, he didn't let it show. "I'll be needing a couple of new sweaters soon," he raised his elbow to show the ragged hole. "I'd hate to come in here alone and pick out the wrong color."

They browsed around Sundance for a while. The owner, a man named Glenn, offered cups of hot spiced wine to Susan and Allie, and then chatted privately with Paul. Then Glenn came over and invited Susan and Allie to take their pick of ski hats as their reward for helping Paul make up his mind before the styles changed again.

Paul was invited for steaks that evening at the Gregorys'. The following morning, Monday, he met Susan for an early breakfast and drove her to her train. He called her at the *Post* that same afternoon. He'd be in the city the day after, and wondered if she'd care to join him for dinner. She said she'd like that. Had she ever been to The Four Seasons? She said she'd love that. On Tuesday evening, as Susan happily picked her way through a menu large enough to roof a small house, a listening device was being installed on the telephone in her 79th Street apartment.

They saw each other often during the weeks that followed. Susan would come to Westport on weekends or whenever her days off fell. Or Paul would drive into the city, sometimes twice a week. He knew the city well. In fact, he seemed to know the Upper West Side better than she did. He took her to West Side restaurants ranging from the extravagantly romantic, such as the Café des Artistes on West 67th Street, to the messy-but-fun, such as Sidewalker's on 72nd Street, where an order of spicy Maryland crab is dumped right onto the paper tablecloth. Susan learned along the way that Paul could order quite comfortably in French and Italian and could make himself understood in German. She was impressed and said so. It seemed like a lot of fluency, even for a travel agent, but Paul brushed it aside, saying that his linguistic abilities were limited to menus and airport signs. Their evening at The Four Seasons notwithstanding, it became clear that Paul preferred to avoid the more famous midtown restaurants. She half-wondered whether The Four Seasons had simply been first-date bait, but she wasn't complaining. The West Side restaurants were fine and, as Paul pointed out, she might as well get to know her own neighborhood.

In conversation, he could discuss the music of Brahms, Count Basie and Bruce Springsteen with equal ease. His range of interests included the French Impressionists, but not so much the Romantics such as Delacroix, whose work Susan adored. He was a student of European and American history, but seemed to have no interest at all in American politics or current world affairs. Revelation piled upon revelation. She might

have found so much sophistication intimidating had he
not been so offhand about his own acquired knowledge,
and had he not shown so much genuine interest in the
things that interested her. His passions included antique automobiles—it was his dream to own and restore
one—and the New York Giants football team, and, of
course, Alpine skiing. They did not as yet seem to include Susan Lesko's body.

Not that she had any intention of leaping into bed
with him. She hadn't even intended to see quite so
much of him or any other man. But each time he called,
even when she had determined to spend some quiet
time alone, she found herself wanting to see him.

Her own intentions aside, she had presumed without
undue conceit that Paul would try to take her to bed as
soon as possible. By their second date, she'd allowed
herself to imagine what he might be like. By the end of
their fifth date, alone in her bed, she found herself
fantasizing about him. He was great. Terrific. In her
fantasies he was warm, funny, affectionate, patient, considerate and excruciatingly sexy. In real life he was all
these things as well, except that at the end of each
evening he would glance at his watch and suggest, as
her father did, that she'd better get some sleep.

"Paul, can I ask you something?" They'd been seeing
each other for five weeks. It was now her second weekend with him in Westport. Except she didn't stay with
him in Westport. He had this perfectly lovely condo-
minium at Beachside Common—they were there now,
with a fire going, the threat of snow outside, what could
be more romantic?—but he'd always take her back to
Allie's for the night.

"Beg pardon?" He was in the kitchen, mixing a
pitcher of hot spiced wine and setting out cheeses.

"I want to ask you something."

"Sure." He came in, setting the refreshments on the
rug by the fire.

"Are we friends?"

"I hope so."

"Pals?"

"Absolutely."

"Just two really good buddies, right?"

"Uh-oh."

"Uh-oh, what?"

"I think I'm about to get hammered for not trying to make love with you."

"Never crossed my mind. But now that you bring it up. . . ."

"Susan," he squeezed one eye shut and looked at the ceiling with the other as if he hoped to find the appropriate response written there. "How about . . . I've wanted you from the first moment I saw you at the garage sale, which is the truth, and that I've dreamt about it every day since, which is also the truth."

"How was I? Any good?"

"Susan. . . ."

"Sorry."

"I suppose I've been waiting for the right moment. I guess I didn't want to blow it by moving too quickly."

"Oh." The old right moment. Most men, she thought, would probably feel that taking a woman out to dinner, then a show or gallery, then some late-night dancing and getting her mildly blitzed would tend to set up the right moment. They'd danced long enough, slow enough and close enough for her to conclude there was plenty of interest down there and for him to conclude that she was probably not a transvestite.

"Want to know what the perfect moment would be?" he asked. "Not that I'd want to wait that long."

"Halftime during the Superbowl?"

"Are you going to be a smart aleck or do you want me to tell you?"

"Tell me. Not that I'm eager, of course. I know it can be a mistake to rush into these things. If, for instance, you'd dropped your pants when I first saw you at that garage sale. . . ."

"Susan, love. . . ."

". . . I guess I would have thought you were the pushy type and I. . . ."

"Okay," he folded his arms, "I won't tell you. I'll just go ahead and do it with Pia Zadora like I planned all along."

"I'll shut up now." She clapped a hand over her mouth.

He poured the wine and handed her a glass. "The perfect moment is about six weeks from today."

Paul smiled at a barely audible "Oh, shit" coming through Susan's fingers.

"The time," he continued, "is about midnight next January ninth. The place is in a private compartment aboard the Orient Express somewhere between Paris and Zürich."

Susan's eyes went blank. Her hand fell away.

"I'm in black tie," he went on, pausing overlong to sip his wine, "and you're wearing an evening dress; black, low cut, it barely covers you from the waist up. You're probably wearing some kind of flapper headband with feathers in it because we'll have just left a dining car that looks exactly the way it did in 1928. . . . No, that's not right."

"No?" Perhaps she said "Oh?" Her mouth hung slack and open.

"No, because right after the dining car we'd make another stop in the bar car. Couldn't very well walk right through. One after-dinner drink, champagne seems right, as we listen to a few Cole Porter tunes played on the black baby grand piano of the bar car. Then we take the rest of the bottle with us, we lurch as elegantly as possible back to our compartment. . . . Pay attention, now." He waved his hand over her eyes. "We're almost at our big moment."

Susan only blinked.

"I'm asking you to go with me." He put his glass down and took her hands. "Perhaps a couple of days in London, then we board the Orient Express and take it almost all the way to Klosters in Switzerland where I have access to a small chalet. Then for the next three weeks we ski our butts off."

"Oh, wow."

"Do you need time to think about it?"

"Oh, wow."

"Not *Oh, wow*. Tickets to a Grateful Dead concert is *Oh, wow*. Making it to the ladies' room on time is *Oh, wow*. Going to Switzerland by way of the Venice–Simplon Orient Express from London is 'Oh, Paul, I'd love to and I'm really sorry for giving you so much grief.' "

"Oh, wow."

Paul let out a sigh and glanced at his watch.

"Paul?"

"Good girl. But you're still stuck on one-syllable words."

"Paul, old buddy?"

"Yes, pal?"

"If you look at that watch one more time and tell me I'd better get some sleep I'm going to sock you right in the mouth."

He was almost everything she'd hoped he'd be. He undressed her slowly. So slowly. For a full hour he explored her body, probing for the nerves that made her shudder and the nerves that made her gasp. And when at last he entered her body, he had absolute control of it and she felt as though she had none at all. She heaved and lashed wildly as he thrust ever more deeply, his lips and tongue finding still more nerve endings on her neck and shoulders. She heard growling sounds coming from deep within her and she heard shouts as her taut body went into mounting spasms and at last exploded into flashes of colored light.

Afterward, after holding her a very long while, talking to her, stroking her back and her hair, he offered her a sip from the glass of wine she'd carried into his bedroom.

"You were yelling before," he said to her. "Want to know what you yelled?"

"Hmm. I'm not sure I do."

"It wasn't anything terrible, exactly."

"Oh, God. What?"

"You're getting warm."

"Oh, wow? I gave you another Oh, wow?"

"More like ten of them."

"Oh wow . . . *shit!*"

"It's okay. You were wonderful all the same."

"Me? You did all the good stuff. I just enjoyed the ride."

"If you think that was good, wait until you try it on the Orient Express."

"Really romantic, huh?"

"It is, but that's not it. All those cars were built in the twenties. They still have their original springs."

A grin spread across her face. "Up-and-down bouncy, you mean?"

"You're beginning to get the picture."

"Oh, rats." The grin turned to a frown.

"What's the matter?"

"We just blew your perfect moment."

"Nope. Rehearsals don't count. Does that mean you'll go with me?"

"The paper owes me two weeks' vacation. I'd have to see about a third week."

"Except for football games and white sales, nothing much ever happens in January, anyway."

"I'll tell my boss you said so."

They made love again. Just as slowly as before, but not as wildly. This time they talked and joked all the while. And afterward, Susan bathed him with warm, moistened washcloths, intending to make love to him in another way. She decided against it. Better to leave something special for the train.

The second time, and then the third, hours later when they woke in each other's arms, were once again all she could have hoped for. Almost all. There was a thing she'd noticed about him in the weeks since they'd met, and she noticed it now in the way he made love. Paul Bannerman always seemed to know exactly what he was doing. No wasted moves. No real spontaneous emotion, at least so far. No wackiness, never early, never late. It was hard to imagine Paul ever losing himself in lovemaking the way she sometimes did. Hard to imagine him ever really giggling, or shouting, or showing any extreme of joy or sorrow. It was hard to imagine him angry.

They spent Thanksgiving at Tom and Allie Gregory's. Susan had invited her father as well, but he begged off, saying he'd promised to spend the day with some of the Gallagher's crowd who had no such place to go. She told him over the phone that she was thinking about a January ski trip to Europe. He seemed genuinely impressed. Even proud.

At first, Paul begged off as well. He spoke vaguely of other commitments that he said he'd try to reshuffle. It was only when he realized that her father would not be there that his *other commitments* were resolved. Not that she blamed him. It was still a bit soon to be meeting family. And she'd known more than one young man whose interest in her diminished considerably after spending an hour or two in friendly conversation with Raymond Lesko. Oh, he was always pleasant enough. But without actually threatening them in any way he would manage to communicate that flossing with a chain saw would be considerably less dangerous than any libidinous lapse involving his daughter. Raymond Lesko did more for male impotence than German measles.

Still, it would have been interesting to see how Paul handled her father. The matador and the bull. Allie said she could have sold tickets.

Allie, by this time, had come to adore Paul Bannerman. What more could Susan want, she asked. He was bright, charming, successful, and one of those men who seemed to genuinely like women. Susan in particular. He was perfect for her. On Thanksgiving day, she said as much every time Susan passed through her kitchen.

Perfect, thought Susan. If not, he was awfully close. What more *could* a woman want? A flaw, maybe. An ordinary human failing. Heck, Paul didn't even snore. He didn't have any family skeletons because he apparently didn't have any family. His father had died when he was quite young, his mother some years later. Each was an only child. So was he. He grew up in California. She saw a UCLA mug on his desk, filled with pencils. No yearbook, though. She'd looked for one among his books, hoping to see what it said about him, who his friends were, what his interests were. Anything.

After college, three years in the Army. Made captain. Stationed in Europe. No Vietnam. Got a master's in international marketing while in the Service. Joined a tour operator afterward, did that for about ten years before opening up his own tour operation and finally a travel agency. Why Westport? A good travel market. And a good local agency was for sale. Not much more to tell, he said. Not especially interesting, he said.

"Ever done drugs?"

"Uh-uh."

"Even gotten drunk?"

"In school a few times. Sure."

"Probably never been arrested, right?"

"Right."

"Ever been in a fistfight?"

"No, but I've written a few strong letters in my time."

"I'm serious."

"Okay. Once, Mary Lou Brickman took my skate key, and when she wouldn't give it back, I punched her in the stomach."

"No, Paul, I'm serious."

"Susan . . ." he asked gently, patiently, "what is it you want to hear?"

"I'm not sure. What would you do if someone insulted you . . . some guy in a bar, for example."

"I'd walk away."

"What if he insulted me?"

"We'd both walk away."

They'd had two or three exchanges like that. And they all went about that way. Paul would start by being flip, trying to keep it light, she'd press him, and he'd either change the subject or his voice would take on a sort of soft, low chill and she'd get mad at herself for being a nag. And for what? What did she really want to know? That he was a real man? Susan never doubted that. She was sure in her own mind that if Paul was ever forced to protect himself, or her, he'd do just fine. But she was also sure that he'd go to almost any length to avoid a confrontation. Which might explain why he'd never been married.

Wait a minute. What is this? Something good had happened to you so there has to be something bad about it? The guy's terrific. And this is Thanksgiving, right? Count your blessings.

As Christmas approached, Susan took it for granted that Paul would share it with her in the city. Her father, no excuses this time, would come in from Queens on Christmas Eve. It was time he met Paul, she decided, and time for him to know that Paul was someone special in her life. And the prospect of seeing how they'd size each other up was getting more interesting than ever.

The three of them could take a long walk along Fifth Avenue, looking at the decorations and the department store windows. Afterward, she'd fix a champagne supper and drag them both to midnight Mass at St. Patrick's Cathedral. On Christmas morning they'd exchange gifts, then Paul and her father could spend the rest of the day watching football and getting acquainted. Her father would leave at about five o'clock because her mother would be coming in from New Jersey for Christmas dinner and there was still too much polite tension between her parents.

But this time it was Paul who couldn't make it. He was sick about it, he told her, but he had business in Florida that would keep him away for the holidays. He had booked a large group onto a Christmas cruise and he was expected to go with them as tour guide and host. Speaking of Christmas, however, he might have an early present for her. If he were to give her a first-class ticket to the Bahamas, how would she feel about joining him there for New Year's? There was a place just off Eleuthera called the Windermere Island Club. Very exclusive, very quiet, very British. Not to try to turn her head, but various members of the royal family owned villas on the club grounds. No telephones or TV, five miles of perfect beach, lots of romantic little coves. The offer, however, would be withdrawn at once if she said *Oh, wow.*

Her disappointment at not sharing Christmas with him faded quickly amid visions of moonlit strolls along a tropical beach. Susan, after a five-second stammer, managed a simple, explosive *yes.*

The Windermere Island Club turned out to be one of those insular anachronisms the British had been establishing since their early years as a colonial power. Once the earliest visitors were satisfied that the trade or plunder potential of a given place could not be exhausted in less than a year, the British would set about choosing a likely spot for a club and shooing away any local who happened to live there.

Since a British club was by definition a retreat, it contained very little that was indigenous to the surrounding area. Native color, to say nothing of colored natives, was specifically excluded. Where possible, a club's ambience and architecture would be distinctly British. If that were not possible due to a lack of suitable building materials, the design of the club would be borrowed from some other colonial post of fond memory. The Windermere Island Club, from the look of it, seemed to have gotten its inspiration in the British occupation of the Massachusetts seacoast. The clubhouse and its outbuildings had a weathered barn look more reminiscent of Cape Cod than of the tropics.

Paul met her at Nassau's International Airport. He waited, already tanned and grinning happily, as she cleared Customs. Taking her bag, hugging her, excited as a schoolboy, he led her through another gate where a Cessna air taxi waited to fly them to Rock Sound Airport on Eleuthera, less than thirty minutes away. He insisted that she sit with the pilot while he sat behind her providing a running commentary on all she saw. They flew over waters of such startling clarity that it seemed they were passing over desert dunes. The only undersea vegetation came in curious round clusters that looked like scattered green oases. Deeper waters ranged in color from aquamarine to turquoise, and as the plane descended, she could make out schools of parrot fish winding through the coral. This was a new Paul. Excited, nervous, at least ten years younger. The old Paul, Mr. Cool, seemed to have been washed away by the gentle surf beneath them.

Landing at Rock Sound Airport, they were met by a smiling Bahamian who led them to a fleet of Ford and Chevrolet station wagons from the early seventies, all in near-vintage condition. After a drive of another forty minutes, they crossed the single narrow bridge that connects Windermere Island to Eleuthera. It seemed to Susan that they'd reached the end of the earth.

"My gosh," she thought aloud. "Is this place ever hard to reach."

"It's deliberate," he told her. "You'll see why."

Crossing the bridge was like going back in time, to the way the islands used to be before the tourists came. The beaches, Paul told her, except for an occasional combing of storm debris, were kept just as they were when Columbus first saw them. A stout wooden barrier swung down behind their car.

The club's manager, an Englishman about Paul's age with an interesting scar beside one eye, was waiting to greet them. His eyes met hers. Appraisingly, she thought. Then they met Paul's. She saw approval in them. Susan wasn't sure whether she was pleased or annoyed. How many other women had been here with Paul?

The manager, chatting amiably, led them through a small forest of hibiscus to the place where they'd be staying. She'd somehow expected a room in the clubhouse proper. But the place was a small villa, lushly furnished, with a well-stocked bar and a terrace that could have accommodated a dinner party. In the living room, a freshly iced bucket of champagne sat on a marble coffee table flanked by a basket of fruit on one side and tray of canapés on the other. The manager, whose name was Colin, said he would be pleased if they would join him for cocktails before dinner. Once again, there was an odd, unspoken communication between the two men. Colin excused himself.

"He seems to know you pretty well," she said, then wished she hadn't.

"I knew Colin in Europe," he said. "We go back a long way." His lips moved again but he said nothing more. She had a sense that he knew what she was asking but did not know how to answer. She turned from him and stepped out onto the terrace overlooking the sea and horizon and miles of pink-hued beach. Not a soul in sight. Not even footprints in the sand.

"You do know how to show a girl a good time, don't you," she said.

He didn't answer. He stepped close behind her, put his arms lightly around her waist and smelled her hair. She shuddered.

"Paul. . . ." She bit her lip. "I feel a little sticky from the trip. How about if I take a shower . . . or we can take a swim?" It was true enough. The clothes she'd traveled in were too warm for this climate. But mostly . . . she could live with not being the first woman he ever brought here . . . but she was damned if she was going to follow the same script.

"Susan. . . ." He brought his lips to her ear. "You are as fresh and as clean as anyone I've met in my whole life."

He trembled as he said that. She felt it against her

back. She'd expected him to say something romantic. While opening the champagne. Something that would lead as quickly as possible to a nice, long, welcome-to-Windermere screw. But she now had a sense, standing there, that that wasn't what Paul had in mind at all. Not just then. And his words. The way he said them. With such longing.

He was making no move to turn her, to run his hands over her body, to loosen her clothing, or even to kiss her. She turned within his arms and held him tightly. He trembled again. She said nothing more.

"Paul?" It was the morning of their second day. They were barefoot, walking slowly along the beach, holding hands. "Do you send a lot of your customers here?" It wasn't precisely what she wanted to know but it was as close as she cared to come to asking about his other women.

"I don't send any," he told her. "There are places I keep for myself. This is one of them."

"It's so lovely here. That seems almost selfish."

"You'll feel the same way by the time you leave. You won't want even your best friends coming here because you won't want anything to change."

"Weren't you afraid that I'd change it for you?"

"You completed it."

They walked along in silence for a while, Susan savoring the compliment. Beyond them, two ladies were approaching from the opposite direction. They were dressed in simple smocks with batik prints and wide-brimmed straw hats. One carried a walking stick. They might have been two elderly members of a British garden club. The ladies smiled a greeting as they passed. Once again, she thought, their eyes lingered appraisingly on her. And once again, they moved on to Paul with that same look of approval. One of them, Susan would swear, even poked him in the ribs as she walked by. Paul spoke before she could ask about them.

"Want to know who you just met?"

"Queen Elizabeth, right?"

"You're close."

"Come on."

"The one on the left is the Duchess of Abercorn. The

other lady, carrying the stick, is the Countess Mountbatten of Burma. I told you. Quite a few of the British aristocracy keep homes here."

"But they were . . ." Susan's eyes went wide, ". . . so sweet." She could not resist a glance back over her shoulder. She straightened quickly. The two ladies were also looking back.

"They're watching us," she whispered.

Paul kept walking. "They've never seen me here with a woman. They're probably saying 'Perhaps that American chap isn't bugger-all queer, after all.' "

Susan's grin stretched to its limit. He'd answered the question she wouldn't have asked.

Her thoughts drifted back to the afternoon before. When he'd held her. For a man who prefers his own company much of the time, a man who doesn't even seem to have any close friends as far as she'd been able to tell, he'd seemed almost desperately glad that she was with him. She was, he had said, as fresh and clean as anyone he'd ever known. Fresh and clean compared to what? She wasn't exactly Linda Lovelace but she wasn't the Flying Nun either. What was he used to? Hell's Angels mommas with tattooed boobs?

But that curious moment had passed. And of course they made love. And Paul was back to his old self again by the time they joined Colin for drinks. Maybe, before they left, she'd take Colin aside and pump him about Paul. What he was like, back whenever *way back* was. Maybe she'd ask. . . .

"Paul?"

"Uh-huh?"

"How do you happen to know a duchess and a countess?"

"I don't. I'm a guest here. So are they. That's all there is to it."

Rats. She wished she hadn't asked. It's more fun to wonder. Now Colin will probably say they met selling vacuum cleaners door-to-door. Better to stay in fantasyland. Like this morning, when she sat by the pool in the same lounge chair used by the Prince of Wales. It wasn't the most sophisticated thing she'd ever done but so what? Enjoy. What's so great about reality?

* * *

The next two days were the most people-watching
fun of Susan's life. Added to her collection of titles were
a baron, two baronets, a viscount and two men who had
The Honorable in front of their names. There were at
least four other people who were entitled to be called
Sir- this or *Lady-* that but she never heard them addressed formally except by staff. The women were some
of the most elegant she'd ever seen, and all of them had
names like Pamela, Cornelia and Fiona. Not a Debbie in
the bunch. Not even a Susan. She'd expected to meet a
Muffy or two and said so to Paul. He pointed out one of
the Cornelias, who'd been a Muffy until that name
plummeted out of fashion in response to popular ridi-
cule. Also a Chip who became a Charles upon his recent
promotion to the presidency of his brokerage firm.

Most of the men were, as her father would have put
it, guys with two last names. Like Prescott Thornton
and Hadley Peale. They wore paisley-patterned dinner
jackets with Bermuda shorts. Susan tried to imagine her
father here. If the other guests saw him wading ashore
they would probably evacuate the island.

Their stay at the club, like most things involving
Paul, was almost perfect in every way. They went scuba
diving—her first time—and snorkeling. He taught her
to sail a sunfish, which she picked up quickly, and they
sailed to a private cove, with boxed lunches and wine,
where they swam naked and made love. They played
three sets of hard tennis every day. The games were
close but Susan had the edge and she took every match
but one, which, to Susan's mild surprise, seemed to
please Paul very much.

Almost perfect.

There was only one odd incident. On the morning of
their final day. They were at breakfast, intending to play
tennis afterward, when Colin came to their table and
told Paul there was a phone call for him. There was
something in Colin's eyes. That unspoken communication again. Paul excused himself and followed Colin.
Susan got up and returned to the buffet for another
sausage. From that angle, she glanced out toward the
pool area and saw that Paul and Colin had stopped,
nowhere near the office phone, and were talking quietly. She could not see Paul's face but he must have

been angry because Colin seemed to be calming him. When Paul returned to the table he said he had a few calls to make, just routine business, and suggested that she go over to the courts by herself where she'd surely find a pick-up game. Whatever was happening, Susan decided not to pry.

She did find a decent game with one of the Pamelas. Afterward, she changed into her swimsuit, Paul nowhere in sight, then spent another hour by the pool working on her tan. Lunchtime approached, with still no sign of Paul. There was a main lounge on the second floor of the clubhouse, octagonal in shape and offering a 360-degree view of the club grounds. Susan went there, hoping to spot him. On her second pass of picture windows she saw him. He was walking toward her, still in his tennis whites, from the direction of the beach. Another man, much older, was walking with him. The older man was surely not a guest because he wore a dark business suit and street shoes. Whatever they'd been talking about, the discussion seemed to be over as far as Paul was concerned. But the older man was pressing, arguing.

They walked nearer. With the sea breeze behind them, Susan could pick up a few words. She heard *Paul.* And *damn it.* And *tolerate.* Yes. Something, something, and he won't *tolerate* it. *It has to stop, Paul. It has to end.* Paul ignored him. He kept walking.

Paul's manner seemed to infuriate the older man. He snatched at Paul's arm. Paul caught his hand, not roughly, and, still holding it aloft, stepped closer so that their faces were only inches apart. Whatever Paul was saying to him, the older man's face turned ashen and his knees began to buckle.

A sound below her. Susan stepped nearer the window. There was another man there. Another dark suit. This one was much younger, about Paul's age except that his hair was thinning. He was moving toward Paul, one hand unbuttoning his jacket. Paul's head turned at the second man's approach. His eyes were shining, his expression . . . frightening . . . almost inviting. The balding man hesitated. Then he backed away, once more out of sight. Paul took no further notice of him. He released the older man's hand but took his arm and guided him up the path. Susan heard him say, "You won't come here again, will you?"

"I will go wherever I. . . ."

"Never again, Palmer. Not even as a paying guest."

Susan stepped back from the window. She wandered through the empty lounge for several minutes, gathering her impressions of what she'd seen and heard. She had, at last, seen Paul angry. All it took, apparently, was a violation of his privacy . . . of the sanctity of his island retreat. She could, she supposed, ask him about it at lunch. He would understand that she didn't mean to eavesdrop. It was probably nothing. Some business rival, some old grudge. Or perhaps she'd better say nothing. Wait for him to bring it up.

He stood up, smiling, as she approached their table. His face betrayed nothing. Pouring an iced tea into her glass, he asked about her morning. She described her game, then mentioned the panoramic view she'd just enjoyed from the room above them.

"Yes," he nodded. "Pretty, isn't it?" He left the lure untaken.

There was movement out toward the office. A group of men walked past the lobby entrance to the dining terrace. Colin and two large Bahamians were escorting the two men in dark suits toward the driveway. After a moment, she heard the slam of station wagon doors.

"Who was that man?" Susan asked, gesturing with her head.

Paul shrugged.

"Didn't I see you talking to him just a while ago?"

"On the beach, you mean." Paul didn't hesitate.

"Yes. He seemed upset."

Paul chewed and swallowed. "It wasn't much of a conversation. He wanted to discuss some old business. I didn't."

"What has to stop?" She asked it less casually than she'd intended.

He hesitated for the briefest moment but his expression gave away nothing. But in that moment she had a sense that his mind had traveled to the upstairs lounge and was replaying whatever words might have been heard from there.

"Susan," he put his fork down. "What you saw was an intrusion that I'm trying to forget. If it's important to you, we'll discuss it. But this has been such a great weekend that I'd. . . ."

"It has," she told him, "and it isn't."

Not the intrusion, anyway. She was less curious about those two men and why they'd come than about this new Paul Bannerman she'd seen. This new Paul could, with a few words, make one of the men turn pale and, with a look, the other back away. But that aside, Paul was right. The weekend had been wonderful. She was not about to let a single minor blemish drop a cloud over it.

Another time.

CHAPTER 5

In Westport later that evening, as the TWA flight from Nassau was passing the Carolina coast, Dr. Stanley Gelman stepped out onto the second floor veranda of the New Englander Motor Inn. There was no movement in the parking area below him, only a cold, wind-blown rain that swept across it in silvery waves. Still, he wished there had been a side exit.

Pulling his tweed hat lower over his brow and bunching his coat collar over his cheeks, he stepped from the veranda's cover and hurried down the exposed fire stairs toward the dark Buick Regal that he'd parked rear-end in, so his license plate would be concealed. Keys in his left hand, he unlocked the door, then paused for a moment to cool the palm of his right hand by holding it flat against the Buick's roof. The palm, still hot and tingling from the spankings he'd administered, was soothed at once. But he held it there a few moments longer. He could still hear the woman's cries, muffled by the pillow in which he'd told her to bury her face. He could hear the odd hooting sound she made as he'd entered her savagely from the rear. And the agonized gasps as he seized her tightly bound wrists and jammed them up high between her shoulder blades. Mrs. Kitsy Sweetzer. A ridiculous name. An absurd woman. His breath was coming fast again.

Dr. Stanley Gelman dried the hand against his coat and slipped behind the wheel. He scanned the parking area one more time before starting the engine. Still no one. Putting the Buick into gear, he coasted quickly to

the nearest exit and blended into the traffic of the Post
Road. His face was glowing. He could feel it.

Gelman was home in five minutes. His house, a redwood contemporary set on a wooded lot off Bayberry
Road, suited the twice-divorced psychiatrist nicely. It
was private, not easily seen from any neighbor's window, it contained every personal comfort he desired,
and it was not unduly ostentatious. His income, even
after the amount his ex-wives extorted from it, would
have permitted a considerably grander home. But let
those two greedy bitches see any show of affluence and
they'd be on the phone to their lawyers. His patients
were another problem. The patients of a psychiatrist,
unlike the clientele of an investment counselor, consider it unseemly if he appears to profit too greatly from
their incapacity to manage their lives.

Stanley Gelman reached to his car visor and touched
the remote unit of his automatic garage-door opener.
His headlights washed over a Mercedes 380SL that he
used when driving anywhere outside Westport. He
tapped the unit once more and the door slid down behind him. On the doorway leading to his kitchen was a
small box resembling the face of a Touch-Tone telephone. He tapped out the digital code that disengaged
his security system and unlocked the door. He pushed it
open, his mind already on a long, hot soak in his Jacuzzi
and wrapping his still-smarting hand around a tall, cold
vodka tonic. His body was beginning to itch from the
touch and smell of Kitzy Sweetzer.

Outside, in a cul-de-sac almost directly across Bayberry Road from Stanley Gelman's driveway, a man and
a woman sat watching his movements through the
streaked windshield of a Subaru station wagon. The
woman was small, no more than five feet two, and
weighing less than a hundred pounds. Her hair was
brown, with a reddish tint, worn in an elfin cut that
made her seem even tinier. She was dressed in jeans
and a sheepskin jacket trimmed with fur. Her skin was
pale but unlined. She could pass for thirty in an advanta-
geous light, although she was well into her forties. Her
face might have been called pretty except that her eyes
were so quick, so intelligent and direct that superficial
observations tended to be discouraged.

"Well?" She shot a glance at the man with the curly gray hair who sat at the wheel. "What do you think?"

"He seems to be alone in there," he answered. Dr. Gary Russo, M.D., surgeon, Johns Hopkins class of 1955, saw that Gelman had passed through what looked like a living room, dark except for the spill of light from the kitchen, and flipped on the lights of a bedroom or bathroom. He lowered his binoculars to wipe away some condensation from the inside of the windshield. He raised them once more. Gelman was returning to the kitchen. He was reaching into a cabinet and now he was pausing at the door of a copper-colored refrigerator. "Looks like he's making a nightcap. How long do you think we should sit here?"

"Until Billy shows up." Carla Benedict gestured toward his mobile phone. "Or until Molly calls to say he's back at Mario's."

Gary Russo smacked his lips irritably. It could be a long night, and he was already feeling pressure from his bladder. The reference to Mario's, a bar directly across from the Westport commuter station, seemed to make it worse. He could always get out and step behind a tree, he supposed. But if old Billy McHugh was anywhere close by, he just might pick that moment to make his move.

"How well do you know this Gelman?" Carla Benedict asked.

"Just by reputation. A real sleazeball." He'd heard stories about Dr. Stanley Gelman almost from the day he'd opened his own cosmetic surgery practice three years earlier. All of them from other doctors, none for attribution. God knows Gelman wasn't the only shrink around who went beyond supportive hugs and hand-holding. But Gelman was much worse than most because the line on him was that he fundamentally despised women. Dried-out Barbie dolls, he called his Westport patients. Self-absorbed whiners. Whenever he had a patient who was at all attractive, and at all unsure of it, sooner or later he'd plant the notion that the acid test of her sexual allure would be a private evaluation by her therapist. How else could he offer remedial advice? Perversely, there were stories of marriages he'd destroyed by advising female patients to cut off sexual contact entirely. There were worse stories. He would suggest to certain of his patients that the key to sexual liberation was to go and seek sexual adventure wherever they could find it. Try the delivery boy. The meter reader. A black man. Try two, even three men at a time. Then try a woman.

The urgent call from Molly Farrell, once she mentioned Gelman's name, had not surprised Dr. Russo in the least. A woman, a regular at Mario's off the 5:44 from Grand Central, divorced, fairly attractive, normally well-behaved if she stayed within her limit of three whiskey sours, had suddenly and most awkwardly begun propositioning some of the male commuters at the bar. Uncle Billy, which was what nearly all the Mario's regulars called the popular bartender, gently took her drink from her hand and led her back to the office for some strong coffee and a good talking-to.

There, to his horror, the woman made a pathetic and near-hysterical attempt to seduce him as well. He ran back into the restaurant, where Molly Farrell was in the process of serving a table of six, and nearly wrenched her arm dragging her back to the woman in the office. The woman, by this time, was sobbing out of control. It took a full twenty minutes, with both Molly and Billy sitting with her, holding and stroking her, for the halting details of her treatment at the hands of Dr. Stanley Gelman to emerge. Billy McHugh listened, his own eyes moist. He stood up, kissed her lightly on the forehead, then turned and left the office. Because Billy had been better these past three or four months, Molly assumed that he'd returned to his place at the bar. She made the woman stretch out on the office couch and covered her with a coat. By the time she turned out the light and stepped back into the restaurant, Billy McHugh was gone. She hurried out the door and, seeing nothing of Billy, crossed to the public phone on the Westport station platform.

Three hours had passed since then. It was more than enough time for Billy McHugh to have picked up his tools, get into his working clothes, and locate Stanley Gelman. Russo had very mixed feelings about trying to stop him this time. If anyone ever deserved Billy, it was Gelman. But Russo had made a promise and he'd do his best to keep it. He owed at least that much to Paul Bannerman.

"Where would you look for Gelman?" Carla Benedict touched his arm. "If you were Billy, I mean."

"I'd have to start right here."

"Then what? What if he wasn't home?"

"I'd stay right over there." He pointed through the windshield. "Back in those trees. Sooner or later Gelman would pop that garage door and I'd go right in behind him."

"But Gelman just popped it. Why wouldn't Billy have done that, too?"

"I don't . . . shit!" Gary Russo ran a hand across his mouth. "Because he's better than that, that's why."

"You think he's already inside."

"Let's go." He snatched his medical bag and stepped into the slanting rain.

Stay calm, Gelman told himself.

Easy.

He could see his bare chest heaving and he willed it to slow down. He willed the terror he felt to ease to a level he could manage, so that reason and then control could follow.

He sat rigidly in the swirling waters of his gleaming brown Jacuzzi, naked, utterly helpless. Where the man came from, how long he'd been there, Gelman could not know. There had been no sound, not even a shadow. Only a stinging tug at his scalp and a black blur as a powerful arm slipped under his chin and tightened against his carotid arteries. The arm tensed when he struggled, it relaxed when he did not. The man said nothing, did nothing else. Gelman did not understand. It was a submission hold and the man was expert at it. He would be unconscious in seconds if that was what the man intended. Or his neck could be snapped. Oh, God. But the man didn't seem angry. Not even excited. He was breathing softly, naturally, against Gelman's ear, his fingers twined tightly in Gelman's thick brown hair.

"Take anything," he said. "Take whatever you want. You don't have to hurt me."

"Finish your drink." It was a gravelly voice. A mature voice. Chillingly calm. Something in the way he spoke suggested to Gelman that the man had made a decision.

Slowly, carefully, Stanley Gelman reached for the vodka tonic he'd set on the Jacuzzi's edge. There was a bottle there, too. He didn't remember bringing in the bottle. He was sure he hadn't. Hard to think.

Burglars. That's all they are. This one is just holding me here while another goes through the house. Okay. Okay, that's fine.

"Finish it," the voice said. The arm tightened against his neck. Gelman drained the glass and set it down.

"Pour from the bottle. Pour a lot," the voice said. Gelman poured two inches over the ice. The arm tightened. He poured two inches more.

"Now drink that."

Okay, thought Gelman. Get me drunk. That's smart. It will buy you more time when you and your friend leave. Very smart. It means you don't have to hurt me, doesn't it? Just get me drunk.

He took the glass and drained it.

"Again," the voice said. Gelman poured four more inches.

Better than any layman, Gelman could analyse and understand his fear. The psychology of torture. Take away a man's clothing, strip him naked, and you take away half the man. Immobilize him, make him powerless, and you take away half of what's left. Hide your face, ignore his pleas, tell him nothing of why this is being done to him, allow his terror to feed upon itself and the torture becomes all but unnecessary. Unless cooperation is not what you're after. Unless you want to break him. To make him hurt.

No, he told himself. That's not the case here. A burglary pure and simple. Cooperate. Do not resist. But wait. There should be other sounds in the house. Drawers opening and closing. Closets ransacked. But there was nothing.

A deadening thought struck him. He's a husband. The husband of one of those women. She had told him things.

Talk to him. Get him to talk. Make him understand

that she's a sick woman. Very sick. Turning on those who are trying to help her. With sick lies.

"If you'll just . . . if you'll only tell me what this is about. . . ."

"Just finish your drink." The forearm tightened, hurting him.

Gary Russo and Carla Benedict huddled against the single side window of Gelman's garage. Using a penlight cupped in his hand, Russo scanned the outside edges of the window's frame. The small circle of light stopped on a half-inch hole, freshly drilled. He looked up at Carla, who nodded knowingly. It had been drilled to fish for the alarm wire. Once Billy had it—there was little doubt he was now inside—he would have spliced a bypass to it. The penlight moved to the window clasp. It was in place but the screws that held it had been torn loose and were probably in Billy's pocket. Carla Benedict tried the window. It opened easily. The clasp fell into Russo's waiting hand.

Russo opened his bag and extracted two pairs of surgical gloves. He waited as Carla removed her rings and put hers on, then helped her through the garage window. Russo followed. The penlight's beam scanned the garage interior. Russo allowed the beam to pause meaningfully on the Mercedes—that would have been where the intruder waited, in it or behind it—then it traced a path to Gelman's kitchen door. He opened his bag once more and withdrew its leather tray of implements and drugs. Under the tray and clamped to the bottom was a Belgian automatic pistol, plus a silencer that was fully eight inches long and as wide around as a half-dollar. He screwed the silencer to the barrel as Carla refilled the bag.

"Go," he whispered.

Gelman's heart jumped. A voice. A woman's voice. And he hadn't imagined it because the arm at his throat went tense and it twisted slightly as if the man had turned his head to look. Then he felt the arm relax and he heard what sounded like a sigh.

"What good is this?" asked the voice at his ear.

"At this point. . . ." Another voice. A man's voice.

"I guess not much." He heard footsteps on the tile. The man. He could see him now, coming around the Jacuzzi. A gun. A long black gun hanging at his side.

"Doctor?" Oh, God. Oh, thank God. "Doctor Russo?"

Gary Russo ignored him. He gestured toward the vodka bottle and looked into the face of the man holding Stanley Gelman. "How much?"

"About ten ounces in ten minutes."

Russo glanced at his watch and nodded. He raised his gun sideways, looking at it as if it were so much useless metal, then stepped to a marble countertop and set it down.

"Wait," Gelman gasped. "What are you doing? Get this guy off me, Goddamn it." Gelman could hear that his speech was slurring. The one holding him was getting him drunk. He understood that. It was some kind of a set-up. But this part he didn't understand at all. That's Gary Russo. He's a fucking doctor, for Christ's sake.

"Billy, what did you have in mind, exactly?" Russo asked the question calmly, clinically. No hint of disapproval.

The man—who the hell is Billy?—seemed to be answering but not with words. Gelman could feel him gesturing. Then he saw Russo nod his understanding and shake his head as if he disagreed. Russo moved closer and knelt at the side of the tub.

"Dr. Gelman, just relax now," he said. "What sedatives do you keep here in the house?"

"Wha . . . sedatives?" Gelman blinked disbelievingly. "What the hell are . . . will you just get this guy the fuck off me?"

"He's not going to hurt you. What about Valium? You must have Valium."

Gelman stared stupidly. This is crazy, he thought. It's like one of those nightmares where you're in terrible trouble but everyone around you is just calmly passing the time of day. You're strapped into the electric chair and the warden and the executioner are making small talk. How's the wife? Kids okay? They sure grow up fast, don't they? Got any pictures? But this wasn't any execution. They're just playing some goddamned game. Okay. You want to play, we'll play. But tomorrow I'm going to have your ass.

"Valium. I have some Valium."

"How much?"

"I don't know. Maybe fifty milligrams, I.V."

"How much was in the vial originally?"

"A hundred milligrams. Hey, so what?"

"Thank you, Doctor. That's fine." Russo looked up at Carla, who was already poking through Russo's medical bag. He held up three fingers and then formed a zero. Thirty milligrams.

Gelman heard the sounds she was making. He'd forgotten about her. That was a woman's voice he'd heard first. She'd said "Uncle Billy" to the guy holding his head. Who is she? A patient? That *is* what this is all about, isn't it? One of those bitches had gone whining to Russo.

"Who's back there?" he demanded. "If that's one of my patients . . . ?"

"Oh, no," Russo smiled. "That's Carla Benedict. She works at the Westport Library. Reference section."

"Hi, Doctor Gelman," she called pleasantly. She was at the washstand drawing a solution into a disposable 5cc syringe. She raised the needle to the light and squeezed off a short stream. Next she brought it around to Stanley Gelman's left side.

"Hi," she repeated. She turned his left arm so the palm was up and she sat on it, pinning it to the Jacuzzi's edge. Gary Russo took the syringe from her and found a vein in the crook of Gelman's arm.

"Wha . . . what are you doing?" Gelman asked.

Russo withdrew the syringe and patted Gelman's cheek. "I just killed you, you little prick."

The doctor used his penlight for a final check of Stanley Gelman's pupils. He'd already checked twice for pulse. Gelman's eyes were staring sightlessly at the churning hot water of the Jacuzzi. His expression resembled an embarrassed grin. No look of fear, no suggestion of panic. It was just about right.

Russo lifted Gelman's chin and peered closely for any sign of discoloration. No contusions. Only a slight rosiness under the health-club tan where Billy had gripped him. Billy had already washed the neck with damp tissues to remove any fibers his black sweater might have left. Everything looked fine. The syringe, with Gelman's prints tamped onto it, still dangled from his arm. Cardiac arrest had come within a minute. Much better, much cleaner than the bathtub fall and fractured skull Billy probably had in mind. Tubs are dangerous. Billy wasn't a young man anymore. In the struggle, he might have slipped as easily as Gelman.

Russo made a final check of the bathroom. Carla had broken down his pistol and returned it to its place. He'd felt sure it would not be needed, but there was always the slim possibility that Gelman could have bested Billy, or that Russo might have needed it to get Billy's attention so that this could all be done properly. The Valium vial, also with Gelman's prints on it, was left on the washbasin along with the paper wrapping from a Plasti-Pak disposable syringe. It had been a small detail, establishing that Gelman had Valium on hand and that the amount was sufficient for him to commit suicide. But it's the small details that could land you in prison.

Carla Benedict was resting on the toilet seat. She'd been on her hands and knees, obscuring any heel marks between the garage window and Gelman's tub. Billy McHugh was waiting for them by the garage window. He'd gone there to resplice the alarm wire, cover the splice with putty, replace the screws in the window clasp with the aid of plastic wood, sweep up the shavings from his electric drill and patch the drill hole with the redwood plug he'd saved.

"Are you ready?" the doctor asked Carla.

She took a deep breath and let her shoulders sag. "Billy wants to know if we're sore at him."

"Let's talk in the car."

"He says he's sorry. He wants us to come back to Mario's for a bacon cheeseburger."

"A cheeseburger." Russo shook his head. "He's sorry I just had to kill a man for him so he's going to treat us to a cheeseburger?"

They hadn't seen Billy McHugh leave. One moment he was a silent shadow moving a stack of firewood to cover any footprints outside the garage window—the rain would do the rest—and the next he was gone. Russo took Carla's arm and led her across Bayberry Road and down the facing street to the parked Subaru. Just another suburban couple leaving a late dinner party. As they approached the station wagon, Carla took a handkerchief from her pocket and began dabbing the rain from her eyes. Russo escorted her to the passenger door and moved to open it.

"Carla?" the low, gravelly voice came from a shadow on a stone wall bordering somebody's yard. "Carla, are you okay?"

Russo paused at the door, not wanting to turn on the inside light by opening it. He saw Carla's handkerchief. Billy must have thought she was wiping tears. He should live so long.

"Go on, Billy," he said softly. "Get away from here."

"He hurt one of my friends, Doc." It was not quite an explanation. More a statement of the obvious.

"Billy, this isn't the place to talk."

"I'll make it up to both of you."

I know, Russo thought. A bacon cheeseburger. But he said nothing.

"Is Carla crying?"

"She's just tired, Billy." At least he thought that's all it was. On the other hand, why the hell should he be reassuring Billy? "And she's sad. She wonders, like I do, whether we'll ever have any peace around here. And whether you care more about some woman in a bar than you do about her."

"Hey, that's crazy. You tell her, will you? That's just not so."

"Forget it, Billy. Go home."

"We have peace here. Especially, we have friends here. I bet in our whole lives we never had friends like since we came to Westport."

"She knows that, Billy. And she understands that we want to take care of our friends. I think she's worried that sometimes we don't take such good care of each other."

"Well, that's not right." His tone was gently scolding. "That's not right at all. There's nothing in the world I wouldn't do for my friends."

"We know that, Billy." How well we know that.

A long pause. "Are you going to tell Paul?"

"I don't know. We haven't thought about that."

"Because it wasn't like you think. I wasn't going to. . . ."

"Billy," he hissed sharply. "Can we get away from here please?"

"Hey," the voice brightened. "What about that cheeseburger. You like it charred on the outside and bloody in the middle, right? I'll fix it myself."

"Okay, Billy. Sure."

"Carla?"

What the hell, she thought. So it's not a total loss. "Sure. I could eat."

"That settles it." the shadow rolled soundlessly over the wall. "I'll see you back there, okay? Hungry is one thing I know how to fix."

Carla sat silently through the first few stoplights during the ten-minute ride back to Mario's. A police cruiser approached from the opposite direction, shushing by on the black wet road. She glanced at it without interest. It would be tomorrow afternoon at the earliest before anyone became sufficiently concerned about Gelman's absence to consider forcing his front door. She had deeper concerns about tomorrow.

"Are we going to tell Paul?" she asked finally.

"I'd hate to have him find out from someone else."

"Molly won't say anything if we don't."

"That's if he doesn't ask her. Molly won't lie to Paul and I don't think I want to, either."

She shook her head. "All we promised was we'd keep Billy out of trouble. We did that, sort of."

Gary Russo drummed his fingers against the steering wheel. "What about next time, Carla?"

"We'll need him someday, Gary. Meanwhile, we just keep working with him."

"Wonderful."

"This time was different. Seeing that woman come on to him and then get hysterical was more than he could handle."

"They were all different," he answered, yawning. "How long do you think it will be before some other woman walks into Mario's who's just been slapped around by her husband? Or some guy who's being fucked over by his wife's lawyer, or some old lady who's had her life savings churned down to nothing by a stock broker? These people are all Billy's friends and he's their Uncle Billy. Sooner or later someone else is going to hurt one of Uncle Billy's new friends and that someone is going to die."

"He's getting better," she repeated stubbornly. "This is the first time since last August."

"It's also a whole new year. We're only three days into it and already he's started thinning out Westport's population again."

"Stop that," she muttered.

"Stop what?"

"Being negative. Billy's come a long way since he's been here. He probably has more friends than any of us."

"Friends," Russo repeated. "I'm getting very tired of that word."

"Anyway, Gelman's a piece of shit. He got what he deserved and he's where he belongs."

"What Gelman deserved," the doctor answered patiently, "was public disgrace and the loss of his license. Where he belongs is in a prison getting gang-raped in the shower room."

"Fat chance. A patient's word against a doctor's?"

Russo ignored that. "And where Billy belongs, if Paul is honest about it, is in Greenfield Hill." He gestured with his thumb in the direction of the psychiatric hospital on Westport's northern border. "The man is just too dangerous."

"Only to people like Gelman," she shook her head. "Ask anyone else, Billy is as warm and kind and generous as anyone they've ever. . . ."

"Oh, for Pete's sake, Carla. Are you listening to yourself?"

She folded her arms and turned away from him.

"What Billy is," Gary Russo softened his voice, "is a warm, kind and generous man who happens to kill people in very large numbers."

"Most of us have killed, Gary. In very large numbers."

"We've killed to protect our own and when we didn't see that we had a choice. It's not the same."

"We did it reluctantly, you mean."

"I think so, yes."

"Gary, if you don't know that's bullshit, you're crazier than Billy. You want us to be honest? You want me to tell you how much remorse you showed when you were shooting up old Stanley back there?"

"Do you want to discuss this or not?"

She looked away again. He tried again. "Carla, honey, I'm trying to sort this out. I can talk to you or I can talk to Paul."

"Go ahead."

"Talk to Paul?"

"No." She touched his arm. It was almost a slap. "I'm listening."

"How much do you know about Billy's background?"

"I don't know." She'd known him, or known of him, for ten or twelve years. "We've never talked much about his personal life."

"He's never had one. None. Do you think I'm exaggerating?"

She didn't answer.

"As far as anyone knows, Billy never had a home, never had a family, and never had more than a few years of grade school education. One day he wandered into a Marine recruiting office carrying a birth certificate. Even Billy isn't sure whether it was his or someone else's. The Korean War was on, so they took him, trained him and shipped him over. From that time on, all the respect, all the approval, and almost all the money he ever got in his whole life came because he was good at killing. First for the Marines, then for Naval Intelligence, then the CIA, and then he also went free-lance working for the Israelis and for British and German counterterrorist units. Killing was not only what they paid him for but practically the only thing anyone ever talked to him about. He had no friends, no idea how to make friends, and no outside interests at all. I wouldn't be surprised if he's never even petted a dog."

"Paul was his friend. And Paul's mother, I heard, was his friend before that."

"Rare exceptions." Russo dismissed those examples with a flick of his hand. "Anyway, even Paul probably never heard Billy string more than five words together, or laugh, or even smile before he came to Westport. And even Paul was wary enough of Billy to keep him stashed at Greenfield Hill the whole first year he was here."

"He wasn't stashed" Carla looked up at him. "Paul gave him a job there. It was just until he could get used to the idea of settling in here."

Russo didn't bother arguing the point. If Billy had worked for almost anyone but Paul, and especially if he had stayed a CIA contract agent, the most he'd have had to look forward to in his autumn years was a padded room with a lifetime supply of Thorazine, or a nice ride in the country and a bullet in the back of his head. Preferably the bullet because the last thing they'd want is Billy's head clearing up long enough to decide maybe he should be mad at somebody.

"Which brings us," said Russo, "to the metamorphosis of Billy McHugh. He's here a year, keeping out of trouble, not bothering anybody, and Molly Farrell has a brainstorm. She needs a relief bartender at Mario's. How about, she asks Paul, we give Billy a try. She thinks it might be perfect for him because that way he's forced to be out and around people, they'll almost all be friendly, and none of them will pay too close attention to him. Paul agrees. We all agree. We say, who knows, maybe there really is a human being in there and anyway Molly would always be close by and she can keep an eye on him."

"It was a good idea, Gary. And it worked."

"Did it ever," Russo fairly shouted. "Beyond anyone's wildest hopes. Here's a man who's never had a close friend in his life," he held up a hand, "who can count maybe two people in all that time who weren't afraid of him and who ever had more than a five-minute conversation with him, and here he's being greeted by fifty smiling people his first day on the job. Never mind that he's a little quiet. He's new. He'll loosen up. Never mind that he doesn't know from daiquiris and mimosas. Hardly anyone at Mario's drinks that shit anyway. Never mind that he talks to himself sometimes. In a crowded bar they'll think he's talking to another customer.

"By the third night he's starting to smile back a little. I saw it myself. I would have thought it was a nervous tic except Billy doesn't have any nerves. By the third night he's actually answering people who talk to him. Then comes the end of his first week and it's his day off but he won't take it. He likes it there. By the end of the second week he's recognizing a lot of the regulars and he gets it into his head that he's part of the reason they come in. They *like* him. He knows that because they keep saying things like 'Hey, my friend,' and 'How's it going, buddy?' Now Molly has to explain to him that having friends is nice but it's not necessary to buy them every other round and a two-ounce drink is generous enough if he doesn't want his new friends knocking down telephone poles on their way home."

"Look . . . I know all this." Carla knew what was coming. Gary's Frankenstein speech. She'd heard it before.

"Don't stop me now," he took both hands off the wheel. "I'm just getting to the good part." A sheet of rain washed over the Subaru's hood. Russo turned the wipers on full. "You want to know how little it takes to create a monster? All it takes is one customer who's been calling bartenders *Uncle-* this or *Uncle-* that all his drinking life to walk in during week three and say, 'Evening, Uncle Billy. How are you tonight?' A couple of minutes later, a woman two stools down calls him the same thing.

"Molly sees that it kind of startles him but it also pleases him and she figures, what can it hurt? She starts introducing him that way and it works immediate magic. By week four it's as if the rest of his life never happened. The metamorphosis from killer slug to social butterfly and everybody's favorite uncle is complete. Suddenly we have Billy McHugh telling jokes. We have Billy McHugh laughing out loud. We have him reading the sports pages every morning in case a customer wants to bullshit about last night's game. But then, God help us, we also have Uncle Billy McHugh starting to listen to the troubles of all his little nieces and nephews. He learns that other people, people who are not his friends, are cheating them, divorcing them, firing them, two-timing them, harassing them and even burglarizing them. All of a sudden we have our Uncle Billy remembering what he's good at, and people start to die."

The Subaru's tires hummed across the grating of the Saugatuck River Bridge. Mario's and the Westport station were two blocks away. "Why do you talk like it's all Billy?" she asked sullenly.

"Who else is it?"

"You've done your share of housekeeping. So have I."

"Yes, but not right in Westport if we could help it. We don't foul our own nest. And we sure don't want any more people noticing that the obituary columns were getting longer than the garage-sale listings."

Carla stared ahead. "You're talking about Paul's new friend?"

"Yup."

"He says that's under control. Is it?"

"Apparently."

"She's with him now, isn't she? Down at Windermere. Why is he still seeing her?"

"Because he likes her, I guess. And yes, she is." Russo turned onto Railroad Place. He saw a parking slot a few storefronts past the entrance to Mario's.

"Come on, Gary. If she's not a problem, why hasn't he dumped her?"

Russo said nothing. He backed the Subaru into the space and shut off the engine. Carla made no move to leave the car.

"Your cheeseburger will get cold," he said.

She looked at her hands. "I don't like Paul getting involved with an outsider."

"A lot of us have, Carla. Paul's entitled. And he's a careful man."

"If he needs to get his ashes hauled, he doesn't need some young kid. Molly Farrell would be happy to oblige him. So would I, for that matter."

"And let's not forget masturbation." Russo threw up his hands. "What the hell's eating you? You're jealous of the Lesko girl?"

"No."

"Of course not." He poked her.

A tiny shrug. She looked away.

"Carla, honey," he took her hand, "It will end soon enough. Paul knows it can't go anywhere."

"I hope he does."

"Give him a break, will you? She makes him feel good. What's the harm?"

"Are you kidding?" She turned to him. "Look . . . granted he's got a right to a private life and I probably wouldn't mind very much if he took up with one of the locals. He could have his pick of all those divorced real estate ladies. But this one's a reporter for a New York newspaper. And her father is even bigger trouble. What if she gets her father snooping around up here?"

"Snooping by either one of them is exactly what Paul is trying to head off. As for her father, he knows nothing about Westport and nothing about Paul."

"How do you know that?"

"Molly's had a wire on her for three months now. The Lesko girl, I promise you, is absolutely not a danger to us." Russo reached for her shoulder and gave it an affectionate shake. "Hey, look. I think you're getting a case of the post-holiday blahs. What do you say, after Paul calms down about the Gelman thing, we hit him for a couple of first-class tickets to a quiet beach of our own. We'll lie in the sun all day and screw our brains out all night."

"So you're definitely going to tell him?"

"Tell you what. We'll wait until he asks."

"He will. And it might be the end of Billy."

"All the more reason to have those tickets handy. What do you say?"

"You might have a deal." Carla opened her door.

CHAPTER 6

The TWA flight from Nassau swung wide over Long Island to take its place in the landing sequence for John F. Kennedy Airport. Paul was dozing. He'd slept through the movie. Susan Lesko dreamily studied the green route map in the rear of TWA's in-flight magazine. Her finger traced a line from the Bahamas to New York, then from New York to London, then from London to the southeast corner of Switzerland. Five more days. They'd be off again.

She found herself wondering whether life with Paul would be like this all the time. Jetting to the islands. Then, tan intact, popping off to Europe for a spot of skiing. Where would they go when it was summer? A cruise of the Greek Islands? A villa in the south of France?

Some life. Not bad for a Polish Catholic cop's daughter from Queens. She'd have to quit her job, of course, but she'd still want to work somewhere. Maybe as a stringer for the *International Herald Tribune.* Or as a travel writer. Another possibility, she supposed, was to work with Paul at his travel agency, but that might be carrying togetherness a little too far. She'd much rather do something that was her own. Separate careers are probably better for a . . . relationship.

She almost said marriage. A number of times now she'd fantasized about what it would be like being married to Paul. The daydreams embarrassed her. They seemed uncool, unliberated these days, even though she suspected that almost every woman still had them.

And she'd thought about his age. He was thirty-nine, he said. Fifteen years older, although you wouldn't know it from the shape he kept himself in. If they had kids he'd be pushing sixty by the time they were college age. Not a big deal. Better to wonder whether she could keep him interested that long. It was a reasonable question that had nothing to do with self-esteem. She didn't even know why he was so interested in her in the first place. Okay, she was good-looking and fairly bright, a pretty good athlete, enthusiastic, with a decent sense of humor and maybe not a bad lover, but so were a lot of women. And okay, he'd more or less answered the question back at Windermere when he told her she was as fresh and clean as anyone he'd met in his whole life. Eye of the beholder. But he seemed to mean it.

Those eyes. They looked so sad just then. What she wouldn't give to see the things they'd seen and to know what was going on behind them.

Strike that. There were a couple of things her own eyes had seen that she wouldn't be crazy about him seeing. She hadn't sprung into existance on the day they met either. Better to keep some mystery in there.

Speaking of mysteries. That conversation this morning with that old man at the Windermere. That man was afraid of Paul. She saw his face after he'd grabbed Paul's arm and Paul turned on him. What it might have been was some personal argument between them that wasn't any of her business anyway and Paul didn't want it ruining their Windermere holiday. That would be just like him. Susan reached toward Paul's lap and placed her hand lightly over his.

"Hi." He opened his eyes. A lazy smile.

"We're almost at Kennedy," she said. The flight attendant had begun moving through the first-class cabin checking seatbelts and getting seats returned to their full upright position.

"Susan," he checked his watch. It was after eleven. "How about coming back to Westport with me tonight?"

"I just can't." She squeezed his hand. "I have to be at work at seven." And the next five days were going to be madness. The paper would wring every last moment out of her in return for that extra week's vacation. Then she had to get her skis sharpened and waxed and decide what she was going to bring and start packing.

Paul was frowning. From his expression it was not a romantic invitation after all. He looked the way her father looked whenever she was going home late and alone.

"Do you worry about me?" she asked. "Living alone in New York, I mean?"

"Of course I do."

"That's nice."

"What I'd really like is for you to stay in Westport until we leave. And after we get back too, for that matter."

Susan's eyebrow went up. If she heard it correctly, that was an invitation to come live with him. But that invitation was even less romantic than the other. That frown. He really did seem worried about her.

"I just have too much to do," she raised his hand and kissed it. "As for after we get back, let's wait and see how things go."

He nodded, saying nothing. More mysteries.

"You know," she told him, "I'm probably one of the best-protected single women in all of Manhattan. My father's a retired policeman. I'm not supposed to know it but he gets the cops in my neighborhood to look out for me."

"That's good to hear. I hope they're just as tough as he is."

She looked at him quizzically. "You know about my father?" Paul had never mentioned him before. Or asked about her family.

"New York's Toughest Cop? Sure. We read newspapers in Westport, too, you know."

"How come you never asked about him?"

"Because you never brought him up. I thought it might be a sensitive subject. Anyway, I was much more interested in his daughter."

"You'd like him, Paul."

"I'm sure I would."

"I have a date with him Wednesday night. A basketball game and then dinner. That's another reason why I have to stay in the city."

"I guess I won't worry about you on Wednesday."

She heard the grinding sound of the landing gear coming down and locking into place. "I haven't told him about you, either. He worries about me, too. Except he gets snoopy and you don't."

Paul said nothing.

"I'm going to tell him about you on Wednesday. But it will be time enough for you to meet him after we get back from Europe. If you'd like to, that is."

"You're not afraid he'll scare me off?"

"I'd like to see what could scare you," she smiled.

At the Marriott Airport Hotel in Miami, Robert Loftus knocked on the door of a third-floor suite. A voice said "Yes?" and he gave his name. The door opened. A man named Burdick, in shirtsleeves, with a shoulder holster, wavy blond hair and dead eyes let Loftus pass and then checked the corridor behind him.

In the sitting room of the suite, two more men sat at a large coffee table that held several thick manila files. One of the files lay open. A photograph of Paul Bannerman was clipped to the inside cover.

The older of the two men at the table, silver-haired, neatly groomed, in a dark suit, in his late sixties, held out his hand for the envelope Loftus carried. Loftus made no move to surrender it. He waited.

"Well?" the older man asked. "Do you have it?"

"Yes, sir." Still, Loftus made no move.

The older man understood. Using facial expressions and gestures, he asked the other two men to wait in the corridor until called. One of these, a prim, wooden-faced little man named Whitlow, pursed his lips in protest but obeyed. Loftus waited until the door clicked shut.

"You're not going to believe who the girl is." Loftus pulled a freshly printed black-and-white photo from the envelope. An attractive young woman in a tennis dress. The courts of the Windermere Island Club were clearly discernible in the background. "Her name is Susan Lesko. Her father is Raymond Lesko."

The older man stared blankly, then his brow knitted as the name registered. "Not that New York policeman."

"The one who killed two of Elena's people and one of ours. Yes, sir."

"And his daughter is now traveling with Paul Bannerman?"

"It gets worse. The girl's a reporter with the *New York Post*."

"For heaven's sake."

"Yes, sir."

"Do you suppose Bannerman knows that she's a reporter?"

"Pending confirmation, sir, this seems to be the same girl he's been seen with since early November at least. He's got to know it."

"What is his relationship with her?"

Loftus wasn't sure how to answer. "It seems to be sexual in nature. They certainly shared a room at Windermere."

"Yes, but how could such a relationship have developed?"

"I don't know if I follow, sir."

"Whatever else Bannerman is, he's a consummate professional and a very deliberate man. Why would he enter into a relationship with a newspaper reporter? Could he be planning to go public about Westport? Perhaps to head off any action I might take against him?"

"In my opinion? Bannerman would never go public. It's not his style." Nor, Loftus thought, does Bannerman seem at all concerned about any "action" this old man might take. He travels freely, never a bodyguard, almost certainly unarmed, although he does avoid predictable routines. Probably out of habit.

"I agree." Palmer Reid rose to his feet and began pacing thoughtfully. "Could she have discovered what's happening in Westport on her own? And Bannerman is merely trying to distract her?"

"It's really not a thing one could stumble onto, sir. She'd have to have been told. If she were told, it would take a lot more than sweet talk from Bannerman to keep her from printing it."

"Yes. Yes, I agree." Palmer Reid paused at the sofa and straightened two throw pillows that the man with the shoulder holster had left askew. "Try this, then. The fact that she's a reporter is irrelevant. Bannerman's real involvement is with the father and his relationship with the girl is incidental to that. Perhaps he used the daughter to reach the father."

Loftus had nothing to offer.

"And if the linkage is from Bannerman to the daughter, to the father, what might the next link be, Robert?"

"From Lesko to Elena, sir. But that doesn't seem very likely."

Palmer Reid ignored the last. "Then from Elena, to her people, to our people, to us."

"Yes, sir." Loftus shrugged inwardly.

"For heaven's sake."

"Yes, sir."

"There's still another scenario." The older man turned, holding the fingers of one hand aloft. He used them to count off the links. "Start with Bannerman, who had been in Westport three years, to Lesko's daughter, to Lesko himself, to Elena who has dropped from sight for almost two years. What if it all goes full circle, Robert?"

"Sir?"

"Could Elena be in Westport?" Palmer Reid's eyes were shining. "Could she be living there right now under the protection of Bannerman and his killers? Wouldn't a hole card such as Elena go a long way toward explaining the man's monumental arrogance? His defiance of the entire United States intelligence community? To say nothing," his voice was rising, "of his insolent dismissal of my own attempts to reason with him?"

Loftus stood silent.

"Robert?"

"Yes, sir."

"Your opinion."

"I suppose that's possible, sir."

"But you don't believe it."

"Sir," Loftus took a breath, his hands clasped behind him. "In my opinion, Bannerman has all the hole cards he needs right now. Secondly, we're almost sure that except for one trip back to La Paz, Elena has been holed up in Europe. Third, Bannerman was never in a position to know anything about Elena, not even that she exists. Fourth, even if he does know Lesko, it seems extremely unlikely that he could connect with Elena through him. Elena was lucky to live through her last meeting with Lesko. She would hardly have kept in touch with him after that."

"But Lesko did have a prior business relationship with Elena, did he not?"

"My opinion, sir, that's just talk. The police didn't believe it, our informants insist there was no connection, and our own people are convinced he didn't even know who she was when he . . . *assuming* it was Lesko . . . shot up that barbershop."

Palmer Reid glared at him. "So it's all one big coincidence then."

"No, sir."

"What then?"

"Sir," Loftus picked his words. "I think there's an answer in all this somewhere. We just don't know enough."

"I want you in New York tomorrow, Robert."

"Yes, sir."

"Get a wire on Lesko's phone and on his daughter's phone. I want surveillance teams on each and I want you to get a third team into Westport. Whitlow will coordinate. Burdick can head the Westport team."

"Sir . . . ?" Loftus held up his hands.

"Yes, Robert."

"We've lost two men dead and two disabled in Westport already. I suggest we go in force or not at all and certainly not with a team headed by Tom Burdick. The man's gun-happy."

"I prefer to think of him as decisive."

"Sir, please." Loftus closed his eyes. "I can give you the wires but I suggest we hold off on the surveillance teams. For one thing, I think Lesko would spot his. And Bannerman would spot any team we put on the daughter if he's with her. Why don't I just go up and look things over myself?"

"It is your conceit, I take it, that you would not be spotted."

"I certainly would by Bannerman, sir. He knows me now." Loftus kept his voice even. "I had Lesko in mind. If he were to spot me, it would not necessarily be a bad thing. We'd see what kind of calls he makes afterward."

"Very well," Palmer Reid waved him off. "I'll want daily reports."

"Yes, sir."

"Bannerman and Elena." He'd resumed pacing the room. "Imagine that."

"Yes, sir."

"He put his hands on me this morning. You saw that, didn't you."

"Actually, um . . . yes, sir." It did not seem useful to point out that it was he who had grabbed at Bannerman.

"And he told me never to go there again. He said that to *me*, Robert."

"Yes, sir."

Reid paused at an ashtray and stared with disgust at the single cigarette butt it held. "Who smokes, Robert?"

"Doug Poole, sir. My assistant. He was here earlier."

"You'll put a stop to that, won't you?"

"Yes, sir."

Reid stared at him. "Bannerman . . . to Lesko . . . to Elena. For heaven's sake."

"Yes, sir."

CHAPTER 7

Doctor Stanley Gelman rarely saw patients on Monday. In consequence, he was not missed until Tuesday. Late Tuesday afternoon, his secretary–receptionist, who had been trying to reach him by phone all day, drove to his house on Bayberry Road. Though the blinds were drawn, she could see that one or two lights were on inside. She rang the bell repeatedly without result. Listening at the door, she thought she could hear running water. Next, she walked around to the window of Gelman's attached garage and, leaning over a stack of firewood, she could see her employer's Mercedes and, beyond it, the dim outline of his Buick Regal. She decided to call the police.

Paul learned of Gelman's death two hours later. An auxiliary policeman named John Waldo placed a whispered call to one Anton Zivic, who operated an antique and interior design firm on Westport's Main Street. Zivic then notified Paul. Apparent cause of death: suicide by barbiturate poisoning. Apparent time of death: sometime the previous Sunday. This was strictly a guess based upon the unreplayed calls that had accumulated on Gelman's answering machine. The parboiled state of his body did not permit a reliable forensic determination. No, said Zivic, there was no reason to suspect that the suicide was anything but genuine. And therefore, no, he saw no reason to confront Billy directly.

On Wednesday afternoon, Zivic called again. Another suicide. A woman named Sweetzer, discovered by her husband when he stopped at home during his lunch

hour. This suicide seemed even more clearly genuine
and was, in fact, related to Gelman's. Mrs. Sweetzer,
known as Kitzy, had left a suicide note that her husband
tried to snatch from the policeman who found it. The
hysterically rambling note suggested a master–slave
sexual relationship with Stanley Gelman, whose own
death had been on the early local news. Kitzy Sweetzer
had slashed several household photographs of herself,
slashed her own breasts and abdomen, then swallowed
an undetermined number of Seconal tablets, whose bottle bore Gelman's name as prescribing physician.

There is no likelihood at all, said Zivic, that Billy was
involved in the Sweetzer death. But there are two troubling factors. First, if Gelman had ill-used Mrs. Sweetzer, he had probably ill-used others and that was the
type of behavior that had prompted an emotional response in Billy in the past. Secondly, Dr. Russo suddenly
has the look of a man with something on his mind.

Paul Bannerman called a council meeting for seven
o'clock that evening. At his office. Attendance mandatory.

Paul readied the small conference room at the rear
of Luxury Travel Limited, then stepped out among the
silent computer consoles and racks of tour brochures so
he could watch the council members as they arrived. If
his concerns had any basis, he might see it on their faces
before their expressions could be masked.

The travel agency occupied a double storefront in
the Compo Shopping Plaza on Westport's Post Road.
Directly across from that busy thoroughfare was another group of shops, the largest being a Herman's
Sporting Goods store that had replaced a failed Finast
Supermarket. A woman at the Herman's checkout
caught Paul's eye. Even at that distance he easily recognized the bushy raccoon coat and Indiana Jones–felt hat
of Molly Farrell. She was chatting animatedly with the
clerk, another Mario's regular. Now she took her
change, waved goodbye while rushing toward the door,
a yellow Herman's bag, with the grip of a new tennis
racquet sticking out of it, in her hand. Now, outside,
another woman called to her. Barely breaking stride,
Molly went to her, touched cheeks, then dashed toward

the Post Road, jaywalking, skipping and dodging
through the evening traffic, answering still another
wave and a honk from a passing car; then, against all
odds, arriving safely at the Compo Plaza parking lot.
Paul shook his head. The gesture was matched by Anton
Zivic who, Paul now noticed, was standing in the parking lot waiting for her.

Zivic, elegantly dressed, slender, of medium height,
with silver hair and mustache, stood sternly erect, his
arms folded, facing Molly Farrell. His posture suggested
severe disapproval. He shook a finger at her. Now the
same finger stabbed in the direction of the pedestrian
crossing at the corner. Paul had to smile. Zivic was, no
doubt, attempting to explain the function of stoplights
and crosswalks. Molly's impenitent response was to kiss
his cheek, pull the tennis racquet from her bag, and
begin an enthusiastic description of its virtues. Zivic
refused to look at it. He would not be derailed: Dashing
across busy, darkened streets is not to be forgiven. He
turns his face from her. Her expression becomes
wounded, contrite. A gloved thumb raises her mouth.
Zivic tries not to look but he can't help seeing. He
throws up his arms, defeated. Molly, her grin restored,
seized his arm and marched him toward Paul's office.

Her eyes met Paul's before she reached the door.
The smile remained, a wave of greeting. He watched to
see if the eyes stayed overlong on his. He thought they
did, for only the barest moment. She was a tall woman,
standing half a head above Anton Zivic, and she moved
with an athlete's grace. She was a lovely woman, Paul
thought. Not traditionally pretty. Just a wonderfully
warm and open face, a wide mouth with laugh lines
permanently etched at the corners, large brown eyes
that seemed curiously sad, almost timid, when in re-
pose. But Paul knew, there was nothing timid about
those eyes. And they missed very little.

Molly entered, Anton following. Behind them, Gary
Russo's white Subaru wagon pulled into the parking lot.
Carla Benedict rode with him. Paul met their eyes as
well. Russo nodded to him, then looked away. Carla
squeezed Russo's arm and, Paul was sure, said something through her teeth. Paul nodded, but the nod was
to himself.

* * *

"Well?" Paul spread his hands when all five were seated. "Who's going to tell me?"

Gary Russo straightened. "I assume you're asking about Gelman."

"Gelman and the woman, yes."

"Woman?" Carla Benedict paused in mid-reach for an ashtray. "What woman?"

Paul glanced at the faces of Molly and Russo. Like most of Westport, they had heard about Gelman. They seemed genuinely surprised at the mention of a woman.

"Her name is Katherine Sweetzer, *a.k.a.* Kitzy Sweetzer. A patient of Gelman's. Apparently sexually abused by him. Killed herself upon learning of Gelman's death."

"It's news to me," said Gary Russo. "I never heard of her."

Paul reached into a folder and produced a photocopy of an enlarged 5 × 7 snapshot. The copy showed crimp marks where the original had been indented by a picture frame and it showed that the photo had been slashed and then taped back together. He passed it to Molly Farrell. "Ever seen her in Mario's, Molly?"

"No." She seemed relieved. "No, Paul, I haven't."

"What about Gelman? Did he ever come in?"

"Not that I know of. Do you have his picture?"

Paul produced a newspaper file photo taken at a charity function a year earlier. It showed several people. Gelman's face was circled with a marker. He handed it to Molly.

"I've never seen him before, either." She shook her head.

"All right," he set both pictures down, "I'll ask it another way. Do any of you have any reason to believe that Billy had anything to do with either of these suicides?"

Russo leaned back. "From what I hear, Gelman mainlined his Valium stash while sitting in a hot tub. That doesn't sound like Billy's kind of work."

"That's right," Carla agreed. "Ask me, all you have here is an unethical shrink who was probably about to get his license lifted and one sappy woman who decided she couldn't live without his cock. Good riddance on both counts."

Paul ignored the observation. "I want to know whether this dead woman happens to have been one of Billy's new friends. Molly?"

"Billy didn't know her," she answered earnestly. "I'm as sure of that as I can be."

"That's right," Carla nodded. She tried holding his gaze. He chose not to ask, even if that were true, how she could have known it.

"Paul." Anton Zivic, his accent vaguely Slavic, spoke for the first time. "If some of us speak too quickly," he glanced toward Carla, "it is because we all wish to believe Billy is innocent. We understand your discomfort. You go away for two weeks and practically on the day of your return there are two fewer people in Westport, each, as before, no great loss to the community. But this time I think the suicides are genuine."

"I'm trying to believe that as well." He studied Carla and Gary for a long moment. "A couple of things need to be repeated. The first is to make sure all our people understand, especially those of you in this room, that no action in violation of any law is to be taken without my express approval. Any question on that?"

"It is as before," Zivic said. The others nodded.

"The second is that Billy doesn't get another chance. If he kills again on his own, or if he's arrested or charged with any previous killing, I'm going to have to execute him."

"That is also as before."

"Molly? Billy agreed to that himself. He hasn't forgotten, has he?"

"He hasn't."

"I'd better have a talk with him. Tomorrow morning."

"Paul, he's my responsibility," she said evenly, firmly. "And I'm telling you that Billy did not kill either one of those people."

Bannerman rubbed his jaw thoughtfully. He felt sure Molly was telling him the truth, although not necessarily all of it. He had no wish to back her into a corner if he could help it. He decided to ease off a notch. "How do you think he's doing generally?" Paul asked.

"He's doing brilliantly," she said, composing herself. "Every week he seems to find a new interest. He reads every word of *Time* magazine. He's studying vocabulary, he's learning to cook . . . and this morning he helped his landlady wallpaper her living room. Last week he even took her out to dinner and a movie."

"Billy had a date with a woman?" Paul almost smiled.

"It was really very sweet." Her expression warned those at the table that she did not consider it a laughing matter. "He got a haircut and bought a new shirt. He wanted to know if he should bring flowers and candy. It was . . ." she almost said *cute*. "It was nice."

"I guess that's good," Paul said cautiously, "as long as you keep an eye on it. If Billy's never dated a normal woman, he's probably never been hurt by one. The only kinds of women he's known are. . . ."

"I know what kind he's known. I'll watch it."

Bannerman saw little use in pursuing the subject of the Gelman–Sweetzer suicides. Part of the truth was clear. The rest he'd get from Billy.

"Let's move on." He glanced around the table. "Any problems with anyone else?" The reference was to the eight men and two women who were under the supervision of the four he had called to that meeting.

Anton Zivic raised his pen. "Harry Bauer asked me to mention two items." Bauer was a certified public accountant, once a German banker, who managed the financial affairs of the Westport group. "All of the retail and service businesses run by our people are showing a profit, with the exception of John Waldo's video rental store. Too much competition from the chains and drugstores. But there is a locksmithing and home-security systems business for sale in Westport. John asks that we buy it for him."

"What does Harry think?"

"The asking price is fair, the business is sound, and John, of course, is already an expert in that field. This same firm, incidentally, installed the system now in place at the Westport town hall. The specifications could be useful to us one day."

"It sounds okay to me. Any objections?"

"He'll still stay on with the auxiliary police?" Carla

asked. "It's nice that John has his toys, but I'd rather have someone inside police headquarters."

"He understands that, I assure you," Zivic said patiently.

"And if business is so bad, how come he drives a new car?"

Anton sighed. Molly looked at the ceiling. Carla, they knew, was still smarting over being forced to cancel a Porsche, a red one at that, that she'd ordered last year on the salary of a part-time librarian. Harry Bauer felt that it would have attracted undue curiosity from the Westport citizenry in general and the Internal Revenue Service in particular. The choice offered her was to either work at an enterprise that might justify a Porsche or drive a car appropriate to her apparent income. Carla opted grudgingly to be poor but unencumbered. Harry found her a Volkswagen Rabbit, six years old, that Carla accepted but which she denied both her affection and routine maintenance.

"Waldo's car is leased by his business," Zivic answered. "Otherwise, he remains a man of modest needs. On this subject, Harry also reminds us that he wants everyone's complete financial records by the end of this month if he is to prepare our tax returns."

"Harry Bauer is a pain in the ass," Carla muttered. Though she had to admit that thanks to Harry none of them would ever be broke. Harry could do with money what Molly could do with electronics or what Gary could do with a scalpel. Except what good was having it if you had to live as if you didn't? It's fine for people like Billy who'd be happy with the price of a cheeseburger and a *TV Guide*. . . .

Billy.

Paul, she realized, didn't fully believe any of them. Except Anton, who doesn't know but probably suspects. She hadn't figured on Paul going around Molly. Maybe she should have let Gary tell the truth after all. Oh, well.

"If there's no other business," Paul said rising, "the bar's open."

"Paul?" Carla didn't move. "Aren't you going to tell us about Palmer Reid?"

"What about him?"

"Anton says you met with him at Windermere."

Paul made a face. "I did not meet with him. He learned I was there and he came uninvited. I warned him not to do that again, especially at Windermere."

"So? What did he want?"

"Just more of the same. He wants us to surrender Anton, he wants me back in the field, or so he claims, and he wants the rest of you scattered and relocated individually. The only new thing he offered was that we can keep the funds we seized and, if you don't want to trust him, he'll put your relocation under the FBI's Witness Protection Program."

"We're supposed to trust the FBI?" Carla smiled.

"It's academic. I said no."

"Reid's not a man to be brushed off," Russo warned. "You don't think he's cooking something up?"

"Reid's always cooking something up."

"I don't know why you don't let us scratch that son of a bitch once and for all," Carla said. "He's going to hit us sooner or later."

"Look . . ." Paul stepped to the bar and poured a glass of wine. "Let's not even think in those terms. Reid's people will never come to Westport in force because they'd never be able to get all of us. He probably isn't even sure how many there are. I don't think he'll try to infiltrate again because I've told him I'll be obliged to kill any agent he sends in. He won't try a snatch on Anton because he knows we'll retaliate— against his family if we have to—and all he'll end up with is a swap. Palmer Reid is frustrated, humiliated and angry, but as long as we keep our heads he has no acceptable options."

Carla was not convinced. "He's going to nail you one of these days. You're going to disappear during one of your trips and he's going to swear up and down he has no knowledge of it."

"I've discussed that with him. He knows that Molly and Anton are to assume he's behind it, regardless of where else the evidence might point, and retaliate accordingly. More importantly, I've explained our structure to him. What we have here is a collaborative that will go right on functioning even if I walk outside and get hit by a truck. He understands that I'm no longer essential to it."

"The heck you're not," Molly Farrell said quietly.

"Don't start thinking that way either," Paul told her. "My personal safety depends on Palmer Reid believing that there's no head for him to cut off."

"So," Anton Zivic chose a cognac, "your assessment is that he will do nothing, Paul."

"He'll watch us, try to contain us, and keep looking for a crack he can exploit. In the meantime, I think his immediate concern is making sure what we did here can't happen in his other towns."

"Perhaps it would not be a bad idea to stir up some trouble in one or two of them," Zivic suggested. "Take his mind off Westport."

Paul answered with a pained expression. It was not a new suggestion. It seemed to come up every time one or more in the group felt restless. None of them, and especially Anton, were accustomed to taking static defensive positions and leaving all initiative to the opposition. But the point was, they were no longer a tactical action group. They were retired. They had new lives, each of his own choosing. As far as Reid's other towns were concerned—there were five other "Westports" across the country that he knew of—what was happening in them was none of their business. So far, Paul had declined even to name them.

Anton Zivic accepted the cue and dismissed the subject with a wave of his glass. Perhaps over a quiet drink one day he would tell Paul that his government—his former government—had knowledge of at least two. One was certainly Wilmette, Illinois, a Westport-like suburb just northeast of Chicago. Another was Palo Alto in California. Suspected were Framingham in Massachusetts, and Fort Worth in Texas.

It would not be very difficult, were Zivic so inclined, to compile a list of towns that were likely candidates. Paul had long ago told him how Westport was chosen. It followed that the same criteria would apply to all. They would be upper-middle-class communities. Not conspicuously affluent, but comfortable, offering a lifestyle that was at least the equal of what the agents had enjoyed in the field. Like Westport, they would all be commuter towns, towns with more or less transient populations where newcomers attracted little notice. No company towns. No one-industry towns such as those in Silicon Valley. No socially competitive towns such as nearby Greenwich or Darien. A primary consideration would be finding places in which people tended to respect the privacy of their neighbors. Westport had that reputation, and for that reason it had attracted many celebrities over the years, particularly those in the arts. People left them alone.

A computer would narrow the list further. First there were all the ordinary quality-of-life considerations. Recreation, cultural activities, affordable housing and so on. Schools were not a factor. Agents were not supposed to have been there long enough to conceive, let alone raise, children. Romantic relationships with the locals were, in any case, forbidden. The computer would also exclude any towns that had career intelligence officers or retired State Department personnel in residence. It would not do to encounter a former case officer while standing in line at the supermarket.

The concept, Zivic supposed, was sound enough in theory. It was like the halfway house, but on a grander scale. Halfway towns. A way to depressurize and rehabilitate certain agents who were being retired from the field. A year or so of learning to live, under close supervision and tutoring, like normal citizens. Then relocation elsewhere under more relaxed supervision but with continued counseling. Then eventually, a more complete reabsorption into ordinary American life. A sound enough concept. It might even be called benevolent. It gave some of these people a chance to save their lives.

The halfway towns were not intended, Zivic knew, for the ordinary CIA or NSA or military intelligence field agent. Not even for those Operations Branch agents of whom so much cloak-and-dagger nonsense is written. Such personnel usually retired to become authors, lecturers, local police chiefs, registered foreign agents or lobbyists, private corporate spies and, occasionally, whistle-blowers. Those meant for the halfway towns were different. Nearly all were contract agents, free-lancers who were bound by no official constraint or code of conduct. Nor were they, like career agents, immune to criminal prosecution by informal convention among NATO countries. Many were operatives who had spent half their lifetimes in deep cover and high-stress situations. These were assassins, kidnappers, expert interrogators, even torturers. These were people who would think nothing of robbing a bank or trafficking in arms in order to finance an operation too sensitive to be funded through identifiable channels. Most were living, breathing weapons. Cocked weapons. Some were borderline psychotics, likely to choose an enemy of their own if one were not regularly provided for them. A few, like Billy, could never be allowed to retire to any environment short of a maximum-security mental institution.

The halfway town concept, first envisioned by Allen Dulles and later expanded under President Jimmy Carter, provided some with at least the chance of being salvaged. But the rehabilitative process was also an evaluative process. Though President Carter was unlikely to have known it, fully one third did not survive the relocation. They simply vanished en route to their promised new locations. Nor was there ever a need to explain their disappearance. They had, after all, been relocated with new identities. It could truthfully be said, to anyone who might inquire, that they no longer existed. Of those who did survive, few of any value were left in peace.

Anton Zivic sipped his cognac, his expression thoughtful as he studied the faces now standing about Paul's conference table. Not one of them, he was certain, would be allowed to retire to private life.

Dr. Gary Russo. An interesting case. Here is a torturer who looks into a mirror and sees an apostle looking back. He steadfastly refuses to regard himself as an assassin. He will acknowledge that he's killed. Many times. But he regards this as a quibble. He is, after all, primarily an interrogator. His way of dealing with the taking of lives is to persuade himself that those he kills were doomed in any case. It's their fault, not his, that they lay strapped to his table. Now, if they will only answer his questions, fully and truthfully, there need be no more pain, no more blood, and he will assist them to their peaceful release. Otherwise, quite a decent sort, actually. But he'd heard the answers to too many questions. Without Paul's protection, he'd have been a dead man years ago.

Carla Benedict. Once one of the very best, although still quite definitely world-class. Tiresome at times, occasionally shrewish, and yet utterly reliable and unquestionably loyal. In recent years, however, she'd developed a habit of toying with her targets. She could take a man to her bed, laugh with him, enjoy him, give pleasure in return, and then, the next morning, cheerily bring him a breakfast laced with strychnine if she hadn't cut his throat while he slept. Perhaps it came of spending too much time with Dr. Russo. He'd taught her to linger. He had not taught her to control her tongue. Nevertheless, as Paul had observed, if one must live near a volcano, it's best to be near one that smokes.

And Molly. Dear, sweet-natured Molly. Had there ever been a nicer, more loving, more generous young lady on the KGB's list of Most Wanted . . . ?

"I'd better think about locking up," said Paul, draining his glass. "Molly, I wish you'd join me for dinner. You could probably do with a change of menu."

He held Molly's eyes to show that it was more than a casual invitation. Zivic saw that as well. He also saw that Carla was making no move to accept the coat being urged on her by Gary Russo.

"What about your reporter friend?" The question was blurted more than asked.

"What about her, Carla?" Paul asked evenly.

"Is that under control or isn't it?"

Paul's voice took a hard edge. "It was until three days ago. We'll just have to hope that two fresh Westport suicides do not rekindle her interest."

"You're taking her to Switzerland, aren't you?"

"Yes, Carla. As a matter of fact, I am."

"Why?"

His eyes flashed. "I beg your pardon?"

"If you're getting serious about her, we don't like it."

"Umm!" Anton and Molly made the sound in unison.

"Okay, *I* don't like it." Carla took a breath and plunged. "It was one thing, cozying up to her to find out what she knew. That turned out to be nothing. Why are you still seeing this kid?"

"All right, now listen. . . ."

Molly Farrell stepped in quickly. "What Carla *means,*" she shot a warning glance at the other woman, "is that you have a perfect right to see anyone you please. I think we just wish it could have been someone other than an investigative reporter who is also the daughter of a dangerous New York cop."

"For openers," Paul checked his temper, "the father's not a cop anymore and Susan is a long way from being an investigative reporter. Secondly, the father doesn't even know I exist because Susan—*like me*— prefers to keep her relationships private. Which brings up a third point. . . ."

"Don't say it's none of our business, Paul," Molly said quietly. "You'd be just as concerned if one of us hit on a combination like that."

"All the same, I . . . what I do with . . ." Paul lost his train of thought because Anton Zivic had affected a pained expression and was rapidly shaking his head.

"Molly," Zivic touched her shoulder, "to the heart of the matter, please."

Molly fidgeted, shrugged, and finally spread her hands. "We're a little . . . sort of jealous." She shrugged again, embarrassed.

Paul blinked.

"She's twenty-four. She's pretty. And she's clean. On the other hand, out here you've got a couple of used-up broads who don't want to lose you, and we get a little possessive sometimes."

"Oh."

"What does 'Oh' mean?"

"It means I don't know what else to say." Suddenly, Paul didn't know what to do with his hands either.

"You've been taking care of us for a long time. We're not saying that's a life sentence but. . . ."

"We've been taking care of each other. That won't change. Ever. I can't believe that you two of all people have been letting this worry you."

Zivic winced. Another shaking of the head.

"These are feelings, Paul," Molly told him. "Who says they have to be rational. We love you, damn it."

Paul's mouth moved but no words came. Carla reddened but was also silent.

Zivic said, in a stage whisper, "The phrase you're trying to think of is 'I love you, too.'"

"Yeah . . . sure . . . well, that goes without saying."

"Almost never," Zivic corrected him. "Also if you know what's good for you, you will not let this 'used-up broad' designation pass unchallenged."

"Well, that's the dumbest thing I've heard tonight." He looked at Carla, whose eyes were down, and at Molly, who pretended to be studying the light fixture. "You're by far two of the most interesting and attractive women in Westport and you're. . . ."

"Already too many words," Zivic interrupted. "Try again, please."

"I love you both. Very much."

"Carla," Zivic ordered, "go hug but say nothing. Then we go eat before I am sick."

Amazing, Zivic thought to himself as he put on his coat. The smartest men are always the dumbest about women. Perhaps he would make Paul a gift of a pint or two of his Russian blood. It couldn't hurt.

CHAPTER 8

Anton Zivic did not take it amiss that Paul chose to dine alone with Molly Farrell. It was their habit never to congregate publicly in groups larger than three. He suggested a French restaurant called Chez Pierre for himself, the doctor and Carla Benedict, also suggesting that they walk there, a passing warm front having turned the weather almost springlike. Paul and Molly fell in behind them. There was a Szechuan restaurant en route that Molly had been wanting to try.

Across the Post Road, in the parking lot just down from Herman's, John Waldo watched from his car as the five dispersed. On the front seat close to his right hand sat a bag of Grand Union groceries. In it, just under a two-pack of toilet paper, was a silenced Ingram M-10 machine pistol. He reached for a small transmitter and with his fingernail made a series of scratching sounds that meant *all clear* and *break off*. Within seconds, another car appeared from the alley behind Paul's office and Glenn Cook, owner of the Sundance Ski Shop, headed home for his evening meal. John Waldo started his engine. He would watch what direction they were taking and then he'd stay with them a while longer until they were safely indoors. But he did not expect trouble now. The best time to move against them had just passed. Nor did he give much thought to the fact that this was the first time in months that he'd been asked to do sentry duty during a council meeting. Or that it was Anton Zivic, not Paul Bannerman, who had asked him.

Paul took Molly's arm as they crossed the Post Road. "Thank you," he said, "for defusing that in there."

"Carla will be okay. And I meant what I said."

"I know. So did I."

Molly said nothing more until they reached the far corner and paused to wait for the light at Compo Road. Zivic and the others had already crossed.

"Susan seems very nice," she said then. "She's certainly crazy about you."

Paul nodded, frowning. He found that he was mildly annoyed, though he knew it was entirely his own doing, that Molly knew so much about Susan. On the second day, after he'd followed Susan and her friend through Westport to the Sundance Ski Shop where he'd contrived to have Glenn Cook introduce them had not Susan startled him by approaching him first, he'd asked Molly to install a dropout relay device on Susan's Manhattan phone. For three months now, Molly had recorded every call that went in or out. During the first weeks he'd listened to the tapes himself but the act became so distasteful to him that he soon asked Molly to provide only verbal summaries. One such summary forewarned him, in time to prepare an excuse, that Susan intended to bring him and her father together on Christmas Eve. He'd also known, before Susan told him, that on this very night Susan and her father would be going to a basketball game. And as of her father's Monday morning call to Susan, that they'd be dining afterward at Gallagher's Steak House. The "she's crazy about you" reference came from a Tuesday call to Allie Gregory during which Susan gushed over her visit to Windermere, and over Paul himself. She made no reference to his encounter with Palmer Reid. It seemed to have left no lasting impression.

"She might be good for you, Paul."

"What?" His mind had wandered.

"Susan. She might be good for you."

A pained expression. "Am I missing something? Weren't you just telling me that seeing Susan was a bad idea?"

"That was Molly, the council member. This is Molly, your friend."

"That certainly explains that." The light changed.

He took her arm. As they crossed, he noticed the car that was coasting to the curb a hundred yards ahead of them on the far side of the Post Road. John Waldo's car. They kept on.

"Don't you think so?" Molly persisted.

"Don't I think what?"

"That it could work out."

Paul took a breath. "She's pretty young, Molly."

"Twenty-four's not so young. And you're not so old."

"She's also not stupid. She's starting to wonder what's real and what isn't about me." Paul told her of the Reid conversation, that Susan had overheard bits of it, and that she'd clearly doubted his version of what was being said. A bigger concern was that Reid had seen her as well and would certainly have identified her by now.

"So what?" Molly asked. "He won't bother her. He wouldn't dare try to recruit her."

"Nothing that overt," Paul agreed. "But he'll look for some way to use her. He'll also waste a lot of time and manpower trying to find out why I'm seeing so much of a reporter. Which is okay, I guess. But when he checks Susan out he'll find out she's headed for Europe and it won't take him long to realize we're going together. I had hoped to spend those three weeks without looking over my shoulder."

"Do you want a couple of us to come? We'll stay in the background."

"I don't think so." Paul's tone suggested that he had considered it. But a pleasure trip wasn't a pleasure trip anymore, once bodyguards were involved. What he wanted was to be with Susan and to enjoy her for whatever time was left to their relationship. As it was, he'd probably have to end it shortly after their return, or whenever he could no longer plausibly avoid meeting her father. Molly and Carla were right about that part. He had to assume that her father would inevitably start sniffing the air.

Molly the council member knew that. But Molly the friend had, in spite of the life she'd lived, somehow managed to remain a romantic, and was now arguing that he and Susan might have a future after all. She'd done it before. Once, when he'd brooded aloud about having lied to Susan since the first day they met, mostly lies of omission, she pointed out that there was no such thing as a totally honest relationship except among dopes. Every man, every woman, had a few things that were better left unmentioned. Susan, being a cop's daughter, would know that better than most. Her father didn't sit down at the dinner table and say "Guess who I shot this morning?" And Susan, being her father's daughter, was probably less fragile than most, as well.

Not that Molly had a particular interest in matchmaking, or even in this particular match. Her point was, being a romantic but a fairly realistic one, that since most romances tend to be short-term anyway, there's no great danger and possibly a lot of pleasure in letting them run their course. She'd had a few affairs herself, mostly with men she'd met at Mario's and those she'd inevitably meet on her own vacations. She wasn't about to set a time limit on them.

Nor was marriage out of the question, at least in principle. Glenn Cook got married last year to a nice girl from Darien who still thinks he's just a former ski bum who was finally ready to settle down and open a ski shop. And Harry Bauer is practically engaged to a widow he met while teaching an investment course. Janet Herzog has had a portrait artist living with her for two years now and he doesn't suspect a thing. Carla has a rich building contractor who's nuts about her although her major interest in him is probably to get him to buy her that red Porsche she wants. Even Billy McHugh, God help us, has a girlfriend.

Paul knew all that. They could afford the distractions. He could not. Especially with Palmer Reid showing signs of getting restless again. It was one of the reasons he had wanted Susan safe with him in Westport this week. Or maybe just with him, period.

They walked along.

"If you'd like," Molly said, "I'm sure we can think of ways to keep Palmer Reid busy over here for three weeks. Then maybe you and Susan could. . . ."

Paul shrugged and shook his head. He knew they could probably throw Reid into a panic just by letting either Carla or Billy be seen in the vicinity of his Maryland home. But better not to risk overreaction. Nor did he want another lecture on his personal life or his lack of one.

"Listen," he said, "if I ever did get hit by a truck, who do you think should take my place? That's assuming you don't want the job."

"I don't. And the answer's Anton."

"You'd bet your life on him?"

"I already have. In Iran. So have you."

"I'm going to ask him to take over while I'm away, with full authority to make all decisions. That's if he'll accept."

"He will."

"When I get back, I'm thinking of asking him to keep the job for the next year or so. After that, maybe we'll rotate. Or have elections."

"You're not going anywhere, are you?"

"Just easing off. You keep telling me I should."

"You're overdue."

"How will Gary and Carla react? To answering to Anton, I mean."

"It'll be fine with Carla. Gary's nose might be out of joint for a while. He thinks of himself as senior to everybody here but you."

"That probably comes with being a doctor. In terms of competence as an operative, he's not senior to anyone. He was never trained for the field. He's also never learned not to let his eyes give him away."

Molly knew what was coming and said nothing. She held onto his arm.

"Anything you want to tell me, Molly?" he asked quietly.

She remained silent for several more steps. "Paul, I'm going to ask you to let it lie."

"I can't function wearing blinders and I can't set a precedent of turning my back. How can I go away without settling this?"

"Please, Paul. Trust me just this once."

"You're not going to tell me?"

"I'll tell you that Uncle Billy didn't kill anyone. That's the truth. And I'll tell you that none of us even knew that woman existed."

"Were you involved?"

"No."

"Was Anton?"

"Not at all."

"What would keep it from happening again while I'm gone?"

"It can't. Not in a million years."

Molly had tried hard to satisfy herself of that. For anything like it to happen again you'd have to find another shrink who amuses himself by sending patients out to solicit men in bars. Then one of those women would have to choose a bar whose bartender happens to be a benevolent assassin. Then of all the men in that bar she'd have to pick the bartender to come on to. Next you'd need Gary and Carla going out to head him off, finding him in time, and then deciding what the hell, the guy's a shit anyway, and finishing him off themselves.

They'd told Molly, as they'd no doubt told themselves, why the killing was unavoidable. And how reluctantly it was done. But their story didn't wash. Paul would have seen through it in a minute. Gelman, by their own account, had never seen Billy's face. Gary could just as easily have injected Gelman from behind and then pulled Billy out of there. When Gelman woke up, the most he could have done was call the police with an incomprehensible story about unseen intruders who took nothing and left no sign of forced entry.

No, Molly felt certain Gary and Carla had killed Gelman because they wanted to. They might say it was to contain the damage. If pressed by Paul, Gary might say his judgment had been colored by outraged professional ethics and Carla might even claim feminist outrage. And, of course, Gary would have found a way to convince himself that Gelman was as good as dead anyway once he hurt a friend of Billy's, so it really wasn't murder. But the truth, Molly knew, was simpler. For the past fifteen years of their lives, most of Gary's and Carla's problems had been solved by killing. Whatever they tried to tell themselves, they had killed Stanley Gelman because killing is what they do.

"I'll think about it," she heard Paul say.

"Are you still going to talk to Billy?"

"Yes."

"Even after I promised he didn't do it?"

"It's necessary. But I believe you."

"Thank you."

They walked silently for a minute or so. Ahead of them, the others were walking three abreast. Gary Russo, Molly noticed, took the curb side, as a gentleman should. Anton took the inside, as a careful man should. Paul was right about Gary Russo.

Not that Gary ever made an issue of it, Molly reflected, but it was clear that he did see himself as intellectually superior, and probably morally superior, to everyone but Paul. All those degrees and certificates. He was liked well enough, and respected generally, but Gary had never had to act alone in a dangerous situation and he'd never even planned an operation. He could never be a leader. The others would trust him in his specialty but that's as far as it would go.

Molly's eyes drifted toward John Waldo's car. He was getting ready to move again after watching their backs. There was another thing about Gary. She'd spotted Waldo, she knew without asking that Paul had, and was sure Carla had as well, but she'd have bet anything that Gary had never noticed him. And if by chance he had, Russo would have asked what he was doing there. The rest of them knew. He was there because Anton put him there. Anton put him there, on his own initiative, because there was a chance, however slight, that Palmer Reid might do something foolish. That was the difference between them. Paul was right about Anton as well.

Anton Zivic. An intelligent man. An elegant man. Nice sense of humor, no more ruthless than he has to be; very decisive, deadly when he ought to be. He was a man to be feared and yet he was not a frightening man. Molly liked him.

Anton, as much as Paul, had helped set up the system that had brought a measure of control to the random violence that marked their first year in Westport. And he had tamed John Waldo. In fact, in that first year, Waldo, Carla, Gary and one or two others were almost as big a problem as poor Uncle Billy was the next. First there was Carla, who walked out of a cheese shop to find a young black busily prying the radio and tapedeck out of her dashboard. She paralyzed him with a thumb driven under the joint of his jawbone, used the car door to crush both his hands, and, when she saw the damage his screwdriver had done, rammed it a full six inches into his colon.

In another automotive incident, John Waldo shattered the right knee of a man who insisted upon making a high-speed shortcut of John's quiet street. A neighbor knew the man's name. She'd asked him to stop it on one occasion, and called the police on another, both without effect. John Waldo, who could move through a darkened house as silently as a night breeze, visited the speeder as he slept off his evening martinis. It was eighteen months before the man could press a gas pedal again.

Westport's first fatality, though it was not a resident who died, was due to massive internal bleeding, and it came at the hands of Dr. Gary Russo, assisted by John Waldo. Russo's home and office had been burglarized. So had another home on Russo's street a night earlier, and a home on a nearby street the night before that. Waldo, a world-class burglar in his own right, agreed that such acts should be discouraged. He caught the two felons after two nights' surveillance as they were looting a large Victorian owned by two vacationing attorneys. Waldo, wearing a ski mask, disabled both men and then called Dr. Russo, who arrived wearing a surgical mask and mirrored glasses.

They chose the less defiant of the two burglars and invited him to watch and listen, tightly bound, as Dr. Russo questioned the other. The one to be questioned was advised that he could kick and scream all he wished, to the extent screaming was possible through a cloth gag soaked in methyl alcohol, but when the gag was eventually removed he would be expected to give his full name and address, that of his friend, that of his fence, and that of every burglar of his acquaintance who had scored in Westport during the preceding year. He was advised, truthfully, that his accomplice had already given two such names and it would be well if at least one of those appeared on both lists.

By the end of a leisurely two-hour interrogation, amid the considerable coughing up of watery blood, the man being questioned managed to sob out a total of sixteen names. Russo presumed the list to be largely accurate since it included the man's father. As he in-

jected 50,000 units of heparin into the vein of the man
he questioned, he explained to the other that they were
now to be released. He was to take his informative
friend back to their neighborhood in nearby Bridgeport
and tell all his sixteen other friends what had happened,
suggesting that in future they practice their trade in
some other Connecticut community. Russo warned that
he would be telephoning a few at random to make certain they had gotten the message. If the man failed to
tell them first, therefore, foregoing the opportunity to
put the best possible face on why he had had no choice
but to name them, they would probably do him additional harm. Though Russo did not mention it at the
time, he felt that the message would be further drama-
tized when the burglar he had injected died of massive
heparin-induced hemorrhaging within four hours of returning to Bridgeport. He was as good as dead anyway,
Russo felt, having betrayed the names of so many dangerous people.

Paul had no prior knowledge of these and other epi-
sodes, such as Janet Herzog torching the home of a
woman who poisoned neighborhood dogs, but he might
have expected them. His people were all specialists.
Most were accustomed to taking decisive action in
threatening situations. Individual initiative had always
been encouraged, although usually within the frame-
work of specific policy or in pursuit of specific objectives.

There was the problem. There was no more policy.
There were no more missions, no more teams. There
was only the implicit objective, actually more of a habit,
of protecting their institutions against hostile interests.
Their primary institution was now the town of
Westport.

Nor would it have occurred to them to seek outside
help, such as by calling the police, any more than it was
in their nature to be passive victims. They understood
the uses of a local police department but also its limita-
tions. Their attitude toward the court system was similar. Both were for people who had no other recourse.

Paul had no intention of discouraging decisive action
against people whose own actions were in need of dis-
couragement. But individual initiative clearly had to be

controlled. An advisory council was set up. Any act in violation of any law, certainly any act of violence, had to be approved by the council in advance. A plan of action would also have to be submitted for review. Under those guidelines, Russo's and John Waldo's action against the burglars probably would have been approved. Waldo's action against the neighborhood speeder would have been approved after a suitable warning was given and ignored. Carla's action against the radio-thief would not have been. It was too spontaneous, it could too easily have been witnessed, and the devastation of a young male thief by a tiny woman would have made her the object of unwelcome curiosity.

Billy McHugh's activities were another matter entirely. While Russo, Carla, Waldo and the others spoke freely within the group of their activities, although always after the fact, and tended to regard them as a form of volunteer community service, Uncle Billy regarded his as intensely private. In nearly all cases, they stemmed from humiliations suffered by his friends. It would hardly do to compound a humiliation by discussing it with others. Molly Farrell's first clue to Billy's uses of his leisure time came when the advisory council had been organized and each member was asked to explain its guidelines to the individuals within his or her charge. Billy listened closely, an expression of concern on his face that Molly first took to be one of sympathetic understanding. But then he started asking questions.

"You mean," he nodded, "if we do something that affects any of us, you got to know about it up front."

"Anything done by any member of the group can affect the group, Billy."

"You mean, if it's something that would get the cops looking for whoever did something. Like shooting a guy or blowing up his car, for instance. Not if a guy just had some bad luck."

"No, Billy. I mean anything at all." She was beginning to get a bad feeling.

"Yeah, but what if it's something personal, like I did my friend a favor and my friend doesn't even know I did, and the cops don't look twice at it and the problem goes away."

"I've got to know, Billy. And I've got to tell Paul."

"Paul's got a lot on his mind, you know. We ought to be more considerate."

"What does that mean, Billy?"

"I don't know." He looked down, fingering the corners of his apron.

"Billy, sweetie, what have you done?"

"In Iran and Rome and like that, I used to do a lot of things for Paul I didn't worry him about."

"Are you talking about killings?"

"And like that. Yeah."

"Billy," she rubbed her temples as if she felt a migraine coming, "have you done anything like that in Westport?"

"Paul didn't need anything here so far. Except if you ask me, he wouldn't worry about so much if he'd let me get that Reid guy off his back." Billy gestured toward her head. "You know what's good for that? Two aspirins and a Bloody Mary with lots of horseradish."

The answer almost relieved her. But she did a mental double-take on the qualifier. "Aside from what Paul needs," she asked carefully, "have you killed anyone at all here in Westport for any reason?"

Billy shuffled uncomfortably. "I helped out some people. But they don't know it was me."

"For Pete's sake, Billy. Who did you help out and how?"

"The people who come here." He swept an arm over the empty bar stools. "They come in here, they look like they're feeling pretty good. But you'd be surprised the problems some of them had."

Had.

Past tense.

"And you solved their problems." Molly closed her eyes. She tried to think of any unsolved murders in the area over the past year or so. But then she remembered how Billy worked. "How many?" she asked. "How many are dead?"

"Is Paul going to be sore at me?" His eyes were moistening. Molly thought of a little boy caught stealing Twinkies. "I mean, it's not like I left them lying all over the street."

"How many, Billy?"
"Eleven, I think."

At an emergency council meeting, a shattered Molly
Farrell took Paul and the others through a recon-
structed list of Billy's victims. She was aided by press
clippings photocopied at the Westport Library by Carla
Benedict and then burned in the ashtray at the meeting's end. It helped only slightly that all eleven were
essentially unattractive people. Two had multiple
drunk-driving convictions, one had two arrests, but no
convictions for sexually abusing a stepchild, two were
wife-beaters and three were divorce lawyers. It helped
a bit more that none of their deaths had been deemed
suspicious by the authorities.

"It's my fault," Molly was near tears, "I promised I'd
control him."

"Let's not waste time assigning blame," Paul said
quietly. "I know him better than any of you and I never
even suspected. And we've all sat around congratulat-
ing ourselves on Billy's miraculous rehabilitation."

Anton Zivic spoke, "It does not seem useful to punish Billy for doing what he has always done, just because
no one thought to tell him that it was no longer appropriate. Nor is it necessary to cover for him because he
seems to have done quite a good job of that by himself."

Paul had to agree. All eleven cases were officially
closed. Nor had Billy ever mentioned them again to the
individual *friends* involved.

"What is indicated here is probation. He now knows
the rules which, in fairness, we must admit were late in
coming. Also in fairness, we should give him a chance to
live by them."

"The problem is," Gary Russo sat back, "for us to
conclude he can't, he has to kill someone else."

"You have an alternative?" Paul asked.

"Keep him sedated," Russo shrugged. "It's not a solution but it might take the edge off."

Molly hated that idea. She looked pleadingly at Paul.

"On the other hand," Russo continued, "we're not
running a clinic for the emotionally stunted here. We
want to help Billy but we can't let him risk everything

we've built. This is the only home most of you will ever get a chance of having."

Paul noticed the use of *you* rather than *us* but didn't bother to comment. He looked at Carla, who hadn't spoken. "Do you have any thoughts?"

"I don't like this drug business," she said firmly. "If we ever need Billy we want his head clear. Let's not have Gary making a zombie out of him."

It was the answer Paul expected from Carla. Although she genuinely liked Billy, she tended to think of people in terms of function.

"Molly," Paul asked, "are you sure that Billy understands the rules now?"

She nodded quickly. "I made him repeat them back to me. No action of any kind without consulting us. The only exception is if we're attacked or taken in which case he has his instructions. Billy is very sorry for any trouble he's caused and he asks for just one more chance."

"He understands that it would have to be his last?"

"He says he's sure he can do it. But if he makes another mistake, he says he'll take himself out."

"Okay," Paul gathered the clippings on the table, "we give Billy one more chance but we all watch him more closely. We're not going to tranquilize Billy because we're not going to start manipulating each other. If you see any problem arising, I want to know about it, but you go to Molly first because he remains her responsibility and we're not going to start going around each other, either. Anyone disagree?"

Molly could have kissed him.

But that was then and this was now. There was still the Gelman matter and Paul would have to resolve it before he could leave Westport again. There were one or two other matters as well.

"Molly," Paul paused at the entrance of the Szechuan restaurant. John Waldo's car was still creeping ahead, fifty yards at a time, showing no sign of breaking off their flank. "I'll call Billy from here and ask him to meet me down at the beach early tomorrow. Just the two of us, okay?"

"Okay," she answered, asking him with her eyes to go easy.

He touched her, nodding, then he took a long look back up the road behind them and then down past John Waldo's car. He was frowning. "Do you smell something in the air?" Paul asked.

"Anton seems to. Does he know anything I don't?"

"Only a few more details about my talk with Reid. I guess it bothers him that Reid went so far out of his way to see me."

"It doesn't bother you, though."

Paul rocked his hand and shrugged. "We can let Reid's mood swings keep us on our toes or we can let them paralyze us. Down at Windermere I probably rubbed his nose in it more than I should have. But it will take a lot more than that to make Reid risk a shooting war."

"There's one difference between you and Anton. You think Reid's a deliberate man. Anton thinks he's unstable."

Paul let out a sigh. "Do you want me to cancel? Or at least postpone?"

"No. Take your vacation. Take your lady and go."

Paul reached for the door, then paused. "Listen, on a related matter, Susan is meeting with her father tonight."

"I know."

"I'll want to know everything she says over the phone about me afterward, and any information she gives about our travel plans."

"Of course."

"Then after we leave, if we leave, I want you to remove that bug."

"You're not going to want to know how she feels about you later?"

"Enough's enough." He opened the door. "Let's eat."

CHAPTER 9

Four in the morning.

Lesko had been dreaming again. In and out. More half-awake dreams.

What it was, was last night at Gallagher's coming up on him like a bad Mexican dinner. Susan was in it. Looking happy. Nice tan. Her life going good. Except in this dream she's not only still talking about all that Westport crap, she's actually making a presentation about it, complete with big charts on an easel.

She's on this one big graph showing suicide and accidental-death statistics by year, and one year goes completely off the chart. Lesko is not paying much attention because he's already made up his mind she's blowing smoke and besides, there are too many other things going on. Most of them aggravating.

First there's Katz, wherever the hell he came from, sitting down at the table with her in his cashmere jacket and Rolex, and the jerk is agreeing with her. His mouth is open and he's nodding up and down like one of those fake dogs in the back window of a car. At another table there's Buzz Donovan taking notes. He's holding his notepad low, the way you'd hold a poker hand, because there's that Loftus guy kind of hovering behind Donovan trying to see what he was writing.

Lesko was about to get up and belt Loftus again just on general principles when he saw someone he wanted to hit even more. This was a guy he'd never seen before, but he knew it had to be Paul Bannerman because the guy was standing behind Susan running his goddamned hands all over her shoulders and down her front. Lesko hated the son of a bitch on sight. A big guy, twice her size and twice her age, and he's got this sneaky, leering face. Lesko decided to smash it in no matter what kind of shit Susan gave him for doing it but just then he glanced toward Gallagher's window and there's Elena standing out there in the snow. Just standing there. Watching. In that same fur coat. She sees him looking at her and she gives him this shy little nod.

Lesko's stomach does something funny. A part of him wants to say, all right, come in, you don't have to stand out there in the cold, but what he says is, look, why don't you just get out of here before I change my mind again. She gives him this sad look like her feelings are hurt and she backs away.

Yeah, well, give me a break. What do you want from me, lady? We should be friends? Anyway, for your own good, get out of here before the Loftus guy spots you.

"Daddy?"

"What?" Susan's calling him over to her charts. All of a sudden everybody else is gone except Katz who's still sitting there with his stupid little smile and nodding.

"Uncle David agrees with me that there's something weird in Westport. He spent three years in homicide and he thinks. . . ."

Lesko glared at Katz and jerked his thumb toward the door. *"Take a walk, David. It's bad enough I have to listen to your shit without you bothering Susan with it.*

"Daddy, he's not bothering me. We were trying to figure out why. . . ."

"I don't want you talking to him," Lesko barked, *"And Katz can't figure out a damned thing because he's dead."*

"Oh, right. Right." Susan remembered. And now her hand was on Katz's arm with the Rolex and she's leaning close and speaking excitedly like she forgot he's been away and they had a lot to catch up on. *"Uncle David, as long as you're dead, why don't you look up some of those people from Westport and and ask how come they . . . ?"*

"The thing is, I'm not going to be dead that long," Katz explained. *"I been talking to your father and I think he's going to help me fix it."*

"In a pig's ass, I am. And if you don't get away from Susan I'm going to take your head off all over again."

Lesko was yelling now. He didn't stop yelling until his feet hit the floor at his bedside.

"Christ!"

Lesko rubbed his face.

What's today?

Thursday.

He looked at his clock. Not even five yet. Less than three hours' sleep since he finally got home from Gallagher's. The dream was receding but the details were still vivid enough. He hated this. Four A.M. dreams. All he needed now was for Katz to walk in with his bagels or Danish. He'd shove them right up his. . . .

All right. Settle down. What's bothering you?

He remembered the Bannerman guy with his hands all over Susan. But that's not it, he told himself. You're always doing that with guys she's seeing. You always think they're creeps until you meet them and talk to them. Then you always think they're wimps. Whatever Bannerman turns out to be, he's nothing like the guy you just dreamed about. In fact, the guy in the dream looks more like you. Because Susan told you he reminds her of you. Which is probably why you don't like him. That's all that meant.

So what else is wrong? It's not that Westport stuff. That's not even worth thinking about. It's not Katz because him at least you're getting used to.

It's Elena.

Face it.

You could have done without hearing her name again. Seeing her look at you. You're never going to see her again but wherever she is, you hope she's okay. Admit it.

It's also Loftus. He bothers you.

But why?

Because he's after Elena? Maybe. But that really isn't it, either. What it is, he should never have told you that. Not if he's a professional, not even after you pounded him a little. And if he's FBI, he went to one of the best surveillance schools in the world and yet he did

the most piss-poor job of tailing you ever saw. Even
Donovan spotted him the first ten minutes.

Donovan.

Donovan would be making his calls today.

We'll see.

Now come on. Get some sleep.

That morning in Westport, three hours later, Billy
McHugh drove past the shuttered gate house at the
entrance to the Compo Beach parking lot. He spotted
Paul's blue Honda among the handful of cars parked at
odd angles along the breakwater. It was the only car
facing away from the water, he noted approvingly. Rear
tires on a solid surface. Not on sand or gravel like the
others.

McHugh chose a spot not far from Paul's and parked
his car in a similar manner. Pocketing his keys, he
stepped onto the rocky beach and saw Paul at once.
Paul had his back to him, though Billy was sure he'd
watched him come. He was sitting on his heels talking
to a black Labrador retriever who was wet and frizzy
and had a coating of sand up to his shoulders. The morning sun was warm; last night's unseasonable weather
was holding. Billy could see two other dogs running free
along the beach, their owners ambling behind them. It
was nice that they did this. If Billy had a dog he would
take him for long walks all the time. Or he could come
down here and go clamming like the men at the far end
and the dog could keep him company.

The black Lab backed off at Billy's approach, then
pirouetted playfully as Billy eased to a squat alongside
Paul. The dog took Billy's scent and, deciding he was
friendly, settled down to watch the two men as they
gazed out over the gray-green waters of Long Island
Sound.

"Did you ever read what it says on that statue up
where you drive down to the beach?" Billy gestured in
the general direction of the bronze statue of a minute-
man and the historical marker that told of a British
landing at this spot during the Revolutionary War.

"I've read it." Paul nodded.

"It says," Billy told him anyway, "they landed for
what they call a lightning raid on Danbury, to capture

stores of rebel arms." He shook his head bemusedly. "Some lightning raid. Forty miles on foot. It took them two days in full pack, wearing redcoats that made beautiful targets every step of it."

Paul ran his fingers through the polished stones at his feet, saying nothing.

"They had guts. I'll give 'em that," Billy said quietly. "I could never walk in a line like that past all those stone walls, never knowing when some farmer was going to put a hole through you." Billy reached for a piece of amber sea glass that he studied for a long moment. "Paul," he said finally, "I would like not to die just yet."

Paul looked up at the bigger man, "I'd like that, too, Billy."

"Is that why I'm here? You're going to tell me it's time?"

"I think I'm looking for a reason not to tell you that."

The bartender from Mario's let out a sigh. "You want me to say I'll never go off on my own again."

Paul gave a small shrug but didn't answer.

"I sure would like to, Paul."

"You don't think you can?"

"Last week I would have. But then that woman came in. Paul, you just can't imagine how she carried on."

"I know. Molly told me." Eventually. At dinner. About the other woman, not Kitzy Sweetzer, who had had one whiskey sour too many.

"I mean, have you ever heard of such a thing in your whole life?"

"Not like that, exactly."

"But I did get hold of myself, Paul. And it wasn't really too late. I had that Gelman feller from behind and I said to myself, this isn't right. I promised Paul. I promised Molly. Then I said, what I'll do is get him good and drunk, then I'll tighten up on his neck just enough to put him peaceful, and then I'll leave. I'm not saying I wouldn't have left his balls in the soap dish for when he woke up but at least he would have been alive and he never would've seen my face."

"Who actually killed him?"

"You said Molly told you."

"She did, but in broad strokes."

"Well," he hesitated, "I'm not sure I should say more. Nobody but me deserves to be tarred for this one."

"Okay."

"What's okay mean?"

"I'll think about this. How are you doing otherwise?"

"Real good. Did you know I've been keeping company?"

"With Mrs. DiBiasi," Paul nodded, a soft smile. "How long has that been going on?"

"I don't know," He shrugged. "We just got to talking more and more, watching TV together, going to the food store and stuff. She's teaching me how to play her piano. She says no one is ever too old to learn about music."

"I think that's great, Billy."

"You know she's not one bit afraid of me? Nobody in this whole town so far is afraid of me. Except maybe the Doc, sometimes."

"Gary is probably a little nervous about all of us, sometimes. He'll come around."

Billy raised one eyebrow at Paul's reference to the future. "Paul, if that means I haven't used up my chance, I sure would like to hear you say it straight out."

"What happens the next time someone hurts one of your friends?"

"I go straight to Molly. Then we sit down with you and talk about what was done and what's the best way to teach that person a lesson if he deserves it and it's not none of our business."

"What if someone harmed Mrs. DiBiasi?"

"The same thing."

"That wouldn't be hard for you?"

"Sure it would. But I know you and Molly would want to fix the guy just as much as me and I know you'd let me be in on it."

"What if you saw some of Palmer Reid's people nosing around?"

"Straight to Molly or you."

"Or to Anton. But not to Carla or Gary for a while."

Billy dropped his eyes, then nodded that he understood. He would never have said anything that would get Dr. Russo in trouble. Or Carla. But they never had to let that Gelman see their faces. They walked in meaning to kill him. And they wanted him to see who did it. Which is bush-league. When you go to kill, you kill. It's not a game.

"What if you can't reach any of us?"

"I disappear. Then I wait to see if it's because Reid got you. Then I make it real expensive for them."

Paul picked up a piece of broken shell and tossed it toward the black Lab, who sniffed it disinterestedly. Then the dog moved forward and offered its head to be scratched. "Billy," he seemed to be searching for words, "I want you to know how much I hate having to talk to you like this."

"I was afraid of a lot worse."

Paul grimaced, shaking his head. "I'm talking to you like a kid. You're a man. A very special man. And you never talked to me like this even when I *was* a kid."

"Different times. Different ballgame." Billy reached for the dog's back and found a spot that started its hind leg pumping. "Most of my life I worked alone. Here, you got thirteen people to think about and I got to think about them, too. I can't screw it up for the rest of you. We got a good thing here and I. . . ." Billy let his voice trail off. He gazed out over Long Island Sound. Come spring it would be covered with sailboats. Come summer he meant to go for a ride on one. And he'd get a suntan. Once in a man's life he ought to get a suntan besides just on his face and hands. "I sure do like it here, Paul."

"I know."

"Mrs. DiBiasi says when it gets warmer we can. . . ." Again the thought faded. "You know who she reminds me of, Paul? Mrs. DiBiasi, I mean?"

"Who?"

"Your Ma. Cassie Bannerman."

Paul nodded slowly. They were nothing alike, at least in appearance. But he could see why Billy would feel that way. They were probably the only two women Billy had ever been with long enough to get to know them. Not counting Molly and the others. Up until Mrs. DiBiasi, Cassie Bannerman might have been all the kindness and gentleness he'd known in his life. She had been, in her way, what Susan was becoming in his own life. Until they killed her.

"You know," Billy said dreamily, "more each year you look like your mother. And you got that same soft and easy way of talking. First time I laid eyes on you I knew you were like her. You remember that day?"

"I remember."

Fifteen years. He was twenty-three. And he'd flown to Vienna to claim the body. They'd had it cremated. Who gave you the right, he asked? She'd expressed that wish, they insisted. Where are her things, he asked? Her belongings. We're sorry, they said. There was a fire. Faulty wiring. When she had her heart attack the oven was on. No one thought to turn it off when the ambulance came to take her away. What ambulance? What doctor? And what kind of a company is this anyway? What exactly did she do for you?

It was a reporter for the German Magazine, *Stern*, who told him. The company was a front. American Intelligence. What did she do for them? We have only rumors, the reporter answered, but she must have been an operative because she had had a code name. They called her "Mama."

What kind of operative? Again, only rumors. Tell me some of them. That she was a coordinator of certain specialists, he answered. That she died of bullet wounds, not a heart attack. That others died in her house as well and the fire was set to conceal the damage done by machine-gun fire. I don't believe a word of that, Paul had told him. I know my mother. She was an art buyer. She bought and sold paintings. Perhaps, the reporter answered, you did not know her so well after all. I will show you where to look for the truth, who to start asking, who her bosses were. Why? Why would you help me? For the story, of course, the reporter answered.

But they would tell him nothing. Only lies upon lies. And then one day he returned for the fourth or fifth time to the burned-out shell of the house at 16 Gruenstrasse and he saw another man standing there, his eyes red, his shoes and pants covered with soot, a charred and sodden book in his hands. Perhaps he knew her. Perhaps he knew something about what had happened. Paul approached him.

"Did you know the lady who lived there?" he asked.

The man turned slowly toward him. Burning eyes. Terrible eyes. It was a full thirty seconds before they flickered in what seemed to be recognition.

"Are you Paul?" he asked.

"Yes."

He held up the book. "She gave me this. It's stories and poems. I read some."

"You were her friend?"

"Still am."

"Do you know what happened here?"

"Not yet." He turned to walk away. "Go back home, Paul."

"I'm staying. So are you, until you talk to me." Paul reached for his arm, jerked it backward, then danced nimbly aside as the older man's foot slashed out toward his knee. Paul was quick. He hooked the man's leg with a kick of his own and spun him. He moved in, expecting the older man to fall, but he was surprisingly nimble. The man used his own momentum to complete a graceful crouching turn, and as he rose out of it a knife had suddenly appeared in his hand. It was a skinning knife, short and ugly, designed for disemboweling. The man held it close against his chest. Paul backed off, stripping his jacket and wrapping it around one arm, and assumed a combat stance. The man frowned and straightened.

"Where'd you learn that?" he asked. "Army?"

Paul may have nodded.

"Don't do that. Use your feet against a knife. Kick or run. Running's better."

Paul waited.

"You look like her. You got guts like her?"

"If someone killed her, I want him."

"No police," he said.

"I've tried the police."

"Let's go." Billy turned once more and walked.

She was not, Paul soon learned, what the reporter from *Stern* thought she was. Not exactly. On the other hand, she wasn't what he'd grown up thinking she was, either. It was never quite clear to him whether she was an art buyer who had been recruited by American Intelligence or an agent who operated under that cover. Or how long she'd been involved with them. Or whether she actually ran field-contract agents or simply operated a safe house at 16 Gruenstrasse. Her frequent trips to Europe had begun while he was in grade school. When his father died, and when he went off to college, she moved there and stayed, flying Paul over during school breaks, meeting him in London, Rome or Paris.

He did, of course, question Billy about her. But every question concerning what she did would be answered in terms of what she was. Kind, brave, smart, pretty, nice. Paul thought at first there might have been a love affair between them, hard as it was to imagine his mother and this silent, frightening man together. But bit by bit, the picture of another sort of relationship emerged. For whatever reason, Billy had come to regard her as a saint. He trusted no one else. No one else could locate him when he was between assignments and not at 16 Gruenstrasse. No one else could talk to him, much less control him. No one but the woman known as Mama.

Of the two men who died with her, one was American, the other a double agent, a traitor to the Eastern bloc who'd been spirited up the Danube from Budapest and was awaiting transport to Washington for interrogation. The killers had come down from Berlin, assisted by two Austrians, one of them a ranking policeman. The double agent was not tracked, he was betrayed. The men who had betrayed him, in favor of a prisoner swap they considered more ·beneficial, were Americans. There were three involved. Billy followed the rumors to the door of one of these, a deputy section chief in Salzburg. Billy questioned him, with the aid of his skinning knife, then burned down his house around him. The other two could wait.

He took Paul with him to Berlin, where they found one of the triggermen living in the British sector. This man knew of Billy McHugh. He was terrified. He begged. It wasn't personal, he said. They were told to take no chances with the woman known as Mama. Paul asked Billy to wait outside, to leave him alone with this man. Billy told him, for the first of many times, "This ain't a game." Then he cut the man's throat.

It was Paul who shot the second triggerman. They followed him into the washroom of a service station off the autobahn. Billy had a gun this time that jammed, or so he later claimed. The man whipped his hat toward Paul's face and clawed at a pistol in his belt. Paul caught the hat in flight, took careful aim and fired. The man slammed backward into the toilet stall. He blinked once and died.

"How you doing?" Billy asked him afterward.

"You let him go for it, didn't you. You wanted to see if I could handle it."

"My gun jammed. How do you feel?"

"I'm not sure. Not bad. Not good, either."

"We got three," Billy said, "The main ones. Go home now, Paul. Get married or something."

There was a girl. She'd driven him to the airport. But now that seemed so long ago. "What are you going to do?"

"I don't know. Hang around."

"You're going to finish it."

"Sooner or later. It could take a while. The others will hear about these three. They'll dig a hole."

"I want them, Billy. It's not even just for my mother anymore."

"What else is there?"

"They set up their own people. You don't do that. You take care of your own."

"You talk like her, too," Billy said, then he sat silent for a while. "She was going to take me to Paris. Show me about art and stuff."

"She took me there. I was eighteen."

"She was showing me from books. But they got burned, mostly."

"Go with me, Billy. I'll teach you."

"No." He squirmed as he said it. "Your mother was . . . she didn't care if she had to go slow sometimes. I'm not that smart."

"Everybody's smart, Billy. We're just smart about different things."

"You wouldn't make fun of me?"

"Let's go to Paris." He put a hand on Billy's shoulder. "We'll teach each other."

It was four months later that they found one of the Austrians. The other one, the policeman, committed suicide two weeks after that. A month later, in Salzburg again, one of the Americans was shot to death at a traffic light. Paul learned of it in the newspaper.

"Did you do this, Billy?"

"No."

"Any idea who did?"

"Guy I know. Johnny Waldo."

"Why?" Paul had learned not to bother asking Billy how he knew things. "What's he got to do with this?"

"I told him what you said."

"What I said?"

"That we take care of our own."

Another ten days passed. Paul was taking breakfast alone in his small pensione off Vienna's Schweitzergarten. He was approached by a young man, American, not much older than himself. His name was Roger Clew, two years out of the Georgetown School of Foreign Service. Clew pulled a handkerchief from his breast pocket. Holding it between two fingers, he let in unfold.

"This is . . . um . . . a white flag," he said. "May I sit down?"

Paul nodded toward a vacant chair, his own fingers resting against the pistol under his arm.

Clew asked if he might reach for his photo ID. Paul nodded. He showed it. "I'm with the American Consulate," the young man said nervously. "I'm not a spy. I have a nuts-and-bolts job with a trade mission. They sent me because I'm no one you should be mad at."

"How did you find me?"

"We . . . they . . . tried to talk to some of your people. They said we'd have to deal through *Mama's Boy.* One of them just called. He suggested I come have a cup of coffee with you."

Paul kept his face blank. *Your people?* Aside from Billy, who could this guy be talking about? And now it's *Mama's Boy?*

"Why are you here?" Paul asked.

"To ask about a truce. To try to make peace with you." He gestured toward the street with his thumb. "And them."

"Them?" Paul's brow was creased.

Roger Clew clearly thought Paul was being cute. "I saw three outside. They let me. I would assume you have at least two more covering the back and one on the roof."

Paul still had only the dimmest notion of what might be going on here. Better, he thought, not to let that show. "What's your offer?"

"For you? Reparations, an apology, disciplinary action against the people involved in your mother's death. That's if there are any left."

"And what do you want from me?"

"The message is, 'Please tell them all it's okay for them to get back to work.' For the record, I don't know what that means and I don't want to."

It was becoming clearer. Billy had talked to a man named Waldo who was obviously not a novice at killing. We take care of our own. He, they, must have talked to others. But how was it possible for anyone to believe that he, Paul Bannerman, controlled them? He'd just turned twenty-four, for Pete's sake. And he'd been in Europe less than eight months. But he was not about to ask that question of Roger Clew. Instead he asked, "Why would I trust you?"

"Not me," he shook his head firmly. "I'm neutral. I don't even like this kind of shit."

"Okay, them then."

"You want my opinion, trust has nothing to do with it. It's a question of need. Whether I like it or not, sometimes our country needs people like your crowd. But now they won't work unless you say so. They don't even want to talk except through you. You've made everybody very nervous."

"I'll have to get back to you."

Roger Clew pulled out a card and laid it in front of Paul. "The sooner you do, the sooner I'm out of this. Call me and I'll set up a meet so you and our spooks can sit down and reason together."

"No meeting, no spooks. Just you."

The young foreign service officer spread his hands. "I told you, this isn't what I do."

"Suit yourself." Paul folded his napkin. "But it's you or nobody."

That was the start of it. Even now, from a distance of fifteen years, it seemed no less bizarre. He'd formed a trade union. The notion had never occurred to him, he'd done absolutely nothing in that direction, but there it was. You want something done? Talk to Mama's Boy. Tell him what, but you have to tell him why. Then he'll tell you who, when, and also if.

"Mama's Boy said no? What does he mean, no?"

"He says it shouldn't be done."

"Okay. Get someone else."

"You don't understand, sir. He says don't do it at all."

Paul's reason for insisting that he would only work through Roger Clew was simple. Paul's instinct told him that at the age of twenty-four he would almost certainly be at a disadvantage, and possibly manipulated, in any direct dealings with experienced covert-operations people. The arrangement had two other results. It made him seem all the more shadowy, mysterious, unknowable and therefore difficult to anticipate, larger than life. The second result was that Roger Clew's unsought role resulted in the rapid growth of his own career until, two years before Westport, Crew was recalled to Washington and promoted to Deputy Under Secretary of State for Political Affairs.

Even more rapidly, Paul grew into his own accidental creation. With the guidance of Billy McHugh and others he was soon dictating rules of engagement, contractual terms; requiring mandatory physical conditioning; controlling the disbursement of funds; curtailing free-lance or criminal activities; even securing medical care and death benefits. Paul originated most of these, and managed all of them. Over the next dozen years he attracted the best of the best. Or the best of the worst, as Roger Clew would characterize them. First Vienna, then Berlin, then Tehran, and finally Rome, where it at last began to wear him down. Roger Clew had gone home. His liaison role was assumed by Palmer Reid, an old-time CIA elitist who had headed the Directorate of Operations for both South America and Western Europe. Reid considered that Paul Bannerman's operation was intolerably lacking in control, specifically his own. Paul ignored him.

The black Lab froze into a point, fixed upon two seagulls who were breakfasting nearby. Impudently close. The dog sprang into a chase, scattering them, then trotted on, pleased with himself.

"Billy?"

"Yep?"

"Did you know I've been keeping company my-self?"

"The reporter lady," Billy nodded. "Were you afraid I'd hurt her, Paul? That why you never mentioned her until now?"

"Come on, Billy." Paul punched him lightly. "That never crossed my mind."

"That's good because it's okay with me. You're enti-tled. She real nice?"

"She is. Yes."

"Why don't you bring her into Mario's? I see what she looks like, I can look after her." Billy winced at his own choice of words. "You know what I mean," he said.

"I know. Anyway, I'm not sure how much more I'll be seeing of her."

"How come? You like her, right?"

"A lot of reasons." Fifteen years of reasons. Paul pushed to his feet.

Billy stood with him. "Paul," he said again, "I sure do like it here. Westport, I mean."

"I know."

"If you say it has to be, you got my word I'll either take the pipe or let you kill me. Even so. . . ."

Paul waited.

"Just to be on the safe side, I'd make it clean and sudden if I was you."

CHAPTER 10

Lesko slept until almost noon. On his belly. No dreams. It was more than he'd hoped for and in consequence he hadn't set his alarm. The telephone woke him.

"You know who this is?" came the voice on the other end. It was Buzz Donovan.

"Yeah," Lesko yawned. Now what?

"I'd like to talk to you."

"So talk."

"Not on the phone. Can you come into the city?"

"I'm coming in anyway in about an hour." He was due to make his rounds of the four Beckwith Hotels in the midtown area.

"Do you remember where I bought you lunch to celebrate your new job?"

"Yeah."

"Meet me there at precisely 1:15. I'll be waiting."

"Okay."

The call left Lesko as much annoyed as curious. Donovan, he assumed, had found out something about the FBI guy, Robert Loftus. Or possibly Lesko was in for some heat for working the guy over. But then why all the dumb cloak-and-dagger stuff? The lunch place would be the Yale Club on Vanderbilt, across from Grand Central Station. Precisely 1:15 meant Donovan would be watching from the second floor to see if Lesko had grown a tail.

Do you know who this is? he says. *Remember where we had lunch?* he says.

Good work, Buzz. Very smooth. Except if it's be-

cause you think my phone might be wired, all anyone
would have to do is hang around outside for the next
hour and see where I go. If you're worried that someone
tapped your own phone, it's a little stupid to think
you're fooling them by not using your name.

Lesko climbed into the shower.

At 1:15, having killed five minutes at a magazine
rack in Grand Central, Lesko crossed Vanderbilt Avenue and trotted up the steps into the raised lobby of the
Yale Club. He ignored the are-you-sure-you're-in-the-
right-place look of the deskman and climbed the stairs
to the dining room, a small overnight bag in one hand.
Buzz Donovan waved him in from his window table. He
was not smiling.

"What's the suitcase, Ray? You going someplace?"

"Bolivia." Lesko held up the bag and rubbed his
fingers together to show that it contained money.
"Then maybe Brazil to lay low for a while."

Donovan frowned. "You're not going to tell me?"

Lesko looked skyward. "I'm staying overnight in the
city, for Christ's sake. At the Beckwith Regency. What
the hell's with you today?"

"All right." Donovan raised both hands and dropped
his voice. Lesko took a chair. "Ray, I asked you last night
if you were involved in anything."

"And I said if I am I don't know it. I'm not any
smarter today."

"Nothing involving the Drug Enforcement Administration? Or any other United States Intelligence
agency?"

Lesko bit back his impatience. "The Loftus guy. You
got something or don't you?"

"Robert Loftus was with the FBI at one time," Donovan answered. "But no longer."

"Is he with the Fed at all? Or has he gone private?"

"He's still with the government."

"Well? What agency?"

"That's what's curious. Very curious."

Lesko showed his teeth. Buzz Donovan. Sweetheart
of a guy. Friend of the family. Known him forever. But
he's a lawyer. Try getting a simple fucking answer out of
a lawyer.

"You want me to guess? I'll guess." Lesko drained a glass of water. "He transferred over to Drug Enforcement. Now you want to know why I think so. Three reasons. One, it's the new glamour agency and a lot of FBI types are transferring over because the DEA beats the shit out of chasing down stolen cars and investigating mail frauds. Second, because you just brought up the DEA. Third, because last night he was asking me about this Elena."

Donovan shook his head. "He's not with DEA. First thing this morning I called a friend of mind at Justice to ask about Loftus. He called back a few minutes later and said Loftus transferred out of the Justice Department five years ago but the computer says his new assignment is classified."

"Then how do you know it's not DEA?"

"Because DEA transfers are not classified," Donovan answered reasonably. "A classified transfer has to involve national security. That's why I also asked you about other intelligence agencies."

"So who's he with? Do you know or don't you?"

Donovan answered with a vague toss of his head.

"You're not going to tell me for a while, right? You want to play secret agent some more."

"Might you have been followed, by the way?"

"No," Lesko snapped, causing heads to turn, "I was not fucking followed. And I'm getting so tired of this subject, I'm not sure I'd even give a shit."

Donovan raised his hands again. Another calming gesture. "My friend at Justice called me back a half-hour later. He was now in a considerably agitated state and demanded to know why I was asking about Robert Loftus. Apparently when he accessed Loftus's file, he set off an alarm somewhere else."

"And someone leaned on him."

"Exactly." Donovan paused as the waiter stopped to take their drink order. Lesko asked for a club soda. "I told him you'd caught Loftus following you and you simply wanted to know the reason for it. He put me on hold for a minute and then came back and said it was a mistake."

"Which is what Loftus told me."

"So," Donovan continued, "since he's an old friend,

and since I'd somehow put him on the spot, I tried to put him at ease. I made light of the Loftus question and asked about his family. Then, after some small talk, I asked what he could tell me about another name, assuring him that the two inquiries were totally unrelated."

Lesko felt a tingling at his neck. "You asked about the Bannerman guy."

"Yes." Donovan paused, not for effect but to choose his words. "The name, I'm convinced, meant nothing to him. He agreed to punch it up. Then, whatever appeared on his console, I heard him mutter 'Jesus Christ.' When he came back on the phone he was clearly uncomfortable and evasive. I told him I wanted an answer and would keep making phone calls until I got one. He said he'd get back to me and hung up. I stewed about this for a while and was about to call you when another call came. This one was from Palmer Reid. Ever heard of him?"

Lesko shook his head.

"Reid is old-line CIA. Princeton, wealthy family, very establishment. Probably considered not bright enough for the family's brokerage business so they steered him into foreign service. With his family connections and his own devious nature, Reid did quite well, rising to the Directorate of Operations for Western Europe and then for South America. The Directorate of Operations is responsible for clandestine activities. I'm told that three different CIA directors have tried to get rid of Palmer Reid because none of them have been able to find much tangible result in whatever he does nor could they even figure out exactly what it was Palmer's people were doing."

"Come on," Lesko snapped his fingers. "Bannerman, Reid, South America, Elena. What's the connection?"

"It's better if I take you through the sequence."

"Okay. So the Reid guy called you. What did he say?"

"He acknowledged that Loftus worked for him but only indirectly. Loftus is attached to a special planning unit and one of its jobs is to plot out a long-range anti-drug strategy. As Reid tells it, and this addresses three of those elements, they picked up a tip that you might have had recent contact with the Elena woman. Loftus

decided to check it out himself. He was not authorized
to do so. He exceeded his authority. Reid says it served
Loftus right that you roughed him up, and as far as he's
concerned the matter is closed."

"You believe him?"

Donovan hesitated. "I have no reason not to. In this
case."

"What about Susan's boyfriend?"

More hesitation.

"Did you ask about him or not?"

Donovan nodded. "The name did not seem familiar
to him. He put me on hold. When he came back he
asked me what this Bannerman fellow had to do with
the other. I said, 'What have you got, and why do you
have a file on him at all?' He answered that there's no
file as such. The only place Bannerman's name turns up
is on a list of what Intelligence people like to call 'assets.'
In Bannerman's case, he's an asset because he's particularly well-traveled and well-connected. People like
Bannerman are useful in making introductions and getting American diplomatic personnel and business exec-
utives invited to the right parties. There are many thou-
sands of people on such lists, Ray, and most don't know
it. Most are never asked to do anything."

"So you think Bannerman is straight," Lesko said
doubtfully.

"Again, no reason to think otherwise."

"Then why did his name shake the other guy up?"

"Perhaps because I'd told him the two were unrelated. Then, lo and behold, they both led ultimately to
Palmer Reid's office, though by different routes."

"It doesn't bother you that Bannerman's on that
list?"

"Palmer Reid pointed out that I'm on it myself."

Donovan watched Lesko as he said that. His friend's
eyes, which had been shining dangerously since his first
mention of Paul Bannerman, had relaxed into their normal glower. Donovan was satisfied that, whatever
might be going on here, Lesko truly did not know about
it and that Lesko, therefore, had not been using him. He
gestured toward the buffet table. "Let's get some lunch,
Ray. You've probably had us both worrying over nothing."

* * *

Buzz Donovan hailed a taxi on Vanderbilt and dropped Lesko off at the Beckwith Regency before continuing on to his own apartment on East 57th Street.

He hoped he'd handled the meeting well, though he feared that he might have told Lesko more than was good for him. Ray Lesko was not a man to agitate, certainly not where his daughter was concerned.

Quite possibly he had said too much. But he'd felt sure going in that Lesko knew more than he was letting on and Lesko'd hoped to draw an admission out of him. In the past, whenever Lesko seemed to be even peripherally involved in a thing, he usually turned out to be right at its center. That did not appear to be the case here. Lesko seemed quite genuinely in the dark.

He didn't like lying to Ray. But it was a very small lie. One of omission. He'd told Ray that his friend had muttered "Jesus Christ" at the mention of Paul Bannerman —he probably shouldn't have said even that—but he didn't mention the almost palpable fear that came back through the phone line. Donovan was sure without question that his mention of Paul Bannerman had prompted his friend's call to Palmer Reid and Reid's call back to him. And yet Palmer Reid had behaved as if he were hearing the name for the first time.

But then, Palmer Reid is a liar. Always had been. Probably pathological. George Bernard Shaw once wrote that the penalty of being a liar is not that one can't be believed, but that one can't believe anyone else. That neatly described the cynical and suspicious nature of Palmer Reid. But it didn't begin to describe Reid's capacity for criminal mischief while cloaking himself in the flag of the United States of America. And if this Paul Bannerman is involved with Palmer Reid he is almost surely cut from the same cloth and Susan Lesko has found herself in very bad company indeed.

Well, Buzz Donovan decided, we'll just have to do something about that, won't we. We'll see what this Bannerman fellow is all about. Two or three more phone calls ought to do it.

Lesko entered the lobby of the Beckwith Regency on Park Avenue at 54th and approached the desk. A

new clerk was on duty. She didn't know Lesko and was
visibly startled to see such a rough, scowling face, and
the body of an aging wrestler, neither of which fit the
Regency's customer profile as described to her during
employee indoctrination. He gave his name and told
her she was holding an envelope for him with a room
key. She found it, he took it, then he proceeded to the
elevator, his scowl deepening.

Lesko didn't like that talk with Donovan at all. Not
that any of it necessarily meant anything except that
Buzz had read too many spy novels and had too much
time on his hands. None of it connected. Take it all
piece by piece and all of it could be explained away.

So Robert Loftus works for Palmer Reid. Who gives a
shit? So the former FBI guy is now probably CIA and
has some new secret job. Who gives a shit about that
either? Anyway, almost everything's a secret with those
assholes. Even the time of day is on a need-to-know
basis. The real reason everything's a secret is that hardly
anything they plan ever works the way they meant it to
and hardly anything they ever find out ever matters a
good goddamn in the long run and if they didn't keep it
all secret everybody else would know that too. Anyway,
Lesko couldn't care less.

Except Donovan had lied to him.

He wasn't sure what the lie was, exactly. But he'd
watched Buzz's eyes. There was something sitting back
there. Then there was all that business about not wanting to talk on the phone. What couldn't he have said?
Whatever it was, Lesko was fairly sure that whatever
Donovan didn't want to say on the phone, he didn't say
back at the Yale Club, either.

Wait a second. Hold it, Lesko thought. I'm getting
like the fucking CIA. A conspiracy mentality. Those
guys don't even take anything at face value. Let out a
fart in public and they'll think it's a secret code. You
know what's doing this? It's those fucking four o'clock-
in-the-mornings, that's what's doing it. Last night
Elena's name comes up for the first time in two years,
from the guy Loftus . . . who is supposed to be a pro
but is very easily spotted . . . and who brings up
Elena's name a little too easily . . . and these things
bother me more than I admit . . . so my subconscious

decides to aggravate me about them at four in the morning. So I get this stupid dream with Susan in it, and Katz in it being a jerk, and Paul Bannerman in it except he looks like me, and Elena standing outside looking like she wants to kiss and make up, and Buzz is watching all this, scribbling in his notebook. I should make sense out of that? I should think the dream was a premonition just because Buzz calls me the next morning and asks what's going on? He asked it last night, too, for Christ's sake. The dream didn't mean shit.

Except he was still aggravated. And except Donovan lied.

What if the lie was about Susan's boyfriend? What if Paul Bannerman is more than just a name on a list of potential assets and is somehow involved with Loftus and Reid? And Elena. And therefore maybe even Katz. That would connect everything, wouldn't it?

Uh-oh.

No.

Lesko didn't even want to think about that. What he wanted was to get up to his room, get some coffee sent up, and then go through this envelope full of security reports so he could start his tour. He wanted to do that before the urge got too great to go up to Westport and look up this Paul Bannerman and bang him against a wall until he told Lesko what the hell was going on here.

At the bank of pay phones just inside the Pan Am building off Vanderbilt Avenue, Robert Loftus sat reading a folded copy of *The New York Times.* He did not look up as a second man, younger but similarly dressed in a dark business suit, approached him and whispered several words. The other man walked on and took a position some distance away. Loftus lowered his paper and stared thoughtfully at one of the phones. With a sigh, he stood up and limped toward it, favoring a painful left knee. He closed the booth and, after another long moment of hesitation, tapped out the area code for Virginia and then a number. A voice said "Yes?" Loftus said his name and asked for extension 004. Another voice said "Yes?" The voice of Palmer Reid.

"Donovan met Lesko, sir. They had lunch at the Yale Club."

"Any idea what was said between them?"

"No, sir. Except that his call to Lesko followed within minutes of his conversation with you. Judging by his tone and his wish to see Lesko immediately and privately, I don't think you threw him entirely off the scent, sir."

"Where is Donovan now?"

"Apparently headed back to his apartment. Your man Burdick is on him. My man, Poole, just rejoined me after Donovan dropped off Lesko."

"They are both *my men*, Robert."

Loftus closed his eyes. "Of course, sir."

"Where did Lesko go?"

"Well, that's an odd thing, sir. He had an overnight bag with him. He took it to the Beckwith Regency Hotel."

"The Regency? That's quite expensive, isn't it? And why would Lesko be staying at a hotel when he lives not thirty minutes away?"

"Doug Poole says he didn't actually check in, sir. There was an envelope with a room key waiting for him."

"So he's meeting someone."

"I don't know, sir."

"Bannerman, perhaps?"

"Sir, I don't think Lesko knows Bannerman. I don't think he even knew Bannerman existed until last night."

"On what do you base that opinion?"

"Lesko's daughter called Bannerman after her father took her home. She told Bannerman that she had finally told her father about him and that her father was looking forward to meeting him."

"That's all?"

"On that subject, yes, sir."

"Robert," Palmer Reid's tone had an edge to it, "I could just as easily conclude from that conversation that the two men do in fact know each other and have kept that knowledge from the daughter."

"I've stated my impression, sir." He closed his eyes again. "But the tapes are on their way to you by courier. With your superior experience, you may catch a nuance I missed."

There was a brief silence over the line as Palmer Reid pondered whether there might be insolence hidden somewhere in that last remark. "I may indeed," he said finally. "What else did Bannerman and the girl talk about?"

"There were some expressions of mutual affection." Loftus was stalling.

"What else?"

"Sir, Bannerman and the girl seem to be planning a ski vacation together. There was a reference to the amount of packing that has to be done by Friday. I assume that's when they're leaving."

"Their destination?"

"They didn't say. It's apparently going to be a trip of some duration. She asked if two ski outfits would be enough for 'that many days' and whether she'd need evening clothes. He answered that the only time they'd dress for dinner was their one night on the train."

"The train, you say."

"Yes, sir."

"That sounds like Europe."

"Yes, sir. But," he added pointedly, "it does sound to me like a pleasure trip."

Reid ignored the remark. "Bannerman makes trips such as this at least annually, doesn't he? Sometimes to the Austrian Tyrol. Most often to the Grisons in Switzerland. And both are reached through Zürich."

"Sir, he travels to a lot of places."

"Zürich, Robert," he said archly. "What is the significance of Zürich?"

"Sir," Loftus gritted his teeth. "If you're referring to Swiss bank accounts, I doubt very much whether Bannerman has one or needs one. His funds are all invested in Westport and they're just as out of reach as they'd be in Zürich."

"Those are *my* funds, Robert."

"Yes, sir."

"And I will pass over the fact that there are others who have funds in Zürich, powerful private interests, criminals and even governments who might find it in their interest to support Paul Bannerman's activities."

Loftus had been afraid of this. If he asked what activities, there being no evidence of any whatsoever, Reid would call him naïve. He said nothing.

"I will pass over that question and get to one that is even more intriguing. We have some reports that Elena is in South America, and others that she is in Europe. If you were to begin looking for her in Europe, Robert, where would you start?"

Loftus closed his eyes again. "Probably Zürich, sir."

"Why, Robert?"

Loftus didn't answer. The question was essentially rhetorical. Elena had been born and raised in Zürich, born of a Bolivian national who was then stranded there when Bolivia declared war on Germany and Italy in 1943. She held dual citizenship, and her mother had married into a large and wealthy Zürich family. Elena had plenty of roots there, plenty of friends. It was, true enough, where one would start looking for her, but if it were up to Loftus they wouldn't bother. She wanted to be out of it and she was. As far as he was concerned, that was all Bannerman and Zivic and the rest of them wanted as well.

He'd tried expressing that view to Palmer Reid and had been ridiculed for it. Reid saw conspiracies everywhere. Every conversation had a hidden meaning, every meeting, a hidden agenda. You couldn't even ask him if he was going to a Redskins game without Reid wondering why you were trying to determine his whereabouts on a given Sunday afternoon.

Not that he wasn't right occasionally. Law of averages. And maybe the country needs a few professional paranoids. Maybe they need to be in positions of power because if they weren't, no one would listen to them. Not that Palmer Reid ever told anyone what he was doing. Certainly no one outside Operations. Certainly no politically appointed director. Imagine telling anything important to a loose cannon like William Casey or a gee-whiz type like George Bush. On the other hand, the smart ones didn't even want to know what Reid was doing.

"Robert?"

"Yes, sir?"

"What is Bannerman up to?"

"I don't know, sir. But I think we should keep in

mind the possibility that he's just going skiing with a lady friend."

"The arrogance of the man."

"Sir?"

"I'm agreeing with you, Robert. For the sake of argument. Bannerman is, in a very real sense, a traitor to his country. He is a mutineer who has expelled legitimate authority from what is in fact a government facility."

"Um, are you talking about Westport, sir?"

"I am." Palmer Reid began to hiss. "He is a man who feels so secure in his treachery that he is free to travel as he pleases, when he pleases, and has the gall to threaten retaliation if he or his killers are interfered with in any way. And now he has the effrontery to be taking off on a carefree, extended ski trip to Switzerland with the young lady of his choice."

"Switzerland is just a guess, sir. We haven't confirmed that."

"*And,*" Palmer Reid ignored the reminder, "that, Robert, is the *best case* scenario. Do you realize that? Even allowing for the most charitable interpretation of his behavior, even imputing no sinister motive whatsoever, that behavior constitutes an utter outrage to every decent American."

"Yes, sir."

"But we don't really believe in best-case scenarios, do we?"

"Sir," Loftus couldn't help himself, "I must tell you that I lean strongly in that direction."

"That's fine, Robert," Reid said after a pause. "We must encourage alternative points of view. If we agree all the time, then one of us is unnecessary. Isn't that so, Robert?"

"Um, yes, sir."

"Try this scenario." Palmer Reid began reflecting aloud, unevenly, as if assembling the pieces as he spoke. "Bannerman has reached Elena. He has done it through Lesko. Let's grant for the moment that the daughter is merely a pawn and that Bannerman has used her to reach Lesko. Elena has told Bannerman everything, all about our relationship with her, in return for . . . money? No. Elena has far more of that than Banner-

man. For protection? For the use of Bannerman's killers
to further cover her tracks? Yes. Quite possibly for that."

Loftus said nothing.

"Bannerman in turn has told Lesko . . . what? Certainly about Westport. Possibly about all the other
Westports. Certainly of our association with Elena. Our
involvement in his partner's death. So that Lesko can
. . . take further revenge? Go public where Bannerman might not? Use his daughter to plant a story in the
New York Post? Help me, Robert."

"I have no idea, sir." Loftus gave up.

"Mr. Donovan is involved, of course. Though possibly as a dupe. Yes. Lesko duped Donovan into using his
Washington contacts to determine how much we know.
You see, Robert? You sniffed them out last night. You
made them break from cover. Donovan calls the Justice
Department, I call Donovan, Donovan promptly meets
with Lesko, then Lesko promptly rushes off to another
meeting, calling attention to himself by going straight
to a luxury hotel we know he can scarcely afford. Rather
clumsy, that. His meeting, quite possibly, is with
Bannerman himself."

"We'll see, sir. We'll watch the hotel."

"For heaven's sake."

"Sir?"

"Or," Palmer Reid continued, his voice stronger, as
if struck by a revelation, "Bannerman has not yet met
Elena but intends to do so in Switzerland. Why else
would he go there?"

"Possibly to ski, sir," Loftus said and wished he
hadn't.

"Robert," Reid said sharply, "how many coincidences must pile upon coincidences before you begin to
suspect a pattern? Has Bannerman ever gone off on a
holiday before within five days of returning from another? Has he ever before been known to travel with a
woman?"

"Offhand, I don't think so. However, Mr. Reid. . . ."

"But the details are really neither here nor there,
Robert. It's Bannerman's ultimate intention that matters. And the worst-case scenario assumes that Bannerman's intention is to bring down everything I've
spent my lifetime building. He could bring down this

nation's entire intelligence system, Robert. Do you realize that? He could bring down the President."

"Sir, I really think we should sleep on that one."

"Of course, Robert. You and I both."

"Sir, why don't I hop the shuttle and come down there so we can thrash this out?"

"Have you been to Westport yet?"

"Westport?"

"You remember, Robert. It's a town up in Connecticut. You told me on Monday that you'd have a look around, yourself."

"Sir, I was referring to the activities of Lesko and his daughter. I can't go to Westport. Bannerman knows me."

"Who's the man with you now?"

"Doug Poole, sir."

"Send him, then. You go to the Beckwith Regency to see with whom, if not Bannerman, Lesko is meeting. If Bannerman is in Westport, or after he returns to Westport, tell Poole I want an hour-by-hour log of his activities."

"Yes, sir."

"In the meantime, you will check with the airlines and confirm Bannerman's destination."

"Yes, sir."

"For heaven's sake."

"Sir?"

"You know, I've just had an idea."

"What would that be, sir?"

"All the momentum thus far has been Bannerman's. Perhaps it's time we gave him something else to think about."

"I'm not sure I follow, sir. What's your idea?"

"It's something else I'm going to sleep on, Robert. In the meantime, when Burdick reports in, tell him I want to see him right away and put him on that shuttle."

"No, sir."

"What was that, Robert?"

"I'm not going to do that. You don't want Burdick yet, sir. Please."

A long silence. "Robert . . . ?"

"Yes, sir?"

"Nothing. That will be all, Robert."

* * *

Charles Whitlow, Palmer Reid's personal assistant, waited until Reid broke the connection before replacing the receiver on his extension phone. He folded his hands across his lap, drew his knees together, and waited.

"Comments?" Reid asked.

"As you've noted in the past, sir, Loftus does shrink from difficult decisions on occasion."

"Recommendations?"

"Presume the worst case. Act decisively. One destroys a chain by destroying a link."

"My thought exactly."

"In fairness to Loftus, sir, he may have a point in not using Burdick. Not much finesse there, sir."

"You have something better in mind, I take it."

"Shall I outline, sir?"

"No, Charles. Execute."

"Yes, sir."

"Decisively, Charles."

"Of course, sir."

CHAPTER 11

Doug Poole was elated. Here he was, Doug Poole, actually in Westport. During his five years in Army Intelligence, and especially in the two years since Loftus recruited him to Reid's unit, hardly a week had gone by without his hearing some wild story about the Westporters.

He knew the old man hated them. But he sure didn't. He thought they were fantastic. They were everything he used to hope his own job would be.

Just being here. On the Post Road. Not fifty yards from the travel agency where Paul Bannerman, Mama's Boy in the flesh, was probably sitting right now. With luck he'd get a look at him. Or Billy McHugh. Carla Benedict. John Waldo. Any of them. These people were legends.

He'd lucked out on this one. Loftus had made it clear that he didn't want him going to Westport. It was the old man who had insisted. Just watch, Loftus told him. Keep your car doors locked, with you inside. Pick a spot where you can watch Bannerman's office, take a few pictures of who comes and goes, don't let anyone see your camera. Don't get out of the car at all. If you have to take a leak, either do it in a cup or drive over the line into Norwalk. If you do spot any of Bannerman's people, for Christ's sake try to resist asking for their autographs.

Loftus. He could be a prick when he wanted to be. He could be patronizing. But Poole knew he wasn't the only one who'd give up a month's leave just for the chance to watch some of these people in action. They were the all-stars. They weren't company people. They were all contract agents. Which was a lot more interesting because between them they had probably worked for every Western intelligence agency at one time or another without ever having to do any of the bullshit work.

Bannerman himself had worked for the CIA and for Army Intelligence, which gave Doug Poole a feeling of special kinship with him, and he'd either worked for the National Security Agency or had advanced infiltration and weapons training with them at Fort Meade. Billy McHugh and Carla Benedict had worked for . . . you name it. The Israeli Mossad, MI-6, and both the French and German counterterrorist units. And Anton Zivic was a full colonel in Soviet Military Intelligence, the GRU. Zivic. There was another one they'd like to get into Fort Meade. Except Zivic would probably never see it from the outside again. Yeah. Fort Meade. That place was the nuts.

Poole, like Paul Bannerman, had trained there. Just in surveillance techniques, though, along with a few other agents and a lot of cops from across the country. But the facility was mind-boggling. Talk about towns being taken over. Fort Meade was a small city, about fifty thousand people living and working there, all self-contained inside three barbed-wire fences. The middle one was electrified. And the barbed wire on top of the other two slanted inward as if to keep people from getting out. No place on earth was more secret, more secure, except maybe the Kremlin. It even had its own TV station and power supply.

Everybody talks about the CIA, Doug Poole thought, but the National Security Agency must have ten times the staff and twenty times the budget. Their main job had to do with spy satellites, long-range electronic surveillance from ships and planes, code-breaking and the like. But almost anything could be going on at Fort Meade. In some ways they had it made. No one looking over their shoulders. No one making movies about them. No congressional hearings, no spy novels. Even Robert Ludlum didn't give a shit about the NSA because he thinks there's no glamour there—and they hardly ever shoot people or get laid.

Doug Poole smiled.

You know what's funny? Robert Ludlum even lives here someplace. Right here in Westport. All this shit going on all around him. Chances are he's even had a pop or two at Mario's.

Hey wait . . . !

That little guy just getting ready to come out. You know who that looks like?

Doug Poole raised his camera and peered through the telephoto lens. That's him, he thought. Anton Zivic. Bad angle for a shot. Too much reflection on the windshield. He picked up his notepad and scribbled in the entry. Thursday, 4:27 P.M., Anton Zivic exiting Luxury Travel Associates. Must have been there since Poole arrived at 3:10.

Have to get a better angle. Can't leave car. Move it. Up to the other end by Herman's Sporting Goods.

Damn.

Poole glanced into his rearview mirror. Some guy was double-parked, blocking him. Poole tapped his horn. Come on. Move. The guy made a wait-a-minute gesture and pointed up ahead to show he was waiting for a space. Hey, schmuck. This is a space too, if you'll back up and let me out. Poole lowered his window.

"Come on, will you? Back up."

"What?"

"I said back up."

"Five seconds."

Zivic was out the door. Shit! Poole snatched up his camera and stepped out of his car, one leg, his eyes on Bannerman's storefront. He stopped. The hell with this. Loftus would see the picture and know it wasn't taken from inside the car and he'd have his ass. That was Doug Poole's second-from-last thought.

The last, as he felt his car door slam against his leg and then something else crunch hard into the side of his neck, was that the crazy fuck behind him must have thought he was getting out to start a fight over a god-damned parking space. The guy was hitting him. Pushing him back inside. And now, through a white sparkly haze, Poole could see his face. It couldn't be a fight. The face didn't even look mad. No expression at all. And now the guy . . . short guy . . . white hair . . . was

helping him sit up straight . . . straightening his head
. . . arms on both sides of his neck.

That was all Doug Poole remembered. Except that
the man was friendly now. Talking to him. Gesturing
with his hands. But that part must have been a dream.

John Waldo kept up an animated chat with the unconscious young man long enough for any passerby who
thought he'd seen an act of violence to conclude that he
must have been mistaken. Just two men talking. The
young one must have slipped. Still some ice on the
ground.

That settled, Waldo returned to his own car, parked
it, then walked back to Doug Poole's car and slipped
behind the wheel. At the Herman's curb cut, he signaled Anton Zivic with his horn, gestured in the general
direction of Gary Russo's home and office, then flipped
his turn signal.

Anton Zivic had agreed without hesitation to assume
Paul's duties during the coming three weeks. He had
just spent two hours being briefed on various matters
that might require his attention during that period, including a review of the instructions each of the others
had in the event of several classifications of emergency.
Paul expected no trouble, he said, although Palmer
Reid almost certainly knew something of his plans by
now and, knowing Reid, just might be emboldened to
try an exploratory probe. But it would be only that, Paul
felt sure, and if it happened Anton should take care that
no one else unnecessarily escalated it into something
more.

As for the question, which Paul raised last, of Anton
taking over all administrative duties for the next full
year, Anton agreed that it was a burden which, in fairness, ought to be shared. He certainly had the experience, having commanded a staff of thirty and run ten
times that number of field agents in his former life. But,
selfishly perhaps, the simpler and more gracious nature
of his present life had far greater appeal. There was also
the question of whether he could ever hope to inspire
the sort of loyalty that Paul enjoyed with these people.
His people. Nearly all of whom were essentially un-

governable, and yet they chose to be governed by Paul. Some who feared nothing on earth chose to fear Paul. Or chose to love him. It was astonishing, when one thought of it. For most of them, a word such as love had scarcely entered their lives. Paul did not fear them and they knew it. He admired them and they knew it. He loved them and they knew it because they saw it in his eyes and his actions and they also heard it in his words. Could the answer be as simple as that? Even with men and women such as these?

On the matter of being the first to rotate into Paul's position, Zivic knew as he departed Paul's office that the answer would ultimately be yes. Fair was fair. And a year was only a year. Also, as he left Paul's office, he saw that his new responsibilities had already begun. Because there was John Waldo driving off in a car that was not his own, with a passenger who should not have been there. A young man—large, blond hair, apparently asleep. John pointing to Dr. Russo's residence. Zivic climbed into his car and followed. "It's all yours, Anton," Paul said to him, offering his hand. "And thank you."

So it begins.

Anton Zivic's reflective mood stayed with him as he wound through the wooded residential streets of Westport. Three years since he had joined Paul here. Almost nine years before that when he had first set eyes on Paul, looking down at him from a hovering helicopter, Paul looking back over the sights of a grenade launcher. It was a face he'd known only from the photographs in a dossier that was astonishingly thick for one so young. Mama's Boy.

Paul had been in Iran for less than two months then, operating under a diplomatic cover, although Colonel Zivic knew that diplomacy was the last thing the Americans had in mind when they brought him in from Germany. Iran was in chaos. The Shah had departed. Reprisals against Savak and many foreigners had begun. Then, as the American Embassy was being taken in Tehran, Paul found himself stranded in the Talish Mountains north of Tabriz where he and his guides had been negotiating with Kurdish tribesmen to establish a secure evacuation corridor into Turkey. The Soviets, whose border was less than twenty kilometers away and who realized he was now trapped there, saw an opportunity to take an important American operative. He would simply disappear, missing and presumed murdered by either the Kurds or the Shiites. Someday, perhaps, he might resurface as part of a prisoner exchange, broken and wrung dry in the meantime. The Soviets had no particular plan for Paul, as far as Zivic knew. Only that he was a bird in the hand and he was close enough to their border for it to be argued that he had crossed it for the purpose of espionage.

Molly Farrell was in Tehran as well and had been for more than a year. Billy McHugh had come with Paul but was not with him on this mission. Zivic had dossiers on both of them as well. Molly Farrell's twin specialties were electronic surveillance and the construction of explosive devices in miniature. The latter skill always struck Zivic as unseemly for a proper young lady from Radcliffe who had also been a nationally ranked tennis player while in college. The American privileged classes were a well-known breeding ground for shrill feminists and unkempt radicals but hardly of amiable and athletic female assassins.

In the midst of the chaos, Molly had remained calmly on station, where she intercepted a coded directive from Moscow to the Soviet Embassy in Tehran. Although she could not decipher it without access to the Cray-1 system in the now-captured American Embassy, she was sufficiently familiar with Russian traffic to recognize the Mama's Boy designation and a set of hyphenated digits that appeared to be map coordinates. Since the message originated in Moscow and not Tehran, she reasoned that it could not simply be information on Mama's Boy's activities. She had to assume they were planning some action against him, at the very least to thwart his mission.

With her own chain of command in a state of collapse, and not trusting it to act quickly enough in any case, she called Colonel Zivic and asked for an immediate meeting to discuss "the man in the Talish Mountains." When Zivic agreed to the meeting, she felt sure her interpretation was correct. It told her that Zivic had to be aware of Paul's activities. Molly had met Zivic on several occasions and considered that their relationship was respectful. But she had no reason to expect his help, or anything resembling professional courtesy, without offering a specific incentive. The incentive Molly offered was that she would take out five KGB and GRU officers at random if anything whatsoever happened to Paul Bannerman.

"All that for a contract agent? You hardly know the man."

"He's my friend."

"In two months' time he has become such a friend? This is a man to be envied." Zivic cared nothing about Bannerman. The plan to kidnap him, though in his opinion pointless, was a matter of indifference to him. Miss Farrell, however, was something else entirely. A most interesting young lady. "Is it permitted to ask if there is a romantic attachment?"

Molly didn't answer. Zivic presumed it to be so. More's the pity. He wondered if this Bannerman appreciated her. As for himself, he did not appreciate being threatened. Not even by a young lady he rather liked.

"My dear Miss Farrell," he asked patiently, "what would have been wrong with asking a simple favor?"

"What would you want in return?"

"Another favor, naturally."

The notion that it might be a physical favor never crossed her mind. "I won't double for you, Colonel."

"Will you sleep with me?"

"Yes."

No hesitation. No qualifiers. Just yes. Zivic was at once excited and disappointed. "As much as this may surprise you, Miss Farrell, I do not regard the temporary use of your body as a personal favor. Nor do I regard treason as a favor." He reached for a phone. "I will see to Paul Bannerman. And I will consider that each of you is in my debt. This is fair?"

"This is fair," she answered.

Within that hour, to Molly's even greater surprise, Colonel Anton Zivic was accompanying her in a civilian Aeroflot helicopter en route to the Talish Mountains and the spot designated by the map coordinates that Zivic plotted for the pilot. Using a loud hailer, Molly announced her presence on board, repeating her message until one of Paul's guides flashed a recognition signal and waved her in. Paul and the rest of his team approached the hovering craft cautiously, then, satisfied that there were no armed men aboard, clambered into the helicopter, which took off immediately and headed into the setting sun. An hour later, flying at treetop level, it landed in a barley field several miles inside the Turkish border. Zivic offered Paul and Molly cognac from a flask he carried. Paul, who had been chatting cordially with Zivic, accepted. Molly hesitated.

"Merely a civilized gesture," he told her. "It is not drugged, I promise you."

Paul nodded encouragement. She took the small enameled cup and sipped from it.

"A thirty-minute walk to the southeast," he told Paul, "you have an airstrip. I would have taken you closer but it is a secret installation and to show such knowledge of it would have been a rudeness."

"I understand." Paul offered his hand. "Thank you, Colonel."

Zivic clasped it, then extended his own hand to Molly. When her hand rose, he kissed it.

"To friendship," he said.

Three months later, at Roger Clew's request, Paul set up a station in Rome. His diplomatic cover was an R-2 rating as a Foreign Service Reserve Officer with the United States Information Agency. His R-1 was a legitimate career diplomat who ignored Paul entirely. Paul's specific charge included all paramilitary and counterterrorist activities from Rome, north. South of Rome, particularly around Naples, the Mafia performed his function with even greater efficiency.

Molly Farrell came with him, as did Carla Benedict, who came down from Germany, and Billy McHugh, who wandered in several weeks after that. McHugh had made his own way out of Iran, doing nearly as much damage to the revolutionaries as Iraqi minefields would do later. Dr. Gary Russo, John Waldo, Harry Bauer and Janet Herzog all joined Paul in Rome. A few months after Paul's arrival, Colonel Anton Zivic showed up under a similarly transparent diplomatic cover. He was, legitimately enough, a Soviet Military Attaché, although he was GRU and not regular Army, and his purpose was neither espionage nor subversion, since these were strictly the province of the KGB, an organization Zivic was known to detest. What he seemed to be, based on the organization he was building and the contacts he was cultivating, was something approximating Paul's opposite number.

"You don't think it's awfully strange that he's here?" Molly asked Paul. "It has to be more than coincidence."

"It's not coincidence at all," Paul told her. "Zivic would have promptly reported to Moscow that he helped us and that we now owe him. They know that if they put him in Rome I'll probably cooperate with him wherever I can. They're right."

Molly understood, though with reservations. She realized that the popular view of rival intelligence organizations was a holdover from the Cold War era. A world of shadowy figures, implacably antagonistic, forever lurking about and hatching plots against each other. In actual fact, they frequently cooperated in situations where their interests coincided. Most knew each other by sight and by name because they attended the same parties. They were on the same guest lists because they all tried to cultivate the same influential friends.

"I promised him a favor." Molly had told Paul everything. "What do you think he'll ask me to do?"

"Possibly nothing," he answered. "He knows he has no hold on you except your word and he won't count on you keeping it now that the need is past. He didn't take your retaliation threat seriously, by the way. He knows you make little bombs but he has trouble believing that you actually use them."

"Then why did he help?"

"The same reason I would. Zivic tends to take the long view. I do owe him now. And by rescuing me he effectively disrupted my mission so he did his own job at the same time. Incidentally, I'm having dinner with him tomorrow night."

"You are?"

"Might as well."

"You've talked to him?"

"Oh. He sends his regards."

Molly made a face. "But he actually told you he didn't take me seriously? That wasn't just your opinion!"

"Don't sulk about it. It's better that way."

"You're taking him to the Ranieri?" she asked idly. The restaurant she named was just off the Via Condotti a few yards from the Spanish Steps. The Ranieri and the Hassler Roof, which was also nearby, were not so much favorites of Paul's as they were favorites of Rome's entire diplomatic and intelligence community, and of high-rolling deal makers of every description.

Paul nodded absently.

On the following evening, just as Paul and Anton were completing their fish course, the maître d' announced that there was a call on the house phone for Signore Zivic. The colonel, now dressed in an excellent Italian suit, took the call in a carved wooden booth resembling a confessional. He brought the receiver to his ear.

"Good evening, Colonel," he heard the voice say. "This is Molly Farrell. Do you remember me?"

"With great affection, Miss Farrell."

"I just wanted you to know that when you helped my friend, you didn't do it for nothing."

"That is my hope," Zivic frowned. He did not know quite what to make of this. Surely she knew that he was dining with her friend and that she was interrupting a productive discussion.

"Is anyone near you?"

"I beg your . . . no, no one is near."

"Would you turn your earpiece to face the wood on your left, please? Keep it away from your face and tell me when you've done it."

"This has the sound of a demonstration, Miss Farrell."

"Please do it. Are you ready?"

He did as she asked. "It is ready."

A popping sound. Not much louder than a wine cork coming free. Zivic flinched reflexively. A small metallic object appeared in the wood panel, deeply imbedded. Now he examined the earpiece. Its surface was barely disturbed. One of the holes seemed slightly larger than the others. He returned it to his ear with some reluctance.

"This is very impressive, Miss Farrell. I am forced to acknowledge that your threat had substance."

"Thank you. And I'll keep my part of the bargain depending on the favor."

"You are a most interesting young lady. *Buona sera,* Miss Farrell.

"Colonel?"

"Yes?"

"When you asked if I'd have sex with you and I said yes. Do you remember what you said?"

"I remember."

"Thank you for that, too." She hung up the phone.

On a professional level, Paul was furious. We are not, he told her, in the business of showing off. What would you have done if he wasn't impressed? Blow up a busload of Russian tourists?

"I realize it wasn't the smartest thing. I just wanted him to know."

"Smart would have been leaving well enough alone. Chances are he'd never have called in his marker. He's also not a man to anger."

"He's not angry. He likes me."

Paul knew that. He saw the pleasure on Zivic's face when he returned to the table, and his obvious enjoyment in telling the story of his phone call. But he was not about to give Molly the satisfaction of hearing him say it.

"Who says so?" he asked.

"He sent me roses today."

Not two weeks passed before Zivic called in his favor from Molly. He handed her a key to his apartment and asked if she would sweep it for listening devices at least weekly.

"That's the favor?" she asked.

"That's the favor."

"Your own people can't do this for you?"

"Yes. But they will take the opportunity to place their own. You, I think, will not."

Several years passed before he called in his favor from Paul. They were wearying years for both men, although Zivic felt that Paul had the better of their two worlds. As a contract agent, as Mama's Boy, Paul could decline assignments that he considered stupid or pointless, or even tedious. Unlike Anton, he did not have to produce reams of intelligence reports, numbing pages of statistics or economic surveys that were seldom read and even less frequently actionable. Nor did he have a quota of business and social contacts to make in the event they might be of some future use. Zivic enjoyed no such discretion. Further, while Paul could choose his operatives, Zivic's were for the most part assigned to him and inevitably included a number of KGB informants and tiresome party zealots.

At last, Roger Clew was recalled to Washington and promoted two grades. Roger and Paul handpicked one of Clew's deputies to become Paul's liaison. At about that time, however, Palmer Reid was named Director of Operations for Western Europe and immediately insisted upon the following: Paul Bannerman would swear an oath of service to the United States of America; he would accept a civil service rating and become a salaried employee; and he would report directly to Reid's assistant, one Charles Whitlow. Paul ignored him. There was no shortage of other governments desirous of his services, including that of Colonel Zivic.

Although Paul's interests and those of Anton were fundamentally opposed, they often coincided. Where they were opposed, Paul and Anton sometimes made a game of them. Paul would, for example, occasionally accept assignments to affect the outcome of the Italian political process. Paul would work to defeat the communist mayoral candidates in Marxist-leaning towns such as Genoa and Turin, while Anton schemed with equal vigor to discredit the Christian Democrats, an expensive dinner or case of wine riding on the result.

Their interests generally coincided in the area of counterterrorist activities. Paul detested these people not so much for the randomness of their atrocities as for the pointlessness of them. He would kidnap suspected terrorists, expose them to the questioning of Dr. Russo, and then, feeling no pity at all, dispose of what was left of them like so much rotted meat.

"What is your cause?"

"Justice for the Palestinians."

"Why do you kill the innocent?"

"No Christian or Jew is innocent."

"What would satisfy you?"

"Justice for the Palestinians."

"Would the killing then stop?"

"Retribution would then begin."

"Against whom?"

"You. All of you."

"When might there be peace?"

"There can be no peace."

"Very well. Who are the members of your group?"

"I tell you nothing. I spit on you."

Within hours they would beg to tell.

Colonel Zivic, Paul knew, had questioned just as many, with similar results. Terrorists, in Anton's view, were no less inimical to the interests of his own country than to the welfare of an Ohio family standing in line at Rome's Da Vinci Airport. They were useless as weapons against United States interests because they were uncontrollable. They were insects and yet they could cause great fleets to move. Zivic feared them more than he feared any American rocket. They could not destroy great cities, perhaps, but they could turn cities into fortresses. Even countries. France was already requiring visas of all foreigners, a patently absurd measure that would not deter a terrorist in the slightest, serving only to inconvenience the innocent. Cruise ships such as the QE2 denied entry to all but ticketed passengers so that no Arab or Irish terrorist or vengeful Argentinian posing as a visitor could bring a bomb on board. A pathetic measure. As if a terrorist organization would balk at the added expense of a ticket.

It seemed to be only the beginning. And it was certainly not just the Arabs. The Red Brigades of Italy and Germany, the Irish Republican Army, the Basque and the Puerto Rican separatists had formed a loose confederacy. One would do the work of the other in return for money or arms. With either of these groups, an interrogator would look in vain for cogent political objectives until he realized that the only real objective was self-perpetuation. But neither Paul nor Anton bothered to look for reasons anymore. They simply destroyed them as they were found. Neither kept prisoners or turned

them over to legal systems, because a live prisoner inevitably resulted in a new act of terrorism intended to
secure his or her release. They were both tiring of the
futility of it, the impoverishment of reason; Zivic more
quickly than Paul.

Colonel Zivic had made up his mind that when the
time came for him to retire, or should he be recalled to
Moscow with even the hint that he might not be reas-
signed outside the Eastern Bloc, he would move immediately to ensure that his declining years were spent as
gracefully and tranquilly as possible. He would disappear quietly if he could. He would defect if absolutely
necessary. But he would remain in the West and enjoy
its decadence as long as it lasted.

Zivic's recall to Moscow came during his sixth year in
Rome. The order was hand-delivered by two new deputies whose primary duty, it was clear, was to watch him
closely. He knew this did not necessarily imply a suspicion of unreliability. It was purely routine, but only in
cases of permanent recall. He invited the two deputies
to the Ranieri on a night when it was Paul's habit to dine
there. Paul greeted him and Anton responded with un-
characteristic correctness and introduced his companions, leaving it to Paul to judge their purpose by their
brusque and wary manner.

"How are your helicopter lessons going?" Anton
asked.

Paul didn't blink. "Quite well," he said. "Have you
ever ridden one?"

"Never."

"Would you like to come up with me one day soon?"

"Alas, I'm leaving on a journey tomorrow."

"Another time then. By the way, Miss Farrell sends
her regards."

Two hours and several vodkas later, the three Russians arrived at the taxi stand on the north end of the
Piazza di Spagna. A prostitute astride a Vespa motor
scooter chatted teasingly with the first driver in the line.
He was an older man, Anton Zivic's age, but he was
blushing like a schoolboy.

"Hey, how about you?" she addressed Anton in Italian. "You want to take a ride with me?"

"Some other time perhaps." He opened the door for

his two companions. The second one hesitated, preferring to have Anton sit in between. Anton gave him a friendly push.

"Last chance." The prostitute revved her motor and slid forward on her seat, showing more of her thigh in the process. "Come, papa. Jump on."

Zivic slammed the door and did. The Vespa was almost out of sight before the two frantic Russians made it clear to the driver that he was to give chase, and only when they attempted to scramble back out did he floor his accelerator and begin a winding, screeching chase of shadows through the darkened streets of Rome. The prostitute was Molly, the taxi driver was Billy McHugh. Within twenty minutes, Anton was safely at an apartment in the Trastevere district, negotiating the conditions of his defection with Paul Bannerman. Molly Farrell and John Waldo were en route to Anton's own apartment to retrieve those personal effects he requested.

By the next morning, Anton was at his bank in Geneva withdrawing his funds and a few securities, leaving intact those funds belonging to the Soviet Union. By noon he was aboard TWA flight 006 to New York City, traveling under a Swiss passport that he'd prepared for this eventuality. At Kennedy Airport he vanished. He would remain in hiding until the conditions under which he had come to this country were confirmed by the State Department to the satisfaction of Paul Bannerman.

Paul arrived in Washington a day later and went directly to the office of Robert Clew, now an Under Secretary for Political Affairs. Clew told him he had a problem. The Soviets, reacting quickly, had offered to permit the emigration of one hundred Russian Jews or to release a western agent of comparable rank if Colonel Zivic were returned before his defection became public knowledge. And that, Clew told him, was only their opening bid. The Administration was getting excited because such a trade would constitute a considerable human rights coup. In the meantime, he said, Palmer Reid was acting as if the defection and any eventual trade were all of his design and he wanted Zivic brought to his Westport facility for at least a few days of interrogation before Zivic realized he was going to be returned.

"Reid has nothing to do with this," Paul told him. "What Westport facility?"

Clew explained that Westport was the latest of several suburban rehabilitation centers that had become operational during the Carter Administration for the purpose of easing burnt-out agents back into something resembling normal lives. Once Reid was satisfied that they could function normally, they were relocated. Some, who had prices on their heads or criminal charges pending against them, were given new identities.

"These are like halfway houses?" Paul asked.

"Halfway towns, actually." It was the first time Paul heard the phrase.

"How many are there?"

"You don't need to know. . . ."

"Oh, stop that."

"Six, counting Westport."

Paul tried to imagine any of his people submitting to a retraining program. "How do you get them to agree?"

"It's a condition of their pensions," Clew answered. "It's really not a bad deal, Paul. A contract agent normally gets no pension at all, let alone help getting set up in a new life."

"Westport. That's Westport in Connecticut?"

"Yes."

"And this is a humanitarian concept, you say?"

"That's the idea."

"A humanitarian concept," Paul couldn't help but smile, "that is run by Palmer Reid."

The under secretary grinned sheepishly and spread his hands. "What can I tell you? Reid volunteered. No one else wanted to touch it."

Paul shook his head as if to clear it, then tapped Roger Clew's desk, indicating a return to the subject at hand. "I'm not going to surrender Colonel Zivic. And nobody's going to trade him."

"It could get messy, Paul. You better have some leverage."

"Tell me more about Westport."

CHAPTER 12

Roger Clew could tell Paul little in terms of specifics. He estimated that about two thousand service employees and contract agents had passed through the system since the Carter years. Perhaps a tenth of those had vanished into new identities. A few, a handful, were judged to be beyond rehabilitation and were institutionalized. There might be a dozen to twenty agents in each of the six facilities at any one time, about the same number of staff and security people; the usual stay was about a year. At the core of each facility was a private hospital bought with federal funds as the administration and training center. These private hospitals did not attract much attention because most of the towns had a half-dozen more just like them—private clinics specializing in psychiatric care and treatment of drug and alcohol abuse by the affluent. The hospitals in turn formed dummy corporations that owned various businesses in the community—shops, a couple of restaurants, a few services—that were used for vocational training and for helping agents become accustomed to dealing with ordinary people and problems in less extravagant ways.

"Who does Reid answer to? Who checks up on him?"

The man shrugged. "He reports to the President's CIA Director."

"I'm serious."

"Nobody. Reid is Reid."

"What about the Inspector General's office or the General Accounting office?"

"They can't go near it. The facilities are classified Top Secret and Reid's funds are discretionary. He doesn't account for them but so what? You don't either."

"Molly?"

"Hi."

"Is your phone secure?"

"Are you kidding?"

"Listen," he told her, "both Reid and the State Department are making noises like they'd rather swap Anton back than give him asylum. I'll make the best deal I can but I'm going to have trouble with Reid. If it gets nasty he might put a freeze on my funds and get State to lift my passport to make sure I'm stuck here. You get up to Zürich first thing and clear out the account." He read her the number and the code. "They'll want to verify, so tomorrow at 9 A.M. your time, I'll be at the Marriott Hotel in Stamford, Connecticut. There's also about two hundred thousand dollars' worth of lire in my safe at the U.S.I.A." He gave her the combination. "Get that tonight but don't leave any signs of a break-in."

"I'll use Billy."

"Bring Carla and John Waldo with you to Zürich in case you need backup. Have them stay with you when you get back to Rome and set up a system of shifts so everybody else is outside covering your street."

"You really do expect trouble, don't you?"

"Better safe than sorry. And you're going to be sitting on almost three million dollars."

"What's in Stamford, Connecticut?"

"That's a whole other story. Have you ever heard of a system of halfway towns that are used to retrain and depressurize agents being retired from the field?"

"Uh-uh."

"Ask around. There are six. Westport is one of them. I'm going up to take a look and that's where I'll meet with Reid. There's a phony dry-out hospital there called the Greenfield Hill Memorial Clinic. If Reid should try to put me on ice, the way to bet is that's where I'll be. I'll call you every day at nine in the morning and six at night, your time. If I don't call, I've been snatched and all of you get over here, fast."

"Gotcha."

"One more thing. Reid comes from Connecticut. He's twice divorced but he has a brother and sister living, I think, in Greenwich, and some other family in Palm Beach. If he snatches me, you snatch at least two of them."

"Speaking of better-safe-than-sorry, maybe I'd better send Billy over now."

"Maybe you'd better. After he cleans out my safe."

"Paul?"

"That's it for now, Molly."

"You said you'd make the best deal you can for Anton. You wouldn't give him up, would you?"

"Are you kidding?"

"Herr Bannerman?" The voice belonged to Karl Vogele, Managing Director of the Bordier–Hentsch Bank on Zürich's Bahnhofstrasse. "How are you today, sir?"

"I'm fine, Herr Vogele." Paul spoke clearly and distinctly, aware that even though the banker knew his voice it was being fed into a voice printer for positive identification. "The transaction is authorized and Miss Farrell is acting as my agent."

"And how is the weather in Connecticut, sir?"

"It's not the South of France." Any other answer, any description of local conditions, would have alerted the banker that Paul was calling under duress.

"Excellent," Herr Vogele answered. "Fräulein Farrell is anxious to speak with you. Shall I connect you to the drawing room?"

"Thank you." Most private Swiss bankers had small, elegant parlor-type rooms for consultations. Conversations in such rooms were never recorded. Paul waited for Molly to pick up.

"All clear here," she said. "Billy got your lire, no sweat. It's converted to dollars and he's bringing you fifty thousand of it, okay?"

"Fine. When does he get here?"

"He's already at the airport. With the time difference he should show up at the Marriott around four this afternoon after a stop in New York to buy weapons."

"Who said we need weapons?"

"Wait'll you hear. You told me to ask around about the halfway towns? Janet Herzog is a graduate."

"Come on."

"Four years ago. It wasn't Westport, it was Wilmette. That's a suburb on Chicago's North Shore. Remember four years ago she decided to pack it in? She heard Reagan was cutting funding for all kinds of programs and she thought she might not get a chance at a pension. They also give you. . . ."

"I know what they give. What did she say?"

"She thought it might be worth all the bullshit they put you through first. You know about that, too?"

"Yes."

"Well, anyway, she said she always felt funny about it because a couple who had left long before she did said they'd write to her but they never did. And some of the others were real damaged goods who she couldn't believe would ever be let off a leash. She left Wilmette after about six months, which was faster than most because she already had a trade—Janet designs jewelry—and they set her up near New Orleans with all new paper. She was there about two months and one of Palmer Reid's people approached her about doing a job for them."

"An assassination?"

"You got it. Somewhere in South America. Janet said get lost. He came back again and got pushy and grabbed her arm, which you don't do with Janet, and she blinded him with her car keys and then backed her car over him. She figured recess was over so she headed back to Rome. You didn't ask what she'd been doing all that time?"

"I did," Paul made a face. "She said she was designing jewelry."

"Ask a silly question."

"You better come over. All of you. Call them. Don't go back to Rome."

"Then what?"

He told her.

Paul drove to Westport in his rented Ford. It was an easy fifteen minutes from Stamford on the Connecticut Turnpike, which ran parallel to the coast of Long Island

Sound. A clear and perfect May morning. He whistled as he drove.

From the Westport exit ramp, checking his map at the light, he made his way to the Greenfield Hill Memorial Clinic on Long Lots Road. It was a huge white colonial, once a private estate. No gate, low stone walls, but there were sixty yards of open lawn up to the house. No cover. He counted two groundskeepers near the stone wall, both idle, and two men dressed as male nurses further on. All probably armed guards.

He continued past the clinic property and began a random two-hour drive through the residential and commercial streets. Pretty. Very pretty. Lots of white and pink dogwoods. Azaleas in full bloom everywhere. Trees fat with tender spring leaves. Comfortable homes, the kind that were meant for living rather than for show. The town had an informal kind of beauty, as opposed to the self-conscious grooming of a Palm Beach or a Beverly Hills. The people he saw seemed relaxed as well. They had an easy this-is-who-I-am look about them. If you like me, great. If you don't, God bless you anyway.

A strange place to find Palmer Reid, he thought. Reid didn't belong here. It was not a place of moves and countermoves and lies.

As he drove, casually exploring, an idea that had begun in idle self-amusement began to sprout and expand like the hemlocks he saw. It had such a sweet irony to it that Paul knew he had to be careful not to be enchanted by it.

Palmer Reid didn't belong here at all.

His only stop was at a bookstore where he picked up an illustrated volume about Westport past and present and a better map than the one he'd found in Stamford. With these he took a roundabout route back to the turnpike entrance, past the golf course of a place called Longshore. His book said it was once a private country club but now anyone could use it. A pool, tennis courts, a handsome Norman Rockwellian clubhouse and restaurant right on the water. And a marina. And then a gorgeous public beach where a hundred healthy young bodies were working on the base for their summer tans or launching small sailboats. Nice. Very nice.

He knew that he was behaving unprofessionally. This was a reconnaissance, not a Sunday drive. There were people at the clinic who had seen his photograph, who might have seen him pass, who might be searching for him even now.

He didn't want them in Westport either.

He drove back to the Stamford Marriott.

In his room, his message light was blinking. He called the operator. The message was the private number, no name, of his friend at State. He dialed it.

"They've clipped your wings, Paul. Your passport's lifted."

"How is it tabbed?" Paul was asking what action was to be taken when he tried to use it.

"Security risk—yellow." That meant apprehend with caution and detain. Reid, Paul assumed, must have learned about that morning's withdrawal in Zürich. He would have ordered that Molly be picked up as well. Paul checked his watch. She should be in the air by now. There was a good chance Reid would know it if she used her own passport.

"Is Reid in Westport?"

"Last I heard."

"I'll see him soon."

"You watch yourself."

"I owe you." Paul broke the connection and dialed the number of Greenfield Hill Clinic.

Palmer Reid, demanding to know where Paul was, and told close by, insisted upon an immediate meeting. Paul said he'd be there at six. He arrived on time, was checked for weapons, and escorted to an office apparently belonging to the facility's administrator. The office had a window overlooking the broad sloping lawn. The building's shadow was lengthening over it.

When he entered on the floor below, Paul caught a glimpse of a woman in a blue jumpsuit being led away by a male nurse. She seemed wooden, docile; probably drugged. Now, below his window, Paul saw that a groundskeeper, a legitimate one, was planting marigolds in a flower bed. As he moved on to another section a stocky middle-aged man, also in a blue jumpsuit, knelt at each fresh planting and began tearing it up. He'd done that to half a row before two more male nurses stopped him and brought him inside.

Reid entered the room, offering no greeting. Paul read his expression. He was angry. But he also seemed pleased with himself.

"You kill a lot of them, don't you, Palmer?" Paul asked quietly.

"A lot of whom?" The question startled Reid.

Paul gestured where the man had been. "These agents. The blue jumpsuits. Here and in your other towns."

"What other towns? There are no other. . . ." He didn't bother to finish. "In any case, the answer is no. That is a despicable suggestion."

"I see."

"Your tone suggests doubt."

"Of course I doubt you, Palmer. You almost never tell the truth."

Reid studied him. "What is the truth, Paul?"

"I think some do get new lives and new paper. But I think they go right on working for you. Not the government. Just you."

Reid was silent for a long moment, then, "They say you were a good man, Paul, until you turned against your country."

Bannerman turned from the window. "How's that again?"

Reid used his fingers to tick off the particulars. "You have consistently refused to take an oath of service, though I presume you've at least recited the Pledge of Allegiance at some time in your youth. You have stolen a great sum of money from your country. You have allied yourself with a dangerous Soviet agent who, incidentally, *has* taken such an oath, except that his is eternally hostile to your country's interests. You have probably brought him into this country illegally and you will doubtless attempt to blackmail your country into granting him unconditional asylum. How am I not to regard such behavior as treasonous?"

Paul had to smile. "I suppose it's useless to point out

that Palmer Reid and my country are not one and the same."

Reid matched his smile. He folded his arms. "I have your Dr. Russo. He was taken two hours ago at Kennedy."

"I thought I saw a twinkle in your eye."

"He will be released, you will both be released, when you surrender Colonel Zivic."

"That's easy," Paul shrugged. "Bring me a written guarantee of asylum from the Secretary of State. He must also guarantee in writing that Zivic will not be asked to compromise his country's interests because Zivic, as it happens, is not a traitor to his country either."

"What, pray, would you call him?"

"Retired."

"Then so are you."

Paul spent the night under close guard. Supper, brought to his room, was a steam-table lasagna and a half-pint container of milk. He flushed them both down the toilet. In the morning, he was escorted back to the office where Reid was already breakfasting. Paul helped himself to Reid's coffee and half a croissant. Reid seemed to be controlling himself with effort.

Munching his croissant, Paul stepped to the window. The morning sun warmed him.

"In view of past service," he heard Reid clear his throat, "I'm considering meeting you halfway."

"I'm listening."

"Bring the Colonel here for one week of interrogation. You may witness it if you like."

"Why would he trust you? I certainly don't."

"I rise above the insult." Reid's jaw tightened. "The fact is, the Colonel's primary usefulness has come and gone. The Soviets believe he's been in our hands for almost a week now and they've surely made adjustments to offset anything he might have told us. Still, he might have some value to me. And of course you'll return the money."

Paul ignored the last. As for the rest of it, the words *some value to me* were the essential ones. Reid, at some level, had accepted the fact that he'd get little of real importance out of Zivic. Anton was a man who loved his country just as much as Reid pretended to love his. He would not betray his homeland and even now he was probably very anxious to get word to them that he had not. What Zivic might do, however, was throw Reid a few bones to facilitate a grant of asylum. He might give Reid the names of Americans and Western Europeans who had sold information for money because Anton detested such people. But they would be minor players. Compromised homosexuals, drug addicts, compulsive gamblers, misfits. Men and women who were no longer used because they were by definition unreliable. But at least they'd be something. And it would be Palmer Reid who got the information. Enough to perpetuate the fiction that it was he, Palmer Reid, who had turned in Colonel Anton Zivic.

A horn honked down on the road. Three short beeps. Paul could not see the car but he knew that its driver saw him. That had just been acknowledged. He pretended to stretch and yawn. Three more beeps. Paul nodded once.

"Stand away from there, please." Reid heard the sound as well.

"Relax, Palmer." His back still to Reid, Paul cupped a hand to his ear, then made a circular motion with his index finger.

"What do you think you're doing?" Reid pushed to his feet, more annoyed than alarmed.

"Waiting for a phone call." He crossed to Reid's desk where he spread marmalade on the other half of his croissant. The phone rang. "That will be for me. Molly Farrell's calling."

Reid snatched up the phone. His color rose when he heard her voice. "He is not available," he said into the mouthpiece.

"Ask her why you should let her speak to me," Paul suggested.

Reid hesitated, then asked. Now his color drained. He looked at Paul, his eyes blazing. "You son of a bitch."

"Trouble at home, Palmer?"

"If you harm one hair . . ."

"Your relatives are in good hands. Ask Molly whose hands."

He did, and the answer caused him to blink rapidly. His lips tried to form the name but he could only sputter.

"Billy McHugh." Paul helped him.

"You son of a bitch," Reid repeated.

A loud sneeze came from the hall outside. "And that would be John Waldo." With a gesture, Bannerman invited Reid to see for himself.

Still blinking, Reid stepped to the door and opened it. The guard he'd posted was on his knees, hands clasped behind his head, staring up at him helplessly. Reid didn't bother to look for Waldo. He closed the door.

"What do you want?" he asked, his voice a choked whisper.

"I want you to go away. Out of Westport."

"I have ten men here, all armed . . ."

Bannerman corrected him with a patient shake of his head. "Them too, Palmer. Have Gary Russo here in one hour. Then you can all leave quietly."

"You . . . you're crazy."

"Go to the Marriott Hotel in Stamford. Wait in the lobby for my call. I'll tell you where you can pick up your relatives, what my plans are for Westport, and why you should try very hard to accept them."

"You really are insane, aren't you? You're as crazy as . . ."

"Billy McHugh," Paul said pointedly, finishing Reid's sentence. "Goodbye, Palmer."

There were only six agents being processed through the Greenfield Hill Clinic and the Westport community, including the two Paul had seen in the blue jumpsuits. The other four were functioning normally outside. The number was a relief. According to Janet Herzog, who was now in Westport with the rest of them, as many as twenty might be in any of these halfway towns at a given time. Paul found the files on the six who were there. Russo was evaluating them now. With his own people, that brought the total number to eighteen. The two in the jumpsuits were doubtful. He might have to make other arrangements for them. On the other hand,

neither seemed much more damaged than Billy Mc-
Hugh.

The dummy corporation that Roger Clew had mentioned was called The Greenfield Foundation, logically
enough, and it owned an impressive array of local real
estate. Paul would need operating control of it.

Palmer Reid, his family members released un-
harmed, was in a cold fury when he called.

"I will grind you down," he said.

"You still have Wilmette and the others," Paul told
him. "Count your blessings." Part of that was bluff. Paul
could not yet name the remaining halfway towns but
Reid had no way of knowing that.

He listened, eyes closed, as Reid vented his rage with
sputtered threats and dire predictions. At last he interrupted, suggesting that he be allowed to summarize the
situation. Paul then patiently listed all the legal and
extralegal measures that were available to Reid, explained why each would fail, and how he, Bannerman,
would respond even to the failures. Most of his responses, he pointed out, would necessarily involve killing because—short of going public about these six
towns, which, he presumed, neither of them wanted—
killing was all that would be left to them.

"Incidentally," Paul told him, "I'll need to be named
executive director of The Greenfield Foundation, with
full power of attorney."

"You have the gall to suggest that?" Reid was sput-
tering again.

"You can certainly refuse. But then I'll take the three
million and set up my own corporation. On the other
hand, if you give me control over yours, you can still
pretend that I answer to you. You can say I'm running a
new experiment on your behalf."

"What sort of experiment?"

"We're all going to stay here. We took a vote."

"For how long?"

"We'll see. If they can function well here, and
they're content to stay, there doesn't seem to be much
point in uprooting them after a year or so. If the experiment works, you might think about trying it elsewhere."

Reid was silent for a long moment. Bannerman

could almost hear the workings of his mind. First would come the reflex rejection of Bannerman's given word. What was he really up to? How did he plan to use these people? Then, last, he would explore the possibility that Bannerman might actually be telling the truth.

"You intend to establish them permanently?" Reid asked. "In Westport?"

"That's what I said, Palmer."

"How many?"

"I'm afraid that's a secret."

"Might I ask . . . why they would agree to this?"

"They suspect that you'll try to retire them as well, Palmer. I think they feel safer if we all retire together."

"Paul. . . ." Another long silence. "On the remotest chance that you're serious about this, and that you have no ulterior motive, can you possibly believe that Westport can absorb that wolf pack of yours without getting eaten?"

Though Bannerman chose not to acknowledge it, Reid had a point. True, they'd been functioning as a group for years, most of them, and true, their habit of mutual support was well ingrained, but they weren't exactly the Junior League. It remained to be seen how soon the fun of having stolen Palmer Reid's town would wear thin.

"Listen," Paul told him. "You go ahead and think this over. I know you'll try to hit us one way or the other so go ahead and do that, too. I'll hit back and then we'll both know where we stand. After that, maybe we can stop the foolishness before too many people get hurt."

Reid, predictably, tested Paul's resolve although not until he was newly incensed by still another outrage. A report reached him that Anton Zivic was seen moving freely about Westport, representing himself as a dealer in art and antiques. Zivic's file showed that he had indeed been a collector and knew his subject, Italian Renaissance in particular. Reid gave orders to kidnap him. The team he sent for that purpose was found the next day in an automobile trunk in Norwalk, both men alive, but barely. Paul called Reid to tell him where the car was parked.

Some months later, two more men came to Westport

for the purpose of assassinating Paul. They came by
boat, docking at Westport's Saugatuck Yacht Club, secure in the belief that two extra pleasure boaters were
unlikely to be noticed in a town that was full of them.
They died aboard their boat, victims of a fuel explosion
that was ruled accidental. To drive the message home,
Palmer Reid's new Grand Banks trawler was simultaneously destroyed by fire while berthed at the Chesa-
peake Yacht Club in Annapolis, Maryland.

During the two and half years that followed, Reid
retreated into attempts at surveillance, though only
from a distance. He tried to put pressure on Paul and his
people through other government agencies. But they,
with the exception of Anton Zivic and Harry Bauer,
were American citizens. They were paying their taxes,
apparently breaking no laws, were wanted for no crime
and made no attempt to disguise their identities. As for
Zivic and Bauer, the State Department suggested, infu-
riatingly, that Reid mind his own business.

During those two and a half years, though Paul kept
his people well prepared for further attacks, none came.
None of Reid's men had even dared step within
Westport's borders. Not until the arrival of Doug Poole.

John Waldo met Anton Zivic at the door of Gary
Russo's home and office. Waldo gestured over his shoulder toward a closed examining room where, Zivic presumed, the unfortunate young man would be strapped
to a table.

"Have you begun questioning him?" Zivic asked.

"Ask me," Waldo answered, "I think we're finished.
His name is Douglas Poole, he works for Robert Loftus.
Loftus is Reid's top guy in the field."

Zivic heard a female voice coming from the examining room. "Why is he here? And who is in there with
him?"

"Molly and Billy were here already. Molly brought
him for his sinuses. As for the kid, all he knows is Loftus
told him to keep an eye on Paul except he shouldn't
leave his car. Before that they were in New York tailing
Susan Lesko's father and a guy named Donovan but the
kid doesn't know why. He doesn't even know there's a
daughter to go with the father."

"He's been here not ten minutes. How did you get all that so quickly?"

"We couldn't shut him up. The kid's a fan."

"A fan." Zivic's expression went blank.

"Like in *gee whiz*. Like in *golly*. The second he recognizes Molly and Billy it was like he keeps a scrapbook. It was disgusting. By him, it was an honor I cold-cocked him."

The door opened. Molly stepped out, grinning broadly.

"What is happening now?" Zivic asked.

"He's shaking Billy's hand," she beamed. "I bet he'd just die to meet Anton Zivic."

Anton brushed that lunacy aside. "Could this young man really be so . . . inept?"

"He's probably competent enough," she shook her head. "He's young and he's star struck. I think it's kind of. . . ."

"Flattering," he said sternly.

"Oh, loosen up, Anton. It's been three years since anyone looked at us like that. He's in awe. I got the same way when I ran into Paul Newman buying vegetables at the Korean's."

Zivic closed his eyes as if in prayer that sanity would soon return. "What do you suggest we do with him?"

"You're the boss."

"An opinion, please."

Her smile faded. "Don't tell Paul. Let him go and enjoy."

"And the young man? This Poole?"

"Let him go, too, before they miss him. Take him back to his car and tell him he's welcome to watch us all he pleases as long as he's discreet about it. Chances are he'd be too embarrassed to report that he was taken so easily and interrogated."

"John?" Anton invited his opinion.

"She makes sense. Keep him or hurt him and you force Reid's hand. Let him watch us and that way we watch him, too, and he sees what we want."

"What do you make of the girl's father being followed?"

Molly answered. "If they know about Susan they know who her father is. If I were Reid, I'd wonder how and if Paul is connected to a man like Raymond Lesko. It's a blind alley. Let him follow it."

"This seems careless."

"To me it seems considerate. Would you want Paul to cancel his vacation over this? He will, you know."

Slowly, frowning, Zivic nodded agreement.

"We must have black-and-white glossies made up." He turned to the door. "Perhaps a team photograph for all future Doug Pooles."

"T-shirts would be good, too," John Waldo growled.

CHAPTER 13

That Thursday evening. Late.

Robert Loftus had spent the afternoon following Raymond Lesko from one hotel to another before it dawned on him that they were all Beckwith properties. He returned to the NSA communications center, housed in the headquarters building of one of the major broadcast networks, where he made some discreet inquiries of the New York City Police Department and listened to that day and that evening's tapes of both Raymond and Susan Lesko's phone calls. Doug Poole checked in at eight, behaving a bit strangely but having nothing to report except that he'd spotted Anton Zivic. Loftus attributed that to having spent an afternoon in Westport and getting out intact. He was more concerned about Frank Burdick, who had not reported in at all.

Wearily, he punched out the number of Palmer Reid's Maryland home. Reid answered on the second ring. He identified himself. Reid said "Report." Loftus could hear the clink of ice cubes against glass. Maybe after this call he could relax with a drink of his own.

"Sir," he read from his notes, "first of all, Lesko wasn't meeting anyone at the Beckwith Regency. He's a security consultant for the Beckwith chain and has been for a year. He spent the afternoon visiting other Beckwith hotels and right now he's back in his room. Room service brought him his dinner and a typewriter. He's probably doing reports."

"Perhaps, but go on."

Loftus resisted an urge to flash a middle finger at the mouthpiece. "Secondly, he did not at any time meet with Bannerman. I continue to believe they don't know each other. Bannerman was at his Westport office when Poole got there. Poole says there's no particular activity in Westport either, although he did see Anton Zivic leaving Bannerman's office. Apparently a routine visit."

"If you say so, Robert."

The finger twitched again. "Finally, Lesko called his daughter an hour ago. That's how I know what he's doing in his room. He told her. Lesko then asked the daughter for the particulars of her travel plans. 'In case someone gets sick' was the reason he gave. They are, it turns out, going to Switzerland but not to Zürich. They're going first to London where they'll board that restored Orient Express train. The train passes through Zürich, but they don't get off. Their final destination is Klosters. Bannerman has rented a chalet there. The daughter says that's where they'll be for the whole three weeks. I have the address and phone number."

"I see." Reid allowed a silence to settle. "So you're satisfied, I take it, that it's all an innocent romantic adventure."

"Unless you know something I don't, sir."

"At the moment, it's more a question of what Mr. Donovan knows. I'm afraid he's been on the phone again."

"Asking about Bannerman?"

"And getting answers. He knows, Robert."

"He knows what part?"

"Who Bannerman is. Or was. He has a call in now to Roger Clew who, fortunately, is in Mexico at the moment."

"Are you sure he knows that, sir?"

"Why would you doubt it?"

"Because I think he would have gone straight to Lesko with that information and Lesko would have stopped that ski trip very damned fast. But I'm sure Lesko didn't know as of an hour ago."

"Good point, Robert. Why would he not have called Lesko?"

"Probably because he wants confirmation first. More

details. But whether he talks to Roger Clew or not, he won't wait past Bannerman's flight tomorrow."

"I've seen to that, Robert."

"Sir?"

"I've had him taken."

Loftus closed his eyes and bit hard into his lower lip. "Burdick?" he asked.

"Among others."

Loftus was speechless. "Sir," he managed, "may I respectfully remind you that Donovan is a former U.S. Attorney? And that Burdick is a fucking goon?"

Reid took in a breath at Loftus's choice of adjectives, but did not comment. "Thoughtful casting was not a requirement, Robert. I merely wanted the man removed from circulation until I can have a friendly chat with him."

"When will that be?"

"Tomorrow morning. Do you know Ambassador Pollard's residence in Scarsdale?"

"Yes."

"You may reach me there if you learn anything else. Your presence, however, will not be required."

"Mr. Reid, I hope you know what you're. . . ."

"Good night, Robert."

Friday morning, after breakfast. Raymond Lesko's mood had not improved much at all.

He glanced at his watch. Susan's flight was in about ten hours. This time tomorrow she'd be on a mountain somewhere. He hated the thought of her being that far away. Right now. Too many things didn't feel right.

One of which was that Buzz Donovan didn't show up at Gallagher's last night, and he didn't answer his phone at home, and he didn't answer it this morning, either. Garage man says his car's still there but no Donovan.

Another aggravation was finding out this morning that goddamned David Katz doesn't just hang around his Queens bedroom. Four this morning, he shows up at the Beckwith Regency.

Damned dreams. Seemed like all night long. With the whole cast of characters. Loftus was in one. Just sneaking around again. Lesko wished he'd squeezed him harder when he had the chance so he wouldn't have to stew about him when he could be sleeping. And Bannerman was there, this time younger and thinner but with slicked-down hair and a pencil mustache. Looked like what they used to call a lounge lizard.

Lesko knew Bannerman didn't look like that any more than he looked like he did in yesterday's dream. Susan wouldn't hang around with a creep like that, anyway. But seeing him that way in a dream didn't help Lesko like him any better.

Another new guy in the dream was Palmer Reid. Lesko's head made up a face for him as well. Guy about Donovan's age, dresses like a Ken doll, gets a haircut every week. He's not doing anything. Just watching. Loftus keeps whispering in his ear. Donovan keeps looking over at him like he can't stand the son of a bitch.

The dumbest part, Lesko winced at the memory, was that not only was Elena there—it must have been Gallagher's again—but Donna, his ex-wife, was there, and Donna's having a high old time telling Elena all about life with Raymond Lesko. He snores, he farts in bed, he never hangs up his clothes—which is not true, by the way—he forgets to flush, and when he eats kielbasa his breath could peel wallpaper. What the hell's that all about? Anyway, it's just like Donna to harp on shit like that when serious things are happening all around her.

Katz wasn't in that dream. He showed up later. Four in the morning. Still with the bagels or Danish, but here he's in the suite they let Lesko use, and he's walking around saying this is nice, this is good, it looks like you finally scored.

"Yeah, well, it's not a score, it's a job. And this isn't mine so don't go touching anything."

Katz's hands went to his hips. *"You can't say hello before you start with the nasty mouth?"*

"You come in here expecting etiquette? Who invited you? Anyway, you're not even here. You're dead."

"You don't have to keep saying that, either."

"Christ." Lesko bunched the pillow against his face.

"You're worried about Susan, aren't you?"

"No."

"You want me to keep an eye on her? Maybe I could do that."

"Keep an eye where? She's going to Switzerland."

"Maybe I could find them," Katz shrugged. *"I don't know."*

"She's with a guy. You think I want you standing around at night watching whatever she does with him?"

"It's just a thought. I thought maybe it could help square us."

"You want to make yourself useful? Go find Donovan for me. After that, you want to haunt somebody, go haunt my ex-wife. Flush the toilet all night while she's trying to sleep."

The dreams stayed with Lesko throughout breakfast and through two more attempts to reach Buzz Donovan. No answer.

Funny how he was getting used to Katz. The conversations they were having weren't all that different from the way they talked to each other when Katz was alive. He could have done without dreaming of Elena, though. Twice in a row now. Bad enough she pops into his head nearly every damned day. And he could also do without his head inventing new Paul Bannermans every night. Maybe he should sneak out to the airport and watch them check in. At least he'd know what the real Paul looked like.

Where the hell is Donovan?

A couple of meetings this morning and then a free afternoon. You know what he might do? Maybe he'd go back to Queens and borrow Mr. Makowski's car and take a ride up to Westport. No particular reason. Just to look around. See if he notices many people leaping out of windows or running in front of trucks.

Irwin Pollard, having made a substantial fortune as an investment banker, contributed generously to the first-term election campaign of President Ronald Reagan. He let it be known that he would appreciate being named ambassador to the Court of St. James or any other comparable post that did not involve dealing with Orientals or Arabs. He was offered Bolivia, but declined, giving the excuse that he did not speak Portuguese.

It was Palmer Reid who persuaded him to change his mind by pointing out how that position could make him considerably richer and that the languages of Bolivia were, in any case, Spanish and Quechua. Further, the currency of Bolivia was not the peso but the coca leaf. Many a great and worthwhile cause could be funded with that money, particularly if a man of vision, a man who was not a lackey of the State Department or the Congress, happened to take that post.

Pollard, who was now on station in La Paz, was a man who knew the value of a dollar. As a further incentive to take the job, Reid offered to pay off the mortgage on Pollard's Scarsdale home and, until Pollard was recalled, pay him a substantial rent in return for the right to sequester people there on occasion. Reid also threw in a state-of-the-art security system, behind which Buzz Donovan, unpressed and unshaven, had just spent a very angry and sleepless night.

"I know you're upset." Palmer Reid entered the Pollard living room, hands raised, palms forward, where Buzz Donovan sat on a sofa watched over by Frank Burdick and an ape of a man named Gorby. "You have every right. It's perfectly understandable."

"Don't dare patronize me, you son of a bitch." Donovan glared at him.

Reid made a show of stopping in his tracks, an expression of confusion on his face. He blinked at Burdick and Gorby, then back at Donovan. "My God," he hushed, "No one's explained to you. Is it possible no one had told you why you're here?"

"Oh, stop it, Palmer." Donovan said disgustedly.

Reid pretended not to notice the cynicism. He looked at Burdick. "Did I or did I not give specific instructions that Mr. Donovan was to be told why he was brought to the safety of this house?"

"We may have erred on the side of caution, sir." Burdick knew his lines.

"No wonder the man is outraged," he snapped. "Get out of my sight."

"Sir, if I could just apologize. . . ."

"Get out. Now."

Burdick and Gorby left the room. Reid sighed deeply and shook his head. Now wringing his hands, he took a seat facing Donovan. "Before I begin," he said, "I must remind you that you are still bound by oath to uphold and defend. . . ."

"Spare me, Palmer. Get on with it."

Reid paused again as if choosing his words. Then he made a damn-the-torpedoes gesture signifying, he hoped, that he had decided to withhold nothing. "A project is now under way," he said quietly, "whose objective is nothing less than the destruction of all South American drug traffic within two years. What is particularly outrageous about that drug traffic is that a number of former government agents seem to be very much involved in it. A trap is being laid for them. You, I fear, are in danger of springing it prematurely."

Donovan waited.

"I tell you now, regretfully, that your friend Raymond Lesko appears to be involved with these people, either directly or as an unwitting dupe."

"Spell it out, Palmer."

"You are, of course, aware that shortly after the death of his partner, Raymond Lesko executed three men in a Brooklyn barbershop?"

"That has not been proven or even charged."

"It may shock you to learn that one of these three men was an American undercover agent. Quite an excellent young man, by the way. Lesko shot him down without a word."

"How could you know that?"

"There was a witness. Her name is Elena."

Reid watched for a light of recognition in Donovan's eyes. Donovan had made up his mind to give him nothing.

"I have it all second-hand, of course," Reid told him, "but the essence is that she survived the shooting because she and Lesko had been in league all along. She's been hiding since the event. I think Lesko knows where."

"That doesn't make him sound like an unwitting dupe to me."

"It's conceivable, I suppose," Reid told him, "that their relationship might be more personal than criminal. But I have reason to believe that a third party is using Lesko to reach Elena. I'm afraid Lesko's daughter is involved in this as well."

"Who is the third party?"

"I'll need your word first."

"To do what?"

"I'll tell you what I know. You'll tell me what you know. You will agree, at minimum, not to tip my hand to Lesko or anyone else. These people are quite desperate, you see, and your phone calls were bringing you closer to making certain connections. It's why I had you taken out of harm's way."

"You have my word that I'll do what is proper," Donovan told him. "The third party, I take it, is Paul Bannerman."

"It is."

"Tell me about him."

"The man is a cancer. An open sore."

"Aside from that."

"Paul Bannerman is the ringleader of a group of renegade former agents. All are dangerous. Most homicidal. All have been dismissed from service for incompetence, disloyalty, and an array of criminal offenses that would strain your credulity."

"Such as?"

"Theft, extortion, atrocious assault. Three of them once kidnapped a little girl and sexually abused her for many hours. The poor child had to be institutionalized."

"I see."

"They all live in Westport, with Bannerman, masquerading as decent citizens. They are also part of a drug conspiracy that is destroying the very fabric of our nation." Reid reached into his pocket and took out a packet of photographs. He held them aloft, his hand trembling. "I want you to see what they're capable of," he said. "I want you to know how hard it's been for me to stay my hand against them until I'm sure I can get them all." Reid spread the photographs across the coffee table.

The first few showed an open car trunk. Two men, bound and beaten, were crammed inside. Other photographs showed that they had survived the ordeal. Still others showed close-ups of their facial injuries. "That was the first surveillance team we sent in," Reid told him, "Now see the second."

The next series made Donovan recoil. Two charred corpses, their arms reaching out. "These men had wives and children," Reid said.

Two more photographs. Each showed the burnt hull of a boat. Donovan looked more closely. They were two different boats. "What happened here?" he asked.

"The second team went in by boat. A bomb was planted aboard. The explosion was made to look like a fuel-leak accident."

"Then what boat is this?" Donovan pointed to the other.

"It's my own." Reid's color rose. "They burned it the same day. A personal insult to me." He picked up the photo.

Donovan's eyes drifted back over the others.

"She was beautiful," Reid said sullenly.

"What was?"

"A Grand Banks trawler. Custom-designed. All-teak decks. Named for my dead mother. I never even got a chance to have her photographed under power."

"The man must be a monster," Donovan said dryly.

"Well?"

"I'm thinking."

The photographs had shocked him. The story of the gang rape and sexual torture of a child had its effect. But Donovan didn't necessarily believe a word of it. Over the years he'd heard too many such embellishments from Palmer Reid. He had a sense that this little girl could just as easily have been a nun or a cripple or somebody else's sainted mother if Reid had thought of either first. The beaten men could have been anyone. The burned men in their boat as well. They may or may not have had wives and children. And he had trouble believing they'd enter Westport by boat, as opposed to a highway ramp or country road, for the relatively innocent purpose of surveillance.

Be that as it may. What ruined the desired effect of all this was Palmer Reid, who had the sensitivity of a mackerel, focusing his only creditable emotion upon his own stupid boat.

"The part about Ray Lesko," Donovan said, "and his

daughter, and their being involved in a drug conspiracy with Elena and this Bannerman. . . ."

"I know. It's hard to believe."

"I think it's the most ridiculous story I've ever heard in my life."

Reid flushed but recovered quickly. He gestured to the photographs as if they proved everything. Donovan dismissed them with a wave.

"I may not know Bannerman," he said, "but I do know the Lesko family and none would ever be involved in such a thing. What I know *about* Bannerman is that he withdrew from government service three years ago but that his reputation for integrity prior to that time seems to have been the highest."

"He was never in government service," Reid said darkly. "He was a contract agent, bound by no code of loyalty or decency, and he. . . ."

"I know what a contract agent is," Donovan glared back at him. "And I know what you are."

"Meaning?"

"That whatever Bannerman is now and whatever he's done, I would sooner trust him—to say nothing of Susan Lesko's judgment of him—than a man who has hardly uttered a truthful sentence in his entire adult life."

Palmer Reid's eyes went dead. After a long moment he slowly shook his head, then placed his hands on his knees and pushed to his feet. Bending over the coffee table, he gathered the photographs, taking care to place them in order, and returned them to his pocket.

"Mr. Gorby." he called to the door.

The big man opened it. "Yes, sir?"

"You have an errand not far from Mr. Donovan's residence, is that right?"

"Yes, sir." Buzz Donovan heard a car starting up in the driveway. He could see the other man, Burdick, apparently off on an errand of his own.

"Take him home, please."

Donovan stood. "Just run me down to the Scarsdale station. I'd prefer the train." While I decide what charges to bring, you son of a bitch.

"I wouldn't hear of it," said Palmer Reid.

* * *

Lesko's last appointment of the morning extended into lunch. He excused himself, went to a phone, and gave Buzz Donovan's number another try. Still no answer.

He was getting worried. Donovan was no kid. Could have had a heart attack, a stroke, maybe he fell down and broke a hip. Lesko found the number of Donovan's building superintendant, identified himself, and asked the super to go open Donovan's apartment and take a look. He'd wait at this number.

The dream he had that morning came back to him. He'd told Katz to go look for Donovan. That's all he needed. Donovan dead somewhere and Katz turning up tomorrow morning with his ghost. Katz with the bagels and Donovan with the coffee. Which would be okay, he could at least get some answers, as long as Donovan didn't make a habit of it. He could ask Donovan. . . .

Hold it.

Steady, Lesko.

Cut that crap right now. Last time you even began to believe in ghosts was when the nuns at Our Lady of Sorrows said all the kids had these guardian angels who hung around all the time watching out for them. You believed that until enough bad things happened to you and your friends to conclude that either an awful lot of guardian angels were asleep at the switch or the nuns were jerking your chain. Even so, it was six months before you could even take a shit in peace.

The phone rang. The super. No sign of Mr. Donovan. No sign he was sick or anything. Lesko thanked him and asked if he'd go back up and leave a note to get in touch as soon as he got in.

Next Lesko dialed a Queens number and asked Mr. Makowski, his neighbor, whether he could use his car for a few hours if he came home now. Mr. Makowski said sorry, not until Saturday. Car's in the shop getting a new radiator. Lesko said thanks anyway.

He'd just about given up on the idea of going to Westport, which didn't really have much point anyway, but on the other hand the prospect of going home to Queens seemed especially lonely. What with Susan going away. Lesko checked out of the Regency and walked with his suitcase to Grand Central. Next train, the board said, was in four minutes. Lesko let out a sigh. If he'd walked slower he would have missed it. So? Make up your mind. Subway to Queens or train to Westport? What the hell, he decided.

The train was more full than he expected. People quitting early for the weekend. Lots of blue suits and briefcases; quite a few womem, some of them half in the bag, having started their weekend with a long, wet lunch. He found a seat and settled back. Straight ahead of him on a bulkhead was a poster for Hennessey's cognac. He'd seen the ad before in magazines. A young guy and a girl in a ski lodge sipping Hennessey's. A fire going, snow outside, both of them covered with nothing but quilts to show they'd just been screwing.

Lesko got up and moved.

The train ride to Westport took just over an hour. He followed the flow of detraining passengers toward a tunnel going under the tracks to the southbound side. Lesko had no plan. He still didn't know why he'd come. But he was here.

Half the people from the train seemed to be headed for either of two bars that stood facing the station. One called Dameon's, the other called Mario's. On the near corner there was a little variety store and newsstand. Lesko went there. He bought a street map and asked where he might rent a car. The counterman said he'd passed a little Avis office on the other side. Lesko thanked him, then went to a phone where he looked up the addresses of Paul Bannerman's home, Bannerman's travel agency, and the Westport Public Library.

As Bannerman himself had done three years earlier, Lesko spent the better part of an hour driving around Westport and gathering impressions. It was more spread out than he'd imagined. He saw no one in pink pants, but they were for summer. Most people seemed to wear ski jackets. Still plenty of ducks on mailboxes, though. And everyone seemed to be driving a BMW or a Volvo. Most of those either had college decals on the rear window or those dumb yellow signs that used to say *Baby On Board* but which now said *Lawyer On Board* or *Ex-Wife In Trunk* so everyone would know they had a sense of humor. Not a bad town otherwise. Not for him, but not bad.

Bannerman's office looked legitimate enough. Lesko crept by it in his car. Three women sitting at computer consoles and another one handing a stack of brochures to a BMW lady. So, four employees at least. Must be making money.

Bannerman's residence turned out to be a condo complex down by the water. There was a manned security booth at the entrance. Lesko got past the guard with no trouble, saying he lived in town and was thinking about going condo now that the kids were gone, and he just wanted to look over the grounds. The guard handed him a card with the realtor's name. Lesko also saw the guard write down his plate number as he pulled away. That impressed him. Most such guards were useless and were primarily for show. He found Bannerman's unit. Number eight. On a corner.

"You see anything . . . ?" He caught himself. He'd almost asked David Katz, on the empty seat to his right, whether Katz noticed anything funny about Bannerman's unit. Habit. Ten years of driving around together, spotting things on the street, thinking out loud.

Katz would have noticed. Of all the units here, there were only two where you had to climb a short flight of stairs to get to the front door or see into the first-floor windows. Of the two, only one had heavy curtains fully drawn. Number eight.

It didn't have to mean anything. Just a thing a cop would notice. That, and the fact that this complex could only be reached by a single road or by water, and the Bannerman's unit had a clear view of both.

The second floor had a deck. Probably off his bedroom. Chances are Susan stayed up there a few times. In his mind he could see her on the deck. Wearing a bathrobe. He blinked the image away.

"Get off her back, Ray. Susan's a good kid." Katz's voice. How many times had Lesko heard him say that? Ever since she started dating boys. Yeah, well, when your Joni gets a little older, we'll see how you act. Any kid licks her ice-cream cone, you'll ask him for a fucking AIDS test. Lesko wheeled the car around and headed back into the town.

His next stop, after a pass of the main shopping street
—they actually called it Main Street—was the Westport
Public Library. Several heads looked up as he entered.
Several heads usually did. He started toward the information desk but was intercepted by a small woman,
attractive, slender, hair in one of those pixie cuts, who
asked if she could help him. Lesko asked if he could see
some back issues of the Westport paper. How far back,
she asked? Just recent. Looking for anything in particular? A story about a friend of mine. She led him to a shelf
where there were two weeks' worth in a pile, then to a
table where three other people, one older woman and
two students, were also researching periodicals.

Lesko wasn't looking for anything special. Just
browsing. Susan's suicide and accidental-death numbers were in the back of his head but he was damned if
he was going to start poring through microfilmed
records as Susan had no doubt done in this very library.
Waste of time. But newspapers can help give you the
feel of a town. He'd just look through a few, then maybe
grab a sandwich and a beer and head back to New York.

The *Westport News* was a biweekly. Published
Wednesday and Fridays. Mostly ads and local news. No
national news at all. He found an ad for Paul Bannerman's company. Luxury Travel Limited. Seemed to
specialize in big-ticket vacations. Which meant he met
a lot of rich people. Which, Lesko guessed, would make
him a pretty good asset. Maybe that's all there is to it.
Maybe Susan could do worse.

The next issue down was from Wednesday, the day
Susan told him about Bannerman. Front-page news was
an argument about whether to tear down some old iron
bridge or have it declared a landmark. Also a debate
over a new truck-weighing station on Westport's stretch
of the Interstate. *The New York Times* it wasn't. He
leafed through it anyway.

Suicide.

The word caught his eye. Two suicides. A psychiatrist named Gelman and a woman named Sweetzer. She
was his patient. Despondent over his death. The *Post*
would have had fun with this one, he thought. Lots of
possibilities. The most likely of which was that he was
porking her.

"Did you find what you were looking for?" The library lady.

"Yeah. Thanks."

"Anything you need, just ask."

"Do you have a pay phone here?"

She pointed. "Right over past the desk."

While Lesko made his fifth attempt of the day to reach Buzz Donovan, Carla Benedict made her second call of the last fifteen minutes to Anton Zivic.

"Describe his manner. His demeanor," Zivic said.

"I don't get you."

"How did he react to the Gelman story? Did he rush to the phone as if he'd made a discovery?"

Carla thought about that. "Actually, no. He's not even taking notes. On the whole I'd describe his manner as bored."

"Then perhaps seeing the newspaper item and making the phone call are not related?"

"Perhaps."

"For the moment," Zivic said after a pause, "we will assume that his visit is nothing more than a policeman's curiosity, to say nothing of a father's curiosity." Zivic knew that Lesko's daughter had just told him about Paul. Lesko's interest in the Gelman items suggested that she'd also told him why Westport had initially caught her notice. Zivic would have been surprised if an experienced investigator took her speculations seriously. From Lesko's manner, he did not. In any case, if the phone call was to his daughter they would soon know what was said. "However," he added, "I will send John Waldo to keep an eye on him."

"I've already called Gary. He's probably outside by now."

"Surveillance is hardly the doctor's specialty." Zivic was annoyed. "Please go to the parking lot and tell him to follow only if John Waldo does not arrive in time. Tell him that if Lesko makes more than two turns in any direction other than toward the turnpike entrance, he is to break off immediately."

Lesko returned to the table only long enough to pack up the newspaper portfolio and return it to its shelf. He slipped into his coat. On his way to the door he passed the library lady coming the opposite way, noticing idly that she'd gone outside without one.

His dashboard clock said 4:30. Too late for a sandwich. He'd wait and have dinner in the city, with Buzz Donovan, if he ever showed up. Checking his map, Lesko chose the most direct route to the station.

A white Subaru wagon left behind him, Lesko noticed. And it was staying with him down Imperial Avenue and right on Bridge Street. It should not have bothered him because he could see from the road signs that his route toward the station was also the most direct route to the Interstate.

"What do you think, David?" he asked in his mind. Without intending to. Habit.

He imagined Katz stretching his arms and clasping them behind his head, because that's what Katz did on patrol when he wanted to look off guard and unthreatening. *"No one left the library when you did,"* he imagined Katz answering. *"No one was walking through the parking lot. What's left is this guy had to be waiting in his car."*

"We'll see." He continued on, over the iron bridge they wanted to tear down, then past the turn-off toward the Interstate, then along a road that curled under the railroad tracks and led to the Avis office on the northbound side. The Subaru seemed to hesitate at the turn-off. Then it followed. As Lesko pulled into the section reserved for rental cars, he heard its engine slow and then accelerate. He glanced over. A man his age was driving. Gray hair, tanned, dark topcoat.

A southbound train pulled in as he was paying for the car. Too late. The next train would be another hour. Lesko remembered the two commuter bars on the other side.

"Gary says he's gone into Mario's." Carla Benedict said into the phone to Anton Zivic. "I don't like this."

"You say his car was a rental?" Zivic asked. "When is the next train into the city?"

"Hold on." She checked the schedule printed in the Westport phone book. "Not until 5:45," she told him.

"Nearly an hour. His choices, therefore, were to sit

in an empty waiting room or to wait where almost anyone else would wait."

"You're betting an awful lot on coincidence lately,
Anton."

"I am *allowing* for coincidence." Zivic asked
whether Dr. Russo had followed him all the way to the
rental car drop-off. He winced when she said yes. Better
send him home, he said. Too late, she told him. He'd
called her from Mario's.

"Is Molly there?" he asked.

"Yes. She recognized him the second he walked in."

"Is Billy there?"

"Lesko's talking to him."

It wasn't quite Happy Hour yet, but it was Friday
and the bar had a fair-sized crowd. He'd passed up
Dameon's next door because its bar was smaller and the
people standing at it were all blue suits. Mario's had a
better mix. More women, more working stiffs from the
town.

Lesko noticed the gray-haired man with the dark
topcoat who entered after he did and went to the
phone.

"Hey, David."

"I seen him."

"Tell me something else."

"What?"

*"How come everyone I run into in Westport either
writes down my license or runs to a phone?"*

"The library lady?"

"And that security guard. Yeah."

"Because you're mean and ugly. What else is new?"

"I ask you a question and you give me your mouth."
Lesko almost blinked him away. But he was enjoying
this. Sort of. *"Four people at that table in the library and
I'm the only one she comes over to check on. Next thing,
she goes outside to the parking lot, no coat on. Next
thing, I maybe got a tail who is, by the way, my second
tail in three days who is hopeless at it."*

*"Maybe we're cops too long. Maybe he's also catch-
ing the 5:45."*

"Maybe."

*   *   *

At the far end of the bar, Molly Farrell had a drink ready for Gary Russo when he returned from the telephone. She beckoned him over. Take a sip, she told him through her teeth, then take your drink into the far dining room, order something, and stay there.

She was tempted to call Carla to make sure Carla didn't show up as well. But Molly knew she wouldn't. Carla was a pro and Molly knew from Russo that Lesko had seen her once already. Nor did Molly want to leave the bar just yet. Susan's father had taken the last seat near the door. He'd thrown his coat over the seat next to it as if he was holding it for someone. And Billy, who she was sure had never seen him, had wandered down to get acquainted. Molly picked up a bar towel and began edging close enough to hear the conversation.

So far this was Lesko's kind of saloon. No college kids on either side of the bar. No crocks of whipped cheddar cheese or bowls of the glazed shit that looks like Chinese health food. Just baskets of popcorn. Not salted so you'll drink more, but unsalted and absorbent so you won't get smashed so quick.

No real décor either except for mementos that were slapped up over the years. A lot of jock pictures on the walls like at Gallagher's. Golfers mostly, but that was okay. At least they weren't pictures of some fucking actor who carries glossies with him every time he goes out for a drink. Behind the bar, on a high shelf, there was a row of about twenty carved wooden statues. Caricatures. He recognized John Wayne, W.C. Fields, The Beatles, two or three presidents, all democrats, no Nixon. His kind of bar.

"New in town?" Billy set down Lesko's beer. "I don't think I've seen you around."

"Just visiting. I got some friends here."

"How 'bout I buy you a shooter with that beer by way of welcome?"

"Absolutely." His kind of bartender, too. Lesko indicated a bottle of Seagram's rye.

The bartender was a big guy, almost as wide as Lesko and a little older. A white short-sleeved shirt, powerful arms, a belly that was rounded but it looked hard. Except that the arms had no tattoos, Lesko would have guessed he was a retired Navy chief. Definitely not a

retired cop. There's a look cops have that they never
lose. His was close to that but different. Maybe Army.
Yeah. He even had that trace of southern accent almost
everybody picks up in the Army but not the Marines,
because the Marines know that and try to sound different.

Billy brought the shot glass. Lesko picked it up, sa-
luted with it, and sipped. "You don't come from around
here," Lesko observed. "An Army lifer, right? Probably
since Korea."

"I got my time in," Billy nodded. "How about yourself?"

"Three years Marines. Then the cops. I'm retired
now."

The woman behind the bar had moved closer. Another patron asked her for three beers. He had to repeat
it. She seemed distracted. As she went back to pour
them, she called "Uncle Billy," to Lesko's bartender,
then shook her head as if she'd changed her mind.
Lesko studied her, trying not to stare.

"You have a very lovely niece. Good face," Lesko
said.

Billy nodded agreement. "But Molly's not my niece.
She's one of the owners. It's just that everyone around
here calls me Uncle Billy."

Lesko looked at her again. She looked back, smiled
shyly, then busied herself polishing glasses. A good face.
Not beautiful or anything. What was good about her
face was that it was open, and kind, and even wise. Big
sad eyes, but not a sad woman. And the look. There was
something about her look, too.

"Nice town here, too." He turned back to Billy. "My
first visit."

"Don't make it your last," Billy answered eagerly.
"Best place I ever lived. But you want to come back
here in April or May because the whole town is like a
garden then."

"How about the people?"

"Good. Good people." His gesture took in all the
patrons and employees. "The thing about Westport is
you're never on your own here. We take care of each
other."

The remark seemed innocent enough to Lesko. The

Rotary Club would have loved it. But Molly with the sad eyes almost dropped her glass. Her smile came right back but what came before it was that look. The same as Uncle Billy's. Maybe close to a cop-look after all. Close but not quite. He would try to remember where he'd seen it before.

On the 5:45 headed back to New York, Lesko chose a seat with an empty one on his right. He did this hesitantly, self-consciously. Having imaginary conversations with Katz was one thing as long as they just popped into his head. Everybody has imaginary conversations. But having them on purpose was something else. If Lesko heard of anyone else doing that, he would decide the guy's elevator wasn't stopping at all the floors.

If Katz was alive though, and sitting there, Lesko would have asked him, *"What did you think about all that?"*

Katz would have said, *"What?"*

He would have said, *"I don't know. The library lady. The possible tail. Those two behind the bar."*

"Ask me," Katz would have answered, *"They made you. They knew who you were."*

Which of course would be crazy. In New York, Lesko was used to being recognized. But hardly ever outside New York. Besides, he'd only stopped at two or three places. What are the odds against him just happening to stop at the two or three places where he'd be recognized? The answer is—enormous. Unless the town was staked out. Which is also crazy when you think of the number of people it would take to do that. Even if they only staked out the places a visitor looking over the town was most likely to go. Which might include the Avis guy to whom he showed his driver's license. The security guard who wrote down his plate. . . .

Nah! Crazy.

The train stopped at Greenwich. A bunch of people got on. Mostly black women, probably working as maids and such and now going home. One of them spotted the seat on Lesko's right.

"What did you think of the bartender?" Lesko asked quickly. *"The guy had this look."*

"*What kind of look?*"

"*A cop-look but different. Seen everything, done everything, can handle anything.*"

"*Like he could have a drink with you one day and snap your spine the next?*"

"*I guess. Yeah.*"

"*But loyal. Takes care of his friends?*"

"*I guess.*" Right. *We take care of each other,* he had said.

"*Then except for that part, you prick, you were looking in a mirror.*"

"*Oh, fuck you.*"

The black woman squeezed in. She sat on Katz's lap. Served him right.

CHAPTER 14

Detective Harry Greenwald, who had worked with Lesko four years in Manhattan South until he made lieutenant, had left calls for him at Gallagher's and at the Beckwith Regency, and had asked the watch commander at Lesko's local precinct to leave a note under his door. Lesko found it when he arrived home from Westport. Forty-five minutes later he was at the Bellevue morgue looking down at the dead, contorted face of Buzz Donovan.

Donovan was on a gurney table, naked, covered with a sheet. His eyes looked past Lesko through slits, his mouth was open, his white hair messed and matted. His expression, it seemed to Lesko, was more one of anger than of pain.

"Preliminary is a heart attack," Harry Greenwald told him.

Lesko reached for the sheet and drew it back over his friend's face. "What do you think?"

Greenwald pulled out his notebook and opened it to a page held by a paper clip. "Doorman says he arrived around half-past two. Gave him the messages you left, which is how I knew to call you. Super says you'd asked him to check Donovan's apartment and it was empty then. Donovan gets home, takes off his clothes and gets into the shower, lathers himself up, which is why his hair is like that, and has an apparent heart attack. Maybe another two hours go by before enough water splashes out of the shower to go through the ceiling below. That tenant calls the super, the super finds him, calls 911."

"Any marks on him? Anything?" Lesko made a gesture of futility with his hands. No matter how much death he'd seen, it was still hard for him to believe that a life, particularly that of a friend, could be snuffed out just like that.

"A small cut on the back of his head, a long scrape down his back, both consistent with sliding down over the shower fittings. He ended up with his face into the shower stream, mouth open. They'll probably find water in his lungs." Greenwald touched the bigger man's arm. "I'm sorry, Ray."

"Where was he?" Lesko asked. "I mean, last night."

"No one seems to know."

"You went through his pockets?"

"Nothing. Just his keys, wallet, pen. The usual."

"How about his notebook?"

"He didn't have one. The clothes, by the way, smelled a little sour, like he slept in them. They were folded across a chair in his. . . ." Greenwald suddenly fell silent, staring into space as if he'd just remembered something. "He always carried a notebook?"

Lesko pulled out his own. "Leather bound, like this one. It's always either in your pocket or where you empty your pockets. Did you look on his dresser?"

Greenwald's mind was clearly on something else. "Ray," he asked, "what was going on between you?"

"Nothing." He was damned if he was going to bring his daughter into this. "He's a friend. I see Donovan maybe twice a week since he retired."

"So why all of a sudden are you so hot to find him? What was in his notebook, Ray?"

Lesko studied him. "Something just got you interested," he said quietly, "what was it?"

Greenwald shrugged. "What I'm asking about. The missing notebook."

"Don't fuck with me, Harry." It wasn't the notebook. That could have been lost anywhere. It would have taken more than that for Greenwald to suddenly ask what's going on and to wonder, which Lesko could see in his eyes, whether it was a heart attack after all.

Greenwald studied Lesko in return. "The messages. The ones the doorman says he gave Donovan to call you."

Lesko's eyes narrowed. "You didn't find them, either."

"Come on. We'll go look."

Robert Loftus had wanted no part in the abduction and illegal detention of Buzz Donovan.

It was stupid. No other word for it.

At the root of the stupidity was Palmer Reid's conviction that he could, given the chance, persuade anybody of anything. At the root of that conviction was Reid's fundamental contempt for any intelligence but his. That was what was so ludicrous. Reid would end up telling Donovan the most transparent lies, never dreaming for a minute that a former federal prosecutor might see right through them. Almost everybody saw through them. Almost always. And when that happened, Reid would regretfully conclude that there was just no reasoning with the man, and that's when Reid would get even more stupid.

The only good thing to say about working for a man like Reid is that you could get rich. No real supervision. Few questions asked. Hardly any financial accounting. Loftus could retire right now on what he had taken out of Bolivia alone, if Reid would let him go. But Reid had told him. You retire when I do, Robert. Not before. Your country needs you. What that really meant, Loftus knew, was that Reid would have the IRS and the FBI inquiring into his affairs within a week, and the DEA would end up confiscating every nickle, every car, every piece of property they could find that could not be explained on an R-2's pay grade.

"Not that it should be any cause for concern, Robert," Reid had told him. "I am entirely confident that you, like myself, have not enriched yourself in any way while in the service of your country."

What was so fucking galling was that Reid's statement was one of his infrequent brushes with the truth. Reid, in all probability, had never pocketed a dime. Of course, having a trust-fund income all his adult life and picking up about four million when his mother finally died just might have had something to do with it.

As for the abduction of Donovan, Loftus had been sure that Reid's "chat" with him would be anything but friendly. What he had feared most was that Reid would then try bullying him, threatening him, or even ordering him kept on ice until he began to see things Reid's way. That would have been stupid enough. But never in his darkest dreams did Loftus imagine that Reid would have Donovan killed.

It was Doug Poole who told him. Poole had been summoned to the Scarsdale house early that morning. Reid's orders. Reid wanted to hear directly from him what he saw in Westport. Nothing, Poole had sworn. Only what he had told Mr. Loftus. The questioning made Poole nervous, both because of his own abduction, which he was not about to admit to anyone, and because the questioning suggested that Reid was losing confidence in Poole's immediate boss.

"Don't worry about that," Loftus told him. "What makes you think Donovan's dead?"

"Well, first of all," Poole explained, "I didn't even know he was there. I got to the house before Mr. Reid arrived and I heard this yelling and banging on a door. I ask Burdick who it is and he says nobody and I should wait for Reid in the library. Mr. Reid shows up and I overhear Burdick saying 'Here's Donovan's notebook.' And he tells Reid he's made copies of all Donovan's keys. Then I walk in and say 'You wanted to see me, sir?' and he looks at me like he forgot and he flicks his hand at me the way he does and tells me to go wait in the kitchen until I'm called. Then he tells Burdick to give him ten minutes with the notebook and then bring Donovan down."

"Could you hear what was said between them?"

"Just some raised voices at one point. Then the door opens, Reid tells Jack Gorby to drive Donovan home. I see Gorby nod to Burdick, who then heads out the front door first and drives away. At first I figure Burdick is going to search Donovan's apartment with those keys while Gorby takes his time driving in."

"What made you change your mind?"

"Burdick showed up about three hours later smelling like someone poured a bucket of Gatorade over him. He goes in with Mr. Reid. I had a bad feeling about that smell so I go and listen at the door. I hear Burdick telling Reid he regrets to report that Donovan suffered a fatal heart attack. Reid just says 'Unfortunate.' Then Burdick says something else I couldn't really hear about Lesko, the father, I think and that's when I got away from the door."

"The smell," Loftus said quietly. "It was amyl nitrate?"

"I'm pretty sure, Mr. Loftus," he said fearfully, "Burdick killed that old man and Reid ordered it."

"You don't know that, Doug."

"I wish I didn't."

"I'm going up there." Loftus kept his composure with effort. "Doug, you stay far away from this."

From Donovan's doorman, Lesko and Lieutenant Greenwald picked up a sample of the message slips he used. There was nothing similar in the apartment. Not in the wastebaskets, not on the dresser tops, not in Donovan's desk or under its mat. They did not search the leaves of every book or the linings of every drawer because it was not a thing Donovan would have taken the trouble to hide. Nor was there a notebook. He and Greenwald had both been right. The notebook could conceivably have been left elsewhere. The message slips could not have been.

Lesko walked to the bathroom where he stood for a long moment gazing sadly into Donovan's shower, envisioning the body as it must have been found. He caught a scent of something. He sniffed the air.

"What do you smell?" he asked Greenwald who came in behind him.

"Deodorant? Maybe the shampoo."

Lesko checked for a room deodorizer. There was none. He looked at the shampoo bottle that remained open on the shower caddy. Head & Shoulders, for Donovan's dandruff. Wrong scent. The soap was Irish Spring. Sort of a heather smell. But what he smelled was fruit. He opened the medicine cabinet. Nothing there that smelled like fruit, either. Nor any medication that suggested a heart problem.

"What are you thinking?" Greenwald asked.

"I'm not sure."

"You think someone else was in here?"

"Let's go talk to the doorman again. The garage man, too."

The doorman had been on since noon. Yes, he said, Mr. Donovan arrived alone. On foot, looking tired, in a bad mood. Yes, he absolutely took the message slip and put it in his right overcoat pocket. Yes, other people he didn't know had entered or left the building that afternoon but all of them were with tenants or were clearly known or expected by tenants.

The garage man had been polishing cars to make some extra money. Had he seen anyone in the garage he didn't recognize? No, he hadn't. Could anyone have passed through without being seen? I guess, he answered, if I was busy. But they couldn't go anywhere.

"How come?"

"They couldn't steal a car without a magnetic card to get past the barrier and they couldn't get up into the building without a special elevator key only the tenants have."

Harry Greenwald took Lesko outside. "I'll have forensics look at his keys. If they were copied recently there'd be fresh impressions from the clamps."

"Also Donovan's lock. There could be fresh shavings."

"But say I find something," Greenwald told him. "What do we really have?"

"I know." Not much. He'd been hoping for a description. Maybe one that fit Robert Loftus. The missing message, plus evidence that the keys might have been copied, would be enough to get the apartment dusted for prints, but Lesko knew none were likely to be found.

"You'll call me on the autopsy?"

"I'll call you. You have to promise to tell me what's in your head, though. No cowboy shit."

"I'll tell you. I know anything, I'll tell you."

Fruit.

Lesko couldn't remember what it was about fruit.

"Are you out of your mind?" Loftus found Palmer Reid behind an antique horseshoe desk in Ambassador Pollard's library.

"You are forgetting yourself, Robert." Reid looked

up icily from a notebook he'd been studying. "Kindly leave this room until you can enter like a gentleman."

"Let's skip the master-servant routine, Palmer." Loftus crossed to the desk and stood glaring at him. "I want to know if you have involved me in the murder of a former United States Attorney."

Reid's expression was unchanged. "I have not the foggiest idea what you're talking about."

"This is a yes-or-no question, Palmer. Donovan's dead. Did you or did you not have Burdick kill him?"

"Buzz Donovan dead?" Reid dropped his jaw. "Dear God!"

"And you can fuck your dear God." Loftus slammed down his hand. "Do you have any idea what you've done?"

Palmer Reid stared at him. "Burdick, you say. You accuse Burdick?"

Loftus made a fist. Here we go, he thought. One of my men must have done it. Acting on his own. Like Henry II didn't kill Becket, his barons did. "Forget it, Palmer. I saw the movie."

"The movie." Reid blinked.

Loftus waved it away. "For two days now, Donovan's been calling all over Washington asking about Bannerman, about you, and goddamn it, about me. Now all of a sudden he turns up dead. You don't think somebody might wonder about that? You don't think Lesko will wonder?"

"His heart . . ." Reid said feebly. "A man that age . . ." he stopped, realizing his mistake.

". . . could go any time." Loftus finished his sentence for him. "If I ask how you could know it was a heart attack, what are you going to say? Lucky guess?"

Palmer Reid rose slowly from his chair, his face flushed, one hand making a small, trembling fist. He turned his back on Loftus and sought to gather himself by studying an English hunt painting on the paneled wall.

"I have always been fond of you, Robert." He cleared his throat. "I find myself more hurt than angered at your behavior. It is beyond despicable."

Loftus wanted to scream. Instead he worked to calm himself.

"It is out of affection for you," Palmer Reid contin-ued, "that I have often tried to distance you from some of the heavier burdens of my office. I had hoped to reason with the man."

"But he was unreceptive." Loftus closed his eyes.

Reid kept his gaze upon the painting. "I sought his cooperation in an entirely forthright way. I appealed to his sense of duty. I extended my hand in friendship and he as much as slapped it away. I made a very hard decision, Robert."

Loftus nodded slowly, as much in resignation as in understanding. It wasn't just stupidity. Or more of Reid's conviction that he could get anyone to believe anything. It wasn't even an act. This man was out of his fucking gourd.

"I understand, sir," he said quietly.

"I hoped you might."

"Could I ask, sir? Was this what you had in mind when you said you'd give Bannerman something to think about?"

"Bannerman?"

"Paul Bannerman." He gestured vaguely toward the east. "Westport."

"Oh, no. That's quite another thing entirely."

Loftus gritted his teeth. "I'd like you to know, sir, that you can rely on me fully. I can only hope that my earlier outburst has not diminished your affection for me."

"We are all heavy-laden from time to time, Robert. Consider it forgotten."

"Can I hope, sir, that whatever you have in mind for Bannerman . . . that I will not be distanced from that as well?"

"You will be among the first to know, Robert."

Loftus's eyes fell upon the notebook the old man had been studying. He picked it up. The notes could only have been Donovan's. There were several names and phone numbers. Washington names. He recognized them all. Several references to Bannerman, some to Reid, two to Elena. Just bits and pieces, but Donovan seemed to be on the right track. Loftus turned the page.

Westport. Community of agents. Bannerman a rene-

gade. Several question marks after that one. Question marks everywhere.

Sexually abused a child. Loftus didn't understand that reference at all. But the order in which the jottings were written suggested that it was Reid who provided the last several pieces. Yes. There was even a reference to the burning of *Reid's stupid boat.*

Then, *What to tell Lesko??? Susan caught in the middle, Bannerman and this lunatic.*

Those were the last entries. The lunatic was clearly Reid. And Donovan was clearly worried about the safety of Lesko's daughter who, as Loftus suspected, probably knew nothing at all. Donovan, Loftus felt sure, never got a chance to tell Lesko anything. Lesko was in Westport while Donovan was being taken home and killed. Loftus had followed Lesko to Westport although he didn't dare risk getting off the train himself. The trip had mystified him. Reid's conspiracy theories aside, there was just no reason to think Lesko was involved with those people. More likely he'd gone to check out Bannerman himself, more as a father than a cop. But Reid wouldn't see it that way. Reid would see it as proof.

Lesko. If he ever finds out Donovan was murdered, there'll be no stopping him, short of killing him. Maybe they still should. Leave him alive and he'll surely try to retrace Donovan's last two days and all the phone calls he made. And, damn it, the first thing Lesko would look for is Donovan's notebook and when he sees it's gone he's going to know Donovan didn't die of any heart attack. But kill Lesko and Bannerman would hear about it right away. It wouldn't take him long to connect the two deaths. He might even know already that Donovan was making inquiries about him. He'd see Reid's hand behind this in a minute and then they'd all be as good as dead.

Jesus.

And as if killing Donovan isn't bad enough, Reid has something else cooking. *Giving Bannerman something to think about,* he said. *Take away his momentum,* he had said. A hit on Bannerman? No. Bannerman had already told him that his involvement would be assumed, whatever the circumstances. A hit on either Lesko or Elena, maybe. They both have other enemies.

And the way Reid thinks, killing either one would break a chain that probably doesn't exist in the first place. He could rig an accident, or he could make it look like the greaseballs did it.

"Sir," Loftus cleared his throat. Palmer Reid had moved to another hunt painting. They seemed to be a series. "Sir, if I'm to serve you properly, I really should know what you're planning."

"My father used to ride, you know. In Philadelphia. I still have his pinks."

"Sir . . . ?"

"They're not just ordinary pinks." Reid still hadn't turned. "He was Master of Hounds. The Master is not normally in on the kill, Robert. But he awards the trophies to the lead riders."

"So there is to be a kill."

Reid cocked an ear toward him. "I said nothing about a kill, Robert. What I've ordered—suggested really—is a distraction."

"But nothing illegal."

"That is always implicit."

Loftus sighed inwardly. A distraction. And Reid doesn't know the details. Which means he left them in the hands of his creepy little assistant, Whitlow. Which means he has deniability if anything Whitlow does backfires. And Whitlow, who's never done a day's fieldwork in his life, thinks he's a mastermind of grand and complex schemes that almost always go wrong.

Jesus Christ almighty.

This whole fucking thing is out of control.

"You say something, pal?" The cab driver looked through the rearview mirror as he cruised along Queens Boulevard.

"No." Lesko blinked. "Long day. Talking to myself."

"I know what you mean."

Lesko looked out the window to discourage further conversation.

"Hey . . . Katz." This time he said it in his mind, though even more self-consciously than when the driver heard him. *"Help me think. What smells like fruit?"*

No answer.

He tried envisioning Katz on the seat next to him. It wasn't working. Anyway, he was embarrassing himself. Maybe there was nothing wrong with a dumb little head game of trying to sort things out like they used to, but now he was starting to act as if he really thought Katz was there.

Knock it off.

A long day.

Just get home, have a beer, maybe take a nap.

Shit.

"Come on, David. What the hell did I smell back there?"

Anton Zivic had arrived at Mario's fifteen minutes after Lesko was seen to board the 5:45 to New York. Carla Bendict arrived separately. She now sat huddled with Gary Russo at the far end of the bar. Molly Farrell motioned Zivic toward a corner table for two. She joined him there.

"Carla's not very happy about this," she told him. "She says he's now seen four of us."

"Seeing is not identifying," he answered patiently. "Anyone who's stopped here for a drink more than once has laid eyes upon that many of us."

"I know. That's just Carla."

"What did Billy think of him?"

"Billy didn't know who he was until after he left. But he wasn't at all surprised. Billy says he could see in Lesko's eyes that the two of them were a lot alike. The only troubling thing is that Billy says he thought Lesko could see that, too."

"But Billy saw no threat in him?"

She shook her head. "Billy kind of liked him. He says they could be friends."

"Better Dracula and the Wolf Man be friends. The world would be safer." Zivic looked at his watch. "Paul has left for the airport. Glenn Cook is driving him. Do you see any reason why he should be told of Lesko's visit before he boards his plane?"

"No. But it's your call."

"Lesko's curiosity would not trouble him. This he would regard as human. His only concern would be overreaction."

"Carla?"

Zivic nodded. "I will talk to her. Lesko is not our enemy unless he defines himself as such. No action is to be taken."

"There's an easier way."

"Which is?"

"Just tell her Billy likes him."

Zivic shook his head wearily and reached for the menu.

"I begin to see why Paul needs his vacations," he said.

"Amyl nitrate," the voice said to him.

Lesko stirred. He thought for a moment that he was in bed. His body felt heavy and it tingled. But now he felt the cool vinyl of his Barcalounger.

"What?" he murmured.

"Amyl nitrate is what smells like fruit." The voice came from Lesko's right, as if Katz had pulled up a chair of his own.

"I asked you that before. Where were you?"

"I don't know." Katz paused before he said that, as if he was trying to remember.

"Never mind. Amyl nitrate?"

"Yeah."

A bit of the fog lifted in Lesko's brain. *"How the hell do you know that?"*

"We took this two-day lecture once in forensics, remember? The guy was telling war stories about ways to kill with toxins so we'd know what to look for. What'd you do, sleep through it?"

"Oh, wait, yeah."

"You spray a guy with hydrogen cyanide . . . what's the other name for it?"

"Prussic acid."

"Right. And it's like he has a heart attack. But you got to hold your breath and you got to spray your own face with amyl nitrate first because it accelerates your blood pressure or something in case you sniff a little yourself. Of course, if the guy happens to sneeze back in your face, you're fucked anyway."

"And that's how Donovan got it?"

"I don't know," Katz shrugged. *"Maybe."*

"Don't give me maybe. Go ask him."

"How do I do that?"

"You're asking me? He's dead, you're dead. Go ask around how you guys get in touch with each other."

"You said you weren't going to keep saying that."

"David," Lesko took a breath. *"Are you going to give me hurt feelings or are you going to try to be helpful here?"*

"You always have to be such a shit."

"David . . ." Lesko made a gesture of his hands that he hoped would pass for an apology.

"Anyway, if somebody killed Donovan, what's so hard to figure who did it?"

Okay, genius. *"So tell me."*

"You had this tail on you, right? Then Donovan makes calls about him, right? Then Donovan gets on to something, right? I figure the Loftus guy."

"After I made him?" Lesko said doubtfully. *"And I've got his driver's license and his address in my pocket, he's going to start killing friends of mine?"*

"Then maybe the Bannerman guy. Donovan was asking about him, too. Ask me, Bannerman's dirty."

"Wait a second. What do you know about Bannerman?"

"Like what? The kind of guy he is, you mean?"

"I guess. Yeah."

"He's like you. Big guy. Ugly. Except he has this little pencil mustache and he's kinda oily."

"That's what I thought."

Lesko kicked the Barcalounger upright and rubbed his eyes. For a minute there, he almost had himself believing that Katz was real. For a minute there it wasn't just a head game. Katz had answers. He knew about amyl nitrate, he knew about Loftus, and he knew about Donovan calling all those Washington guys. But he only knew what Lesko knew. Even if Lesko had forgotten that he knew. What blew it was the way Katz described Bannerman. Katz didn't know shit about him. The description was just a jumble of the ways Lesko himself had imagined Bannerman.

There wasn't any Katz. Just Lesko talking to Lesko. But maybe that wasn't so bad. Maybe it was better than nothing.

Lesko got up, stretched, and walked over to his phone. He made two calls. The first was to Lieutenant Harry Greenwald.

"Remember the fruit I smelled, Harry? Amyl nitrate smells like fruit. Check his clothing for traces, also his skin and respiratory system for traces of prussic acid. . . . No Harry. I don't know anything. I only know that things were missing that should have been there and that amyl nitrate smells like fruit. . . . Because I just remembered, that's why. And because it's very convenient that he happened to fall so the shower would keep washing his face and maybe fill up his lungs . . . Harry . . . I know nothing else. Zero. . . . Yeah, I'll be here."

The second, not counting one to Directory Assistance, was to a number at 21 Mayfield Road, Arlington, Virginia.

"Mrs. Loftus?"

"This is she."

"My name is Raymond Lesko." He spelled it. "I'm trying to reach your husband on a very urgent matter."

"I'm afraid he's not available, Mr. Lesko."

"I won't ask you to tell me where he is." He knew she wouldn't anyway. "But if you could get a message to him, I promise he'll be glad you did."

"Does he know you, Mr. Lesko?"

"Yes, ma'am. And it's very important."

"Very well. What's the message?"

Lesko gave his address and phone number. "Please tell him this," he kept his voice friendly, "If I don't see him here by tomorrow morning, he should assume that I'll see him there."

"There? Does that mean here?"

"Yes, ma'am." Lesko lowered his voice to a hoarse whisper. "It means I'll come and meet the family."

He broke the connection.

CHAPTER 15

Susan Lesko was excited, exhausted, in love and in London. She had not stopped grinning, not since an hour after sunrise when she first sighted the Irish coast from the window of the first-class cabin.

She grinned through Customs and baggage claim at Heathrow and at the sight of her first London taxi which, at Paul's request, took them on an early morning tour through Knightsbridge, past Buckingham Palace, down Piccadilly and back through Mayfair before pulling up at the entrance of the Grosvenor Hotel.

By the time the bellman had closed the door of their suite behind him, Susan had said "Oh Wow!" seven times by Paul's actual count and a truncated "Oh W . . ." six times more. She didn't care. She was in London.

Paul thought a nap might be a good idea. Then they'd shower and dress, see a bit more of the town, have dinner at Mirabelle, visit a club or two, then get a good night's sleep before boarding the Orient Express in the morning.

"Are you daft?" Susan turned from their window where she was already leaning out taking snapshots of everything in sight. She had also acquired an instant British accent somewhere during the taxi ride from Heathrow. "Yes, I'm afraid you've gone quite bonkers." She ducked back inside and handed him his coat. A shove toward the door made it clear to Paul that no part of her one day in London would be wasted in bed. Especially not on a nap.

By taxi, tube and double-decker bus, they spent the next six hours prowling through Westminster, the Tower, Soho, stopping for lunch at Claridge's and tea at Fortnum & Mason, peeking at 10 Downing Street and watching the horse parade at Whitehall. Strolling through Belgravia, in the general direction of Harrods, Susan spotted a placard in a small public garden that read:

LADIES AND GENTLEMEN WILL NOT,
AND OTHERS MUST NOT,
PICK THE FLOWERS.

She loved this town.

At Harrods, Susan began hunting for the accessories that would turn the drop-waisted dress she had brought along into something resembling a 20's costume to wear for tomorrow's boarding of the train. The brochure had suggested it. A floor manager in a swallowtail coat quickly guided her to just the things. A simple cloche hat, a black osprey plume, and a four-foot string of imitation pearls, to be worn doubled-up and knotted. These would do nicely.

Another woman, Susan noticed, seemed to be shopping for much the same items. They'd exchanged looks, polite smiles, but did not speak. Susan paid for her purchase, nodded once more, and went off to collect Paul who had wandered into the food halls. Finding him, she announced that it was his turn to be done over. She led him to the menswear department where she selected a colorful shirt with wide stripes, a brass-knobbed walking stick and an inexpensive Panama hat. These, she decided, would go well with his blue blazer and cream-colored slacks. He argued, uselessly, that she was dressing him in a 1920s summer outfit in the middle of winter. She didn't care.

There, looking at men's shirts, was that woman again. And once more, Susan had the impression that she was considering similar purchases. The woman looked away, but not before smiling and nodding what Susan took to be approval of her choices. Susan winked in return. The woman watched them leave.

* * *

In Lesko's Queens apartment, at the same hour, but five time-zones earlier, the telephone rang. He let his answering machine take the call.

"You called it, Ray." Harry Greenwald's voice. "We have to wait for a lab workup but the M.E. thinks he has traces of cyanide. You get back to me fast, all right? We have to have a nice, no-bullshit conversation about this."

It rang again 20 minutes later. Lesko waited for his recorded message to play. No voice followed. Just a long hesitation. Then the connection was broken.

Lesko couldn't be sure—the hangup could have been anyone—but he had to assume that Robert Loftus, a very angry Robert Loftus, had heard from his wife and would be paying a visit. But an angry Robert Loftus was not likely to trot up the front steps and ring the bell. Lesko went to his clothes hamper and scooped out an armload of soiled laundry. He stepped into the hallway, double-locked his apartment door, and walked down the three flights to the laundry room in the back basement.

There was a yellow plastic chair in the room facing two washers and two dryers. He moved it next to the machine farthest from the door, piled his laundry on the machine, then found an empty detergent box in the trash can. He tore off what remained of the top and inserted his fist, which was wrapped around a cocked automatic pistol. Next, he sat in the yellow chair in such a way that all but his head and shoulders were protected by the washing machine. He sat, not moving, for only ten minutes before he heard the service door outside being quietly opened and closed.

No other sound at first. Then slow, careful footsteps on the basement cement. One pair of feet. Lesko lifted the detergent box with its bath towel muffler and took aim at the laundry-room doorway. The yellow chair creaked as he leaned forward. Lesko cursed silently. The feet stopped.

"Lesko?" came a male voice. Loftus's voice.

Lesko waited.

"Lesko? My hands are empty."

Lesko chewed his lip. What the hell, he thought. "Come in slow, Robert. The hands first."

Loftus entered, nothing in his hands, but he held them defiantly at his sides. "No guns, Lesko," he hissed, "I'm here to beat the shit out of you."

Lesko's brow went up. He rose from the yellow chair and allowed the wrapped detergent box to fall from his pistol. He glanced pointedly at the weapon and then at Loftus. "How's that again, Robert?"

"This time it's personal, you bastard." He stripped off his coat and motioned Lesko forward. "I'm going to take you apart."

"Well," Lesko shrugged and stared, "I certainly wouldn't want that, would I, Robert?" He took two quick steps and whipped the automatic pistol against the side of Loftus's skull.

On Main Street in Westport, in the shop operated by Anton Zivic, the former GRU colonel was showing a mountainscape of the Dolomites to a lady who felt that the wall over her piano needed more drama. A sales assistant interrupted. A Miss Farrell, she said, was calling from New York. She says it's urgent.

Zivic took the call in his office. He knew that Molly had driven to the city. She'd gone, as Paul had asked, to remove the listening device from Susan Lesko's phone. He pressed a button and picked up the receiver.

"Hello, Molly. Any difficulty?"

"I got in and out, no trouble. Susan's wire is lifted." Molly took a breath. "Anton, I found another one."

"Another bug?"

"Actually, two. Living room and bedside. Both are infinity transmitters."

"I see." Infinity transmitters, unlike the device Molly had planted, could pick up any sound in the room whether the phone was in use or not. They were obviously better than a drop-in relay, but Paul would never have permitted the bugging of Susan's bedroom. "Were they installed before or after yours, do you know?"

"Definitely after. I did a sweep when I installed mine. I guess whoever installed this one didn't bother."

"Palmer Reid, you suppose?"

"Who else?"

"Did you leave them in place?"

"Sure," she answered. "But they'll know someone

found them, Anton. I have to assume that the noise I made handling them was enough to set off the voice activators. Reid's people would know that the apartment's supposed to be empty. Should I wait around to see who shows up to check?"

"No, it's not useful." Someone would surely come, but probably not a familiar face. "Better you come back to Westport, Molly. Something I don't like is in the air here."

"Did something else happen?"

"Perhaps. Perhaps not. You know this young man, Doug Poole?"

"The superfan. What about him?"

"On Thursday his manner was one of enthusiastic admiration. On Friday he did not appear, but he is back today. Today he sits low in his car and his manner is sullen. I saw fear in his eyes when I came to open my shop."

"I'll be there in an hour. We'll take him to lunch."

About two hours after leaving Harrods, Susan saw the woman again. Susan and Paul, having changed for dinner, were having a cocktail at a bar just off the lobby of the Grosvenor Hotel. The woman had also changed and she was now with a pleasant-looking man of middle age, probably her husband. They sat in the lobby proper, chatting, people-watching, enjoying the atmosphere.

"Do you see that couple?" She touched Paul's arm.

"The woman from Harrods," he nodded.

"What'll you bet they're going on the train tomorrow, too?"

"You're probably right." Paul was sure that at least a dozen of tomorrow's passengers would be staying at the Grosvenor. It was a first-class hotel and it was immediately adjacent to Victoria Station. He had chosen it for that reason. He knew that other travel agents would have done the same.

"Why don't we ask if they'd like to have a drink with us? Maybe even join us for dinner."

Paul hesitated. "I was hoping we'd have this night to ourselves. Anyway, Mirabelle is booked solid. I made our reservation a month ago."

Susan dropped her eyes. Her expression became distant.

"Does that disappoint you?" he asked.

"Oh, no." She straightened. "Nothing like that."

"What is it, then?"

"Well . . ." she began pushing an ice cube around her glass. "Paul . . . you know, you're really a very neat guy."

"And don't you forget it."

"You're great fun to be with, interesting, a world-traveler, and a wonderful lover, but you're also a very mysterious guy."

"What's so mysterious?"

"You jumped right past wonderful lover. When a woman says that, you're supposed to blush and say something modest."

"That's because it isn't true. That body of yours could excite a stump. Now what's so mysterious?"

"Lots of things," she shrugged.

"But you're going to make me pry them out of you one by one."

Susan made a face, half-wishing she hadn't brought it up, half glad that she finally had. But okay, she thought, let's start with the easy ones. "How come a neat guy like you doesn't seem to have any. . . ."

"Go on."

"The only people you and I have ever been out with are my friend Allie and her husband Tom. And that was only twice, both times at their house."

"You're saying you'd like to socialize more."

"Not exactly."

"Come on, Susan," he said gently. "Just spill it out."

"How come I've never met a single one of your friends?"

"You mean like drinking and poker buddies? I don't have any."

"And you don't have any family."

"No immediate family, no."

"And you're always traveling, mostly alone, and you never miss a thing . . . like recognizing that woman over there . . . and you let people get just so close to you and no closer."

"Including you?"

"Sometimes I feel that way. Yes."

"Susan, you know what I think?"

"What?"

"I think the Orient Express is getting to you. Spies, scoundrels and international intrigue."

"I'm serious, sort of."

Paul sipped his drink, letting Susan wait. "You know," he said finally, "I'm almost tempted to let you believe I'm a spy."

She said nothing.

"Because what I really am is basically boring."

"What are you, Paul . . . really?"

He set down his glass and took her hand. "What I am," he looked into her eyes, "is a travel agent who's been running around the world for more than 15 years. I travel 10 times as much as the average person and I've probably met 10 times as many people. Some became friends but they're scattered throughout other countries, because that's where they live. All this is true, Susan."

"Okay."

"As for Westport, you're right that I don't socialize much. By the time I return from a trip I usually have a pile of work to catch up on and I've had my fill of crowds, cocktails and restaurant food. I've also gained about five pounds, so my free time, when I'm not seeing you, is spent trying to sweat it off. This is true, too."

"Oh, I can understand that." However . . . she took a breath . . . in for a penny, in for a pound. "But you still act like a spy."

"How so?"

"You have a habit of scanning faces every time we enter a public place. You always pick a spot, like now, where you can watch people come and go. And I think you look away whenever someone points a camera at you."

"I do all that?"

"Sometimes."

"You left out that I don't carry a gun. That's another dead giveaway. It means that I can kill with pocket combs, credit cards and little tubes of nasal decongestant. You know what I'm going to do from now on?"

"What?"

"Every time I see a camera I'm going to run up and grin into the lens. I'm going to do that until you beg me to stop."

"I take it back about the cameras."

"Too late. I'm also going to walk right over to that couple and ask them to have a drink with us." He raised his hands to the sides of his head, forming a pair of blinders. "And I'm going to walk over just like this so I can't scan a single other face on the way."

She grabbed his sleeve. "Um, I was sort of hoping we'd have this night to ourselves."

"You're sure?" He kept his hands in place. People at nearby tables were beginning to turn.

"I'm sure," she grinned, reddening. "Now quit it."

"You know, Susan," his voice became a stage whisper, "you're a neat lady but you really ought to learn to be more sociable."

"Oh, good grief." She reached for his hands, to try to pull them down.

"You've got to loosen up." He dropped his hands but it was only to pick up a bowl of potato crisps, which he was now balancing on his head.

Susan hid her face.

For the second time in less than three days, Raymond Lesko sat waiting for Robert Loftus to clear his head. Lesko was reasonably satisfied that he'd come alone. Upstairs sounded normal. Just the mixed noise of two different TV sets and the Murphys on the second-floor front having their regular Saturday-morning argument. Lesko drew his yellow chair up close to Loftus, who was slumped against a Maytag dryer. His hands covered his face. He waited, as he had on Wednesday night, for the pain to reach a level at which he could function.

"Lesko," he whispered hoarsely. "I'm going to tell you this just once."

"What would that be, Robert?"

"You ever call my wife again, you go anywhere near her or my kids, I'm going to start by shooting off both your fucking knees. You understand me?"

Lesko leaned closer, showing his teeth. "I know how

you feel, Robert, being a family man myself. We had a nice talk about this the other night."

Loftus looked up at him. "No one bothered your family, Lesko. No one was going to. That happens to be the truth."

"Maybe." Still the teeth. "But you do other bad things, don't you, Robert? You blow dust in old men's faces and they die."

Lesko expected a denial, a look of surprise, some kind of bluff. But Loftus held his gaze and said, "No, Lesko. The fact is, I don't."

Lesko's impulse was to ask the obvious. Who did? But for the moment he was more interested in Loftus's odd behavior.

"Why did you come here, Robert?"

"Your family's out of this. You keep mine out of it."

"You had to sneak in my back door to tell me that? You couldn't have called? If all you're here for is a personal asskick, why didn't you just ask me to meet you someplace?"

Loftus didn't answer. Lesko suddenly understood.

"Robert," he sat back, "could it be you wouldn't talk on my phone because there's a wire on it?"

Loftus tried to sidestep. "There's always that chance."

"If I'm wired," Lesko told him, "and anyone but you heard the calls I made lately, they know I talked to your wife and they also heard me telling the cops about prussic acid. Robert, I don't think this personal chat is strictly between us anymore."

Lesko had been watching him closely. Loftus stiffened at the mention of the prussic acid. Then he stared past Lesko at a face only he could see, and his lips curled into a silent curse.

"Who killed him, Robert?" Lesko asked quietly.

Loftus slowly drew up his knees and folded his arms across them. He took a deep breath and released it slowly. "You ever get really tired, Lesko?"

"Once or twice."

Lesko bit his lip. Careful, he told himself. Go easy. Robert Loftus was suddenly getting that confessional look. He'd seen it a thousand times. The look of a man

who wanted to talk. But when it comes, you have to give
the guy room. He has to do it his own way.

"My wife . . ." Loftus stopped himself. He didn't
seem to know what to do with his hands. He ran the
fingers of one of them over the dryer. Maybe his wife
had one like it. "Her name is Katherine," he said finally.

Lesko waited.

"She teaches high school English."

He said nothing.

"I've got two kids. Both in high school, not the same
one. My daughter wants to play classical piano. My son
wants to be just like me."

Lesko didn't want to hear this. But he knew Loftus
needed to say it. He nodded that he understood.

"I'm not what I want my son to be, Lesko. For him,
for my daughter, I want nice, I want clean. They think
I'm a great guy. Even a hero." He took another deep
breath; another long silence. "Lesko," he said finally, "if
I had known what was going to happen, I would have
stopped it."

"What do you want from me, Robert?" Lesko asked
gently.

"I don't know."

"I believe you about your family. I think I believe
you about Donovan. But if you're looking for a pass on
this, you'll have to give me something pretty goddamned good."

Loftus looked up. "The line on you is you're straight.
How straight are you?"

"I give my word, I keep it. If you're asking am I dirty,
the answer is no. I hurt cops who are dirty."

"You're so straight, how'd you get friendly with
Elena?"

Lesko had seen that question coming. Normally he
hit people who asked it, but from Loftus it was probably
reasonable. "I saw her exactly once. Two minutes'
worth. But I made an impression."

"The barbershop?"

Lesko shrugged. "How's she figure in this?"

"If you're as straight as you say, I'm not sure she
does. It's a matter of someone adding two and two and
getting six."

Lesko started to ask who. But he found himself wanting to ask something else. "You know her? I mean, personally?"

Loftus nodded.

"Tell me about her."

"A classy lady. Ballsy. In her own way, she's also very straight."

Lesko sniffed at that. Calling a drug trafficker straight is like calling a rapist romantic. "If you know her so well, why did you have to ask if I'm friendly with her?"

"It's complicated." Loftus waved off any further questions and rose to his feet. "If you want to make sense out of this, Lesko, I'm the only one who can help you do it."

"I'm listening."

"First we talk deal."

"Bullshit. Because you're such a wonderful parent I'll try to see you don't get hurt any more than you got coming. That's your deal."

"Not enough, Lesko."

"What's enough? A character reference?"

"I might need you to kill some people. You might want to by the time I'm finished."

CHAPTER 16

Doug Poole could not believe he was doing this. Sitting in Mario's with Anton Zivic and Molly Farrell. Before yesterday, it would have been exciting. Today he was too upset to eat.

They'd walked up to his car. Hi, Doug, how are you? What do you say we grab a sandwich? What was he supposed to do, roll up the window?

They offered him a drink. He should have said no but he had one anyway. Just wine. And then a bacon cheeseburger fixed by Billy McHugh himself. He picked at it, claiming a queasy stomach, and Molly Farrell reached over and took a couple of big bites so Billy's feelings wouldn't be hurt.

By the time coffee came, Doug Poole was almost beginning to believe that the lunch really was just a friendly invitation to break up a useless surveillance. Colonel Zivic telling funny stories. Like how Molly Farrell dressed up as a scooter hooker to get him out of Rome, and how two Russians chased after them in a taxi, never dreaming that Billy McHugh was driving. Molly laughing. Such a nice smile. And she's one of these women who reach out to touch you when they talk. Her touch is warm and soft. Just like anybody's.

But then came the questions. Colonel Zivic sort of glided sideways into them, first telling a John Waldo story that led to an apology for John's roughness the other day. Then to the talk they had had when he regained consciousness.

"Doug," Zivic dropped his voice, "you assured us

230

that Palmer Reid's interest is purely a curiosity about a possible relationship between Paul Bannerman and Raymond Lesko. Is that correct?"

Here it comes, Doug thought. "That's what I'm told. It's really all I know."

"You also said you don't believe any such relationship exists."

"My boss, Mr. Loftus, doesn't believe it." Doug wished he had another glass of wine. "But he says almost anything Paul Bannerman does makes Mr. Reid crazy. Mr. Loftus is trying to keep him from overreacting. That's why he sent me here. Just to keep Mr. Reid happy."

"The tap on Susan Lesko's phone, Doug. This is for the same reason?"

Poole's jaw tightened. He sipped his coffee. "Please don't insult me, Colonel Zivic," he said into his cup.

"It is simply Anton now, Doug. And I do not understand the insult."

He lifted his eyes. "Sir, I'm not in your league, but I'm not a jerk, either. Don't think you can buy me a sandwich and spring any question you like on me just because I admire you."

"No insult was intended," Anton said earnestly. "If Mr. Reid is as curious as you say, the first thing he would do is tap Mr. Lesko's phone. This should surprise no one. If Susan Lesko is believed to be a link in this connection, her phone would be tapped as well. This is not common procedure?"

"I guess." He relaxed a notch.

"And are you satisfied, Doug, that there is nothing sinister happening on our end? That we wish only to be left in peace?"

"It seems a waste of talent. But I guess, yes."

"And that it would be tragic, therefore, if a false premise led to aggressive measures and then to retaliation?"

"Yes." Poole was beginning to perspire.

"And of all Palmer Reid's people, you realize that you are the most accessible to retaliation?"

Molly knew where Anton was headed. She placed a hand on the young agent's arm. "You're not on a surveillance, Doug. You're live bait. Whatever Palmer Reid is up to, his first sign that we're on to him will be when you fail to report in. Can't you see that?"

"Mr. Loftus doesn't operate that way."

"Can you say that about Mr. Reid?"

Doug Poole's heartbeat answered for him.

Molly picked up a fresh napkin and dipped a corner of it into Doug Poole's catsup. She folded the napkin and stuffed it into his breast pocket. "That's catsup from a Billy McHugh cheeseburger. As far as you're concerned, it's better than lamb's blood."

Doug Poole blinked, confused.

Anton had seen Molly do this before. An effective bit of theater. "Miss Farrell has just offered you a considerable gift, my young friend. If you accept it, whatever else may happen, the angel of death will pass over your house."

Poole ran his fingers over the bulge. He felt just a bit silly. He also felt safe. "What do you want from me, Mr. Zivic?"

"When first we talked, you were not afraid. Today you are. Tell us why this is."

Lesko stuffed his laundry into one of the machines, borrowing some detergent from a box another tenant had left behind. That done, he took Loftus's service revolver from his own back pocket, shook out the cartridges, and handed both to Loftus. Better safe than stupid.

"Talk to me, Robert," he said.

"What I'm going to do," Loftus snapped the weapon into his shoulder holster, "is tell you a story. What you have to do is try to listen, believe what I'm telling you, and not draw any conclusions on your own. People drawing conclusions is how we got into this situation in the first place."

"So tell." Lesko backed away a prudent distance.

"Two years ago, back in that barbershop, there was a young guy wearing a suit, the one they listed as an unidentified Hispanic male. He was one of ours."

Lesko remembered. The good-looking one who had moved for a gun and died first. "He was undercover?" Lesko frowned. He could have lived without knowing that.

"Not exactly. We put him there but they knew it."
Loftus hesitated as if looking for the simplest way to
explain this. "Would it surprise you to know," he asked
finally, "that the agency skims a lot of money off the
South American drug traffic?"

It didn't. Not unless it was the DEA. "What agency?"

"It's not really that clean. Basically we're talking
CIA, but it's the old-line CIA, the guys who are used to
making their own rules. Several of their operations have
been folded into the National Security Agency, where
it's easy to get lost."

"And who gets all this money? The CIA or dirty
agents?"

"You're drawing conclusions, Lesko. Try not to do
that."

"I'm listening."

"No matter how much manpower this country puts
up to stop drug traffic, the best they're going to do is
slow it down. The DEA does its best and those guys are
mostly all straight. The CIA works with them. The CIA
people, no matter what you might think of them, are
mostly straight, too, but you have to understand they
have different priorities. They have their own activities,
having nothing to do with drugs, that have to be funded.
The days are long gone when the CIA didn't have to
account for the money it spent. So for certain activities
that are too sensitive to tell a bunch of Congressmen
about, it looks for other ways to fund them."

No shit, thought Lesko. He felt a yawn coming on.

"Now, almost none of this is spy-novel stuff," Loftus
continued. "I'm talking activities that are necessary but
politically dicey. The best example would be domestic
activity, which is forbidden by law even though you and
I know there's no way an intelligence service can operate without at least some of its activities coming back
across the borders of this country. One source of the
funding, the major source lately, comes from protecting
some of the more reliable drug traffickers in return for a
slice of the pie. Like I said, we're not ever going to stop
them. The thinking was that we might as well get some
use out of them."

"All in the name of patriotism, right?"

Loftus's face hardened. "Let's not talk morals,

Lesko. We all make hard choices. You want to talk
morals, we'll talk about where your cop oath says you
can take personal revenge."

He had a point, Lesko supposed. But at least Lesko
hadn't taken any money. "Are you going to tell me, with
all this drug money around, none of you guys lined your
own pockets?"

Loftus looked at him evenly. "There might have
been some spill. I wasn't going to flush it down the
toilet."

Lesko said nothing. Busting balls was not the way to
keep Loftus talking. "The guy at the head of this is
Palmer Reid, right?"

"Yes."

"And Donovan found out?"

"No. Don't get ahead of me, Lesko."

"Then back to the reliable drug-traffickers. That was
Elena?"

"She was one of them."

"I want to know about her."

Lesko listened without interrupting for the next five
minutes.

Her full name, Loftus told him, was Elena
Betancourt although she also used the name Elena
Brugg. Both were legitimate. She was born in Zürich
during the war to a Bolivian mother who'd been sent to
school there. The mother got pregnant by a Swiss national named Karl Brugg and married him. After the
Nazi surrender, mother and daughter returned to La
Paz for a visit. The Betancourts, old-line Spanish blood,
kept her there and got the marriage annulled. The
Betancourts were landowner Catholics, the Bruggs
were financial wheeler-dealers and the nearest thing, in
their eyes, to Jews.

Elena was raised as Elena Betancourt, but her
mother always told her that she had a whole other family in Switzerland. Elena grew up, got sent to Wellesley
for her education but promptly transferred herself to
her mother's school in Zürich . . . "I told you she was
ballsy" . . . and renewed ties with her Swiss father and
his family. After graduating, she returned to La Paz but
she spent her vacations in Switzerland.

The Betancourts grew coffee and corn. They also

grew coca leaves and allowed their tenants to grow crops of their own just as they'd been doing for hundreds of years. The production of coca was and still is perfectly legal. It was also their most reliable cash crop. The end uses of coca were also legal right up until cocaine fell into disuse as a medication/anesthetic and gradually became the drug of fashion, with no law against its use. Then several things happened in the mid-sixties. One was a near-collapse of the Bolivian economy after a series of coups in which Palmer Reid was very much involved. Next, the bottom fell out of coffee and corn prices so the Betancourts had to greatly increase their production of coca paste for export. They were still not getting rich. What really made the profits start rolling in was the classification of cocaine as a controlled substance under the Harrison Narcotics Act. Cocaine was now both hip and hard to get. Supply-and-demand took over. Prices quintupled almost overnight.

When Bolivia's best cash crop was declared illegal by the U. S. government, growers throughout South America were hardly in a position to abandon that source of income. If one grower did, his neighbors would not. The transition from the legal to the criminal was a gradual process. By their own lights, and in fact by their own laws, the Bolivian growers were never criminals at all. America's drug epidemic was America's problem. No one was forcing Americans to snort cocaine.

Elena, by this time, being sophisticated, educated and multilingual, was a natural choice to become the connection between her family's interests and the international marketplace. She dealt with the Colombians who bought the raw paste, refined it and distributed it. She also handled the family's banking and investment interests through the Bruggs, who were not at all involved in drug trafficking but who could hide assets and launder cash with the best of the Bahnhofstrasse gnomes.

Big profits led to greed and greed led to a numbingly brutal war of attrition between rival factions. Under attack, Elena fought fire with fire, hiring guns of her own as guards, avenging hijackings and murders whenever the attackers could be identified, but it was a losing battle because her position was essentially defensive.

Palmer Reid, meanwhile, saw that some of these enormous profits could be used to fund his own activities. Elena was approached, in part because of her overseas connections, and offered protection in return for fronting certain of their transactions and channeling funds back to them through Switzerland. Palmer Reid ended up with an untraceable cash flow that was bigger than the total of U. S. foreign aid to Bolivia.

"It was that neat?" Lesko asked doubtfully. "Palmer Reid to the rescue?"

Loftus smiled. "Nothing with Palmer Reid ever goes in a straight line. Understanding that can keep you alive."

"So Reid probably set up the hits on Elena."

"Some of them," Loftus nodded, "after she initially told him to fuck off. Reid had the Bolivian Army in his pocket, one colonel in particular. It was him who kept hitting her until she had to take Reid's offer."

Initially, Loftus explained, Palmer Reid's protection consisted of guaranteeing her shipments against seizure, providing protection when she traveled, and directing all antidrug activity away from her and against her competitors. The Betancourts prospered greatly for a while but the cocaine wars soon grew totally out of control. There were three warring factions; criminal, establishment and radical. The distributors were the criminals in that all their activities were illegal. The growers were the establishment in that their activities were not only legal but essential to their respective economies. But to complicate matters, a third faction arose. It was a Soviet-aligned left-wing insurgency called The Patriotic Union.

The Patriotic Union, founded in Colombia, declared war on all traffickers, outlaw or otherwise. Bands of them, including many policemen and soldiers, began burning refineries, bombing cars and laboratories, and leaving dozens of *traficantes* nailed to their own front doors or doused with gasoline and set ablaze in village squares. Since they were a left-wing group, Palmer Reid and the CIA found themselves firmly allied with the *traficantes,* and began mounting paramilitary operations against the Patriotic Union. The outlaw *traficantes* were more than happy to tell the CIA who was

Patriotic Union and who was not. It took Reid the better part of two years to realize that almost everyone who was fingered as Patriotic Union, including judges, political leaders, journalists and clergy, also happened to be a sworn enemy of the *trafficantes.*

"Hold it." Lesko raised a hand. He wasn't especially interested in what the greasers did to each other or whether the CIA had painted itself into another corner. All he'd asked about was Elena. "You're telling me Elena was just this nice lady who was only trying to keep the family farm from going under. She lives in a tough world, she had to protect herself, so she goes and shoots my partner in the head."

"It *is* a tough world, Lesko."

"It's also a very confusing world," Lesko showed his teeth, "because now you're telling me a CIA guy killed Katz."

"His job was to protect her interests but you can't call it a CIA hit. Elena gave the order."

"So she told me."

Loftus studied him. It was Lesko's first clear admission that he'd ever actually spoken to her. "Lesko, how come you left her alive?"

"I still don't know."

"Personally, I liked the lady. Maybe you did, too."

Lesko started to deny it. Why bother? "Where is she now? Do you know?"

"My guess? Back in Zürich. After the barbershop, she had enough."

"So how do I still figure in this? And how did it lead to Donovan being dead?"

"Elena kept you alive, Lesko." Loftus said this with a shrug that said her motive was a mystery to him. "Her friends wanted to hit you. They might have even gone for your daughter first. Some of our people wanted you nailed for blasting one of ours and because we figured you had to be in it with Katz. But Elena told Reid, if you go, so does he."

Lesko's eyes glazed over. He was seeing Elena as Loftus spoke. Standing there with death all around her. Very scared. Her chin quivering a little. But brave. No begging. No apologies. *We live by our wits and we accept the risks, Mr. Lesko.* Then she tries to buy him off with cocaine. Not all of it. Some of it. *Lady, why wouldn't I just shoot you and take it all?*

Because there would be no honor in that, Mr. Lesko.

He blinked the scene away. So she protected him. He was supposed to be grateful? "The other night," he said, "you told me word on the street says I've been seeing her since. Where'd that come from?"

"No hard information," Loftus admitted. "It's just that the way she warned people off you and your family, it was hard to believe there wasn't more between you."

"You said people drew bad conclusions. That was one of them?"

Loftus nodded.

"So I ask Donovan to check on you, that check leads to Palmer Reid, Donovan talks to him and the next day he's dead. Why did that happen, Robert?"

"More bad conclusions."

"Reid killed Donovan?"

"He ordered it. An agent named Frank Burdick did it. You just heard me say that for the first and last time."

"You won't testify?"

"No way."

"Why are you telling me?"

"Because I want out of this. The only way I can walk is if Reid gives his blessing or he's dead."

"You don't have enough on him? You can't leave affidavits with a lawyer and tell Reid they go to the press if he touches you?"

"Come on, Lesko. You haven't heard a single thing about Reid that he couldn't deny or explain away. You couldn't even get him on a tax rap because he never personally profited. The man's untouchable."

"But on your word I'm supposed to run out and shoot him." Lesko began pacing the laundry room. "Robert," his eyes narrowed, "let's say I believe you. But if Reid is so untouchable, why would a little nosing around have gotten Buzz Donovan killed?"

"If he'd just asked about Reid and me, or even about Elena, nothing would have happened."

Lesko waited, uncomprehending.

Loftus saw the blank look. It was what he'd hoped for. "You really don't get it, do you?"

A light went on. Slowly. Lesko's face grew slack.

"Bannerman, Lesko. He asked about Bannerman."

The hair on Lesko's neck began to rise. He felt light-headed. He took a step toward Loftus, who could see the rage building behind Lesko's eyes.

"Take it easy. That's a mistake, too."

Bannerman. The name was screaming now in Lesko's mind. And he heard David Katz shouting at him from a distance, his voice an echo. *I told you. Didn't I tell you? The guy's dirty.* And Donovan. He'd been sure Donovan had held something back about Bannerman. And here it was. Bannerman and Reid. Reid and Elena. Elena in Switzerland. Bannerman in Switzerland. *With Susan.* And this son of a bitch knew it all the time. He let them go.

"Lesko! Schmuck! Listen to me."

Loftus was shouting at him through a red haze. Backing away. His hand reaching for his empty gun and holding it like a billy.

"Lesko, don't. It's all a mistake."

Lesko charged him.

The woman in the lobby of the Grosvenor watched them leave. She was in her late fifties, slender, expensively dressed, but there was an easy, earthy quality about her. She touched the hand of the man with her and spoke in a soft southern drawl.

"Hon, don't you think we should tag along? Keep an eye of them?"

"Darlin'," the man shook his head. "I think they've seen just about enough of us for one day." He had quick, mirthful eyes, a ready smile. He was of medium height, with the sort of shape that used to be described as prosperous. "Ask me, that feller was just on the edge of walking over here until he decided he'd rather balance a bowl on his head."

"Good to know he has a sense of fun," she smiled, "if we're going to be traveling with them. Though I wouldn't mind knowing a bit more about him. Anything strike you about the way he moves, sweetheart?"

"He does seem a bit watchful, doesn't he. Could be a lot of things, though. Could be he has a wife someplace. Could be he's afraid she has detectives on him."

"Maybe we ought to call and ask for a profile?"

"Then they'd know where we are, darlin'. Best if they don't. Best if we can fade in and fade out as it suits us."

The woman squeezed his hand to signify that she agreed. "We'll find out tomorrow. Tomorrow we'll sit them both down and get them to tell us all about themselves."

"Well, just don't go gettin' too fond of them, darlin'. That talk-show feller last June in Dallas, you must of moped two whole weeks about it."

"Then like last June," she picked up his hand and kissed it, "all you need do is keep buyin' me presents till you see I'm smilin' again."

"That's fine for you," he pretended annoyance, "but it sure would be nice to turn a profit every now and then."

"Oh, hush." She tugged at him. "How about us seein' if we can find a dish of ribs in this town?"

Lesko was on his knees, dazed. A stream of blood ran down across one cheek and dripped onto the laundry-room floor. He could hear the sounds of brass cartridges being clicked into their cylinders and the cylinder clicking into place but he could do nothing to prevent it.

Minutes ago, seconds ago, he wasn't sure which, both his hands were around Loftus's throat lifting him off his feet. He remembered the gun butt coming down across his temple. Once, twice, more times. He barely felt it. But he remembered Loftus's face retreating farther and farther away and then there was only the cement floor.

"Lesko?" Loftus's voice.

He felt a hand on his shoulder. It pushed him, not roughly, but enough to make him roll onto his back. He looked up, his eyes gradually coming into focus, first on Loftus's face and then on the revolver that was pointed at his forehead.

"I could blow your thick head off, Lesko. Agreed?"

Susan. The son of a bitch had involved Susan.

"Come on, Lesko. Shake it off. Are we agreed I could kill you?"

Lesko nodded slowly. He pushed to a sitting position as the fog receded and was replaced by a throbbing pain. Loftus stepped past him. He walked to the washing machine, opened its lid, and pulled out one of Lesko's wet bath towels. He held it at arm's length until Lesko took it and pressed it against his head.

"I'm getting a little tired of you belting me every time I see you, Lesko. On my card, you're still one up on me."

"What about Susan?" Lesko glared up at him.

"She's in no danger. So don't go crazy anymore, all right?"

"Bannerman. The guy she's with. He's part of this."

"Bannerman is part of a mistake. It's all a stupid mistake and people are dying for nothing."

Lesko eased to his feet with the help of the clothes dryer. Loftus backed away, his gun aimed at Lesko's right knee. Lesko glared at it for a long moment, then made a dismissive gesture with his hand. Loftus lowered the weapon but did not holster it.

"Tell me," Lesko said quietly.

"Paul Bannerman used to be our top contract agent in Europe. He worked for several of our allies as well. A few years ago he decided to take a walk."

"So he's not really a travel agent."

Loftus considered how much to tell him. No point in mentioning the rest of that crowd in Westport. It would only make Lesko crazy again.

"He is," Loftus answered. "That's a legitimate business. The only thing you really have to understand about Bannerman is that Palmer Reid hates him and is afraid of him. On Bannerman's end, all he wants is to be left alone."

Lesko wasn't ready to feel better about this yet. "How does Susan figure in this?" he asked. "How did she get hooked up with Bannerman?"

"I don't know. They could have just met someplace."

"In a pig's ass."

"Now, you see that?" Loftus waved his gun in exasperation. "That's how this whole fucking thing got out of hand. People like you making connections that were probably never there in the first place."

"Bad conclusions." Lesko remembered.

"That's right, goddamn it."

"Tell me."

"Accept for the moment that Susan and Bannerman just happened to meet like any other two people. Maybe there's more to it, maybe there isn't, but let's start there."

"Go ahead."

"Reid finds out that Bannerman is down in the Bahamas. He goes there to try to talk to him because Bannerman has warned him to stay far away from Westport. Reid only wants to talk. There's some unfinished business between them that shouldn't matter to you."

"So he talks to him. So what?"

"Reid sees he's there with a girl. He naturally asks for a make on her. The girls turns out to be not only a newspaper reporter but the daughter of Raymond Lesko. This Raymond Lesko may or may not have something going with Elena Betancourt. Elena can tie Palmer Reid into direct CIA participation in the South American drug trade. If Elena decides to talk, to Susan's newspaper for example, she can set off a scandal that could blow Reid and the whole CIA right out of the water."

"How much of this does Susan know?"

"My guess? Zero. More to the point, I don't think even Bannerman has a clue. He's probably never even heard of Elena." Loftus, waving his gun, realized it was still in his hand. He holstered it. "I told you," he continued, "that Reid hates Bannerman. From Reid's point of view, what's going on here is conspiracy by Bannerman to destroy him. Bannerman got to you, whether or not through your daughter, so he could get to Elena so that he could get the goods on Reid. You, Lesko, are central to this conspiracy against Reid. If any part of it is news to you, none of the rest of it can be true, either."

Lesko, his expression profoundly sad, lifted the end of the towel to his head and dabbed at the remaining traces of blood. Donovan did die for a mistake. He also died because Lesko asked him to make some phone calls.

"You got some more in your ear," Loftus told him.

"Donovan." Lesko whispered the name. "Just for digging around he got killed? How much could he have found out on the phone?"

"He connected Reid and Bannerman. That's all.

Reid's big mistake was ordering Donovan picked up
and taken to this house in Scarsdale. Reid met him there
and tried to feed him a cock-and-bull story about a conspiracy by a renegade agent to discredit our country's
intelligence service. He even said it was Bannerman
moving all the drugs and you and your daughter were in
it with him. Donovan didn't much like Reid either. You
can guess how he reacted."

Lesko didn't have to guess. Donovan would have
come straight to him. Knowing Donovan, he probably
made the mistake of saying so.

"The one who killed Donovan," Lesko asked softly.
"What did you say his name was?"

"Frank Burdick. He's at this place in Scarsdale."

"Why are you giving him to me?"

"The way I feel about Burdick," Loftus looked into
his eyes, "is the way you'd have felt about another cop
who'd kill anyone the commissioner asked him to. Don't
assume you're the only one with principles, Lesko.
We've both done things we shouldn't have."

Lesko had to give him that much. But he had more
than Burdick on his mind. "You said Susan's is no danger. Help me to believe that."

"No one cares about her. If you're worried about her
getting into the line of fire, I promise you that Reid
won't go after Bannerman. He's too afraid of him."

"That's not a good reason to kill him?"

"All I can tell you is that Bannerman has that covered. If a tree happened to fall on him, another one
would fall on Reid within a week."

Lesko wasn't sure he liked the answer. It could have
meant that Bannerman has a standing contract out on
Reid as insurance, but what's to keep the hitter from
keeping the money and lighting a candle for him instead. More likely, Bannerman either has a godfather or
an organization of his own.

"Just how dangerous is this guy?"

"Bannerman? Very. But not to you and not to your
daughter. Believe that, Lesko. But if you want to be
sure, the cleanest way to end all this is to take out Reid."

"And Reid's right now in Scarsdale?"

"So's Burdick."

"Come on upstairs." Lesko opened the laundry-room door. "You're going to take that wire off my phone so I can make some calls."

Loftus held back. "You tell anyone else about this, Lesko, and you do it without me."

"Relax." Lesko reached for his arm. "I had in mind my old pal, Elena."

CHAPTER 17

At Ambassador Pollard's house in Scarsdale, Frank Burdick sat in the darkened library restlessly switching from one cable-TV offering to another. He'd chosen a seat from which he could see the headlights of any car turning into the driveway.

He didn't like this. Reid going back home to Maryland. Leaving him alone with Loftus and Poole, wherever the hell they were. Poole would be no problem but Loftus was sure to give him a lot of shit about the Donovan thing. Burdick could already hear it. You work for *me*, Burdick. You don't do anything except through *me*.

Yeah, well . . . bullshit. You have a complaint, take it to Mr. Reid. He says do something, I do it and I don't shoot off my mouth to him. Anyway, Loftus, you're almost history. Yesterday you shot off your mouth to him once too often.

"It's clear upstairs."

The words, the voice, shocked him. He froze. Someone was behind him, off to his left, somewhere near the staircase. Very slowly, he eased his right hand toward the gun under his armpit. Drop and roll, he told himself. Use the chair as cover. His fingers closed over the butt of the weapon.

"Uh-huh."

It was a second voice. Directly behind him. A gloved hand settled upon his shoulder. Slowly, carefully, Burdick spread his own hands in front of him.

"Your name Frank Burdick?"

The voice made him shiver. "Yeah. Look I. . . ."

"Stand up now, Frank. Walk over to those stairs."

245

Burdick obeyed. He saw the man by the staircase now. Short. Dressed all in black. A fringe of gray hair showing from beneath a wool knit cap. *It's clear upstairs,* he'd said. He'd been there. Burdick could not believe it. Both these men had been walking through the house all this time.

"Who are you guys?" he asked.

"Walk." The man behind, his hand still on his shoulder, guided him forward. This man was bigger. Much bigger. Burdick knew that from the size of the hand and the direction of his voice. It was downward.

One in front, the unseen man behind, they led him to the master bedroom, and then through it into the ambassador's dressing room and bath. The man behind reached around and took Burdick's gun. The one in front turned on the shower.

"Get in," he said.

The words struck his stomach like a blow. This was about Donovan.

"Look," he tried to take a step backward, "this whole house is wired like a bank. You guys are already on videotape."

"Thank you. Get in." The man behind pushed him.

Burdick reached a hand into the spray from force of habit. It was cold. Another push. He stepped into the shower, arching up onto his toes as the spray went through his shirt and flattened it against his skin. He turned his head now to see the second man, and this time his stomach throbbed like a drum.

"You . . . you're Billy McHugh," he sputtered. "Oh, God. Hey, listen. I'm not the one you want. I just do what they tell me."

"Get wet. All over." Billy lowered Burdick's gun to his side. He held it loosely, carelessly, as if the need for it had passed. Burdick saw that and his terrified mind found hope in it. Maybe this wasn't what he thought. Maybe they weren't going to leave him in the shower the way he left that old man.

"Now get your face wet," John Waldo told him.

"Oh, Jesus . . . Jesus . . . please."

"Will you stop?" John Waldo's voice was pained. "And don't splash out here. That's how you get mildew."

That was funny, Burdick's brain screamed. They're messing around. They're only trying to shake me up so I'll tell them. . . .

"Frank," Billy took a step closer, "wet your face. I have to ask you again?"

"Okay . . . okay." He closed his eyes and turned his face into a spray that felt like sleet. "But you gotta give me a chance. It wasn't me. I'm the one who said don't do it."

"Frank . . . wash your mouth out."

"Wha . . . ?"

"Gargle, Frank."

He did, face up.

And then his head exploded.

In Zurichsberg, an elegant suburb overlooking the city and the lake beyond it, a telephone rang. Near it, a woman in a painter's smock stepped back from a palette-knife oil of a mountain scene and wiped her hands. She reached for the receiver.

"Yes?" she answered.

"Good evening, Elena." It was the voice of a cousin on her late father's side. He spoke in the Swiss–German dialect of the Züricher.

"Good evening, Josef."

"Elena, are you aware that an American has been . . . ?"

"A Mr. Lesko," she interrupted. "Yes, Josef. I have been told."

"He seems to be calling every Brugg in the Zürich directory, asking each of us to get a message to you."

"I know, Josef. Thank you."

"This Lesko. He is a friend? He has the voice of a gangster."

"He is neither. Do not concern yourself, Josef."

"You don't want his message?"

"It is only his phone number, no?"

"To me he said more. I wrote it down."

"What is it?"

"He said, 'Tell Elena this is about my daughter. Tell her she once said there will be no lies. Ask her if that still goes.' "

"Did you tell him you know me? That I am here?"

"It is obvious that he thinks you are. It is possible that my manner on the telephone confirmed his belief."

"It's all right, Josef. Thank you."

"This is trouble, Elena? Do you want your bodyguards again?"

"There are two sitting in my kitchen right now. Uncle Urs has already sent them over, whether I want them here or not."

"Mr. Lesko?"

"Yeah." His mouth suddenly went dry. "Yes."

"This is Elena speaking."

Her voice. The sound of it caused a stirring inside him that he had not expected. "How . . . ?" He paused to swallow, glancing toward Loftus with a look that was part acknowledgment and part self-consciousness. "How are you, Elena?"

"I am well. What is it about your daughter? Has she been harmed?"

"My daughter's okay but she might be in danger. Another man, a friend of mine, has just been killed. The killing is connected to what happened between you and me and your involvement with a man named Palmer Reid. I know there's no reason why you should help me. But I have been told things and I have to know that they are true before I act upon them."

"Tell me then."

Lesko sat back. With one eye on Loftus he gave her a five-minute summary of all that Loftus had told him. He mentioned Paul Bannerman, characterizing him only as an enemy of Reid's and a friend of his daughter's.

"I know nothing of this Bannerman," she told him.

"How about the rest of it?"

"It is true. We functioned under Reid's protection. In return we paid him millions. How does this endanger your daughter?"

"I'm not sure. Maybe I'm just nervous. You're in Switzerland. She's on her way to Switzerland."

"And you fear that I might harm her." Her voice sounded weary. Maybe hurt. Lesko wasn't sure.

"No, Elena. That came out wrong. I heard that you protected Susan when some of your people wanted to get even with me through her. It's just that Switzerland keeps coming up."

The line was silent.

"That was decent of you. Protecting her, I mean. If I knew a way, I'd make it up to you."

"It is not necessary." Another long silence. "And what of you, Mr. Lesko? You are well?"

"Not too bad. I'm not a cop anymore."

"I know. I have inquired. You are a man not easily forgotten, Mr. Lesko."

"I don't meet too many like you, either."

"Well . . . good bye."

"Wait a second. If I need to call you again, how do I get you?"

"As you did this time, I think."

"Direct-dialing would be quicker." To say nothing of cheaper.

"Perhaps it is best we keep some distance between us, Mr. Lesko."

"I guess." He tried to envision her. Back straight. Chin high. Eyes direct and a little sad. "Listen . . . Elena. . . ."

"Yes?" Her voice was small, expectant. But he had no idea what he wanted to say to her. Or why he wanted to keep her on the phone.

"You take care of yourself, okay?"

He heard the soft sound of her breathing.

"Mr. Lesko," she said finally. "If you wish it, I can arrange to have your daughter watched while she is here."

Lesko hesitated, then realized he was doing so. "I'd appreciate that," he said. He told her where Susan would be staying.

As he replaced the receiver, his expression distant, he turned toward Robert Loftus and saw a look of amused amazement on the other man's face.

"What's with you?" he scowled.

"What's with me?" Loftus shook his head as if to clear it. "What's with you and Elena?"

Lesko threw him his coat. "Come on. We're leaving."

"You're blushing, Lesko. I'm fucked if you're not blushing."

"No, asshole, it's called getting mad."

"You see Elena exactly once, you shoot everybody around her, and now you look like you want to ask her to your Junior Prom."

Lesko looked for something else to throw. Instead he snatched up his own coat. "You got a car outside?"

"Around the block, yeah."

"Let's go. You're driving me to Scarsdale."

"Talking to you is one thing, Lesko. But once they see us together, I'm dead."

"You're going to show me how to get inside. The talking's over."

Susan hated to leave London, having seen so little of it, but was even more reluctant to cut into her three weeks in the Swiss Alps. We'll come back, Paul promised her. If you get tired of skiing, or if we get some bad weather, we can always fly back and wait it out. Can we really? Anything you like, Paul told her.

But one fantasy at a time. Here it was Sunday morning and, dressed in their costumes from Harrods, Susan and Paul entered Victoria Station and followed the signs to the waiting Orient Express. Other passengers had already arrived, their heads turning toward each new arrival, cameras ready for those who came in 20's dress and for any celebrities that might appear. Several passengers snapped Susan's picture. Paul grinned grotesquely into several lenses until Susan noticed and jammed her elbow into his ribs.

The Orient Express was actually not one train but two. One for the English leg of the trip, the other for the longer continental portion. The first, called the British Pullman, was entirely made up of vintage dining cars, their exteriors painted in tones of brown and cream which gave them an antique sepia look. On the inside, however, each car had its own distinctive design and history dating from the late 20's. Paul had chosen a car that had been a particular favorite of Winston Churchill's who had used it to entertain visiting heads of state. A steward seated them in upholstered wing chairs facing a table set for lunch. Champagne was poured at once. A light lunch of Scottish salmon was served as the train whispered through the Kentish countryside toward the Channel port of Folkestone.

Arriving at Folkestone, the British Pullman eased onto a long jetty extending out over the tidal basin and delivered them within yards of a British Ferry the size of a small cruise ship. Once aboard, they were escorted to the vessel's first class lounge. Paul steered Susan to the port side of the lounge and a booth which offered the clearest view of the Channel coast and the white cliffs of Dover.

Their fellow passengers, who had thus far been speaking in hushed voices as they might in a museum, enlivened considerably with the service of tea and cocktails on board the ship. Most gravitated toward the sound of their own language in search of kindred traveling companions. Obvious honeymooners endured cooing questions and surreptitious snapshots before escaping to the promenade deck. A group of luxury train hobbyists began arguing the merits of the Orient Express versus Spain's equally fabled Andalusian Express.

The passengers, Susan guessed from the accents she'd overheard, were about one third American and another third British, the rest being a mix of other European nationalities. About one woman in five was in some sort of 20's costume including a few that were genuine antiques and several that appeared to be designer originals commissioned for the occasion. Most were like her own, made up of selected accessories, such as the one worn by the woman from Harrods who, with the man from the Grosvenor lobby on her arm, was now crossing the lounge in their general direction.

"Hello there." The woman's eyes lit up in sudden recognition. "You two mind if we share your booth?"

Paul stood as the man extended his hand. "Name's Ray Bass," he said. "This here's my wife Caroline." Caroline offered her hand in turn. "Seein' as how we've run into each other all over London," she smiled, "seems time we met."

Susan liked the Basses instinctively. It pleased her that Paul, normally shy among strangers, seemed entirely comfortable with them as well. The first few minutes of conversation showed Ray and Caroline to be outgoing, warm, enthusiastic and down-home funny.

Down home, as it turned out, was Lumberton, Mississippi where they owned a pecan farm and New Orleans where they kept a town house. Questioning them, Paul learned that the Basses took two or three vacations a year, the most recent being to China, not counting occasional weekend theater trips to New York. For all their easy charm, however, Susan could not help being mildly disappointed that the first new people she met were Americans. Caroline Bass seemed to read her mind.

"Truth be told," she drawled, "I sorta hoped you'd be English. Lady Twiddlethorpe or some such. And this handsome feller would be James Bond even if he does wear bowls of chips on his head in hotel lobbies. On the other hand, I know you didn't come on the Orient Express just to meet a couple of Mississippi farmers."

"See?" Susan nudged Paul. "James Bond. Everyone thinks you look mysterious."

"Um, I think the word Caroline used was 'silly.' "

"What line are you in, Paul?" Ray Bass asked.

"I'm a spy," he deadpanned.

"Oh, good," Caroline clapped her hands. "And you're on a caper, right?"

"Darlin'," Ray corrected her. "Detectives have capers. Spies have missions."

"Well, whatever it is, what is it?"

Paul leaned close, dropping his voice. "I could tell you. But then of course I'd have to kill you. Suffice it to say that civilization as we know it depends on my getting the formula to my contacts in Switzerland before midnight tomorrow."

"That's if you can get past the KGB, of course," Ray offered.

"No problem. Susan here will use her body to distract them."

"Paul . . ." Susan punched his leg.

"Hey, this is gettin' good," Caroline said in a stage whisper. "Do you know which ones they are?"

"The honeymooners," Paul nodded gravely. "No one ever suspects honeymooners."

"Makes sense," Ray Bass agreed. "They can disappear for hours at a time and folks'd figure they're off gettin' acquainted. But how does Susan here get rid of the bride long enough to use her wiles on the groom?"

"My department. On top of being mysterious, I'm also a great lover."

"Oh, brother," Susan rolled her eyes.

She'd asked for it.

In Lesko's Queens bedroom a six-hour time change earlier, David Katz was yelling at him.

"Dumb, Lesko. You're a real putz, you know that? You call me stupid. You want to know what's world-class stupid?"

"It really wasn't very wise, Ray." Donovan now. Complete with his Gallagher's table, which was now in Lesko's bedroom. *"How on earth could you trust a woman who'd order poor David's head blown off? Just look at him. He doesn't even have a face anymore."*

Katz started to rant some more but Donovan's words made him stop. *"No, look,"* he said to Donovan. *"I got a face. I got it back."*

To Donovan, if not to Katz, this was an irrelevancy. *"Whether you have or haven't is not what's at issue here. The issue is whether Ray should have told Elena where Susan and Paul Bannerman are staying."*

"What's the big deal?" Lesko heard himself asking.

"For two years now, Elena couldn't have looked Susan up in the phone book if she wanted?"

"I'm not sure it's the same as having Susan more or less in her clutches, Raymond."

Lesko didn't even want to think that way. He was getting annoyed. *"Elena's okay, all right? She found Jesus or something. Leave her alone."*

"That's real nice, Lesko," Katz sulked. *"Me and Buzz are . . . passed on, but do you give a shit? Nah! Forgive and forget, right? Why don't you and Elena go fucking dancing? You can go out for a couple of shots of tequila schnapps or whatever the hell Swiss–Bolivians drink."*

"Just a minute." Donovan was tugging at Katz's cashmere. *"What was that about 'passing on'?"*

"Don't pay any attention," Lesko told him. *"He gets all out of joint when you say he's dead."*

"Yes, but he included me as well. I'm certainly not dead if I'm sitting here speaking to you."

"Oh, Christ," Lesko muttered disgustedly. He started to roll over but Elena, who was in bed with him

and still wearing her mink coat for some reason, rubbed his back affectionately and said, *"Don't you pay any attention either. It is something they must work out between themselves."*

"While they're at it," said Loftus, sitting atop the clothes dryer, which was also now in Lesko's bedroom, *"they can figure out how Burdick got dead, too. And if you didn't do it, Lesko, who did?"*

Oh, yeah. Burdick. Lesko remembered now. They'd driven to this big house in Scarsdale. Loftus snuck up in the dark to short out the alarm system. Then he comes back, spooked and sweating, saying someone already rigged a bypass on it. Loftus wants to bag it but Lesko went in anyway. The only light on the first floor was from a TV that no one was watching. But there were lights on upstairs and he could hear the sound of a shower running. Quietly, Lesko followed his gun up the stairs to the bathroom where he finds a stiff on the floor of this big shower stall, legs twisted under him, his face in the stream of water. It was just like they found Donovan except this guy was fully dressed and he had a .38 jammed between his teeth and a hole through his head. There was a bigger hole higher up, blasted into the tile. The guy's brains were still dripping down the wall in pink streaks.

Lesko went back out for Loftus and made him come look. Loftus said it was Burdick and now he's really spooked, which seems funny considering that the whole point of coming up here was to make Reid and Burdick dead. Loftus seems to want to believe that Lesko had done it even when Lesko pointed out that there had been no gunshot and no time to do this either unless Loftus thought he just happened to surprise Burdick while he was taking a shower with his clothes on. Next, Loftus wanted to know who Lesko had talked to when he went up to Westport the day before. Lesko asked what the hell that had to do with anything.

"Did you tell anyone there about Donovan being dead in his shower?"

"No, shithead. I didn't even know about Donovan then." Anyway, the only people he'd talked to at all were a nosy librarian, an I've-seen-everything type bar-

tender, plus maybe the guy at the Avis rental. But hearing that didn't make Loftus any happier.

"*Okay,*" said Katz, leaning between them. "*Let's look at the possibilities.*" They were not in Lesko's bedroom anymore. They were in Loftus's car, and Katz and Donovan had joined them in the back seat. Elena was gone. That depressed Lesko because he didn't know when she'd ever climb into his bed again, and the least he should have done was take the opportunity to talk things out. "*Killing Burdick,*" Katz continued, "*was definitely a revenge hit for Buzz here, right?*"

"*Or made to look like one,*" Donovan suggested.

"*Let's keep things simple here, all right? Forget you're a fucking lawyer.*"

"So talk," Lesko said.

"*Buzz was making calls to Washington about Reid and Bannerman. Then suddenly he's zapped.*" Katz threw an apologetic shrug at Donovan for his use of the word. "*One possibility is Buzz's friends in Washington decided to even the score for him.*"

"*No,*" Donovan shook his head. "*They're simply not that sort.*"

"*Good,*" said Katz. "*That makes it simpler. All that's left is Bannerman.*"

"Loftus?" Lesko asked. "What do you think?"

"I don't know."

"*Don't give me I don't know. Katz is right. If this whole thing is because Reid is afraid of Bannerman, who else could it be?*"

"*Listen, I have other things on my mind, okay? I've got another one of my men who's six hours late reporting in. He's clean but he could be dead, too. I also have to get rid of all of you, then go back and go through the motions of finding Burdick's body and calling Reid so he doesn't know I'm part of this.*"

"*Ray,*" Buzz Donovan touched his shoulder, "*Hasn't Bannerman been in transit all this time?*"

"*He could have heard about you when he got to London. He could have set this up by phone.*"

"*But with whom?*"

Lesko hadn't thought of that. "*Maybe he has friends of his own in the Fed.*"

"*But Loftus says he's retired. He wants to be left*

*alone. He's hardly likely to have a skilled assassin at his
disposal. He's even less likely to have known that Burdick was the specific culprit."*

Loftus had a funny look. Lesko saw it. The look suggested that a revelation had struck him. Loftus got the
same kind of look when Lesko told him he talked to a
bartender in Westport. And Loftus says Reid is afraid to
go to Westport, right? Afraid of one guy? Or does the
guy have muscle up there?

Funny looks.

Looks.

The bartender had a look. Like a cop's but not quite.
The lady bartender, too.

Lesko wanted to ask Loftus about these people but
Loftus was suddenly driving away with Katz and Donovan still in the backseat. They must have dropped him
off right at his bed because that's where he was.

He rubbed his eyes.

Shit!

He didn't bother looking at his clock. He knew what
time it would show. He did look at the side of the bed
where Elena had been and immediately felt stupid for
it.

What was today?

Sunday.

Susan would be on that train somewhere. Probably
safe enough. But it would be another whole day before
he could give her a call. And before Elena could start
keeping an eye on her.

CHAPTER 18

At Boulogne, on the coast of France, the blue-and-gold carriages of the Continental stood waiting on a track inside the terminal of the Channel ferry. At the entrance to each of the restored sleeping cars, a young steward, also in blue and gold, waited to show the passengers to their cabins. Paul and Susan's steward—his name was Andrew—handed Paul a cable message and directed him to a telephone kiosk just inside, cautioning him that the train would depart in fifteen minutes. It took Paul six of those minutes to get through to Anton Zivic.

Zivic used another four to tell him about the bug on Susan's phone, his subsequent lunch with Doug Poole, Poole's revelation of the Donovan murder, and Zivic's decision to execute an immediate reprisal against Palmer Reid's man, Burdick. Anton, knowing that public phones at border points are sometimes tapped, kept his language as obscure as possible while still conveying the sense of what had occurred. A man had died, Paul understood, and now another, because Palmer Reid imagined a conspiracy between himself and Susan's father.

"Do you think the father is in danger?"

"I will see to him," Anton promised. "But you be careful. Perhaps the reprisal scared the Old Man off but perhaps not. With your permission, I would like to send Mama's Boy some traveling companions."

"No. Absolutely not." Paul couldn't bear the thought of it. "Colonel, you might give our friend at State a call. Have him ask the Old Man why these two are dead. The

question alone should be enough to make him put his
activities on hold. Otherwise, use your own judgment.
Don't feel you have to consult with me."

A brief silence on the line. Paul instantly regretted
having said that. Anton was right to alert him and he
was not a man who needed hand-holding.

"There is another reason for this contact," Anton
told him. "The bartender is anxious that you know he
acted on my authority."

"Tell him he did fine." Paul heard a rapping against
the glass of the terminal window. It was Susan, pointing
at her wristwatch. He held up one finger. "Listen, Colonel . . . will you check out a couple of names for me? A
Raymond and Caroline Bass from Lumberton, Mississippi. Both in their late fifties, early sixties. He's about
five nine, full head of graying hair. They're passengers
on this train."

"You think someone else has sent traveling companions?"

"Not at all. It's just nice to know who your friends
are."

"I'll call you in Klosters."

"Only if you have to, okay? And Anton . . ." Susan
was jumping up and down. "Tell Billy I'm proud that
he's my friend."

Bannerman ran for the train.

On Lesko's street in Queens, on a rooftop four buildings away and down the block, Glenn Cook of
Westport's Sundance Ski Shop sighted through the
scope of an Armalite carbine at the traffic turning off
Queens Boulevard. Two delivery trucks came through,
then several older cars, a lunch wagon, then two late-
model cars, but they were driven by women.

A new-looking Chrysler turned onto the street.
Charcoal brown. Driver, a man in his mid-thirties wearing a business suit. Perfect, he decided. Glenn Cook
squeezed the trigger.

The brown Chrysler veered wildly, braking first and
then accelerating before its wheels could be straightened. It slammed into the rear quarter-panel of a car
parked at the curb.

Glenn Cook fired again.

He collapsed the stock of his Armalite and jammed it into a sling underneath his ski parka. Picking up his brass, Cook walked unhurriedly across two more rooftops and then disappeared down a stairwell.

From a gas-station phone booth two blocks away, he punched out Palmer Reid's Maryland number, spoke three sentences to a recorded message and hung up. Then, after stopping for a container of coffee and two chocolate doughnuts, he drove back to Westport.

Susan was enthralled. She barely heard a word as Andrew the steward demonstrated the switches and knobs of their private compartment. She stood with a glazed Christmas-morning smile as he explained their dining car choices, and the hours of service, then collected their passports. He'd no sooner closed the door behind him than Susan let out a whoop that had several startled passengers peering out into the corridor. "Americans," the steward explained with a smile.

"This," she announced, semi-composed for the moment, "is the single most romantic thing I've ever seen in my life." Every panel, every fitting, every thread of fabric was exactly as it had been a half-century before. On a table near the large viewing window sat a bucket of iced champagne and a mound of Iranian caviar the size of an ostrich egg. From a baseboard grille she could feel the heat of a charcoal stove rising against her legs.

"You don't know the half of it." Paul grinned at her pleasure. "This particular car sat out World War Two on a siding in Lyons. It was used as a brothel for German officers."

She closed one eye. "Are you making that up?"

He shrugged. "I'm sure they've changed the sheets since then."

"And repaired the springs?"

"I guess we'll find out."

Susan ran her fingers over the embroidered settee, then over the wall above it, trying to imagine where the other bed was and how this day cabin converted into a sleeper. She decided to let Andrew worry about that. Her eyes darted about the compartment, resting for only a moment in one place before dashing to another. Another whoop. A jump up and down. A wave through

the window to some passing French children, who
smiled and waved back.

"I wish you'd climb out of your shell," he said dryly,
"show a little enthusiasm."

"Oh, shut up," she said happily. She dipped a
thumbnail into the caviar, ignoring a low groan from
Paul. "Does everyone get all this?"

"Nope," he smiled. "Only when you special-order
for a special lady."

Paul opened a set of curved mahogany doors that
revealed a hidden wash stand and towels. "If you want
to freshen up before we dress for dinner, I'll go and take
a short walk. There's not much room for both of us to
move around in here."

"I don't want to wash up now. I want to explore."

"You wouldn't like some time to yourself? To unpack?"

"Uh-uh," she shook her head. "Let's go check out the
bar car. No, wait. We have champagne. You have to
make a really romantic toast."

"I'll open the bottle."

"And then how about a quickie?"

"A quickie what?"

She batted her eyes, pretending to blush.

"Susan," he made a show of wincing, "one has quickies in the backseats of cars or in apartment elevators.
One does not have quickies aboard the Orient Express."
He reached for the door latch. "You make yourself comfortable. I'll be back in three minutes."

Her face fell. She said nothing, only staring for a
brief moment and dropping her eyes.

"Oh-oh," he said. "What's wrong."

"It's okay. Three minutes."

"Susan," he leaned backward against the door.
"What just happened?"

Her lips moved, haltingly, as if trying out words and
rejecting them. "You're going to case the joint, aren't
you? See who's next door. See if anyone new got on at
Boulogne."

"And bribe Andrew to show me their passports?"

"Are you?"

"Actually, I was going to the bathroom. It's down the
hall."

Susan brought her hand to her face, but she couldn't stop the laugh. "I'm sorry. I don't believe I said those things."

"I thought we settled all that. I'm not mysterious. I'm boring."

She stepped toward him, put her arms around him, and leaned her face against his chest. "Can I say just a couple more things?"

He answered by holding her.

"There's something about you, Paul. It's a very special quality that I've never seen before except in my father. I know what made him that way. Whatever made you that way, it's more than what you've told me, and I hope someday you'll feel you can."

"Are you sure I even know what it is?"

"Yes. I'm sure."

"You're not just letting your imagination run wild? After all, you're a reporter. You're also your father's daughter."

"Paul?" He felt her chest rise. "Paul, I think I love you."

"I love you. I don't have to think."

She fell silent. He could see the beginning of a tear at the corner of her eye. "That's the first time you've said that."

"I know. It felt good."

She held him, listening to his heartbeat. "Maybe love comes faster than trust. I guess I can wait."

"Thank you." He knew that was the wrong thing to say. It implied acknowledgment. He said it anyway.

Susan heard it. She eased herself away from him, looked about their compartment, and then up into his eyes. "Paul," she said, "this is all very heady stuff for me. These trips, being on the Orient Express, finding out I love you. I'm not especially sophisticated. I'm pretty easy to dazzle for a while. But I'm proud. And I'm not stupid."

"I know. I know all that."

"I guess I want you to know that I'm not just some empty-headed plaything who's along for the ride."

Paul's expression became cool. "You're not stupid, Susan. But that remark was."

She didn't blink. "Tell me why."

"For openers, it's just as offensive as if I told you I'm not some stud who's along to pick up the tab."

Susan winced. "Oh damn," she said.

"Oh damn, what?"

"It's more polite than 'Oh shit.' "

"How do we get out of this?"

"Would it help if I tore off my clothes?"

"Hold that thought for later."

Back in Queens, it was a morning for cops.

It started, as usual, with Katz. Lesko had drifted in and out of sleep after that crazy dream that had everybody including Elena turning up in his bedroom. There were a whole string of small dreams after that, about Susan, about Elena, about the barbershop. That one woke him up. Mostly. He lay there, eyes closed, thinking about his last conversation with Loftus.

There was no question in his mind by now that Loftus knew, or at least strongly suspected, who had killed Burdick. The look on his face had said so. Lesko knew that Bannerman had to be somewhere behind it. Because, besides himself, no one but Bannerman would have a revenge motive after the killing of Donovan. But Bannerman was in Europe. Therefore, friends of Bannerman must have done it. Lesko's instincts told him, and this is where the logic became shaky, that Bannerman's friends were at least two, and maybe four, of the people he'd chanced upon in Westport.

It was more than shaky, Lesko knew. If he'd happened to take an entirely different route during his Westport visit he would have seen or met an entirely different group of people. True, the ones he met had this *look* that kept bothering him. But so what? Lots of people have a look. Ex-cops, ex-cons, some Vietnam veterans, even priests and nuns dressed in civilian clothes.

"Ask me, it's nothing." Katz was there with the Danish.

"I guess," Lesko muttered.

"What it is," Katz was clanking around the kitchen, looking for a clean cup, *"they just stick in your mind when you think of Westport because they're all you saw there."*

"Probably."

"Except you know what?" Katz came in squinting. *"Maybe it's logical you saw those people."*

"What's that supposed to mean?"

"If you want to look over a town like Westport, you do what you did, right? You drive around, you stop at the library, you look through the local paper, then you go check out the places where people hang out."

"Okay. So what?"

"Maybe they know that."

"I don't get you."

"Maybe they got it set up so they spot anyone who comes snooping around because they know just like us where people are likely to snoop."

"Maybe," Lesko said doubtfully. It might make sense but it was an awful lot of trouble to go to. And it would take more than four people to do it right.

"And I'll tell you something else," Katz said brightly. *"When Susan started looking that town over, I bet she went to all the same logical places. And they caught on to her. And Bannerman worked out a way to get to know her to see what she was up to."*

"Up to what? You mean all that suicide and fatal accident crap?"

"I don't know. It could be."

"Which reminds me." Lesko opened one eye. *"How come you never see any dead people except maybe Buzz? How come you don't go find some from Westport and settle that once and for all?"*

"Come on, Lesko." Katz began an instant pout.

"What come on? That's a logical question."

"I already told you I don't know how. Anyway, I don't hang out with stiffs,"

"Well now, David," Lesko's teeth bared against his pillow, *"as a rule, I don't either. Except you don't give me the same choice you have."*

"Anyhow it wouldn't do any good. If they're all like Donovan you can't talk to them because they don't even think they're dead. Donovan still thinks he's in fucking Gallagher's."

"David . . . are you listening to yourself?"

"Don't say it."

"*Not that I begrudge you, David, but one of these days we really ought to face facts here.*"

"*You want to face facts? You really want to make sense out of me coming here?*"

"*I can't say it's at the top of my list, but I guess, yeah.*"

"*Then make sense out of this.*" Katz's voice was becoming shrill. "*Last night you had Loftus here and he's not dead. You had Elena in the sack with you, which incidentally I didn't give you any shit about, and she's not dead. You had Donovan here with his table and his fucking table sure isn't dead.*"

"*Yeah? So what?*"

"*I'm telling you, there's a way out of this. Maybe next time they're here, I'm going to try sort of sliding over next to them and when they walk out, maybe I can walk out with them.*"

"*What the hell,*" Lesko shrugged. "*Give it a shot.*"

"*I'm going to.*"

It was mostly a morning for live cops. The first one came after he'd dried off from his shower and was on his second cup of coffee. A sergeant named Mosconi from the local precinct, where they all knew Lesko and where he lived, knocked on his door and asked him whether he'd seen what had happened on the street an hour or so earlier.

"No, what? I was asleep."

"We had a sniper incident." Mosconi asked if he could enter and then led Lesko to his window where he pointed up toward Queens Boulevard. A brown, late-model Chrysler had plowed into a parked car two down from Mr. Makowski's fifteen-year-old Chevy. There was a four-inch hole high on the windshield. Five patrol cars, their blue lights strobing, had answered the call. Two of them sealed off both ends of the block.

"Anyone hurt?" No ambulance yet. One man in a suit waving his arms, talking to two uniforms.

"No." Mosconi nodded toward the man being interviewed. "He's a salesman. Dry-cleaning equipment. He's on his way to LaGuardia and he's trying to cut over to the Parkway. Never been down this street before."

A random victim.

"You didn't hear any shots, Ray?"

"No. Nothing."

"Neither did anyone else so far. I came up here because I figured if anyone on this street would make a decent witness, it's you."

"I can't help you," Lesko shook his head. "I don't even know who owns a rifle around here."

"How about veterans? You know any real good marksmen?"

"How good do you have to be to hit a windshield?"

Mosconi showed a mirthless smile. "Both shots are through the rearview mirror, one on either side of the stem. One while he was moving, the other after he crashed. I'd call that good shooting."

I'd call it leaving a message, thought Lesko.

But as for the who and the why of it, Lesko had no idea. It crossed his mind, recent events considered, that the demonstration might have been for his benefit. But no. No way. Demonstrations are useless if they're too subtle. It's why loan sharks break legs.

Sergeant Mosconi declined a cup of coffee and left. His uniforms would be going door-to-door and checking rooftops all morning.

The next cop was Detective Harry Greenwald, who heard the squeal about a sniper on Lesko's street and drove out from Manhattan.

"Any chance that could have been for you?" he asked.

"None at all. I just been through that with the Queens cops."

"They have anything?"

"Nothing. No shell casings, no witnesses, no motive. Ask me, it's probably one of those psychos who read *Soldier of Fortune.*"

"I wonder," Greenwald said, then stood waiting.

"You came out for nothing, Harry. Don't waste your time."

"You know what else I wonder?"

"What?"

"Three days ago one of your oldest friends got murdered. You called it yourself. You know I'm conducting the investigation but you don't call to see how it's going, do I have any leads, have we made an arrest. How is that possible, Ray?"

Lesko realized his mistake. "You're asking if I'm out looking for the guy myself. I give you my word, I'm not."

"And you have no idea who killed him." Greenwald looked into his eyes.

What the hell. "Nothing I can prove."

"Try me."

"Prussic acid," Lesko said. "Sounds a little like the CIA, doesn't it."

"Do you have something or don't you?"

"Last time I saw Buzz he was trying to get a line on some big intelligence guy in Washington. I think there was hard feelings between them."

"Give me a name."

"Palmer-something. Yeah. I think it was Palmer Reid."

CHAPTER 19

Caroline Bass watched as Paul entered the bar–salon car, pausing just inside, his eyes sweeping over several passengers in evening dress who were crowded around the black baby grand piano and the bar itself.

"There he is, darlin'." She touched Ray Bass's arm. "And there are those careful moves of his again."

Ray Bass didn't turn. He knew what she meant but he was sure that it signified nothing. Why, back home, he thought, you couldn't sit in one of them Yuppie bars for twenty minutes before noticing that everyone who walked in the door would hold up for a minute to check out the action, as they say. "Pay it no mind, sweetheart. Time comes, he won't be around to worry about."

Caroline raised a hand, waiting for Paul to look in her direction. "Bannerman," she said his name softly. "That name doesn't ring even a teensy little bell with you?"

"Can't say it does." He shook his head. "You know what I bet? Bannerman is one of those manly-type names they always give to detective shows on the TV. I bet that's why it sounds familiar."

"Maybe. Maybe so."

Now Ray Bass turned and stood. "Hey there, Paul. Got a seat for you right here."

Paul heard Ray Bass's voice before he picked him out of the tuxedos. He made his way into the salon part of the car, which consisted of plush Art Nouveau chairs in conversational groupings, each grouping highlighted by the tasseled shade of a brass Orient Express lamp. All but two of the chairs were filled by passengers sipping aperitifs as they awaited the first dinner seating.

"My," Caroline smiled at Paul, who was in black tie as well, "I swear you look more like James Bond every time I see you. What'd you do with Susan?"

"She's drying her nails." He slipped into the seat nearest the window. "I thought I'd scout ahead."

"Matter of fact, Caroline was just remarkin' on the way you size up a room. You wouldn't be one of them TV detectives, by chance, would you?"

Paul sighed aloud, smiling. "Would you believe Susan remarked about the same thing? I didn't believe her until now."

"What line are you in, Paul?" Caroline asked. "For real, I mean."

"I run a travel agency back in Connecticut." He waited as the waiter set down two more glasses and poured champagne into his from the Bass's bottle. "As for that habit I seem to have, I guess I've met so many people over the years that I'm always just a little surprised if I don't run into one of them any place there's a crowd."

"Happens to me all the time." Ray Bass agreed, throwing an I-told-you-so wink to Caroline.

Paul sipped his champagne and nodded appreciatively. "What brings you two to Europe in January?" he asked. "You don't strike me as die-hard skiers."

"Heck," Ray Bass laughed, "I don't even walk real good." He paused to refill Caroline's glass. "Seems like I've been hearin' about this train most of my life, and last month Caroline here says, Ray, ain't either us or that train gettin' any younger. Let's call up, pull our soup-'n-fish duds outta the cedar closet and let's get 'er done. Besides, we heard there's no sight in the world to take your breath away like the Alps in winter and no more comfy way to see 'em."

"Speakin' of sights to see," Caroline pointed toward the bar, "here comes Susan now. My, look at all those turnin' heads."

Susan had chosen a long, filmy black dress, almost backless, arms and shoulders bare except for two tapering strands that flowed up over her breasts and tied behind her neck. Her skin was flawless and richly tanned, her jewelry understated, her color rising with each step she took. Paul and Ray Bass rose as she approached.

"I think I may have overdone it," she said through her teeth. "Why don't I run back and get a blanket."

"Don't you dare," Paul pulled her seat back. "You're absolutely lovely."

"Honey," Caroline told her, "if I could wear that dress I'd steal it first time you turned your back."

Ray Bass chuckled. "She turns her back, it disappears all by itself." He flinched as Caroline threw an elbow.

"Sorry," he grinned. "I couldn't help that. It's a source of great pride to me that the two handsomest women on this whole train are sitting right here at my table."

As Caroline muttered something about snake-oil salesmen, Paul reached for Susan's hand, which she had shyly crossed over her breast and shoulder, and lowered it in his. "By the way, where are you two headed?" he asked, only partly to ease Susan's discomfort by getting off the subject.

"We're ticketed through to Venice," Ray Bass answered. "But we might just get off for a spell at St. Anton, rent a car, and work our way down through some of those jet-set playgrounds like St. Moritz and such."

"Then you'd be passing right through Klosters, where we're going," Susan said. "Why don't you look us up?"

"Might be a fine idea," Caroline brightened. "Ray, you take down their address and phone number just in case."

He used a business card for the purpose. Paul asked for another for himself. The Bass Pecan Company. Lumberton, Mississippi.

"Pecans," Paul nodded. "They come from hickory trees, don't they."

"They do indeed. So does the walnut, which is a kissin' cousin but ain't nearly so refined."

"Don't get Ray started on pecans," Caroline warned. "It's not a subject he's bashful on."

"Fact is, it's a real interestin' nut." Ray Bass chose

not to be denied. "If we were in some low roadhouse and the company weren't so elegant, I'd tell you about the sex life of the pecan. The little devils are hermaphroditic, you know. That means they go both ways and don't care which."

"But you're not goin' to tell, of course," Caroline jabbed him, "us being so elegant and all."

"Their botanical name," he pressed on, "is *Carya illinoensis*. That's if you want the real nutty-gritty. It's the Cree Indians called them pecans. Ate them by the treeful, and you couldn't find a healthier bunch of Indians. They were a little stupid about real estate, however."

Paul, smiling, made a time-out sign with his hands and slid his chair backward. "Of course, I don't want to miss a word of this. . . ."

"Count that day lost when you don't learn something, Paul."

"But I'd want to give it my full attention."

"Understood and you're excused. We'll mind Susan for you."

Paul stepped from the table and made his way back past the bar before anyone could tell him there was a facility much closer. He continued on to the sleeping car where he found Andrew the steward busily transforming the compartments into sleepers. He peeled a £50 note from his pocket. It caught Andrew's attention.

"Andrew," Paul spoke softly, "there's a Ray and Caroline Bass in the bar car. They're very nice but I'd like to be sure they're who they say they are." He held up the fifty. "How about a quick peek at their passports?"

Andrew glanced up and down the corridor. "I'm sure they're in order, Mr. Bannerman. They're checked at every border we cross."

"Just a glance, Andrew. I'll feel better."

Andrew beckoned Paul to a small service compartment at the end of the car. He unlocked it, then slipped a key into a padlocked wooden cabinet. The Basses, listed alphabetically, were near the top. Paul took them and studied them. They seemed legitimate enough. Issued in New Orleans. But only this past December. The only entries were a French transit visa and a Heathrow immigration stamp. That bothered Paul. He'd like to

have seen more of a travel history. On the other hand,
his own passport, being recently renewed, didn't tell
much about him, either, and Susan's was also new in
December. It could mean nothing at all. Nor had he any
reason to wonder about Ray and Caroline except they
seemed to go out of their way to make contact. But he
saw no wariness in their eyes; none of the involuntary,
searching looks that would have suggested a prior
knowledge of him. And Ray Bass certainly knew his
pecans; their sex life had probably served him well at
cocktail parties over the years.

"Everything on the up-and-up, Mr. Bannerman?"

"Everything's fine, Andrew." He handed back the
passports, forcing the £50 on him as well. "I think I've
been reading too much Agatha Christie."

Susan was right, he thought, turning back toward
the bar car. He's got to learn how to relax.

In a far corner of the smallest of Mario's three dining
areas, Molly Farrell poured coffee for Anton, Carla,
Gary Russo and herself, then wiped her hands and sat
down with them.

Carla's eyes were shining. Although Anton's expression gave nothing away, she was sure something was
happening. She'd seen John Waldo parked at the entrance onto Railroad Avenue, a bag of Grand Union
groceries at his side, which she knew concealed an Ingram machine pistol. She'd seen Janet Herzog standing
at the station door, directly across, as if waiting to be
picked up, hugging herself under a thick fur jacket that
would nicely conceal another Ingram. Then, upon en-
tering Mario's, a perfunctory nod from Billy at the bar
as he kept his attention not on her but on her back. Hot
dog, she thought to herself. Maybe it's show time.

Zivic glanced around the room, although it was otherwise empty, and leaned forward. "Have any of you
heard the name Elena?" he asked. "The connection
would be with Palmer Reid, with traffic in cocaine, or
with Susan Lesko's father."

No reply. Just shaking heads.

"What about a Mr. Brendan Donovan, also called
Buzz Donovan?"

They looked at each other. Nothing.

"Then we appear to have a mystery on our hands," he said. "Palmer Reid believes they are all somehow involved with us. He's had this Donovan killed. As a matter of policy I have asked John and Billy to retaliate."

"No offense, Anton," Gary Russo said, "but have you talked to Paul about this?"

Molly winced. "As it happens, Gary, he's *alerted* Paul. This is Anton's call."

"I said no offense. But if there's likely to be trouble, he should either get back here, or a couple of us should be over there with him."

Anton knew that Russo was right. He could only repeat what Paul had told all of them from the beginning. That he would not live his life under guard. That if trouble comes to him, so be it, and the rest of them must go on with their lives. That he is not their shepherd any more than they are sheep. Next, he repeated, for the benefit of Carla and the doctor, what he and Molly had managed to learn from a scared and sickened Doug Poole. Then he told them of the subsequent execution of Reid's man Burdick, and of the method he had chosen to protect Susan Lesko's father from immediate harm.

Carla understood at once. She liked it. "The cops and reporters will be all over that street all day, which protects Lesko. Reid, meanwhile, is thrown off balance because he thinks Glenn is not only dangerous but crazy."

"Yes, but what protects him tomorrow?" Gary Russo asked. "Do we keep on baby-sitting him?"

Anton shook his head. "His continued welfare is not our concern."

"Then why the retaliation for this Donovan? What's he to us?"

"Reid acted upon a connection he believes to exist," Anton explained patiently. "Whether it actually exists is not the point."

"But you don't even know what's going on here."

"It doesn't matter," Carla told him. "Any time Reid hits, we hit back fast and hard. You can't let that wacko hold the initiative."

"I want all our people alerted," Anton rapped the table. "They are to remain as mobile as possible during the next thirty-six hours, which I suspect are the critical ones. I am sending Billy and John Waldo back to the Scarsdale house on the chance that Reid continues to use it as a base. Molly, Janet Herzog and Glenn Cook will drive to Maryland this afternoon. Glenn will keep Reid's home under observation. Molly and Janet already have their instructions."

"Janet?" Carla's face fell. "What about me?" She knew better than to ask what the instructions were but if they were finally getting around to popping Reid, seniority ought to count for something.

Zivic understood. "No harm comes to Reid while Paul lives. That policy is unchanged. You know Klosters, do you not?"

Carla nodded expectantly. "I know that whole part of the country."

"I am authorizing the vacation you and Gary have requested. You are to travel under your own passports and without weapons, first to Zürich and then to Davos. Davos will leave you within twenty minutes of Klosters in case you are needed, but you are to stay away from Klosters otherwise."

"We might as well be decoys," Russo protested. "If Reid's people don't spot us at Kennedy, they will at Zürich."

Carla patted his hand. "I think that's the idea, sweetie."

Anton acknowledged her assessment with a quick, appreciative smile. This was a professional. She knew that they would almost certainly be spotted and that their very presence in Switzerland would cause Reid to rethink any plan he might have in effect. If they were found traveling with false documents, Reid could easily arrange to have them detained by Swiss authorities. As it was, Reid would see that their checked baggage received special attention in the hope that they had brought in weapons and would, without risk to himself, be consigned to a Swiss prison for the next two or three years. But Carla was nothing if not resourceful. She would arm herself if necessary. And Paul would have help close at hand if needed but, with luck, would never know it. Russo, with luck, would never know that he was being sent where he could do no harm.

Moves and countermoves.
Confusion to mine enemies.

Lesko's phone rang an hour after nightfall. He
snatched it up on the first ring, then waited until he
heard Loftus say his name.

"Loftus," he barked into the receiver. "Where the
hell have you been?"

"Saving your ass, for one thing. You were a prime
suspect for killing Burdick until I said I was on your tail
all night."

"Tell me where the Reid guy is and I'll give him his
own ass to worry about."

"You can't touch him. He's holed up down at Fort
Meade. When he sticks his head out again he'll be three-
deep in bodyguards."

"Robert, let me ask you a question."

"What?"

"You know who killed Burdick, don't you?"

"No."

"It wasn't you or me. You say it wasn't Bannerman
because he was on a plane and besides, he's a nice person. Who's left, Robert? Who are the other players?"

"Lesko . . . we're talking on a fucking telephone."

"Which you made clean. Besides, we're just two innocent guys trying to figure what's happening, right?
But that's hard, Robert, because you're keeping
secrets."

"Look . . . I'm trying to stay on top of this. I'll call
you when. . . ."

"Robert," Lesko growled, "answer me. Bannerman
has friends in Westport, doesn't he? And Reid doesn't
like them, either."

Loftus drew a long breath. "Yes."

"Talk to me, Robert."

Another long pause. "According to Doug Poole, you
already met a few."

"Would two of them be bartenders? One a woman?"

"They're a lot of things, Lesko."

"But we're not talking about the local Rotary Club,
are we, Robert? We're talking about an organization of
some kind and it includes shooters."

"It's not like you think." Lesko had said *organization*

like he'd say *Mafia.* "The fact is, Bannerman's friends have offered Doug Poole sanctuary. Why they did it is a long story. The offer includes me. If Poole can arrange it, you might be safer up there, too."

"Did you take the offer?"

"I told Poole to take it. Me I've got a family, remember? Anyway, I want to be able to move around."

"Yeah, well, don't get smart, Robert. A Fed who didn't like Burdick much either and who also knew how to get around that Scarsdale security system makes just as good a suspect as I did."

"Yeah . . . listen, I have to go."

"Loftus? Don't hang up. I want to know more about. . . ."

"I'll be in touch. You sit tight, damn it."

"Loftus," he shouted. "Do not fucking hang up. . . ."

Loftus broke the connection.

Loftus stood thoughtfully at the open-air phone outside a Mobil gas station on Scarsdale's Main Street. He'd considered telling Lesko that the sniper from this morning was one of Bannerman's Westport friends and therefore one of his. But then Lesko would know both too little and too much about Bannerman and was likely to go charging off to Europe like a wild man. Let him stew, he'd decided. It would make Lesko crazier when Loftus needed him crazier.

Off to one side, away from the lights and the traffic flow of the pumps, his car waited with its lights on and motor running. Another car was behind it. Doug Poole waited in the second car, his face toward Loftus, his expression pained. Loftus walked over to him.

"You better get back to Westport," Loftus told him. "Find a motel room and stay there; the closer to the middle of town, the better."

"They said you can come, too," Poole looked up at him, the agony of what he'd done showing in his eyes. "Colonel Zivic said we can even keep our weapons."

"You go," Loftus shook his head. "Anyone ever asks, I told you to maintain the surveillance there. You don't even know about Burdick."

"Mr. Loftus . . . I'm really sorry."

"Don't lose any sleep over Burdick. We don't need people like that."

"I mean about telling them. I don't know how to explain it. They were like really good friends. Even now, except for you, I feel like they're the only friends I have."

"Get going," Loftus ordered gently. "Check in with me when you're settled. Let Zivic know where you are at all times. If you get lonely, they'll probably let you hang out at Mario's."

Loftus watched him go. He watched for any sign that Poole was being followed. There was no one.

He didn't blame Poole. He wasn't even sorry Poole talked to them. Poole was young, not much hard experience, involved in his first killing. Even a good killing would have been rough on him, but Donovan's was murder, pure and simple. The result of a slap to an old man's ego as much as anything. Knowing that had torn Poole apart. Zivic had seen that. The fear. The vulnerability of just sitting there outside Zivic's shop all day. Add a dose of hero-worship, some patient questioning, a touch, maybe even a hug, from Molly Farrell. A sandwich made by Billy McHugh himself. Three of the best operatives in the world treating him as an equal. Believing him. Offering their friendship if he wanted it. Their protection because he needed it. The funny thing was, Loftus thought to himself, they'll probably keep their word. Crazy world. The good guys are the bad guys. The bad guys are the good guys. Except what the hell did all this make him?

Seventy-five yards away, in the parking lot of an all-night supermarket, the man named Gorby stripped off his earphones and disconnected the shoulder stock of a parabolic microphone. There was a large, open briefcase on the backseat at his side. A tape recorder, red eye glowing, lay inside. Gorby shut it off, then snapped the microphone parts into felt-covered spring clips and closed the lid.

"That little creep, Whitlow, was right," said the man at the wheel, half-turning. "This is bad shit."

The driver's name was Walter Burns, the other half of a team called in to dispose of Burdick's body, remove all evidence, and restore the ambassador's bathroom to its prior condition. They'd done this many times.

"It's worse than bad," Gorby muttered. "Sounds like old Bob has been working both sides right along."

"Hard to believe."

"We just heard it."

"So? What's first?"

"Loftus, but not here. He's probably headed back to the Pollard house. We'll give him a few minutes."

"Do me a favor, okay?" Walter Burns said. "No more bathrooms. It took me three hours to replace the tiles after Burdick. Not on Pollard's rugs, either."

"Why don't we just lay down some newspapers? Loftus asks what we're doing, we'll say we want to work the puzzle."

"I don't need sarcasm," Burns told him. "Just a little consideration."

"Shit," Gorby grumbled. "Come on, let's go."

"And no head shots. Not unless it's near a hose."

"What do you want from me? A *Good Housekeeping* seal? Start the fucking car.

Amid the wine-fueled gaiety of the bar–salon car after dinner, as the train hummed on toward the Swiss frontier, the inner voice that had often caused Susan to wonder about Paul became stilled.

They'd dined by themselves, having declined an invitation from the Basses to share a table. This time it was Susan who begged off. She more then enjoyed their company but this was a special night and she wanted at least this part of it to themselves. During the meal, and during the fashion parade that preceded it through each of the dining cars, Paul pointed out a countess, an arms dealer and an Italian film actress. It was not until he identified a fallen-away mullah and a Russian KGB agent in drag that she realized he was making it all up. She would have thrown a roll at him if so many people were not eyeing them as well.

"What do you think they're saying about us?" she asked him.

"The men are thinking how lucky I am and the wives are threatening to pour wine in their laps if they don't quit staring at you."

Silver-tongued devil.

But it brought a smile to her face that lasted through dinner.

Now, taking coffee and liqueurs in the bar car, a group of passengers had gathered around the baby grand singing show tunes. Somewhere in the mix, louder than the rest, Susan could hear the unmistakable baritone of Ray Bass. They picked up their liqueurs and moved closer, acknowledging smiles and greetings as they passed. The Italian pianist was standing at the bar, a Campari in his hand, smiling down on Ray Bass, who had bought him a drink as the price of taking over the keyboard.

"Hey there, Paul," Caroline Bass waved them on. "You play this thing?"

"A little," he shrugged, smiling.

"Well, slide in and take a turn. Ray here thinks if it aint foot-stompin', it ain't music."

Paul wavered but Susan pushed him forward. Ray Bass making room, Paul sat, thought for a moment, and then with his right hand picked out the first four bars of Cole Porter's "Puttin' on the Ritz."

"The very thing." Ray Bass clapped his hands and burst into song, making Paul rush to catch up. From that song he swung into a Cole Porter medley, playing tunes straight through if the passengers knew the words, stopping at sixteen bars if they didn't, giving Susan a solo of "Night and Day," which Susan sang without hesitation in a confident glee-club alto.

Susan hadn't known that Paul could play. Another new dimension. On the other hand, he hadn't known that she could sing, either. Or know that she could play a fairly decent guitar. Someday she'd surprise him with that.

Later, after a nightcap with the Basses and a British couple celebrating an anniversary, everyone said they hoped they'd meet again soon, and she and Paul retired to their cabin. Susan would have liked the magic of the train to have gone on forever, but their stop in the morning would come early. And it would still be a while, Susan hoped, before they let the train rock them to sleep.

"Susan." He turned her and held her as she began to undress. "I do love you, you know."

"Me, too." She loosened his tie.

"And I want you to trust me."

"Shush." She touched her fingers to his lips.

"I mean, I know you wonder about me sometimes."

"Paul, dearest . . ." she began on the studs of his shirt.

"But please don't wonder if I'd ever hurt you."

She leaned her cheek against his chest. "Will you shut up now?"

He'd told her, several weeks earlier, about the up-and-down motion of the train's aging springs. For two tired people, the springs were everything they could hope for.

"Head games," Billy McHugh muttered to himself as he crouched invisibly within the spread of one of Ambassador Pollard's juniper trees.

He did not like head games. Not that Anton wasn't smart. And not that Billy didn't understand about confusing the enemy, giving him other things to worry about. But shooting half his people did that, too.

Instead, now we have pretend shootings. Glenn Cook thinks that's great because it gives him a chance to show off. Carla wouldn't have pretended. She'd have popped Reid the first time he took out the garbage. Which is probably why Zivic wants her and Russo out of the country.

The only one doing anything useful was Molly. That's if she's doing what he thought she was doing.

Billy liked Anton. Except maybe for the head games. Which he knew Anton couldn't help because he was still a Russian. Basically, the Russians are good at games. The Israeli's aren't bad, either. The British are lousy because they always get too cute, probably because they're mostly fags. The only time they were good was against the Germans because the Germans always used logic and they thought everybody else did, which is why nothing they ever figured out was ever right.

Paul plays head games sometimes. But his are different and he probably doesn't even know he does it. What he does, he tells the truth and he never bluffs. Nobody ever believes him so they go and get ready for him to do something besides what he said. Which explains Reid. Reid always loses to Paul. Reid even knows it. But he thinks as soon as he starts believing Paul, Paul will pick then to start lying to him, and then Mama's Boy will have him by the balls again.

A shadow moved.

Waldo. Down by the house.

He'd never seen anybody who could move as quiet as Waldo. Janet Herzog was close. And he wasn't too bad himself. But nobody was like John.

Billy waited.

"Two men." He heard Waldo's voice before he saw him. "They got a third tied up and they're working him over."

"Could you see who?"

"I just heard. They're in the kitchen. I think they're killing him."

"What'll you bet it's that guy Loftus?"

"We're here. Let's go ask."

"Zivic says report first."

"We ask. Then we report."

Loftus knew he was dying.

The voices, the lights, were becoming distant. He couldn't tell whether he'd stopped hurting so badly or whether the hurts had all come together into one throbbing mass. His face was wrecked.

We're sorry about this, Gorby had said. If it was up to us, if we had anything with us, we'd have given you some pills to knock you out first.

That told Loftus he was dead. This wasn't punishment. This was so it would look like Bannerman did it and Reid would have another photograph to show, probably in another car trunk just over the Westport line.

Son of a bitch. His wife would have to identify him. She'd have to see what they did to his face before they pulled up the sheet. Then Reid at his funeral service. Giving a speech. His arm around Katherine. Telling the kids: Anything you need, you just call your Uncle Palmer. Son of a bitch.

Burns, the bastard, isn't sorry. All Burns cares about

is not making a mess. Use the kitchen. The kitchen floor.
Then he sits down and laces on an old pair of work
shoes. Kicking shoes. Each kick measured. Taking his
time. Nothing personal, Mr. Loftus. Don't try to duck.
It'll be over quicker.

Hallucinations now. Shadows moving. Burns starts to
throw another kick but a shadow falls across him and he
freezes. His hands go up to his throat. Like he's choking
himself. Blood squirting through his fingers, pouring
down his shirt. Loftus knew it must be all in his head
because now Burns is doing this tap-dance. This shuffle.
And his feet are kicking out again but they're going
every which way. Slipping, sliding, splashing in his own
blood. Good, you prick. You're so worried about messes,
how do you like that one?

Another shadow. Another voice. Gorby down on the
floor. A shadow on his back, too. That one's moving now.
Getting up.

"I'll ask you again." John Waldo stepped away from
Gorby's writhing body. He waited for Gorby's eyes to
focus on Walter Burns, to watch his partner finish dying.
"Why are you doing this?"

Gorby's mouth was open in a silent scream, one hand
on his knee, the other at his face. His left knee was
ruined. His nose was crushed and torn. Two quick
blows. He had barely sensed another presence in the
room when they came. Now he looked up through
wet eyes at the smallish man who had done this to him
and the other one who had sliced Walter Burns's head
halfway off. Two layers of black stocking covered and
flattened their features, but he knew they had to be
Bannerman's people. He could guess, to his horror,
which two they were.

"This . . . this isn't about you," he managed. "He's
one of ours."

"My question was why."

Waldo made a motion to Billy, who nodded, then
allowed Walter Burns to fall across Gorby. Pinning him.
Soaking him. Then Waldo found the utensil drawer. He
sorted through it until he found a corkscrew, then
leaned over and showed it to Gorby. Satisfied that
Gorby recognized it, he climbed astride Walter Burns

and pressed the utensil into Gorby's ear. Gorby
shrieked, more in terror than in pain.

"One turn," Waldo said quietly, "for every bad answer. One turn when you make me repeat myself."

"No," Gorby choked. "No, wait, I'll tell you." He
wanted to tell them. But a rush of panic seized at his
insides as he realized that the truth would earn him no
less than he had intended for Loftus. God damn Whitlow. Whitlow said it was Loftus who did Burdick. Only
Loftus could get inside here. Or tell how to do it. They
never would have come back to this house if they had
any doubt it was Loftus. The drugs, he thought desperately. Maybe they would understand about the drugs.
"Loftus . . ." he tried to point, feebly, "Loftus went
free-lance. He was dealing cocaine with this cop . . .
Lesko."

Waldo looked at Loftus, asking by way of a shrug if he
could hear, and with a nod if it were true. Loftus tried to
speak but could not. With effort, he shook his head.
Waldo turned the corkscrew. Another soundless
scream.

"Try again," Waldo rasped.

Gorby's voice, when he could speak, sounded like
escaping steam. "It's what they told me . . . them and
a woman named Elena . . . maybe Bannerman, too.
Don't hurt me for what they told me."

Billy turned to Loftus and knelt close to him. "Can
you talk at all?" he asked.

Loftus made a sick, wet sound. He shook his head
again.

"If we get you fixed up, can you straighten this out?"

Loftus nodded. Billy gestured toward Gorby. "Do
we need this guy?"

Loftus hesitated. Another shake of his head, he was
sure now, would mean that Gorby would die. A part of
him almost wished that he could argue for sparing him.
But in his mind he had seen Katherine looking down at
his body as Gorby and Burns had left it. He had seen
Palmer Reid showing snapshots of it. Along with his
fucking boat. He had seen Palmer Reid with his children.

Loftus shook his head.

Then he closed his eyes.

CHAPTER 20

Monday morning. Chevy Chase, Maryland.

As Palmer Reid's limousine paused at the electric gates leading to his sprawling Tudor house, he glared over the driver's shoulder toward the windows of his study. He'd ordered Whitlow to wait for him there.

Reid was seething. He had just endured an entire Sunday at Fort Meade, well into the night, attending an unimaginably soporific seminar on advances in cryptography, filling a notebook with phrases that meant less to him than doodles—"Digital Applications of Junction Technology," "Analog Optical Computing," and, most arcane of all, "Magnetic Bubble Memory"—for the sole and specific purpose of remaining plausibly isolated from the weekend's events in New York's Westchester County.

"Leave everything to me, sir," Whitlow had said.

Leave everything to me, sir, indeed.

That morning, he had no sooner opened his copy of *The Washington Post* over breakfast when a sealed note had arrived from Whitlow, urging him to call home at once. He did, Whitlow answered, and then Whitlow played for him two messages that had accumulated on his answering machine. There on the machine, for anyone, including household staff, to hear, was a message from one Glenn Cook promising that he would shoot the eyes out of any other Palmer Reid agent who appeared within a block of the Raymond Lesko residence. Then, not two hours later, a message from that pup, Roger Clew, saying, "You're not awfully good at returning calls, Palmer, so I'll tell you what this one's about. It's to ask what you know about the murder of Buzz Donovan last Friday in New York. It's also to tell you that if anything should happen to a man named Lesko or to any citizen currently living in Westport, Connecticut, I'm going to be all over you like a fucking rug."

Reid slammed the phone down and called for his car. It took all of the thirty-minute ride to Chevy Chase for his blood pressure to reach an acceptable level.

Roger Clew, he fumed. The gall of the man. Paul Bannerman's lackey. Now his protector. Imagine such a man rising to a position of responsibility in the State Department. Imagine him practically accusing *Palmer Reid* of complicity in a murder. Imagine him referring to Bannerman and his crowd as citizens.

Whitlow, his expression more pinched than usual, opened Reid's front door as the car pulled up. Reid strode past him without a word and walked directly to his study, where he replayed both messages, his color again rising.

"This Cook," he said, pressing the *erase* button, "He's the marksman, isn't he? One of Bannerman's killers?"

"Yes, sir." Whitlow told him about the sniper episode on Lesko's street. Whitlow had, in fact, he informed Reid, made contingency plans for Lesko's removal should Lesko become troublesome, but they had not been acted upon. "The point is that Bannerman is protecting Lesko, which can only mean that you've been right, sir. They've been in league all along."

"And now they've somehow enlisted Loftus," Reid stared.

"It would seem so, sir." There was that call from Lesko to Loftus's wife. There was Loftus showing inappropriate concern about the Donovan matter. There was Loftus a bit too anxious to provide Lesko with an alibi for the murder of Thomas Burdick. "Sir," Whitlow grasped his knees, "I'm afraid we've had some additional losses."

Reid closed his eyes. "Report, Charles," he said stiffly.

Whitlow told him of a call that had come while Reid was en route from Fort Meade. The bodies of Gorby and

Burns were discovered that morning in the kitchen of the Pollard house. Moreover, both Loftus and his young assistant appeared to have vanished. The physical evidence at the scene—specifically, broken teeth and spattered blood that did not seem to be either Burns's or Gorby's—suggested that they may have disposed of Loftus and perhaps Poole as well before being killed in retaliation. That, however, was by no means certain.

Reid's eyes remained closed. "By Bannerman's people?" he asked.

"It would seem so, sir."

"Charles . . . ?" It was a wonder, thought Reid, that he had any stomach lining left at all.

"Yes, sir."

"Leave everything to you, Charles. Is that what you said?"

"Sir, I could hardly have anticipated. . . ."

Reid raised a hand, waved it, then used it to cover his brow. Three of his men dead, he thought. Two more men, dead if he's lucky, captured or gone over to the enemy if he is not. A lunatic with a rifle threatening him on his home telephone. A State Department undersecretary doing the same. That old fool Donovan, avenged three times over, perhaps by Bannerman's people, perhaps by this Raymond Lesko who is, by all accounts, only slightly less of a berserker than Billy McHugh. Bannerman off to Switzerland, not a care in the world, very possibly to have a nice long chat with Elena.

"Charles . . ." he lowered his hand, "do you sense that we might have lost some initiative during your brief stewardship?"

"No, sir," Whitlow's chin came up. "Not entirely."

"Reassure me, Charles."

"You asked me to arrange a distraction for Bannerman. I have done so. It is a diversionary attack through a third party. If all goes well, we'll have Bannerman's people, Elena's people and Raymond Lesko all killing each other within three days."

"An attack upon whom, Charles?"

Whitlow hesitated. He had taken pains to place at least two layers of insulation between Reid and the event. "Are you certain you want to know, sir?"

"Yes, Charles," your recent success rate considered. "What sort of attack would bring that happy result?"

"Upon the girl, sir."

"The girl," Reid repeated blankly.

"Lesko's daughter. She's going to die."

On the Capitol Beltway, three miles north of Palmer Reid's house, Molly Farrell pulled into a rest stop and coasted to a small bank of pay phones. Janet Herzog, wearing a spandex jogging suit and red sneakers, dozed in the passenger seat with a towel over her face to block out the low morning sun. Molly stepped out of the car, closed the door quietly, and walked to the nearest phone.

Janet's jogging suit and sneakers, like Billy McHugh's black woolens, were her working clothes. Upon first arriving in Westport and observing the early morning stream of joggers on almost every residential street, she quickly concluded that her kit would not be complete without a jogging outfit of her own. In Westport, and possibly the whole Northeast for all she knew, a jogging suit was ideal for scouting neighborhoods while seeming to belong there. Even better, she realized, no one in the suburbs ever so much as turned around at the slow slap of jogging shoes approaching from the rear or gave a second thought to why the woman passing had a towel tied over her head. Somewhere, someday, those footsteps would be the last sounds someone heard on earth.

Molly punched out Anton Zivic's number using a credit card. At the second ring, he picked up and said his name.

"It's me," she said. "We're finished here."

"No difficulties?" he asked.

"We could have slept in his bed. He just got home an hour ago." Enough time, she thought, to have buried a bug so deep they'd have to tear down walls to find it. Even a TV camera. That would have been nice. But Anton had told her not to risk leaving any sign that his home had been penetrated.

"How is he behaving?"

"He's getting spooked." She told him about the calls from Glenn and Roger Clew that were on his machine.

Janet was still in the house when Whitlow played them and then called Reid home from Fort Meade. She left by a back door as Reid arrived at the front. She went jogging. Thirty minutes later, two cars, each bearing two of Reid's men, arrived and took up sentry positions along both approaches to his house. Janet jogged past both of them, slowing to scowl suspiciously, as any local matron should, at the sight of strange men sitting low in their cars. On her second pass she brazenly stopped to ask one driver what business he had on her street. He wearily flashed a badge, inviting her to call the police if she felt she must. Both men, she noted, wore flak jackets and were armed with nothing heavier than machine pistols.

"Glenn will keep an eye on the house?" Zivic asked.

"Yes." Molly smiled to herself. Glenn had already gone to the local humane society where he had bought a dog. Although he appreciated Janet's approach in principle, Glenn Cook hated jogging. The same result could be achieved by walking a dog, with the added pleasure of watching it urinate against the tires of surveillance vehicles. "Janet and I are heading home."

"I have a request of you. It is compassionate in nature and therefore strictly voluntary." Anton outlined the events at the Pollard house the night before. He gave her the address of a home in Arlington, Virginia. "The woman's name is Katherine. There are two children."

"How much can I tell her?"

"You have the number of the clinic?"

Reid's phony dryout hospital in Westport. "Yes."

"Call it from Arlington. Her husband will tell her."

During the winter months the Orient Express reaches Zürich an hour before dawn. It then turns southeast toward the town of Landquart, where passengers bound for Klosters and St. Moritz connect with the red cars of the Swiss Mountain Railway, while the Orient Express continues on toward Austria.

Paul had asked Andrew to bring their breakfast tray at seven. That left them an hour to dress and pack, then sit sipping coffee as the sun rose over the still-distant

Alps, bringing the color of the sky to the string of lakes
that followed the tracks for most of the journey.

At Landquart, despite Andrew's suggestion that
they wait in the warmth of their cabin until their luggage was brought from the baggage car, Susan dragged
Paul onto the platform, where she breathed deeply of
the Alpine air, grinning happily at the realization that
she was actually, finally, in Switzerland.

She searched the windows of the train, hoping to
wave good-bye to the Basses or to any of the other
passengers they'd met since leaving London. But only
three or four faces appeared. It was still early, the morning was cold, and the beds in the cabins were warm. A
few others disembarked in scattered pairs. Susan wondered aloud where they were heading. Paul told her
they would all be going to St. Moritz. She was about to
ask him how he knew that but she could see it now. The
St. Moritz passengers had twice their luggage, mostly
Gucci or Louis Vuitton. All of the women and some of
the men wore expensive furs. Two of the women had
already dressed in designer ski outfits and one wore
matching earrings. Neither, from what Susan could see,
had bothered to bring skis.

A soft gong signaled the arrival of the Klosters train.
Susan and Paul shook hands with Andrew, gave a final
wave to the Orient Express, and hauled their suitcases,
ski bags and boot bags aboard for the one-hour climb
into the Parsenn range. Through most of the ride, her
excitement fought a losing battle with the altitude, and
she struggled to keep from dozing. The snow seemed
deeper with each passing mile. A two-foot mantle of
white crowned every farmhouse and chalet. A fragile
lacing on branches and wires said that fresh snow had
fallen during the night. By the time they reached Klosters, two feet had grown to three.

Arriving there, as they passed their bags to the platform, Paul noticed a Swiss police-cruiser parked at the
station. Two uniformed officers sipped coffee from
steaming cups. Glancing around him, he saw that no
other passengers had gotten off at Klosters. He also saw,
inside the glass doors of the waiting room, a man in a
fleece-lined coat and fur hat who stood idly gazing out
onto the platform. The presence of the police, and of

the man, did not alarm Paul. He simply noticed them.
Nor were they taking any particular notice of him. Still,
he wondered. He stepped to a large yellow board cap-
tioned *Abfahrt* Klosters and looked to see how soon the
next train would be coming from either direction.
There would be none for almost an hour. Now he wondered what the man in the fur hat could be waiting for.
He glanced once more toward the policemen, then,
looking out upon the main street, began scanning to see
whether any more of the locals seemed to have time on
their hands. A white blur, a snowball thrown hard,
whizzed past his face. Susan. He turned, in a half
crouch, expecting to see her packing another one. What
he saw was Susan, hands on her hips, with a look on her
face that said *You cut that out. Right now.*

Paul, with an expression of injured innocence,
claimed that he was only considering whether to show
her around the village then or later. Their apartment
was a hundred yards in one direction; the village center,
half that distance in the other. They could take a walk
through town, put some life back into their legs, then
pick up their bags on the way back. "Good thinking,"
she said. Fast thinking, she thought. But she took his
arm and steered him toward the main street. Within
less than a minute, the village of Klosters swept the
incident from her mind.

Klosters, or at least the village center, was barely two
New York City blocks from end to end. Towering mountains seemed to rise in every direction, their lower
slopes dotted with private homes and apartments well
into the tree line. Every building, new or old, was done
in some variation of the chalet style; carved wooden
balconies on every floor, flower boxes at every shuttered
window, roofs gently pitched to hold the snow. The
guidebooks she'd read described Klosters as a quaint
Alpine village that had managed to keep its charm. That
was true enough from a distance, she supposed, but not
from up close. The place had the look of money. She
counted four banks, enough for a town ten times this
size, each with the exchange rates of all major curren-
cies posted in its window and each posting stock prices
from the various world markets. There were two jewelry stores displaying Rolex and Patek Philippe watches,

some priced at more than she'd pay for a car. And each
of the five ski-clothing shops displayed modish outfits
whose cost would dress her for an entire season.

The people, however, were different. No one on the
street seemed dressed for show. Most wore ski clothing
that looked well-used and functional. Everyone looked
fit and relaxed, and nearly everyone smiled and nodded
as they passed. If they had money it was quiet money.
Like the town itself, except for a few store windows,
there was no neon about them, nothing that shouted.
What Klosters seemed, more than anything to Susan,
was *safe.* She repeated the word to herself. Perhaps it
was the wall of mountains that made this place seem so
like a womb.

She thought of Paul. He was walking at her side.
Leaving her to her thoughts. She wondered if she would
have thought of Klosters as safe if she had come here
with anyone but him. Or if she'd never known him. Paul
did seem to like safe places. Windermere Island, for
example. Westport, for example. Even his condomin-
ium there. Guarded. Hard to reach.

Hold it, she told herself. Now *you* cut it out. Everyone here has a buck or two. And everyone here has
made his own comfortable little world someplace.
Paul's no different. Don't start.

"Beg pardon?" he put an arm across her shoulders.
She looked up at him questioningly.

"You've been talking to yourself." he said.

"Have I? I have not."

"My mistake."

"What did I say?"

"Safe. You said it three times."

She shrugged. "Doesn't it strike you that way. This
place, I mean?"

"You may not think so when you see some of the
runs."

"You know what I mean. Down here."

"I suppose. Now that you mention it."

Paul looked away. But he had to smile. They'd just
passed a jewelry store window where, a few years back,
two young backpackers, Dutch kids, decided to finance
their travels by pulling a midnight smash-and-grab at
the Rolex display, probably too stoned to remember

that almost every Swiss male was an army reservist and all of them kept NATO rifles in their hall closets. The two young men barely got fifty feet from the jewelry store before they were bracketed by automatic-weapons fire from half a dozen different balconies. Paul was sure they'd never have made it out of Klosters in any case. This was a valley town, with just one road in or out, easily sealed at either end. That's why Britain's royal family came here to ski. Security's easy. No reasonable hope of escape if you came with bad intentions. It was also why Carla Benedict moved to nearby Davos a few years back after some East Germans—whom Billy eventually discouraged—had put a hundred-thousand-dollar price on her head.

The station was just ahead, their baggage where they left it, the two policemen gone. So was the man in the waiting room. He had not followed them. Paul was sure of that. Probably just someone who stopped in to get warm. Speaking of that, he thought, the temperature felt like it was dropping. The air smelled of new snow. He stepped up to a weather station mounted on the outside wall near the glass doors. Temperature −2 Celsius. Barometer falling sharply, edging down to where it said *sturm* in Germanic script. He looked at the sky.

"More snow coming?" Susan saw the thickening clouds.

He nodded. "Maybe we'd better unpack and get a couple of runs in while we can. If it snows more than a foot or so they'll close the trails."

"Let's do it," she said. "Can we get help with these bags?"

Paul hesitated. His intention had been that they'd carry the luggage themselves, all but the ski bags for which he'd have to make a second trip. That would give him a few minutes alone to call Anton for an update.

A better idea, he thought. Don't call. Don't interfere. Don't second-guess. You're on vacation. Don't. . . .

"Don't what?" Susan asked.

"Beg pardon?"

"You're talking to yourself."

"No, I'm not."

"My mistake."

He pinched some snow off the top of a parking meter and flicked it at her.

"Come on." She took his arm and steered him to the luggage. "Let's go skiing."

Palmer Reid's morning had not improved.

The single bright spot thus far was his own deniability of any foreknowledge of Whitlow's Byzantine plan for the mutual destruction of the Bannerman/Lesko/Elena axis. The agent of the plan would be a particularly repulsive Bolivian named Ortirez. Ortirez would make all arrangements. Even Whitlow did not know the specifics. He, Palmer Reid, would be at least four layers removed from any reasonable suspicion of involvement in the events Whitlow had set in motion.

Reasonable suspicion. There was the rub. Bannerman, for all his cold-bloodedness, could not be expected to behave reasonably upon being presented with the corpse of the Lesko girl. No amount of insulation, be it four layers or fifty, would keep him from suspecting that Palmer Reid, for all his innocence . . . genuine innocence . . . was somehow behind it. He would not look long for proof.

But Whitlow, manipulative little weasel that he is, had thought of that as well. "What, sir," he asked, "would an innocent man do in your position? Would he not be legitimately concerned that Bannerman might suspect his hand in it? Would he not, therefore, contact Bannerman immediately upon hearing of the girl's death, express that concern, express utter outrage, and insist, your past differences notwithstanding, upon helping him to track down those responsible?"

"Bannerman's not stupid, Charles," Reid said thoughtfully. "An innocent man might do that. So might a guilty one."

"Yes, but he'll have other things to think about. It will be quite clear, sir, from the manner of her death that the girl died for her father's sins. Lesko and Bannerman will blame each other, both will blame Elena, Elena will blame Ortirez. You, sir, need only sit back and enjoy the carnage until, at last, you put

Bannerman firmly in your debt by presenting him with the body of General Ortirez."

Or yours, Charles. Or yours.

Within two hours of that conversation, however, the inner glow Palmer Reid was beginning to feel—Paul Bannerman's comeuppance finally at hand—was rudely extinguished by a summons to an immediate conference at the office of Barton Fuller, the second most powerful man in Washington, and fourth in line for the presidency of the United States.

"Good morning, Mr. Reid." The Secretary's executive assistant looked up from her desk but did not smile. "Mr. Fuller will see you at once."

Whitlow moved toward the door with him.

"Mr. Fuller asks to see you alone, sir."

Whitlow hesitated, one eyebrow raised as if in protest, his hands balled into little fists at the end of arms that never seemed to bend or swing even when he walked quickly. The Secretary's assistant's young son had electric toys that reminded her of Charles Whitlow.

"I won't be long, Charles." Reid indicated a seat. Whitlow waited until Reid stepped through the door before he took it. Once there, he reached into his shirt pocket and fingered a pack of cigarettes but did not take one. The assistant knew that Whitlow never smoked. She also knew that the cigarette pack almost certainly contained a recording device and that Whitlow was switching it off.

Palmer Reid closed the door behind him and waited for Barton Fuller to rise. He did not. Fuller made a final note on a paper he was reading and slid it into a file.

"I have very little time," Reid said coldly.

"Then we'll move right along, Palmer." Fuller stood now, revealing his exceptional height. He stepped around his desk and approached to within a foot of Palmer Reid's chest. "Palmer," he asked, looking down into the smaller man's eyes, "could you be up to anything that might, just possibly, cause embarrassment to the president?"

Reid could feel his breath. God, how he detested this man. Nothing in Fuller's background, in Reid's view, qualified him for the position of Secretary of State. Attended Kansas State University, of all places, on a basketball scholarship. Traded upon a gold medal, won at the 1960 Rome Olympics, to gain entrance into Harvard Law School. Made the Law Review, went into investment banking, took time off to manage two of the president's campaigns for lesser office, ultimately left Wall Street to head the Agency for International Development, finally worming his way into this job. All from a stupid game that no gentleman ever played. "You have, I hope, a specific question?" Reid asked. The gall of the man.

"Sure." Fuller smiled pleasantly. "Why is Buzz Donovan dead? Is that specific enough for you?"

Reid sucked air through his teeth. "How dare you talk to me like . . ."

But Fuller turned away from him. He walked to his desk where he pressed a button. "What say we skip the bullshit, Palmer?" The smile was gone. "One day Donovan's calling all over Washington asking questions about you and Paul Bannerman. The next day you clear your calendar and fly to New York. That same man, meanwhile, has disappeared. The following day, he's found dead of a heart attack that the New York City Police Department is now calling murder."

A side door opened before Reid could speak. Roger Clew stepped into the room. He offered no greeting.

"You two know each other," Fuller said. "Roger seems to think you've been doing bad things, Palmer."

The sarcasm was too much. "You will change your tone," Reid said icily, "or I will leave at once."

"Do what you want. But you walk out of here and I call the Attorney General. I'll have the FBI offering all assistance to the NYPD within the hour. I will also have them looking into the apparent disappearance of one of your men." He turned to Roger Clew. "What's his name?"

"Burdick."

"And Burdick is one of your special nasties, isn't he Palmer? What am I to conclude from his disappearance right on top of Buzz Donovan's death? What am I to conclude from the fact that you spent most of the weekend holed up in Fort Meade?"

"I will account for my actions, as always," Reid

hissed, "to appropriate and competent authority in the proper circumstances."

"That authority, Palmer, is the National Security Council, of which I, need I remind you, am the ranking Cabinet member."

Reid looked at the ceiling.

"Let me ask you another question." Fuller sat on the edge of his desk. "If I had time, I'd work on a more polite way to phrase this. But do you imagine that I'm the only person in this administration who knows what a dangerous old fool you really are?"

Reid's eye developed a violent tic. His lips tried to move but he was momentarily struck dumb by the appalling gracelessness of this prairie bumpkin, this party hack. And to be so insulted in the presence of Bannerman's. . . .

"Why is this man here?" he asked hoarsely.

"For the purpose of checks and balances, Palmer. You've heard of the concept. I'm going to ask you some questions. You will lie to me. He will tell me the truth."

Reid stared at Fuller and then at Roger Clew with undisguised loathing. He knew perfectly well the under secretary's role and why he was there. It was Clew, he'd long known, who'd caused Bannerman's passport to be reinstated over his own violent objections. It was Clew who engineered that the State Department take a policy of expressed disinterest in Colonel Anton Zivic, even ignoring the fact that he was, at the very least, an illegal alien. It was surely Clew who'd told Bannerman about Westport three years ago and was therefore just as much a traitor to his country.

"You dare," he curled his lip, "the two of you, to call yourselves Americans."

"Oh, Christ, Reid." Fuller was smiling again, sadly.

"When one realizes that the United States Senate," his voice had found its strength, "has confirmed a man who would condone and protect the most heinous of criminal acts. . . ."

"Ah," Fuller clapped his hands. "We're ready to talk criminal acts. Tell me about them, Palmer."

"Treason," Reid sputtered. "Murder. Theft of government property. Arson."

"Arson?" Fuller turned questioningly to Roger Clew.

"I suspect he's talking about his yacht. There's been talk that Bannerman may have taken some retaliatory action a couple of years ago."

"Retaliation," Fuller repeated. "But against what? Certainly not against any action Mr. Reid here might have taken on United States soil because Mr. Reid, as we all know, is specifically constrained by law against any domestic activity."

"There may have been a lapse or two in that regard."

"I see." Fuller stepped close to Reid again. He fingered the smaller man's lapels. "I know you're busy, Palmer, so we'll cut this short. It seems clear to me that the way to avoid having your boats burned in the future is to leave Paul Bannerman the hell alone. Do that, Palmer, and whatever else might be happening right now might just possibly die down without anyone getting indicted. Is that clear or shall I express it another way?"

"You, sir," Reid tried to brush his hand away, "would do well to reread your oath of office."

"Okay," Fuller said wearily, "how about this?" He took a firmer hold on both lapels as he considered whether to lift Reid to eye level. "Go near Westport again, go near Bannerman again, interfere with him in any way, and I will personally have your ass."

"A bad meeting, sir?" In the backseat of Reid's limousine, Whitlow switched on an harmonic device that thwarted most forms of electronic eavesdropping.

Palmer Reid had the look of a man who'd been slapped. Eyes closed, he waggled his fingers as if to say; *Let me get my thoughts together.*

"That man's a pig," he said finally.

"Yes, sir."

"I'll want to see a file on him, Charles. I'll want it today."

"I've seen it, sir. I'm afraid you won't find much that's useful. Fuller's personal history has been very closely examined."

"A nigger sport," Reid muttered.

"Sir?"

"Basketball. It's a nigger sport."

"Yes, sir."

"Suits him. He was probably a drug user just like the rest of them."

"Um . . . I'm afraid there's no indication of that in his file, sir."

"What is his relationship with Bannerman?"

"None at all, sir. There's no indication that they've even met."

"What is Fuller's interest in him then? Why would he protect him?"

"I'm sure I don't know, sir. Unless. . . ."

"Unless what?"

"One protects those who are useful, sir."

Reid stared at his shoes. "Of course," he whispered. "Of course."

"But how would he use Bannerman, sir? More to the point, would Bannerman permit himself to be used?"

"Think, Charles. What do assassins do?"

"They assassinate, sir."

"And what do trained operatives do?"

Whitlow's lips moved to say *operate* but he didn't say it. It would have risked a scowl. "Sir, I really don't imagine that Barton Fuller is putting together his own death squad. But an occasional exchange of favors might not be out of the question."

Reid nodded slowly, still staring at nothing. "Charles, until I get to the bottom of this I want all operations against Paul Bannerman put on hold."

"That may be difficult, sir. I'm not sure if we can recall. . . ."

"Do it, Charles."

"Sir," he said firmly . . . must he explain again about the layers? "You must understand this. All I've done is provide Ortirez with the girl's itinerary, suggested that punishment of the father is overdue, and that Elena's wishes with regard to the daughter are no longer of concern to us. We are not involved in any arrangements Ortirez might choose to make although I did suggest a method that is classically Bolivian. When they take the girl they will. . . ."

Reid raised a staying hand. He could do without an

image of that young girl nailed to a door or whatever other gesture might be in favor with those animals these days. The shine of anticipation on Whitlow's Himmler-esque little face was sufficiently graphic. But Whitlow, Reid supposed, had done well. The girl's death will be seen as a case of Lesko's chickens coming home to roost. Lesko, in a killing rage if all goes well, will look first to Elena and then to Bannerman, who led Susan into harm's way and then failed to protect her. Whitlow is right. They'll all be feeding upon themselves within a matter of days. Pity he hadn't thought of a way to leave a trail leading back to the State Department.

He touched his fingers to his lapels. Wrinkled. He could never wear this suit again. Ever.

"He put his hands on me, you know," he said distantly.

"Sir?"

"That man, Fuller. He put his hands on me."

"For heaven's sake."

"Can you imagine such a thing?"

"A basketball player, sir." That would seem to explain it.

"Has it occurred to you, Charles, that he might be protecting Bannerman because he fears him?"

"Um . . . as opposed to using him, sir?"

"He fears him, Charles. And he hates him. Given a chance, he would probably punish Bannerman any way he could."

"Sir. . . ."

"Well done, Charles. Very well done, indeed." Perhaps, he thought, his heart quickening again, there could be a way to lay that trail after all.

CHAPTER 21

In the solarium of her Zürichberg villa, Elena stared at her still-unfinished painting of the distant mountain-scape. Two days ago she was pleased with it. Now she was not. It had lost its . . . serenity. Each stroke of the palette knife she'd added since her call to Raymond Lesko seemed somehow more severe, more jagged. Even putting Brahms on the record player had not helped.

The telephone rang. She glanced at her watch. Lesko's daughter, she assumed, must have arrived safely in Klosters. She wiped her hands and picked up the receiver.

"Elena?"

"Yes, Uncle Urs." She listened to the familiar grunting sounds that said he was settling into his wheelchair for a conversation of some length. A fall while rock-climbing had fractured his spine some twenty years before. He was head of the family then and even more so since. There were those, not least Urs Brugg himself, who considered his fall a mixed blessing. The Brugg family's holdings had more than quadrupled during the two decades in which they had received his full attention.

"Josef has called from Klosters," he told her. "The Lesko girl and this Bannerman have arrived. Josef pointed them out to two of our friends with the police of that canton. They will watch out for the girl as best they can. Josef has taken a room from which he can see both the station and their apartment."

Elena frowned. "So much trouble, Uncle Urs? I asked Josef only to. . . ."

"This man, Bannerman," he interrupted her. "You asked me to make inquiries. You say you know nothing of him?"

"Only what the girl's father said. That this man is his daughter's friend and Palmer Reid's enemy. What have you learned?"

"Would it surprise you that this young man, also known to me as Mama's Boy, has for more than ten years directed an elite mercenary group that was employed by various European governments as well as by American counterintelligence?"

Elena was stunned. "You know him?"

"Only by reputation. I've heard stories of Mama's Boy over the years but I never knew his true name until today. My information is that his entire group scattered three years ago and then reassembled in a community near New York where they are said to live in peace. Make of that what you will."

"You say he worked for the Americans." Elena was becoming alarmed, "That means he worked for Palmer Reid."

"He did, but only in a broad, organizational sense. When I asked whether Bannerman might now be allied with Palmer Reid, the question was met with laughter. Lesko was right. They are clearly enemies."

Elena remained troubled. "You have confidence in your sources, Uncle Urs?"

"One is German Intelligence, one is Interpol, the third is KGB. All say the same. All say that Bannerman is a man to be feared, and yet they speak of him with respect."

"What of the Lesko girl? How is it that she is involved with such a man?"

Urs Brugg let out a breath, the equivalent of a shrug. "She cannot be involved in Bannerman's past because she is so young. But it's difficult to imagine that she knows nothing about it. Is she a stupid girl, Elena?"

"Lesko's daughter? I would not think so."

"All these names." Urs Brugg sounded puzzled. "Raymond Lesko, Susan Lesko, Elena Brugg, Palmer Reid, and now this Mama's Boy, Paul Bannerman. They float in the air bumping against each other. It seems that they should connect and yet I am assured that they do not."

They connect, thought Elena. It is only a question of how. It would be reckless to believe otherwise. But it would be equally reckless to act upon so little information.

"Elena?"

"Yes, Uncle Urs."

"You will tell me someday why this girl is our concern?"

"Someday, yes." When I understand it myself.

"This Lesko must be a man of great charm. He is handsome as well?"

"He is . . . a man."

"Aha. Not so handsome. Then he is a romantic?"

"Good-bye, Uncle Urs."

"Of course it is none of my business but . . ."

"Uncle Urs. . . ." She cleared her throat. "Thank you."

"Good-bye, Elena."

For a long moment, Elena's fingers stayed on the receiver as she thought about Lesko and the wisdom of dialing his number. She should tell him, perhaps, what Uncle Urs had learned about the man who was with his daughter. Or she could tell him simply that his daughter had arrived and was well. But the first would only alarm him, possibly to no purpose. As for the second, a simple report, what would she say next? What more could they say to each other? An exchange of banalities at best.

Perhaps, someday, she would write him a letter.

Perhaps he would answer.

Susan had just finished unpacking, hanging out wrinkled clothing, and was about to take a quick, hot shower before dressing for the mountain, there having been no shower aboard the overnight train, when the phone rang. She picked it up and heard her father's voice.

"Hi, daddy," she said brightly. Then, suddenly conscious that her breasts were exposed by the traveling robe she'd thrown on loosely, she covered herself. It was silly, she realized, but she closed the robe anyway.

"Hey, sweetheart. You got there okay?" His voice echoed through the cable.

"We got in two hours ago. Daddy, it was wonderful."

She listened as he assured her that he had no particular reason for calling, just to see ". . . you're okay, didn't lose your luggage or anything like that. . . ." A long pause. "How's it going with your friend?"

"His name is Paul, daddy."

"Yeah, right. Paul."

"I'd let you say hello but he's down stowing our skis and checking in with the lady who manages the building. The fact is, I'm sorry you missed him."

"He, um, still reminds you of me?"

Susan thought she heard a certain pregnancy behind the question but she chose to skip past it. "More than ever. Listen. While I'm over here, you get out and see people, okay? And I don't mean just boozing every other night with Mr. Donovan. If I ever get a few dollars together I'm going to take you on the Orient Express and introduce you to a countess."

"I could picture it. I'd hold out my pinkie drinking tea and I'd probably poke her in the eye."

"Come on, daddy," she scolded mildly. "I told you not to talk about yourself that way."

"Yeah, well, you just take care of yourself, all right? Ski slow."

"We're going up as soon as I change. They're forecasting heavy snow tonight and tomorrow so we're getting in a few runs today."

"Make sure you dress for it. Don't catch a cold."

"Love you, daddy. I'll send lots of postcards."

"Good-bye, sweetheart."

The phone rang again as she turned on the shower. A Mr. Zivic calling from Westport. She covered herself again. Nice-sounding man, very apologetic, spoke with an accent. Very reluctant to disturb either of them but he was unable to find some airline tickets Paul was to have left for him. No problem, said Susan. He has your number?

She stepped into the bathtub, smiling over her father's call. Ski slow. Don't catch cold. He was sounding more and more like Uncle David these days. It would be early morning back there. A little after four. The time when daddy's gremlins came. That might explain it. Maybe Uncle David had dropped in on him again. She paused thoughtfully in the midst of lathering herself as it suddenly occurred to her that the other call had been made at around four in the morning as well. Her father she could understand. But a routine call about some airline tickets?

Anton Zivic, Paul told her, was an antique dealer in Westport. A nice man, a valued client, but a chronic worrier. Sorry about getting a business call, he said, not twenty minutes after walking in the door. He hoped it would be the last.

But, though Paul tried not to show it, the intrusion had noticeably soured his mood. During their walk to the gondola, skis slung over their shoulders, she did her best to pull him back up, to make his eyes, not just his mouth, go soft again. In the end, more than any playfulness or cajoling, it was her undisguised delight in virtually everything she saw that made the difference.

Most breathtaking of all was the ride to the summit. The gondola was a two-stage lift that began just yards from the train station and ended less than ten minutes later five thousand feet above the village of Klosters. To the north she could see the low black clouds of the promised snow advancing rapidly behind darting strips of cirrus. In all other directions she could see nothing but wild, snow-covered mountains marching toward horizons nearly sixty miles away. Looking down, she strained to pick out their chalet in a village now shrunk to postcard size. She gasped and pointed as she suddenly noticed a hang glider soaring two thousand feet below them, riding the wind like a giant red seagull. Roads and the single-track railway had become thin black lines as if painted on with eyeliner.

"How are your legs?" Paul asked as the gondola docked. He was gazing toward a still higher peak in the direction of Davos.

"A touch knock-kneed," she looked up at him eagerly. "but I always thought if I wrapped them around one guy often enough. . . ."

A woman standing near them made a choking sound, then turned and translated for her companion, who laughed aloud. Paul's color rose. He made a gesture meant to deny that he and Susan were together. But a grin split his face and remained until they followed the crowd onto the snowfield and prepared to step into their skis.

"One sport at a time, okay?" he said, still with a trace of the blush that she enjoyed having caused. He spread his arms, one pointing toward the higher peak, the other in the opposite direction far up the valley floor. "From there to there," he said, "you're looking at the longest single piste in the Alps. It's about eight miles, all the way to Kublis. Think you can handle it?"

"Ah . . . for our first run?"

"I guess you're right." He looked to the north. "If you have trouble keeping up, we might be in heavy snow by the time we're halfway down."

"Me being just a girl and all."

"I didn't mean. . . ."

"Lead the way, hotshot."

He hesitated. She pushed off ahead of him.

She realized within ten minutes that no trail map, no aerial photograph, could have prepared her for the scope of these mountains. Far above the tree line, a network of T-bars took them across vast snowfields to the distant peak Paul had pointed out to her. They paused at the highest point for a final tightening of their boots. The entire world seemed below them. The valleys and towns were no longer in sight. The clouds were getting closer. Paul looked to the north, his expression now doubtful. "Maybe that long run isn't such a hot idea," he said. "There won't be many people on it."

"That way?" She pointed with her pole to a steep mogul run. Her pulse was already racing.

"That way," he sighed. "After you."

Almost at once, she began to regret her rashness. The first mogul run had the tops of her thighs burning. A snowfield with a gentler pitch gave some relief, but ahead she could see a series of long, fast chutes where other skiers tucked low for added speed. One, a woman, lost her nerve or her balance. She fell backward. Her momentum carried her onward, sprawling, bouncing, sliding for what must have been two hundred yards. She stopped at last, not badly hurt, but with her skis and poles scattered far behind her.

"We can bypass the chutes," Paul told her. He gestured toward a blue trail that wound to their right.

"This way's fine." She chewed her lip.

"We have plenty of time. Don't push yourself if you don't feel ready."

"Let's go."

Hitting the chute, she sucked in a breath and held it. Tuck low, lower, she told herself. Skis apart, elbows in. Legs supple, take the shocks, lean into it. Oh my God. She was doing it. She saw Paul now, wearing the parka she had picked out for him a hundred years ago, his weight giving him more speed, passing her. He was slowing now at the top of the chute, braking, waiting for her. She dug in her edges, spraying snow up to his waist.

"Nice going," he was grinning broadly, pleased with her. "You ever skied that fast before?"

"I hardly even drive that fast," she gasped.

"That's just about true. Want to know how fast you were going?"

"There's still another chute?"

"Two more."

"Better tell me later."

The others were easier. Just as fast, but her confidence was building. Then, a much more gentle stretch over winding trails that must have been three miles long. Beautiful. Wonderful. Her legs were screaming now but they'd reached the tree line. Must be halfway down at least.

Paul led the way most of the time but he wasn't pressing. He'd pause, stop and wait at a turn in the trail, then Susan would bring her skis together and boom on past him. She knew she was being foolish. She'd pay for it tomorrow. But she was not about to be the first to ease off.

They'd entered the low clouds and the first flakes of snow. Paul was calling from behind, asking her to wait. He pointed down through the trees at what seemed to be a restaurant. A dozen skiers were sitting on its deck. Paul stopped at her side, breathing hard, looking exhausted. She had a sense that he was acting.

"How about taking a break," he said. "I can't keep up this pace."

He was barely perspiring while she was soaked

through. She realized that he was being gallant. "If you like," was what she said. Bless you, was what she thought.

The restaurant, called a schwendi, was unlike any Susan had even seen, in that it was not near any lift. It could only be reached by skiers taking this trail or by hikers during the summer. Just ahead, a small knot of skiers paused on a bluff overlooking the schwendi as if preparing for their final approach. The faces on the deck below all seemed to be turned up toward them.

"Watch." He touched her arm and gestured toward the other skiers. "You'll see why they stop here first. It's the only place on the mountain where they're skiing in front of an audience."

What it was, he explained, was a sort of ritual. The skiers, most of them as tired as Susan, had been struggling down the mountain. With the schwendi in sight, and with all those eyes upon them, almost all would brace themselves for an approach in perfect form. It's the only time all day, Paul told her, that most of them try to parallel ski. For those already down and sipping a beer or hot wine, it provided an informal entertainment.

She watched them go. Some did well. Others crossed their skis and tumbled, their humiliation almost palpable. Susan didn't laugh; she could feel her own body stiffening and her confidence draining. She took a breath and pushed off.

Within seconds, Susan had cause to hate Paul for his lesson in human nature. She hadn't fallen since they started. She fell twice in full view of the schwendi's deck. Her second fall drew applause.

"Paul, darling," she smiled her father's smile as they stepped out of their skis at the restaurant's entrance, "I'm going to get you for that if it's the last thing I ever do."

She felt better after a bowl of goulash washed down with a beer. Susan, not herself exempt from the laws of human nature, joined the applause for some of the more spectacular tumbles of the skiers that followed, until the thickening snow obscured all but the nearest skiers, and Paul suggested that they'd better move on.

The orange trail markers were by now barely visible.

They were skiing almost blindly and yet, if Paul hadn't been pressing before, he was pressing now. When at last they reached a clearing in the pines and could see the town of Kublis taking shape, she was immensely relieved but no less exhilarated. In another ten minutes they had reached the Kublis train station. It was all she could do not to lie down on the platform.

"Hang in there," Paul told her, checking the train schedule, "we'll be home in half an hour."

"Tell me again about your advanced age," she said darkly. "Tell me again how hard it is to keep up with me."

"Tree skiing is dangerous," he said innocently. "I like to get it over with."

Her expression went blank. "That certainly makes sense."

He looked away. "I know we pushed too hard. But we might not get another chance for a few days. Tomorrow you can get a massage at one of the health clubs. You'll be good as new."

His eyes were becoming distant again. "Paul?" she asked. "What's on your mind? It's still that phone call you got, isn't it?"

He shook his head.

"What, then?"

"You."

"What about me?"

"You were terrific back there."

She studied him curiously. There was something else behind those eyes. Coming down the mountain he was skiing as if . . . she wasn't sure what. At the start he seemed to be testing her. Then he'd changed his mind. Eased up. But on that last run he was attacking that mountain with all he had, taking foolish chances, plunging through those trees like a frightened deer. She wanted to ask him about that. It seemed so unlike him. But all she said was, "Thank you."

She was asleep, on their living-room couch, not ten minutes after squeezing off her boots and leaving them where they tumbled. She'd needed both hands to lift her legs to the cushions. A glass of wine remained untouched at her side. Paul fetched the bedroom quilt and gently draped it over the woman he had deliberately exhausted. He needed time to be alone with his thoughts and the deep, gnawing anger that he'd fought all day to control.

He'd lied, of course, about the effect of Anton's call. What bothered him most about it was not the news of Palmer Reid's people, the Scarsdale killings, the grant of sanctuary to two of Reid's agents. It was not even, though he hated to think of it, that Anton had gone against his wishes and dispatched Carla Benedict and Gary Russo to Davos. He knew he would have done the same in Anton's place. It was the insanity of it all that he despised. People were dying because of a plot that did not exist—between himself, Susan's father, whom he'd never met, and some woman in Zürich whom he hadn't even known existed before this morning.

Palmer Reid.

In Paul's dark mood he almost wished he'd listened to the others and let them finish Reid at the outset. They'd all urged it except Anton. Most of them volunteered. Even Molly. But Paul knew, as Anton knew, that Reid would soon have been replaced by someone very much like him. Perhaps by someone younger, more clever, more stable, whose powerful friends had not all died or had not yet been betrayed. Better the devil you know.

And in Paul's heart, though he never spoke of it to anyone but Anton, he could not help feeling a certain sympathy for Reid. There had been a time when Reid and others like him probably served their country well. During the war years. Then the Cold War years. But, like Hoover, he'd stayed too long. Too many moves and countermoves. Too many lies. A conspiratorial mentality taking permanent hold. Then, inevitably, a growing contempt for any elected official who embraced a world view other than his own. They'd tried to get rid of him, retire him, and in doing so they marked themselves as dangerously naïve at best, or communist tools at worst. Like Hoover, Reid began to gather files on them. As with Hoover, his files, real or imagined, kept him in service long after his time had passed. Like Hoover, the actions of his later years blotted out all else that might

have been admired. But sympathy, like love, has its
limits.

Susan.

What to do about Susan?

He was so proud of her today. Staying with him. Not
complaining. Even during that last stretch through the
trees when he himself had almost panicked. When an
hour of brooding over Anton's call left him wondering
whether Reid might actually make an attempt against
him here. When his mind ruled out all the ways in
which it might be done except for on a narrow, lonely
ski trail during a snowstorm where he and anyone with
him could be quietly and quickly killed and their bodies
pulled off the trail, and many days might pass before
they were found.

It was not a reasonable fear. He knew that. If he'd
been alone it would have been a fleeting thought at
most. Nor would he have stuck to marked trails. But he
was with Susan. So he'd raced on, straining to keep no
less than twenty yards between them in open stretches
and shielding her body with his own in places of possible
ambush. But Susan didn't know the game. She thought
she was being tested. She would stay with him if it killed
her. And that was the problem, he thought sadly.
Sooner or later, it very well might.

At Windermere, and again on the train from London, he'd almost managed to make himself believe that
a future with Susan was possible. Even a future measured in months. But each time, something had happened to slap him back into reality. At Windermere, it
was Reid's visit. Here it was Anton's phone call.

There would be other women. But from now on he'd
pick them more carefully. They'd be closer to his own
age. Women who've been around the track a few times.
Less trusting. Less vulnerable. Easier to let go when
they began to ask questions. Or will he and Molly Farrell, God bless her, look at each other one day and say:
We might as well face it. You and me. Like it or not.
We're all we're going to get.

Apologies to Molly, the thought made him sick.

"Ask me," yawned Caroline Bass, "those two have
called it a day."

She passed the binoculars to her husband who slouched behind the wheel of the black Saab sedan. They'd rented it at Zürich that morning after slipping off the train. A blue plastic ski pod, empty, was mounted on its roof.

"Which shows they got more sense than us," he sighed. Ray Bass raised the glasses and focused them, through Caroline's side window, upon the outline of Paul Bannerman. The better part of an hour had passed since they watched him gently drape a quilt over Susan. Now Paul was outside, on his second-floor terrace, sometimes pacing, mostly sitting, oblivious to the snow-flakes swirling around him, staring into the night. "Old Paul looks like he has a thing or two on his mind."

Caroline nodded. "I still have a funny feeling about him. Just can't put my finger on it."

"Well," Ray Bass shrugged, "as far as I can tell, he's exactly what he says he is." He'd placed a call to Westport, mostly to satisfy Caroline, getting the number of Paul's travel agency and asking to talk to the head man. The lady who answered was real talkative, real friendly. If Mr. Paul Bannerman and his travel agency were anything but the genuine article, no question it was news to her. "Anyhow, look at him." Ray gestured toward the terrace, "sittin' up there all wide open and back-lit like he is. Where are those 'careful moves' of yours now?"

"No harm in wonderin', sweetheart."

"About all he's got on his mind is how much it's going to snow and whether to wake her up and go to supper. See the way he keeps peekin' in at her? Be nice if he'd decide to go eat by himself. We could be done here and back up to Zürich before midnight." Ray Bass was silent for a moment, then he chuckled. "Might have been a real feather in our caps if we did her on that fancy train. Wasn't much chance, I realize, but it sure would have been fun to brag on doin' a real-life murder on the Orient Express."

"It might *be* new but it wouldn't *sound* new, darlin'. You want to brag on somethin'," she chuckled with him, "figure a way to do grand theft—auto on the Orient Express. Now that would be a whole new wrinkle."

Ray made a face. "I'm not sure people would line up

to hear about that one. Might as well do insider trading
on the Orient Express." He clapped his hands gleefully,
"Or how 'bout *Revenge of the Nerds* on the Orient Express? Wouldn't that be a stitch?"

"Steady, sweetheart." She patted his thigh. "Let's
think about how we're goin' to get the girl alone real
soon. A town this little, one of them's like to spot us
sooner or later."

"That happens, we just whoop and holler and act
like we been lookin' all over for 'em. Say we lost the
paper with their address but came down anyhow. Then,
if we can't get 'em separate, we'll just have to get 'em
together."

"Paul's not on the list, sweetie. Ain't no bonus money
in him."

"Well, don't you worry." Ray Bass took her hand.
"Tomorrow, next day for sure. Susan's going to go off to
get her hair done, or to shop, or to go to the food store.
We'll have her stretched out in that ski pod before she
knows it."

"Speakin' of food . . ." Caroline held her wristwatch up to a streetlight.

"Soon as Paul goes back inside, darlin'." He used his
free hand to wipe the glass. "It wouldn't do to have him
wonderin' why this car backs out without anyone
walkin' up and gettin' in it."

"I want a piece of fish, breaded and fried. Don't take
me any more places where it comes all white and they
make little vegetable doodles all over your dish."

"We'll drive over to Davos. We ought to know the lay
of it anyhow in case we want to leave through the back
door."

"That's if we don't get snowed in first." She turned
her head toward the terrace. "Go on, Paul. Go take a
pee like a nice fella."

"And there he goes," Ray Bass grinned. "Shows what
positive thinkin' will do, darlin'."

They watched as he stepped through the sliding
door, paused to look down at the girl, then walked the
length of his living room and was lost from view. Ray
Bass counted to ten, then started his engine.

* * *

Bannerman had seen the car. His eye, like his wandering mind, had passed over it several times but always, as if of its own accord, it found its way back. It was the window. The one on the front passenger side. The windows of all the other cars facing in the same direction were snow-covered. That one had no snow on its bottom half, as if the window had been partially lowered to clear it. And the bottom half was steamed. From the inside.

There were no recent tracks leading to it. No footprints. The tire marks were at least an hour old. And there . . . a hand wiping a circle in the condensation.

If he were anyone else, if he were normal, he realized, he would probably think nothing of it. Someone waiting for a train. A couple of young lovers. They'd shut off the engine, perhaps, because they were low on gas. Or because they were warming each other.

But he wasn't like everyone else. So here he sat, seeing shadows in the woods again. Wondering whether any of a thousand people who might wish him harm could be sitting in that black Saab with the blue ski pod on top. And here he sat, refusing to let that car make him go inside, yet ready to dive to the terrace floor if whoever was in it should roll down that window.

Another thought struck him. This one made him angry. What if the hand that wiped that window belonged to Carla Benedict or Gary Russo. Taking it upon themselves to check up on him, ignoring Anton's instructions to stay out of Klosters. Hard to imagine Carla being so obvious, and parking head-in like that, but Gary might.

Damn, he sighed.

To hell with this. If you want to know who's in that car, go look. See what they do when they see you walking toward them. And if it's Carla or Gary, by God, make them wish they'd never. . . .

Abruptly, he stood up. He stepped from the terrace and through his living room, pausing once to be sure Susan was asleep and again at his kitchen where he plucked a carving knife off its magnetic wall strip.

By the time he reached the street, the Saab was disappearing into the lights of Kloster's shopping district.

Bannerman stood in the falling snow, the knife held hidden against his thigh. He felt foolish. A fat lot of good the knife would have been if he'd indeed had anything to fear from whoever was in that car. And if they turned out to be Carla and Gary, how tough could he really have been on people who wanted nothing more than to keep him safe and well? He walked on, following the Saab's tracks to no purpose. He reached the train station, then stood for a long moment staring at the public telephone mounted on the wall. He walked over to it and began to dial the number of Anton Zivic's shop. He broke the connection. Then he began again.

"No, everything's okay," he said upon hearing the concern in Anton's voice. "I'm just having a little trouble unwinding."

"Who could blame you?" Anton sympathized. "However, things on this end seem to be quieting down nicely." Roger Clew, Zivic told him, had reported on the meeting between Reid and Barton Fuller. Reid seemed chastened, even frightened. He was holed up at his home, apparently afraid even to risk a forty-minute drive back to the safety of Fort Meade. The Pollard house had been cleaned up, closed down, and all of Reid's people withdrawn. Reid's man, Loftus, was in stable condition but Dr. Russo's skills would be needed to rebuild his face. Molly and Janet Herzog picked up Loftus's family and then, in order to avoid possible interception, chartered a plane in Virginia that had just landed at Bridgeport, Connecticut. "And your Mr. Lesko is visiting Mr. Loftus even as we speak."

"Susan's father? How did he find out about the clinic?"

"He appeared at Mario's this noon and announced to Billy McHugh that he would either be taken to Mr. Loftus or he would begin heaving furniture into the street. Billy's position regarding the latter was that he would feel obliged to prevent it. The choice forced upon me was either to rush down and claim a ringside seat—while it remained indoors—or to prevent the destruction of a Westport landmark. My intervention was roundly booed by the entire luncheon crowd."

"You probably prevented the destruction of Raymond Lesko," Paul grimaced.

Anton hesitated. "Have you seen this man?"

"I've seen Billy. I've never seen anyone last ten seconds with him."

"Envision the heavyweight wrestling champion of Transylvania and you have some idea of this Lesko. Your Susan is clearly adopted."

Paul had to smile. "I take it he's quieted down nicely, too."

"For the moment. There was murder in his eyes when he saw what was done to Loftus but his mood improved when Loftus described Billy's retaliation. I think, however, he'll go straight after Reid if we don't prevent it."

"It's your call, Anton, but I'd keep him there."

"My thought, as well. Incidentally, I have a report on that couple you met on the train."

The Basses. He'd almost forgotten. "Yes?"

"They appear to be genuine. Solid citizens, well-known, well-liked, travel extensively. They're definitely on holiday in Europe."

"Do you have a description?"

"Yes." Paul heard a rustling of papers and then a rundown on their ages, coloring, physical dimensions and personality types. No distinctive markings or speech patterns other than a regional accent. "I'm waiting to hear from one other source but I expect no surprises."

"That's them. Thanks. Anton. Have you heard from Carla?"

"I just phoned her."

"In Davos? When was that?"

"Not twenty minutes ago. I had her paged in the dining room of the Des Alpes hotel. Why do you ask, Paul?"

"It's nothing. I thought I saw her in Klosters a few minutes ago."

"Not possible. But if it were my call, as you say, I would give her more latitude. Let her come to Klosters. She will stay out of sight."

"I don't know. . . ."

"She's professional, Paul. Give her something to do."

What the heck, he thought. It was a foolish notion, anyway. Thinking that for three weeks he could live as if fifteen years of his life had never happened. Pretending that he lived in a little white world where the snow never got dirty and there weren't any people like Carla. Or Billy. Or even Anton. Trying to pretend that he wasn't just like them.

"She'll stay out of sight?" he asked.

"You'll never see her."

"But not Gary. He might as well be carrying a sign."

"We'll both rest easier, Paul."

"Okay. Thanks, Anton." He broke the connection. Sure.

Why not? Let someone else look for the shadows.

He turned back toward his building, toward the lights that marked his apartment. A nightcap, a glass of wine, followed by a good night's sleep. That sounded just fine. He could relax now. Maybe even be decent company again. He'd get back to Susan, and he'd hug her and hold her, or maybe he'd save that until morning and let her sleep. Tomorrow they'd start fresh. Make a vacation out of this yet.

The carving knife, which he'd tucked out of sight inside his parka, jabbed into his hip. He drew it out and slid it, blade first, up into his sleeve. Susan might be awake when he returned. That's all she needs, to see him walking around with a. . . .

"Paul?"

He hadn't seen her. She'd been standing there. How long, how much she'd heard, he couldn't ask. He couldn't even speak.

"It's time we had a talk," she said.

CHAPTER 22

Tuesday morning, Klosters.

Susan Lesko slid her stiff legs from the couch on which she'd spent the night. She rose unsteadily, but quietly, and made her way to the bathroom where she closed and locked the door behind her. She sat on the bathtub's edge and turned the hot water tap on full, breathing deeply of the rising steam, waiting while the events of the night before sorted themselves out from the dreams that troubled her sleep.

She'd insisted they have a talk and they did. It made matters worse. As he calmly explained his odd behavior —just a business call, some forgotten detail at his office, he didn't want it to disturb her sleep—in her mind she marveled, sadly, at what a smooth and practiced liar he was.

Damn you, Paul. I heard you mention my father. And who is supposed to stay out of sight? And after you've explained it all away and poor, dumb little Susan says, "Oh. Makes sense to me, Paul. How could I have ever misunderstood?"—tell me how it is that considerate Paul Bannerman goes out to make a routine phone call with a kitchen knife tucked up his sleeve.

She soaked for almost an hour, during which time she thought she heard movement outside the bathroom door. When she finally emerged, having tried to imagine what he might say to her, or she to him, she saw that the bedroom door was open, the bed where he had slept was made up, and he was gone. There was a note on the

316

kitchen counter. It said, *There's no coffee. Gone to shop for groceries. XXX. Paul.*

XXX. Sweet of him. Don't you feel terrible? Here's good old Paul trudging through the snow to get you breakfast and all you can think about is a few teeny white lies and a dumb old bread knife.

She dressed quickly in a parka, furry boots and jeans. She scribbled a note and left it next to his. *I've gone for a walk. I want some time alone.* She underlined *alone* three times.

In the coffee shop of the Alpina Hotel, directly across from the Klosters station, Caroline Bass touched her husband's arm and gestured toward the road outside. "First him, now her," she said.

Ray Bass twisted his head to look. Susan was approaching the village. There was something peculiar, he noticed, about the way she was walking. She was moving in spurts, peering ahead through the still-falling snow, staying close to a row of railroad utility sheds. Suddenly she paused, then backtracked a few feet and stepped out of sight behind a small freight warehouse. Ray Bass turned his head in the other direction. There was Paul. A plastic shopping bag in each hand. Heading her way.

"Know what I think?" Ray smiled

Caroline nodded. "From the look of it, those two had a tiff. Seems like Susan wants no part of him just now."

"Could be real convenient, she keeps her distance from him for a while. Why don't we tag along and see where she goes?"

Caroline watched as Paul went by the freight warehouse. He was thirty yards past it when Susan reappeared and resumed her walk to the village. "Let's wait a bit, darlin'," she suggested. "Like as not, Paul will see she's gone and come lookin' for her."

Ray Bass wiped the window for a better look at Susan. "Can't tell whether she's sad or mad. Of course, one's as distractin' as the other. I bet a couple of friendly faces like ours would be real welcome right about now."

Caroline nodded again. "We meet up with her, let's do it from the car, not on foot."

Ray Bass agreed. "Take her on a nice ride, let her cry

on your shoulder about whatever mean thing Paul did. I wouldn't mind findin' out a little bit more about him either."

"Whyn't you go to the front door, sweetie? See which way she goes. I'll sit here and keep an eye out for Paul."

In a corner room two floors above them, Josef Brugg, who had also seen the daughter of Elena's policeman hide from the man known as Mama's Boy, quickly put on his coat and hat. He too could see that the girl was distracted. Though he saw no particular peril in it, it could do no harm, he decided, to keep an eye on her. At least he would get some exercise.

Susan had no destination in mind. She might, she thought, pick up a dozen postcards although she knew she was in no mood to write breezy messages to friends. Or she might just keep walking. Pumping strength back into her legs. Or find a place to sit and give her thoughts a chance to settle. Maybe in one of these little patisseries, although she didn't feel much like eating either. Or maybe in a movie theater, if one were open at this hour, and if Klosters had one. It didn't seem to.

She passed a storefront that appeared to be a chamber of commerce office. Racks of brochures, things to see and do, posters. One poster listed the movies showing that week in Davos. Four cinemas to choose from. All current films, most of them American.

Davos. Not a bad idea. A much bigger town. Time to herself without looking over her shoulder for Paul, half hoping he'd be there, half hoping he wouldn't. She turned back toward the train station.

"Paul's come lookin' all right." Ray Bass slid back into the booth with Caroline. Together they watched.

Susan had gone directly to the station, where she stood studying the yellow *Abfahrt* Klosters sign. Paul nearly walked by her. But he saw her now and approached her from the rear. Caroline saw Susan stiffen, her shoulders heaved as if in a sigh, and she turned to face him. His manner seemed conciliatory, and he gestured in the direction of their apartment as if asking her to come back to it, but Susan was more than adamant.

Twice he reached to touch her and twice she recoiled. At last she turned away. She stood facing the tracks, glancing now and then toward the north. Paul stood watching her for a minute or two, his manner one of helplessness. He approached her one more time, spoke to her briefly, and she nodded without turning. He walked away.

"The way she's lookin'," Ray Bass said, "she's waitin' for a southbound train. Not much down that way except Davos. We could be waitin' when she gets there, darlin'."

"Oh, shoot." Caroline touched his hand. "Paul's gonna try again."

She watched as Paul retraced his steps but he did not approach Susan. For a long moment he stared at her back, then, with a gesture of resignation, he stepped to a telephone that was out of Susan's line of sight. As he dialed a number he patted his pockets until he found a pen. He waited, then scribbled what must have been a phone number on the telephone casing. He dialed again, his expression grim, and spoke into the phone. As he did so he rubbed out the number with his thumb. He broke the connection and walked away. He did not look back.

"Funny time to make a call," Ray Bass frowned. "Unless Dear Abby has a hotline from over there."

Caroline nodded. "Considerin' his own phone ain't but two minutes away."

"Still, we got a bird in the hand here. That train comes, we're gonna lose her."

"Let's go." Caroline picked up her purse.

With their attention upon Susan and Paul's actions, neither Ray nor Caroline noticed that Susan had been followed to the station. A large, middle-aged man in a fleece-lined coat and fur hat had taken a position near the newspaper kiosk. Paul, with his mind on Susan, and his own carelessness the night before, and on his phone call, made with the greatest reluctance, for Carla Benedict's room in the Des Alpes hotel, also failed to notice that the same man who'd watched them arrive was now there again as Susan left.

* * *

Caroline Bass, having explored Davos on the preceding evening, found that it was a long and narrow town, almost a city, that had grown lengthwise along the valley floor. Its shops, hotels and cinemas ran along a single one-way street called the Promenade. She'd seen that the Promenade ran parallel to the railroad tracks but had been cut through rock some eighty feet further up the slope. For passengers detraining in Davos, the shops were reached by climbing a single winding street. The way was clearly marked.

The place to wait for Susan, Caroline decided, was in their black Saab on the Promenade itself. From it they could watch the train pull in. If Susan was in fact aboard she would almost certainly follow the signs to the Promenade. It would not do to wait for her outside the station because the street she must climb ran the wrong way against them. They would not be able to follow in their car.

Carla Benedict, however, was on foot. And in foul humor. She'd been in bed when Paul rang their room, having unenthusiastic sex with Gary, mostly to stop his whining about his having to stay by the phone in Davos while she went up to Klosters. To look things over. To see if any familiar faces were showing up in town. To see who might be driving a black Saab with a blue ski pod on its roof. But now she wasn't going. Instead, she fumed, she now had to play chaperone to Paul's pain-in-the-ass little play toy. Make sure she doesn't get lost, or slip on the ice, or get sold a Japanese watch. Paul owes her for this, by God. A week in Hawaii. Two weeks. Without Russo. No more mercy-fucking.

She spotted Susan at once. Stepping off the train. In a fog. Following the crowd down the steps and through the underpass to the street. Then standing there trying to figure out where to go next. Come on, dummy. Follow the signs. Why do you think everyone else is. . . .

But everyone else wasn't.

The one in the fur hat. Hands in his pockets. He was waiting. Moving only when Susan moved. Waving off a taxi driver who looked at him questioningly but keeping his right hand in his pocket. Now following her. Up the hill.

Carla began humming to herself.

There was a large variety store at the top of the hill, positioned to get first crack at the tourists' money. All the window displays had *sale* signs in German. Susan went in. Carla watched as she browsed, finally stopping at a display of carved wooden heads that wore fierce expressions and had long, wild hair fashioned from horses' tails and real horses' teeth and were said, by those who sold them, to ward off evil spirits. Susan was smiling now, trying to choose among them. At last she selected one, paid for it with a credit card, paused twice more to look over a food display and a rack of junk earrings, then left the store. The fur hat followed. Carla brushed past him at the entrance, her fingers nimbly tracing the outline of an automatic pistol in that right-hand pocket.

Now she was sure. He was a tail, no question, and he was armed and ready. But why would he be following the girl? And who was he?

She considered watching and waiting. But that went against both her habit and her temperament. When in doubt, take 'em out. Or at least force the issue. Hadn't Anton told her to make her presence felt? To let it be known that Paul was not alone in Switzerland?

Her humming picked up in tempo.

Josef Brugg had fallen to a prudent distance behind the Lesko girl. The red plastic bag she carried made it all the easier to pick her out among the shoppers and strollers.

"Excuse me." He heard the voice, a woman, American, behind him. He turned. A tiny woman. Wearing a fur jacket that seemed too large for her.

"No English," he lied.

"Are you a policeman?" she asked, wide-eyed.

He frowned. "Nein. Nicht polizei. No English."

Josef tried to step past her. She sidestepped with him, babbling something about being lost. But then she slipped on the snowy surface. She would have fallen had they not grabbed each other. He moved to straighten her but now she seemed stuck to him. Her left hand, he was shocked to realize, was suddenly in his pocket. It had gripped his pistol. He felt the movement of her thumb as it snapped off the safety, now twisting it violently so that the muzzle was lined up against his crotch.

"How would you like your pecker shot off?" she asked in German.

He stood frozen.

"Put your arm around me. Walk with me." She cocked her head toward a service alley between two shops. "That way."

"There she is," Ray Bass pointed. "Got a red bag."

Caroline saw. Susan was ambling along, reading a map or pamphlet as she walked. Now she was stopping, making half turns as if to get her bearings. She lifted her head, focusing on a point halfway up the western slope of the valley. "Come on, honey. Keep comin' this way. You got some old friends to visit. . . . Oh, darn." Susan was crossing the Promenade. Now she was leaving it. "What's up where she's goin'?" Caroline asked.

Ray checked his own map. "Not much. Just houses. Oh, wait." He traced his finger over the grids. "There's a tramway there goin' to a restaurant up the mountain." Ray reached for the door handle. "Let's go, darlin'. We'll have to leave the car."

Caroline hesitated. Something down the road had caught her eye. "What's all that, you think?" Looked like a man and woman dancing. Or wrestling. A crowd started to gather.

"Maybe it's how the Swiss have babies," he said impatiently. "Darlin', let's get this done."

They hurried on foot down the Promenade, rehearsing as they went. *Susan? Susan darlin'? . . . My golly, I don't believe it! . . . Ray here says, look, there's that pretty Susan, and I said can't be . . . but sure enough here you are. My golly, I just can't believe . . . Ray here losin' your address and all . . . Where's your handsome fella? . . . He is? . . . We'll go surprise him later. . . . Meanwhile it's almost lunchtime and me and Ray were headin' up this tramway to try some of that hot raclette cheese they got, and why don't we all . . . ?*

"Let go or shoot," the big Swiss said to Carla.

He had her in a bear hug, lifting her a foot off the

ground, her eyes now level with his, her arms pinned to her sides, the knuckles of one fist digging into her lumbar vertebrae.

Shit.

Hardly one man in a hundred, she thought disgustedly, wouldn't have followed meekly at the thought of his balls sprayed all over the sidewalk. She had to pick one who'd been neutered.

"Let go," he repeated, "or shoot."

She considered it. But his muscles were tensed and ready. Without a killing shot, not possible where the gun was pointed, those knuckles could snap her spine. His eyes promised it. But she was not about to release the gun. And she couldn't dangle here all morning. She decided. Carla drew back her head.

"Fuck you," she snarled. She slammed her forehead against his nose. Once, then again. In the same moment wriggling violently, tugging on his gun to free it from his pocket. That was a mistake. For an instant it became knotted in the fabric of his pocket. His right hand came down and covered hers. She could feel his thumb close over the hammer. With her other hand, still pinned against him, she clawed desperately at the soft flesh around his crotch but now, with a growl, he seized her hair and tore her free of him.

People around them had stopped. Some were shouting. But she saw only the face of the big Swiss, advancing on her now. She feinted a jab with her fingers at his eyes, then threw a spinning kick against the side of his knee but her footing and her leverage were poor. He had her again. One hand gripped her coat and the other slammed a fist into her ribs. She gagged.

"Stop this." A shouted voice in German. A woman. Carla, blinded with pain, could hear the sound of blows against the big man's back. A clattering sound. Like an umbrella. The big man raised an arm to ward them off. Another man, a passerby, seized it. Now still another grappled with him. The big Swiss was shouting, trying to explain. Carla heard the word *meuchel*. Assassin. She freed herself and aimed a final well-timed kick. Josef Brugg gasped and sank to his knees.

She turned to her rescuers so that they might see what this beast of a man had done to her. Her face was streaked and splattered with the blood from Josef's nose and from her own tears. She backed away from him as if in terror, now breaking into a run as two men seized and pummeled him.

Down the Promenade she ran, searching through the crowds and the falling snow for the red shopping bag, peering into every shop she passed. Susan Lesko, damn her, had disappeared.

Paul Bannerman tried reading, he tried watching television, but mostly he paced. From the silent telephone at one end of the room to the terrace door at the other. Watching for each arriving train. Hoping to see Susan among those walking from the station. Wanting to go to Davos, to look for her, not wanting to leave the phone in case she called.

The only call had been from Carla. She'd lost Susan. But so had the man who'd been following her. No, Carla had no idea why. Or who he was. Possibly a policeman. Possibly something worse. She had watched him for a while after failing to find Susan. As soon as he freed himself from the people who were berating him, he rushed to the nearest phone and reported. To whom? Who knows. Should she watch him or keep looking for Susan?

Look for Susan, Paul told her. She doesn't know Davos. The way to bet is she'll stick to the shopping streets. You find her, get her back here no matter how much you have to tell her.

He watched one more train arrive, then picked up his phone. He dialed three Westport numbers before reaching Anton Zivic at the clinic.

"Anton," he said, after relating the substance of Carla's call from Davos, "Is it possible that Susan's father arranged to have her watched?"

"By the Swiss police, you mean?" Anton sounded doubtful. "I suppose it's possible. Policemen around the world do favors for each other, but. . . ."

"Is there a way you can ask him without alarming him?"

Anton sighed meaningfully. Unless Lesko was in fact having her watched, the answer was clearly no. "In any case, he's asleep. We agreed it was best to keep him here. I had to use chemical means."

Paul sucked in a breath. He knew that he was reaching. And that Anton could hear the edge of desperation in his voice. "Anton, see if you can bring him around. Ask him. Just be ready to put him back under if you have to."

"You'll stay by your phone?"

"I'll be right here."

Elena, too, was pacing. First the call from Uncle Urs telling her of the attack on Josef—that he had been bested by a small woman, to say nothing of being belabored by the umbrella of a Swiss grandmother—then another, telling her that Raymond Lesko had called, asking about a man seen following his daughter. Was this, he asked, the man Elena said she would send to watch over Susan?

Uncle Urs had assured him that this was the case. But he thought it wise to say nothing of the attack on Josef. Or of the woman who attacked him even though she too seemed more intent on protecting the daughter than on harming her. Very possibly, thought Uncle Urs, this woman is a member of Bannerman's group. But Lesko was in far too agitated a state to deal with conjecture. Moreover, said Uncle Urs, his speech was slurred and his head did not seem clear. He may have been intoxicated. No cause for alarm, Uncle Urs promised, as he took down the number where Lesko could be reached.

Elena was in her kitchen, helping her cook prepare the evening meal, when the phone rang again.

"Elena?"

His voice seemed pained. "Uncle Urs. What has happened?"

"Terrible news. Someone has tried to kill the girl. They may have succeeded. Josef saw the ambulance and went to investigate. She has been taken to Davos Hospital."

"Oh, God."

"She was found . . . beaten. Then someone threw her off the footpath that leads down from the Schatzalp. Do you know the place?"

"I know it. Yes." The mountain restaurant, reached

by cog rail or hiking path. "Could that woman have done this?"

He hesitated. "Perhaps. I don't think so."

Elena heard the hesitation, and the other before he had said *beaten.* What was he holding back? Surely she had not been raped. Not on a hiking trail during a snowstorm. "Uncle Urs, what are you not telling me?"

A silence. Then, "It was done with cocaine, Elena."

She couldn't speak.

"Cocaine was forced into her mouth. She was made to swallow it."

Elena closed her eyes, placing one hand against her kitchen doorjamb as if for support. "*Trafficantes,*" she whispered. She knew two others whom they had killed in this manner. She had heard of a half-dozen others. She'd heard of none who survived.

Elena stepped through the door, closing it behind her so the cook could not hear.

It was always done for vengeance. But it was seldom the guilty who were murdered in this way. First came family. Loved ones. Wives and even children. This was vengeance against Lesko? After two years? Did they wait for the daughter to be in Switzerland where her death would touch Elena Betancourt as well? She gathered herself.

"Uncle Urs, listen to me. Call Davos Hospital. Tell them they must carefully examine the girl's vagina for evidence of a suppository. If they find one it is also cocaine. It is there to kill her if the other does not."

"I understand."

"The man, Bannerman. Does he know?"

"By now, I think. Josef gave the Klosters address to one of our friends on the police."

"The father. We must tell the father." How she dreaded the thought.

"I will do it, Elena. He gave me his number."

"Tell him . . . whatever I can do, whatever he needs. . . ."

"I will see to it."

Urs Brugg promised to report all developments, then broke the connection. He would call the father now. And he too would offer assistance. He had an idea, however, that this Mama's Boy and his associates would be providing more than enough.

By the time the last direct sunlight began creeping up the eastern slopes, Paul Bannerman was becoming more angry than worried. Angry at Carla for losing Susan. Angry at Susan herself. In the end, he was sure, it would turn out that his whole day of pacing and waiting had been for nothing. She'd show up laden with shopping bags. Saying she had lost track of time. He would point out that all she had to do was look out a window to know the sun was going down. And the Swiss public phones were not so mysterious that an American college graduate couldn't at least reach an operator.

He rehearsed these and a dozen other things that he would say to her. He knew that he'd probably say none of them. Or get a chance to. Women never follow the script.

He found himself watching the cars that came down the street in his direction. Watching for a taxi from Davos. Or any car that slowed and stopped outside his building. Maybe she'd met another American shopper. Maybe she got a lift.

He saw a police cruiser approaching. Slowing. He willed it not to stop. If they were coming to see him, if it's about Susan. . . .

The slow-moving cruiser disappeared around the side of his building. Bannerman held his breath and counted to twenty. More than enough time if they were coming. . . .

The door buzzer. Its sound cut through him like an electric shock. His mouth went dry and a lead weight dropped into his stomach. The buzz sounded a second time and then a third before he could make himself move toward the door.

CHAPTER 23

She was alive. There was that at least. The police had tried to prepare him, to encourage him, during the ride to Davos. Still, the sight of her was devastating. He found her in the intensive-care unit, on a respirator. Her lungs had ceased to function on their own. A crusted tube ran from her nose, held in place by tape. There were others in each of her arms. The right side of her face was badly bruised. One eye was blackened and swollen shut, the other, partly open but seeing nothing. There were fresh sutures through her eyebrow. On the cheek below it, near her mouth, Paul could see the imprint of fingers.

"Are you the husband?" A doctor appeared at his elbow. The two uniformed policemen waited beyond a glass partition.

Paul moved his head vaguely. "How is she?"

"It's not very good, I'm afraid." His accent was faintly British, a Swiss who'd studied abroad. "Have the police told you?"

"Cocaine overdose," he nodded. His lips drew back over his teeth. "That girl has never taken a drug in her life."

"This drug was forced upon her." The doctor laid his hand gently over the imprint of fingers much smaller than his own. "She was beaten first. Probably knocked unconscious. Then thrown into deep snow off a hiking path. A dog found her. Two boys with the dog climbed down to see where the dog could have gotten a plastic shopping bag with a wooden carving in it. But for that dog, and those boys. . . ."

"How is she?" Paul repeated.

"She's in a coma. A comatose patient's condition is always listed as grave, but there is more hope here than with many. We've pumped her stomach, her breathing is being assisted, we're monitoring her vital signs and I'm awaiting a laboratory report on her blood and gastric contents so we may know how much she ingested. The next twenty-four hours will tell."

"Tell what, exactly?" Paul closed his eyes.

"Whether she wakes up at all. Whether there is brain damage." The doctor, being Swiss, made no effort to hedge or evade. "There is some good news. Her convulsions have ceased and her pupils are responding to light, although not as much as I'd like at this point. But the cocaine also brought on a type of pneumonia. It's called aspiration pneumonia. It deprives the brain of oxygen, and that may be the greatest danger at this point. We must wait and see."

"Brain damage," Paul said numbly.

The doctor stepped to a plastic IV pouch and adjusted the drip rate. "There were no suppositories, incidentally. Neither vaginal nor anal."

"Suppos . . . what?" He wasn't sure he'd heard correctly.

"Ah, yes. You're not the man who called, are you?"

"Doctor, what are you talking about?"

"We received an anonymous call that the person who did this might have inserted a cocaine suppository as added insurance. But there was none."

Paul stared at him, his mind spinning. Who could have known to make that call? Someone who knew about cocaine, about killing with it. But why cocaine? And why Susan? Killings like that are meant to leave a message, like the dead bird stuffed in the mouth of an informer, and yet he would bet his life that Susan had no connection with drugs. Who was the message for?

A barrage of thoughts, like random rocket bursts, fired off in his head. Cocaine. Susan's father was involved in cocaine. The woman in Zürich. He had forgotten her name. Did Anton say she was involved in it too? Is it possible that Susan is dying for their sins? If that turns out to be the case, they will both damned well die

for their own. And yet, who called? Who tried to save
her?

"This call," Paul asked, "did you take it yourself?"

"The switchboard took it. Then there was a second
call to the nurses' station to make sure the message was
delivered."

"Where is the switchboard?"

"It was the first door on your left as you entered."

"Excuse me, Doctor." He squeezed Susan's hand
and left the room.

Down the corridor, Bannerman found a young,
plain-faced woman seated at a metal desk with a call
director and card file. He explained his relationship to
the patient Susan Lesko in Intensive Care, then asked if
she had taken the call that warned about a suppository.

"I did. Yes."

"Who made that call?"

"A man. Just a man. He would not give his name."

"Was he Swiss?"

"Oh yes."

"What sort of voice?"

"A mature man. A deep voice. A kindly voice."

"Kindly?"

"He seemed very concerned. He called again to confirm that the message was acted upon."

Bannerman pulled two hundred francs from his
pocket. He held up half of it.

"All you must do to earn this," he told her, "is to pay
close attention whenever anyone calls to inquire about
her condition. Ask if they would care to leave their
names. Otherwise, make a note of what time they call
and write down a description of their accents and
voices."

"This is a matter for the police, no?" she asked, un-
certainly.

"It is a personal matter. But you may tell the police
anything you feel they should know." He held up the
second hundred. "This is for the person who relieves
you. You will give her the same instructions?"

"I will do it. Yes."

"Thank you." He handed the money to her. "Where
can I make a private call?"

She pointed him to a visitors' waiting-room halfway

up the corridor. He shut the door behind him and dialed
Anton Zivic. This time Paul tried the clinic first. Anton
came to the phone at once.

"Paul? Anton. How is Susan?"

"She's . . . how did you hear about it?"

"A man named Urs Brugg called to tell Lesko. He is
the uncle of Elena Brugg. Lesko was asleep. He told me
what had happened. I am so terribly sorry, Paul."

"Urs Brugg. Describe his voice."

"A deep baritone. A gentle manner. Cultivated.
Why do you ask?"

Paul told him about the anonymous call. It could
well have been the same man. "Did you find out if
Lesko had someone watching Susan?"

"If you mean the man who tangled with Carla, Urs
Brugg volunteered that as well. The man was his
nephew. Herr Brugg was concerned that Carla might
have been the one who attacked Susan until I in turn
confirmed that she is one of us."

"One of us? He knows about us?"

"He knows of Mama's Boy. He's heard rumors about
the rest."

Bannerman gritted his teeth. This was turning into a
Chinese fire drill. Two bodyguards cancelling each
other out. Goddamned Carla. And goddamned Lesko
for giving out their address. And now here's Anton com-
paring notes with . . . "Who the hell is this Urs Brugg
anyway? And when did you start trusting a voice on the
phone?"

The line went quiet, then, "He made inquiries, Paul.
So did I. Urs Brugg is a formidable man, head of a powerful family, but he is a fair man by all accounts. If you
are looking for an enemy, I suggest you look closer to
home."

"Oh, Christ," Paul erupted. "You're talking about
Reid?"

"The man hates you, Paul," Zivic kept his voice measured. "You are an obsession with him."

"So you think the attack on Susan was an elaborate
act of spite? So he can go home tonight feeling smug?
That's bullshit, Anton. This is about drugs, it's about her
father and it's probably about your new friend in Zürich."

"Paul . . . listen to me."

"And the only powerful families these days are ass-deep in the drug trade. Urs Brugg called this hospital because he . . . I don't know. Maybe because he found out who I was and got cold feet."

"Paul, this is nonsense."

"I'll tell you what's nonsense. Nonsense is. . . ."

"Paul . . . *shut up.*"

Zivic's words came like a slap. Bannerman blinked rapidly. He also heard the echo of his own words. He hadn't realized he'd been shouting.

"Paul?"

"Yeah. Yes, Anton."

"I've just heard more profane language from you than in the entire time of our acquaintance. Also less self-command. I understand why this is. Do you?"

"Yeah. I do." Susan. One eye staring at nothing. He'd put her there.

"Susan is still alive. You must assume that the killers are paid for results and will try again. Your first concern is to protect her."

Protect her, he thought bitterly.

"I suggest . . . I *order,* that you post Carla and Gary wherever they can help you. I am sending Molly Farrell and Billy McHugh on the first available flight. The father is also entitled to be there."

"No, wait a second. . . ." He rubbed his eyes. "Lesko will just . . . he probably doesn't even have a passport."

Zivic ignored the objection. The concern over a passport was frivolous. "They will be there by morning. See that Susan is guarded. You get some rest. If you stay the night with her you will be more than useless tomorrow. You will be a danger to the rest of us."

"Okay," he said meekly. "Look, Anton, I know I was . . ."

"Get some rest, Paul. Clear your head."

"Yeah."

Bannerman returned to the Intensive Care Unit. He stood at Susan's bed but would not look at her. At the foot of the bed was a bulging plastic bag with the hospital's logo on it. Someone had packed up Susan's personal belongings. He picked it up. The doctor entered.

"You have notified her family?" he asked.

Bannerman nodded. He glanced toward the two policemen. "Will they be here all night?"

"Only until they question you, I think."

"Is it possible to hire a security guard?"

"I can see to it."

"But no visitors without my approval. No one gets close to her."

"As you wish."

Paul scribbled the number of his apartment. "I'll be there when I've finished with the police. You'll call if there's any change?"

"Of course. But you are free to wait with her."

There was a hint of disapproval in the doctor's eyes as he spoke. Paul understood it. He was regaining control. Detached efficiency did not become a distraught husband. But there would be no control while Susan's battered face remained in sight or in mind.

"Thank you, Doctor."

He turned and walked away.

Elena Brugg composed herself, then picked up her phone on its fourth ring, expecting to hear the voice of Raymond Lesko.

"Hello?"

"Good evening, Elena." An oily voice. Hispanic. Ortirez? No. Not possible.

"Who is this, please?"

"You forget old friends so soon, dear lady?"

"Ortirez." She spoke the name drippingly. "Where are you?"

"At my house," he said, his manner cheerful. "In La Paz. Enjoying a fine lunch on this beautiful day."

She could hear children in the background. She could hear birds. "What do you want, Colonel?"

"Ah, but I am now a general. And I live in a house as grand as that of the Betancourts. It is, in fact, the very same house, dear Elena."

"What do you want?" This man, a general. The uniform must have cost him millions.

"You will recall that you left us under circumstances that were, at the very least, questionable?"

"I gave my reasons. Among them, Ortirez, was that you are scum."

"Brave words from such a distance."

"Then come to Zürich. I will say them to your pig face."

"Ah, but I am there in spirit, Elena. This very day I have made you a present of the daughter of Detective Lesko."

Elena put a hand to her mouth. It was as she feared. She had suspected the *trafficantes*, certainly. But Ortirez? He was a fool, a lout, who did nothing except for profit. And a brute. Not given to poetic methods. He would have poured gasoline upon the girl and watched her dance.

"Did you hear what I said, great lady?"

"I heard you."

"And when your detective has suffered enough pain, I will make you a present of him as well. I will save you for last, Elena. I will. . . ."

"Do I hear the laughter of children, Ortirez?" she asked calmly.

The line went silent. He had covered his mouthpiece.

"Ortirez, do you know what a perpetual trust is?"

He said nothing. Even his silence sounded stupid.

"It is a fund of money that carries out one's wishes even after death. This fund will contain two million Swiss francs. Do you know how much that is in pesos, Ortirez?"

"Tell me about your fund," he said scornfully, "and I will laugh at you."

"Oh, the bounty will not be upon your life, Ortirez. That would be too merciful."

He waited.

"First it will be for the eyes of your children and the noses of your women. I will keep them here in a box where I can count them. Next it will be for your disease-ridden cock, Ortirez. I will dry it and frame it so that all who come into my house may make jokes about the great General Ortirez."

Lesko's lunch made him sleepy all over again. He couldn't understand it. Had trouble staying awake ever since he got here. Must be run-down. Too many four-in-the-mornings. Too many aggravating dreams.

He dozed off and on in a deep leather chair, in what must have been a recreation room, back when this place had patients. Now there was only Loftus. And his wife and kids. And that other guy, Poole.

Katz was there for a while. Sitting with him, watching a fight on cable. Lesko didn't mind as long as all he talked about was the fight. And about some of the other ones they saw when they used to go out to the old Sunnyside Gardens on Friday nights. But then one of Loftus's kids came in and took Katz's seat and he had to leave. Elena came in a couple of times, too. Or he thought she did. He wanted to get up and change the channel so she wouldn't think all he watched was boxing. But when he woke up enough to do it, she'd be gone, too.

Something cold touched his wrist. Then something rubbed it. He opened one eye.

Loftus. Face all bandaged. Nudging him, saying his name through wired teeth. Billy the bartender, pulled up in a chair. Zivic, the Russian, putting away a needle. A needle?

"Come on, Lesko." Loftus patted his cheek.

"What . . . ?" Lesko looked at this wrist where the cold spot had been. "What was that?"

"Just a stimulant," Zivic said. "To help you wake up."

"Lesko." Loftus patted him harder. "You have to concentrate. Can you hear me?"

"Yeah, goddamn it." Lesko slapped away the hand. "What?"

"You're going to Switzerland. Right away. This afternoon."

"How come?" He could feel his heart beating faster. "What happened?"

Loftus held up a finger. "First you have to promise me. You stay calm. You listen. You go nuts like you did with me, Billy here will have to break your knee and you don't go."

He looked through hooded eyes at Billy McHugh. For a moment he thought this must be another dream because Billy's face had changed. The friendly bartender was gone. His face showed no expression. His eyes looked cold and dead.

"Tell me," he said quietly.

"Tell me about yourself, Mr. Bannerman." An inspector from Zürich had joined the local police at the hospital.

"Let's save time," he said crisply. "You know who I am, where I'm from, and you know my personal history. You know, or will learn, that neither Susan Lesko nor I have ever been involved in drugs. We came on a ski holiday. Nothing more."

"And your two friends, also from Westport. They too are here on holiday?"

Computers, thought Bannerman. They did for anonymity what the Xerox copier did for confidentiality. He got out none to soon. "I have enemies. They were concerned about me taking this trip unprotected. They came in my interest."

"Bodyguards? And yet they claim to be unarmed."

"You've detained them?"

"We're questioning them. As for enemies, evidently Miss Lesko has one or two as well."

"Evidently," he scowled. "Up where she was found, did you find any tracks or bootprints where she was thrown off that trail?"

"All signs were obscured by the rescuers." He pointed to the bag Paul carried. "I would like to look through her belongings."

Paul carried it to a bench and carefully doled out its contents. There was the red plastic bag that might have saved her life. A carved wooden head, bought on a credit card. A brochure from the Schatzalp Restaurant. A small bag containing two Klosters ski pins in the shape of snowflakes, one of them probably for him. Maybe she wasn't all that mad at him anymore by the time she. . . .

Not much else. Keys. A dozen postcards. A package of mints of the sort one finds at restaurant cash registers. A blue American Express receipt. For seventy one Swiss francs. About $50 American. He stared at the receipt, at Susan's signature, until the inspector took it out of his hand.

"Seventy one francs," the inspector said, frowning. "It would be hard for two people to spend so much for a simple raclette at the Schatzalp. More likely three. Perhaps Miss Lesko plus two American assassins allegedly retired to the peaceful environs of Westport, Connecticut."

"Take that up to the Schatzalp. Ask the waiters if they remember three people who had raclette. Until then, you're wasting your time. And mine."

"In your opinion."

"You want a second opinion? One you'll like better?" The inspector waited.

"Call Urs Brugg."

Bannerman didn't know what made him say that. Or even, clearly, what it meant. Perhaps it would give the inspector something to think about. Keep him busy.

"As it happens, Mr. Bannerman," the inspector said coldly, "Urs Brugg is the only reason all three of you are not already under lock and key."

He stopped once more at Susan's bedside as a nurse was drawing the bed's curtain for the night. He took her hand. He had to force himself to look at her.

"I'm so sorry," he whispered. He tried to say more but his throat became full.

Bannerman reached to her good eye and closed it. It seemed to flicker at his touch. Perhaps it did not. The eye was now still.

The nurse released the curtain, still not fully drawn, and hurried away. Later, hours after he was gone, she would tremble at the look she saw on this man's face.

Back at the Klosters apartment, Bannerman called the Des Alpes Hotel to leave messages for Carla and Gary. He had no idea how long the police might detain them. He wanted to alternate them on station at the hospital's front entrance, security guard or no. If they were not released soon, he would have to go himself. He might in any case. He would rest if he could, as he'd promised Anton.

It felt odd, he reflected, to hear Anton giving him an order. Of course Anton had every right. He had the job now. The final authority on anything affecting the security of the group. And cool, collected Paul Bannerman had been right on the edge of losing his grip. Having Anton take control had felt more than odd. It felt good.

The telephone rang. Carla, maybe. He picked it up and said his name.

"This is Lesko," said the voice on the other end. "How is she?"

Bannerman would have known the voice from Molly's wire taps. Except now it was pitched lower, little more than a hoarse whisper. He could hear a rage and a hatred held barely under control. And he heard pain.

Bannerman told him all that the doctor had said. Coma. Waiting for tests. Twenty-four hours would tell. He chose not to mention the battering of her face.

"Who did it?" Lesko hissed.

"I'm not sure."

"Then fucking guess. Who did it?"

"Lesko," Bannerman sighed, "it depends on whether this was done to you or to me. Nobody was mad at Susan. I don't know whether Susan had worse luck being my friend or your daughter."

Lesko took a breath. He had the sound of a man biting his tongue. "What about who did the hit? You got anything there?"

"No."

"No? What's no?"

The question caught him off guard. He had, he realized, answered it almost dismissively because the habit of his fifteen years was rarely to concern himself with triggermen but rather those who sent them. Chasing after dime-a-dozen hired hands was a waste of time and energy. But a policeman, he realized, would not think that way. In this case, and in the case of his mother, come to think of it, neither did he.

"There are no witnesses so far. No descriptions, but the police are working on it," he said lamely. "There seem to have been two of them. It looks like Susan had lunch with them just prior to. . . ."

"Lunch? So someone saw them together?"

"We don't know that yet." Bannerman explained about the American Express receipt and the other contents of her purse that helped to trace her movements.

"So who did Susan know in Davos?"

"No one," he said, frowning. "Unless she ran into
. . . I don't know. Someone she knew from the States."

"Come on, Bannerman. Wake up." Lesko's voice was
rising. "Her friends from the States don't hang around
Davos and they don't try to kill her. Who did she know
in all fucking Europe well enough she'd buy them
lunch?"

Bannerman felt the blood drain from his face.

"You there, Bannerman?"

"I'm here."

"We're going to the airport right now. I'll get there
in about ten hours. Do you think you can maybe give
this a little thought in the meantime? Maybe keep an
eye on her for a change?"

"I'll see you in ten hours." He replaced the phone.

Bannerman was splashing water on his face, trying
to stop the burning, trying to separate the sting of Lesko's words from their content, trying to see more clearly
the picture that was forming in his mind when the ring
of the phone jolted him again.

"Paul?" The voice on the other end took a hesitant
breath. "This is Palmer Reid."

"Yes, Palmer." With effort, he kept his voice even.

"Paul, I've heard about the Lesko girl. The Swiss
cabled a background check on you and two of your
people. I saw the traffic. I picked up on it just to see what
you were up to. Then when they. . . ."

"Palmer, why are you calling?"

"I'm calling to give you my word of honor that neither myself nor my people had anything to do with it."

Paul remained silent. Waiting.

"Damn it, Paul, this is the truth. Whatever our differences, and even though I would happily see you and all
your killers in your graves, I would not dream of harming that girl."

"I believe you, Palmer."

A pause. "Do you?"

"Yes." For the moment. Until I learn differently. But,
in fact, he could not imagine what Palmer Reid could
hope to gain by harming Susan.

"Paul, I'm offering you a truce. And even though you
may reject it, I'm offering any assistance that's mine to
give. Men, money . . . anything."

"Thank you, Palmer. I'll let you know."

"I mean it, Paul. I have family of my own."

Whom he didn't want visited by Billy McHugh again. "Palmer, I said I believe you."

"Is it true that cocaine was used?"

"Yes."

"Will she recover?"

"I don't know."

"Paul, cocaine dealers have been known to kill that way. They have also been known to kill family or loved ones to heighten the suffering of their primary victim. Are you aware that Susan's father slaughtered several drug traffickers two years ago?"

Paul understood what he was suggesting. "But why now, Palmer? And why in Switzerland when they had two years to get her back in New York?"

"Because Switzerland is where Elena is."

"Where who is?"

"Elena, Paul. If you want my opinion, it was done either to teach her a lesson as well or it might even have been done at her direction."

"Palmer . . . what are you talking about?"

A long pause. "You're saying you don't know her?"

"Who is she?"

"For heaven's sake."

"Palmer . . . ?"

"She ordered the death of Lesko's partner. Lesko killed three of her Bolivians to avenge him but left Elena alive at the scene. There has been talk that she and Lesko had been in league all along. There's also talk that they've fallen out. Either way, the attack upon that lovely young girl seems to be a case of Lesko's chickens coming home to roost."

"I see."

"Paul . . . do you know why I called you?"

"To keep me from coming after you."

"There's a better reason. I despise these people, Paul. They are destroyers of children. They corrupt all that they touch. Some of my own men, I'm afraid, have succumbed to temptations of money, of drugs, of perverted sex. They have been bribed with the bodies of young girls, Paul. Innocent little girls, made to suffer the most appalling sexual abuse and then strangled so they could not identify their tormentors."

"Un-huh. I see."

"We can wipe them out, Paul. Working together, your people and mine, we can descend upon them like the wrath of God."

"Let me think about that."

"Until we talk again, the truce is in force. No action will be taken against any of your people. Will you make the same promise?"

"If yours behave? Same as always, Palmer."

"Paul?"

"Yes."

"My prayers are with Susan."

Paul set the phone in its cradle and sat back, staring out into the night. Palmer Reid, he thought. He's never been able to resist that one extra trowelful. Now it's abused children.

As for Elena, Paul had pretended no knowledge of her on general principles. When Reid makes a call such as this he usually talks from a prepared script and does not react well to surprises. He'll now spend the rest of the day revising his assumptions. Moves, countermoves.

As for the offer of a truce, that nonsense about striking a blow for decency aside, it had to mean that Reid was frightened. With good reason. Anton had already hit him hard even before the attack on Susan. That attack could not have been an act of retaliation. It had to have been set up well before. But Reid knew he'd have top billing on any enemies list, and that was reason enough to make the call. Guilty or not. Moves and countermoves.

As for Paul saying that he believed him, it was less a means of disarming or reassuring Reid, than it was an encouragement to get Reid past the protestations and on to the point. Paul had no interest in sorting out what was true and what was not in what Reid had to say. Reid had, at best, a psychotic's concept of truth. Truth was a tactic. He did not so much tell it as retreat into it.

We'll see. First things first. The call that had shaken him was Lesko's. And still no word from Carla. Susan there alone but for a bored, possibly napping security

guard who may or may not have even arrived. There
would be no sleep. He reached for his coat.

The phone rang a third time. He answered.

"Hey, James Bond." Caroline Bass. "How are you,
handsome?"

"Caroline?" He forced gladness into his voice.
"Where are you?"

"Me and Ray are up in Zürich at this fancy hotel
called the Dolder Grand. Day we got off the train we
stopped in for lunch and for Ray to steal an ashtray, but
the food was so good we ended up stayin'. Time to move
on, though. I'm about to split a seam."

"Where are you heading next?"

"Well, Ray wanted to drive down to the French Rivi-
era to see some more beautiful people but this really
isn't what you'd call high season at those topless
beaches. I said we know two beautiful people right
down in Klosters and why don't we drive down come
morning and see if we can't get you and Susan out for
lunch."

"I'm afraid it's not a good time, Caroline. Susan's had
an accident."

"Oh, shoot, no." Her voice fell. "One day there and
she busted herself up?"

"Something like that, yes."

"How bad, Paul?"

"Listen, Caroline . . . are you in your room?"

"Down at the bar."

"There's a policeman here. Can I call you back in
five minutes?"

"You better." She read him the number.

Paul put down the phone and stared at his watch.
Three minutes. Enough time. He dialed information
first, then the hotel switchboard and asked for their
room. No answer. But now he knew they were registered. He dialed the number of the bar and asked for
Mrs. Bass.

"A policeman? Paul, how bad is it?"

"She's umm . . ." Paul paused and swallowed hard,
as if to keep his voice from breaking "She's in a coma.
They're not sure whether she'll come out of it or not."

"Oh, dear Lord," Paul heard the sound of a loud,
frantic whisper. She was calling Ray Bass to the phone.

He could make out the words *alive,* and *coma,* and *head injury.*"

"Caroline. . . ."

"Paul, this is Ray."

"Ray, it's not exactly a head injury. It's . . ." he stopped himself. "Look we're not going to know anything until at least tomorrow afternoon. I know you're concerned but it's not a pleasant situation and it might be better if you two just go and enjoy your vacation."

"I know you don't intend the insult, Paul, but that's what it is. What hospital's she in? Map looks like we could be down your way in two hours."

"It's already half past nine. I've got to get some sleep. Why don't you do the same and, if you still feel like it, meet me at Davos Hospital first thing tomorrow?"

"Try keepin' us away. Meantime, we'll be prayin' real hard, Paul."

"You're good people."

"You just get some rest."

Bannerman held the phone against his chest. His eyes were blazing. He looked at his watch. Two hours. He could safely sleep for most of that. Then he'd go sit with Susan and wait for the two people Susan knew in all fucking Europe—her father's words—well enough to buy them lunch.

He still wasn't sure. He'd wanted to ask Ray what he'd be driving but he could think of no way that would not be transparent.

But if they should turn up in a black Saab with a blue ski pod on its roof, good old Ray and good old Caroline were going to die very hard.

CHAPTER 24

It being a midweek flight, Lesko, Molly Farrell and Billy McHugh had the curtained first-class section on the Swissair 747 largely to themselves.

Lesko had an aisle seat, Billy the window, and Molly the aisle seat opposite. He had little to say to either of them. The flight attendant had served a meal that Lesko barely touched, and they'd shown a movie he didn't watch. He drank through both of them, more than he should have. Now the plane was darkened, windows covered, although the morning sun was still far to the East.

Molly Farrell was asleep. According to Loftus she'd been up all the night before, driving down to Virginia, snatching his family before Palmer Reid could grab them and use them for leverage. Loftus owed her for that, he said. In his eyes that made her okay. But Lesko didn't owe her shit. She'd tried to be friendly. He wasn't having any. He knew he needed them. He'd be lost in Europe by himself. But that didn't make them pals.

He had one too many pals already. Fucking Katz was along. Lesko would doze or his mind would wander and there would be Katz, kneeling on the empty seat in front of him, arms folded over the back, grinning at him like some jerk kid all excited about being up in a plane.

"Dumbrowski," Katz kept snickering. It was the name of the fake passport they had given him. Katz thought this was hilarious. *"I bet they picked Dumbrowski on purpose. It suits you, you dumb shit."*

Mostly Lesko ignored him. Earlier in the flight he'd tried to get Katz to help him think. Asking him the same

344

question he'd asked Bannerman. Who could have done it? Who did she know so well that they could catch her off guard? But Katz was no help. Anyway, he still had a bug up his ass about Elena. Katz heard him call her from the airport. First Bannerman, then her. Telling her he'd be coming. Did she know who did this? She hedged. Will she help him find out? Yes. Can you get me a gun? She answered with silence.

"What are you, out of your mind?" Katz railed at him. *"How do you know it wasn't her who set Susan up? If she did this to me, you don't think she'd give a little taste to Susan for what you did?"*

"It wasn't her. Forget it."

"I was right, wasn't I? You got the hots for her. She gives you a little sweet talk, probably just to throw you off, and all of a sudden, by you she's Doris Day."

"Listen . . . Katz. I got other things on my mind, all right?"

"I know," he said, softening. *"Me, too. I'm her Uncle David, remember?"* Then he brightened. *"Hey, you know what? Maybe I can talk to her. A coma's like being asleep, right? Maybe I can ask her what happened."*

"You do that."

"And God forbid she doesn't make it, I can take care of her, I think."

The thought brought a clammy sweat to Lesko's face. *"David . . . shut up about that."*

"All I'm saying is if. . . ."

"That happens," Lesko said darkly, *"I'm going to shoot everybody involved, starting with Bannerman and the Reid guy, then I'm going to bite it myself so I can get my hands on you because none of this would have happened if you weren't dirty."*

"Shhhh." Lesko heard the sound. "Mr. Lesko." A woman's voice. Molly Farrell. She was shaking his arm.

He stayed quiet. And awake. In an hour the shades were lifted and the pilot announced that they had crossed the coast of France. The sky was still a deep purple. The flight attendant brought orange juice. Billy McHugh leaned close to his ear.

"Can I ask you something?"

Lesko was mildly surprised. The bartender–killer

hadn't spoken since they left Westport. He'd been all business. "What?" he said.

"Before, were you dreaming or were you talking to somebody?"

Lesko closed his eyes. "Drink your juice."

"Don't get embarrassed. I do that, too."

"You do what, too?"

"Talk things over with a partner. It's good to do even if people think you're nuts sometimes. Even Paul does it. He told me."

"That's very interesting," Lesko squirmed.

"Anyway, you don't want to shoot Paul."

Lesko moaned to himself. He'd said it aloud. That's why the shushing. He wondered if the washroom was free.

"You can't shoot him now, anyway. Molly and I both heard you. Don't take this personal, but either of us, we'd kill you the first time you looked cross-eyed at him."

Lesko considered this. It brought up something he'd been wondering about. "You, I can believe," he said. "But the lady with the sad eyes, she doesn't look so tough."

"See?" Billy turned in his seat. He was warming to the subject. "That's another thing I always thought. Some people think looking big and ugly like us is bad, but it can be good. It can save you a lot of trouble, right?"

Lesko had to nod.

"People who look like Molly, and like Paul, too, they surprise you. People like you and me only surprise people when we're nice. That's funny, isn't it?"

Lesko resisted rolling his eyes. This was like talking to Katz. But he didn't mind. Maybe he could even learn something. "What kind of guy is Bannerman?"

"The best. You don't want to shoot him."

"Who do I want to shoot?"

"You already said it. Palmer Reid."

"I said that, too? Out loud?"

"Yeah."

Lesko glanced across the aisle at Molly Farrell, whose hand was pressed against her mouth and whose eyes were shining. She was pretending not to listen but it was clear that she found this exchange amusing in the extreme.

Billy nudged him. "Your partner's name is Katz, right?"

"Listen," Lesko lowered his voice. "What do you say we get off this subject."

"And he gets jealous," Billy nodded understandingly. "I had one like that. I had another one who didn't like to work when it's hot."

Lesko looked at him, scowling. "You're jerking my chain, right?" From across the aisle he heard a heave of Molly Farrell's chest.

"It's true," Billy insisted. "You shouldn't be embarrassed, either. Paul had an Indian named Running Wolf and a girl in blue jeans named Jennifer. He told me."

Lesko looked skyward. This conversation was approaching lunacy. All the more so because he now had no doubt of Billy's sincerity. He tried again, dropping his voice still further. "This Palmer Reid I should shoot. I know I should shoot him for Donovan but how about for my daughter?"

"For everything. It's always Palmer Reid."

"There aren't times when it's someone else?"

"When it looks like someone else, that's when it's Palmer Reid the most."

"Let me see if I got this." Lesko looked pained. "We go down to Davos, we figure out what happened and who did it, and if the answer isn't Palmer Reid we know it's Palmer Reid."

"Lesko," Billy's eyes turned dead again. "You don't want to make fun of me."

Lesko matched the look. "My daughter's in a coma. I look like I'm in the mood for jokes?"

"You asked me, I told you. You do what you want."

The seat belt sign came on.

Bannerman returned to the hospital just before midnight. He'd napped, off and on, for two hours. Better than nothing. And it helped to clear his mind.

He was even less certain than before that the Basses were responsible for the attack upon Susan. It was a possibility, nothing more. If they were the ones, however, they might well not wait until morning to make

another attempt. Granted they would have to get past
the security guard and the night nurses. But a resourceful professional would always find a way. Better not to
take the chance.

He checked the little room where the call director
was. No one on duty. The security guard, however, was
in place outside the glass partition in full view of Susan's
curtained bed. He went in to look at her. Her face was
different. There was a frown, a grimace, that had not
been there earlier. A hand twitched. A leg quivered. He
walked to the nurse's station.

"The cocaine is wearing off," the duty nurse told
him. "Her body is trying to purge itself of the poison."

"She looks like she's in pain. Isn't that a good sign?"

"Perhaps," the nurse said. But her eyes told Paul
that it meant very little. A bodily function. A mechani-
cal process involving her brain's circuitry but not its
intellect. He returned to the corridor and sat.

An hour passed. His head had begun to nod when he
heard movement at the outer glass door of the hospital.
He stood up, tensed and waiting. Carla Benedict
pushed through the inner door, Gary Russo following
close behind. She approached him, hesitated, then
hugged him. Gary Russo put his arms around them
both.

They stayed for half an hour, Russo checking Susan's
charts and talking to the duty nurse, Carla more sub-
dued than usual. She'd blown an assignment, she knew
it, but it was not within her to express remorse. Paul told
them both to go. Get a few hours sleep. Carla was to
take the first morning train to Zürich Airport. Be there
to meet the flight. Report at once if they are detained by
Swiss police or Immigration. Gary was to be back at the
hospital by six. Watch the main entrance from outside.
Warn him of any suspicious activity. Keep an eye open
for a black Saab with a blue ski pod on top. If he sees
one, let Paul know at once. Bannerman told the security
guard he could quit at five. He found a coffee machine
at the rear end of the main corridor. He settled down to
wait.

It was half-past six, not yet full daylight, when he saw
the young switchboard operator enter the front door
and walk to her office. He stood up, walked toward it

from the opposite direction, and as he did so, he noticed two figures standing in the half-light outside the hospital entrance. They stood motionless for a second or two, then, abruptly it seemed, pushed through the doors. Caroline entered first, Ray Bass close behind. Ray carried a box marked with the logo of the Dolder Grand Hotel. Caroline approached Paul with her arms extended, embracing him. They'd been up half the night, she said. Sick about this. No use trying to sleep so they came on down. Ray held up the box. Got the hotel to pack up some coffee and rolls for you, he said. How is she?

He guided them to the bench where he'd been sitting. "I didn't tell you last night," he said, "because I didn't want to involve you, but now you're here. Someone tried to kill Susan. They used cocaine. They stuffed it into her mouth."

"Dear Lord," Ray Bass whispered. "Who on earth would hurt a girl like Susan?"

"I don't know."

"But she's going to be all right?"

"She's beginning to show signs of coming around. But she has a long way to go. And even then . . ." Paul shook his head, unwilling to finish the thought.

"Cocaine." Caroline found her voice. She spoke the word as if it were something vile.

"Paul," Ray Bass looked at him levelly, "I have to ask. You're not involved with that stuff, are you?"

"Absolutely not. Neither is Susan. That's what's so hard to understand."

"Mistaken identity, maybe?"

"I thought of that. I guess it's possible. The police tried to track her movements but they haven't had much luck."

"Paul," Caroline touched his arm. "Would it be all right if I went in and sat with her a bit?"

"Give me just a second. I'll go in with you." Leaving them on the bench, he walked fifty feet to the message office. The girl looked up as he entered, then reached into her drawer for a note pad.

"There were several calls," she said. "One man said he was her father. One gave the name of Reid. One said he was a friend but left no name. These were Americans. There were three other calls and they were all Swiss."

She showed him the log. There were scrawled notations after each listing. Lesko's call had come at 18:22 the previous evening. Reid's, at 19:44. The other American, at 20:02. Two of the Swiss calls said *polizei* after them. The other was from a Frau Brugg, who'd called at 20:55.

"What does this say?" He pointed to the notation after the American who had left no name.

"Cowboy," she said.

"Cowboy? What do you mean?"

"Like in American westerns."

"I'll be right back."

He walked quickly to the front door, where he looked for Gary Russo. He heard the short tap of a horn and turned his head toward its source. Gary was in the hospital parking lot, where he'd found an unlocked car and was seated inside it. Bannerman hurried over to it.

"Have you seen that Saab?"

"It didn't come by here," Russo answered.

"A middle-aged couple went in a few minutes ago. Did you see them park?"

"They were on foot. They came down that hill," he pointed.

"Thanks, Gary. Keep your eyes open."

Bannerman walked briskly back to the door, slowing to a stroll when he came within view of the Basses. He asked them by hand signal to bear with him. He returned to the message office and asked if he might make a call.

"Yes?" The voice was sleepy. It was one in the morning in Westport.

"Anton, it's Paul."

"Susan?" Alarm leapt into his voice.

"Susan is holding her own. Anton, those people from the train. The Basses. One of them's a hitter. Probably both. They did this."

"Intuition or evidence?"

"Mostly intuition. I know it, Anton."

"From this end it seems extremely unlikely. Their identities have been confirmed. The Basses are definitely legitimate and definitely on holiday."

"The pecan farm couldn't be a cover?"

"Definitely genuine."

"Then these people aren't the Basses."

The sound of a sigh. "Paul, you are too personally involved. Please do nothing until Molly arrives with Billy. It should be . . . two hours."

"Anton, I have to go." He broke the connection.

Cowboys. Southerners. All the same to a Swiss. And if that cowboy was Ray Bass, he'd called the hospital more than a full hour before he was even supposed to know that Susan was in it.

The phone rang as he left the room.

At Zürich Airport, in the long corridor leading to Passport Control, Lesko stopped at the first phone he saw and got an operator, who put him through to Davos Hospital. Susan's condition was unchanged. He communicated that information to Molly Farrell through a shrug and pressed on toward the line of passengers waiting for a passport check. Lesko walked on numbly, his mind filled with thoughts of Susan.

Billy nudged him. "Watch yourself. We got company."

Lesko followed his glance to two men standing wide apart, grim-faced, hands in their overcoat pockets, watching them. Billy drifted past, toward one of them. Molly Farrell, Lesko saw, was already in position to move on the other.

"Mr. Lesko?"

He followed the sound. And then he saw her. She had moved into the center of the corridor. His stomach took a hitch. She looked very much as she did when he last saw her, wearing a fur, gloved hands folded, chin high but more than a little frightened, but minus the dusting of cocaine that his shotgun had sprayed throughout the barbershop's back room.

"They cops?" He gestured toward the two men.

"They are my cousins." She held his gaze. "Hello, Mr. Lesko."

"Hello, Elena."

"That phone call. It was to the hospital?"

"She's still alive. It was your old pals, wasn't it?"

"They were never my pals."

"Whatever. Do you know who did it?"

"A Bolivian army officer has called to claim credit. He says you will be next. Then I will follow."

"You going to give me his name?"

"If we live long enough I will give you more of him than that. But our concern now is Susan. He did not know that his people missed. They will try again."

"Then I better get going."

"I am going with you."

She turned away before he could object. He saw that she was leading him past the lines. He followed, pausing briefly at a glass booth where an immigration official nodded respectfully to her and then gave only the briefest glance at Lesko's passport.

"You have baggage?" she asked.

"Only what I'm carrying." He hefted a small borrowed bag.

"Come. I have a car."

"Hold it. I got people with me."

"Those two?" She gestured with her chin toward Molly and Billy, who were standing within a kick of Elena's friends. "They are reliable?"

"They're Bannerman's people. I guess I trust them."

Elena waved them forward. The officer put out a hand to stop them but dropped it when he followed their eyes to Elena. He didn't look at their passports at all.

Molly and Billy stopped short of Elena. Molly beckoned Lesko to a private conference.

"I assume that's Elena Brugg," Molly said.

He nodded. "The other two are bodyguards. She wants to drive me to Davos."

"We've arranged a car of our own. There will be weapons in it. How reliable is she?"

"She asked the same about you. Anyway, you saw she has clout around here. Unless you have more, we can probably use her."

"I agree," Molly said crisply. "Stick with us until we get our car. We'll follow her to Davos. You will want to see Susan immediately, but you must give us time to evaluate whatever situation we find there. You will be given a weapon when I see evidence of cooperation. Not before."

Lesko was impressed. A new Molly. The friendly, sweet-faced bartender was gone. But he wasn't so impressed he was going to follow her around like a puppy.

They passed through the customs gate marked *Nothing To Declare.* Again, no one stopped them. A knot of people were waiting beyond the gate to welcome passengers. Some held up signs. In the front row was a hard-eyed young man wearing a leather jacket. His sign, crudely hand-lettered, said *Mario's.* Lesko might have dismissed it as coincidence. But standing next to him was a woman, as small as Elena, who was a Westport librarian the last time Lesko had seen her.

"Fucking Old Home Week, isn't it," he said to Billy McHugh.

"I did not expect a motorcade." Elena peered into her rearview mirror at the two BMW sedans that were following close behind. Bannerman's three friends were in the first. The leather jacket disappeared after he showed them to their car and handed them a satchel that no doubt contained small arms. Elena's two cousins brought up the rear.

"I didn't expect you," Lesko said. "Thanks for greasing us through. You don't have a spare gun, by chance."

She hesitated, then shook her head.

Neither spoke for the next several miles. Their lips would move occasionally as if searching for words. Many times during the past two years, Lesko had thought of Elena, imagined conversations with her, but he had never imagined how they might begin. He could think of no opening that would not sound hollow. Finally, he retreated into being a cop.

"Listen," he cleared his throat. "You got so much pull with immigration, can you get a list of Bolivians who entered the country the last few days?"

"It won't help," she said. "They would not have sent Latins to a European ski resort. Your assassin is far more likely to be American or British."

Lesko grunted. "Which did you used to use?"

Her eyes closed briefly and her hands tightened on the steering wheel. Lesko noticed.

"Sorry," he muttered. "Cheap shot."

"Do you think we could have a long talk some day,

Mr. Lesko? I don't require your affection but I do not feel I deserve your contempt."

"I said I'm sorry." He stared at the road. "You want to know the truth, actually I . . ." Oh, Christ.

"Actually, you what?"

"Like I said on the phone . . . you made an impression." He could feel heat rising on his cheeks. His mind recalled the dreams he'd had, the ones with Elena beside him in his bed. They were dreams, not fantasies, so he had no need to be embarrassed by them. Still, if she ever knew . . .

"Thank you," she said.

"Don't make a big deal."

Now he felt a pounding at his temples. He covered the one nearest her lest she notice. This was humiliating. The closest he could remember feeling like this was way back when he worked Vice and a couple of times he met hookers he couldn't help liking, and they liked him too because he was straight and he never hit on them for sex or money. Up to him, he'd have left them alone to make a living. On the other hand, none of those hookers ever killed his partner.

"Do you ever think about Katz?" he asked. Shit! Stupid question. The words just came out.

She frowned. "No."

"You don't . . . um . . . you don't by any chance ever dream about him?" How he wished he hadn't asked that, either. "Never mind," he said. "Just wondered."

"Mr. Lesko," she said softly, "if you're asking whether I feel any remorse, we had this discussion two years ago. As for bad dreams, I assure you that I have enough devils of my own without Detective Katz."

"It's just Lesko," he murmured.

"Please?"

"You don't have to call me Mister. It's Ray or it's Lesko. Unless it's me who's impolite calling you Elena."

"Elena is fine. Which do you prefer?"

"Lesko's okay."

"Lesko, then."

The pulse at his temples eased a bit. "Elena, I want you to know I appreciate this."

"You are entitled. I owe you a debt."

He turned to look at her. "How do you figure?"

"Two years ago I bargained for my life. You did not take it, nor did you take payment. I consider that the debt remains."

"Oh, for . . ."

"Please?"

"Will you stop with that? You and that weird logic of yours? I didn't shoot you back then because I didn't feel like it. I didn't feel like it because . . . Ah, the hell with it."

"Lesko?"

"What?"

"I admire you as well."

"Ahhh . . ." Shit!

He never said he admired her. He said . . . kind of . . . that he liked her. A little. Mostly she just made him crazy. What he should be feeling is hating her guts because if there wasn't any Elena, there probably wouldn't be any Susan lying in a coma up in those mountains there.

"I take it," Elena searched for a change of subject, "that you have dreams of Detective Katz."

"Forget it."

"If his death still troubles you, if you want to talk, I don't mind."

"It's nothing like that." Lesko shifted uncomfortably. "It's not like regular dreams. Sometimes, even when I'm awake, I catch myself arguing with him like I did when we were partners. It's more like a habit."

"I understand, I think."

"What? That I'm nuts?"

"It sounds like the behavior of a lonely man."

"Hey. I'm not so lonely."

His reply carried not much conviction and he knew it. He raised a hand before she could say more. Next she'd ask him how he spent his time and she'd start sounding like Susan. He wasn't so lonely. He went to ball games. He still had friends. He went to Gallagher's.

"How much further?" he asked.

"Ninety minutes. Perhaps less."

"Elena . . . my daughter's all I got."

She didn't answer.

"Elena, what's going on here?"

"I am . . . I am not sure."

"Yeah, but that should have been an easy question, shouldn't it. I killed some Bolivians and blew away their shit. My daughter gets found with the same shit stuffed down her throat. Then you get a call from some greaseball, no offense, who says you and me are next."

Elena understood him. That much, however unpleasant, was reasonably straightforward. "But you know there are others involved."

"Bannerman and Reid," he nodded. "Bad conclusions. Connections that don't connect. Bad blood between Reid and Bannerman. But if that's where the answer is, why is the victim still Susan? Could Reid hate Bannerman so much that he'd kill his lady friend out of meanness? And if the answer is yes, why make it look like something else?"

"Lesko, may I give you some advice?"

"Go ahead."

"You are a very direct man." She reached to touch him as she said this. "You will never understand a man like Palmer Reid because he does nothing except circuitously. Also, you are trained as a policeman. You think in terms of gathering evidence and making arrests. It is true you have killed, but only, I think, when your blood was hot. You are not a killer."

"What's your point?"

She gestured toward the car behind her. "Those people are killers. Go see your daughter, Lesko, but stand back from this. Leave it to those whose heads are clear and who are not encumbered by a policeman's rules."

"That's good advice. Thank you."

Elena screwed up her face. "I beg your pardon?"

"I mean it. When you're right, you're right."

Makes a lot of sense, he thought. It was more their style. Let them kill each other off. As many as possible. Then he'd go clean up whoever was left.

CHAPTER 25

On the second floor of Palmer Reid's home, shortly after two in the morning, Charles Whitlow tapped on the door of his superior's bedroom. He was fully dressed, having seen it as his duty to remain in control of events while Palmer Reid slept. He tapped again, more loudly, then entered at the sound of Reid's voice. He carried a cup of steaming tea that he placed on the bedside table, then sat primly in a straight-backed chair as he waited for the older man to signal that he was sufficiently awake.

"The girl?" Reid rubbed one eye.

"Still alive," Whitlow answered dismissively. "We have several more urgent concerns. Some may be opportunities as well."

"Just report, Charles." Reid sipped from the cup without acknowledging its source. "I will evaluate."

Very well, Whitlow sniffed inwardly. See what you make of these. He produced a note pad, folded open. "Raymond Lesko has arrived in Zürich in the company of two of Bannerman's top agents. They were met by one more, plus some young hoodlum who apparently left after bringing them a car. They were also met by Elena Betancourt herself, accompanied by two bodyguards. As we speak, this entire retinue is probably just arriving in Davos."

Reid blinked. "For heaven's sake."

"Your suspicions would appear to be vindicated. A conspiracy, if I dare offer an opinion, has clearly existed all along."

"Elena knew them? All of them?" Reid straightened.

"So it would appear. Her greeting of Raymond Lesko was characterized as guardedly affectionate. As for the others, we had asked that any of Bannerman's people be detained for questioning. Elena waltzed them right through. They proceeded to the parking lot and departed in three cars as a group."

"Impossible."

Whitlow, smugly, tapped the notebook with his index finger.

"Bannerman doesn't know Elena. He assured me of that himself. He'd never even heard the name until I mentioned it."

"Bannerman's 'assurance,' you say. You don't suppose he might have been fibbing."

"I know the truth when I hear it, Charles."

"Of course, sir." Whitlow kept his expression blank.

"Could it be possible, Charles, that Bannerman is being duped by his own people? That they've begun a drug enterprise right under his nose? That the girl, under the direction of her father—you'll recall that I suggested this scenario—seduced Bannerman in order to distract him?"

Whitlow could hardly bear it. If it weren't for the money, the power. . . .

"There is certainly some confusion here, sir. But there is also the fact that four of Bannerman's key operatives are now with him in Switzerland." He ticked them off, including Dr. Russo who had been questioned and released by the police, again in spite of his own request to the contrary. "Whatever else may be afoot, such a gathering would seem to seriously deplete Westport's capacity for effective resistance."

"My order stands, Charles." More's the pity, he thought, because Whitlow undeniably had a point. "There can be no action against Bannerman or Westport while that damned basketball player is breathing down our necks."

Whitlow pursed his lips. "That brings up another problem, sir. General Ortirez's people are still at large. He claims he cannot withdraw them unless they contact him and he does not expect them to do so."

"A moot point, I think. Bannerman and the girl

would seem to be adequately protected for the moment."

"One would think so, sir. Ortirez, however, has demanded the immediate execution of Elena Betancourt. He insists that it be done within the next twenty-four hours."

"Ortirez *demands?* Ortirez *insists?*" Reid conjured a vision of this beribboned and pomaded little spic and then shook it away as too distasteful to contemplate at such an early hour. Still, the idea had its attractions. If Paul Bannerman didn't know Elena before, he was now at the point of making her acquaintance. A cozy exchange of information between them would not be to his benefit.

"It seems, sir, that he made an ill-advised call to Elena. He thought the girl was dead. He called Elena to boast of it. The call was intended to unnerve her, but I'm afraid she got the better of the exchange. She responded with a threat or two of her own and now Ortirez wants her killed before she can put them into effect."

"Get Ortirez to Washington, Charles. It's time I clarified our relationship."

"He's quite beside himself, sir. I'm not sure he'll leave the protection of his compound."

"Then redirect his concerns, Charles. Get him thinking about his place in world affairs."

"Sir?"

"In eighteen months his country will need a reliable presidential candidate. Whisper to him, Charles, that the United States would consider its interests well-served if he would accept the burdens of that office. Promise him a secret meeting at the White House. Anything. Just get him here."

"Yes, sir." Whitlow liked that. Not only would it fetch Ortirez, but he might even shave for the occasion.

"In the meantime, arrange whatever is necessary to give him peace of mind."

"I'm afraid nothing short of. . . ."

"You do follow my meaning, Charles."

"Yes, sir." Whitlow snapped his notebook shut.

"You're a very good man, Charles."

* * *

Susan was dreaming. She was on the mountain. With Paul. But he was skiing too fast again. He wouldn't wait. It was because they'd had an argument. She couldn't remember about what.

But Caroline stayed with her. And Ray. Caroline tried to make her feel better. Saying life's too short to fuss over every little thing. Especially between two people who like each other so much. Plain as day. Written all over both your faces.

Caroline tried to make her smile. Pushed her into a snow bank. Threw snow in her face. Funny that Ray and Caroline are skiing in their street clothes. Then suddenly she couldn't see. Her cheek hurt. She was dizzy. Now her eye hurt. And she couldn't breathe. Caroline? Caroline, help me.

Better now. Feels good. Feels won-der-ful. Oh, wow. Oops. Have to stop saying that. But it feels soooo good.

Not now, it doesn't. Hurts. Face, nose, chest. Everything. Caroline? Oh, you're here. Why are you staring? Is something wrong with my face?

"Come on, Susan." Caroline Bass leaned over the bed and kissed her forehead. "You're gonna make it. You're gonna be just fine." She turned to face Paul, who'd drawn up a chair to the opposite side of the bed. "I believe she's comin' back, Paul," she smiled warmly.

He nodded hopefully. The breakfast from the Dolder Grand was balanced on his lap. He'd touched none of it for all Ray Bass's repeated urgings that he get something in his stomach. In truth he was ravenous. He'd barely eaten since a late lunch Monday. He couldn't take the chance that the rolls or coffee were doctored. Nor would he leave the bedside though his bladder had settled into a dull, crippling ache.

His last opportunity to relieve himself came an hour earlier when a nurse came in to give Susan an alcohol bath. But before he could stir, Caroline Bass asked if she could bathe Susan herself. She'd been, she said, a nurse's aide in Mississippi. It would occupy her mind while helping her to feel useful. The nurse had no objection. Paul said, "Not yet. Let's wait a while."

Now Caroline picked up the alcohol again. "Why don't you two boys get a breath of air? Give the ladies a few minutes' privacy."

"Sounds good to me," Ray Bass stood and stretched. "Come on, Paul. Do you good."

"Not just yet, if you don't mind," he said. "Every now and then I'm getting a little squeeze from her hand."

"That's sure a hopeful sign. But when that girl wakes up and gives you a proper squeeze you'll faint dead away, the rate you're goin'."

"Just a while longer. Please."

Another forty minutes passed. A waving white-clad arm caught his eye from the nurses' station. The nurse was holding up a phone. He rose gingerly and walked over to it, trying not to waddle.

"It's Molly, Paul."

Thank God.

"We're parked at the Davos station. We have a small army here."

"Who?"

She told him briefly. He did not take time to ask how the various Bruggs came to be with her. It was enough that Molly seemed comfortable with them.

"I want you to stall Lesko for a full fifteen minutes and then let him come see his daughter. There's another American couple here now. Pleasant-looking, medium height, late fifties. She's wearing a light-colored fur and he has a tan cashmere overcoat. If they leave the hospital in those fifteen minutes, they'll have just tried to finish Susan off."

There was barely a pause. "Take them or follow them?"

"Take them, but quietly."

"Fifteen minutes," she acknowledged. "It's a long time to hold Lesko if he doesn't want to be held."

"Tell him his daughter's getting a bath."

Crisp and efficient was fine, Lesko thought, but Molly was becoming a pain in the ass. They'd pulled up all three cars at the railroad station and then waited while she made a phone call. Then she says sit tight while the three from Westport go scout the hospital for signs of a stake-out. What Lesko wanted was to see his daughter, and he wanted to see her now. But he couldn't argue that looking the place over made sense.

Just ten, maybe fifteen minutes. Besides, Elena agreed with her. Elena also agreed that her two cousins would be strictly back-up. Good, then give me one of their guns. No, said Molly. Why the hell not? Because you're too worked up. The librarian gets one but I don't? Fact is, she doesn't get one, either.

Bullshit.

But she left before he could argue.

Ten minutes. Twelve. Almost fifteen. Then Molly returned alone and drew up alongside Elena's Mercedes.

"Susan has visitors with her," Molly said. "I think they're just leaving."

"So what? I'm supposed to wait my turn?"

"Then Susan's getting a bath. Paul thought she'd prefer to be cleaned-up before you see her."

"Yeah, well, fuck him, lady." What the hell is this? He turned to Elena. "You going to drive me over there or do I get out and walk?"

"Susan's all set, Paul." Caroline found them sitting in the front lobby. "Clean as a whistle. I brushed her hair and gave her a dab of Shalimar behind the ear."

Paul saw that she'd put on her coat and was carrying Ray's over her arm. "Thanks, Caroline. Are you leaving?"

"Just to take a walk. I think I breathed in as much of that alcohol as I splashed."

"Take your time. It'll still be quite a while." He walked back toward Susan's bed.

Elena gripped Lesko's arm as they climbed the steps of Davos Hospital and pushed through the double doors. The couple, approaching them obliquely from the lobby's-sitting area, caught her eye. The woman in the light fur suddenly began to weep. She turned her head into the man's chest and he buried his face in her hair, comforting her. Something about them. Vaguely familiar. Lesko tugged her toward the information desk. Elena pointed to a sign showing that the Intensive Care Unit was just down the corridor. She led Lesko in that direction.

*   *   *

"You get a gold star for your timing, darlin'." Ray Bass patted Caroline's shoulder. "I would say we now have one too many fellers named Ray around here."

"That was him all right," she glanced over her shoulder. "Who'd have thought a big, ugly brute like that would have such a pretty daughter?"

"Well, my own daddy was plain as a post and you see the fine-looking gentleman he produced. You do know that was Elena with him, don't you, love? Though I don't believe she recognized us."

"She didn't get much of a look, not now or back then, either. You covered us real smooth, by the way."

"Thank you, darlin'. But I think we have to assume we might have rung a little bell and at least that Elena didn't come here without some kin. What do you say we use another door?"

"Then what, precious?"

"Let's get at least an hour away, down toward Italy," Ray said thoughtfully. "Then we can call like we're still here in town and get the bad news about poor Susan. It's a shame, though."

"Now darlin'," she gave him a squeeze, "you keep tellin' me not to go makin' this personal."

"Oh, I don't mean about the girl. I mean we just had all three of 'em standin' practically within the swing of a cat."

"Everything in its time and place, darlin'. . . . Goodness, what was that?" A loud crash echoed down the corridor. A woman shouting in German. White-clad people running.

Susan was naked. And she was lying in a snowfield under a bright, warm sun. Her skin felt cool, not cold, and fragrant. She could smell spring flowers in the air. It was so much better now.

Caroline had undressed her. Was massaging her. Cold hands. She could feel them rubbing lightly over her breasts and stomach, then lower, probing now between her legs. Caroline? What are you doing? Caroline . . . I don't think this is such a good idea. Caroline, don't. Don't touch me there.

Oh, wait. It's all right. It's Paul. Paul, honey, for a minute I thought you were . . . never mind. Paul, sweetie? Not so rough, okay? Gently. And not in my ass, damn it. I don't like that. Paul, stop. My father. Not in front of my father.

"You fucking creep. . . !"

Her father's face over Paul's shoulder. Now grabbing Paul, by the hair, flinging him out of sight. Crunching sounds. Smashing sounds. A woman shouting. Susan wanted to cover her nakedness but her arms were too heavy to move.

"Here. I got it." A man in a loud sport coat drew the sheet over her.

"Uncle David?"

"How you doin', kid?"

"I'm fine . . . I . . . Uncle David, they're fighting."

"Your old man's just feeling parental. Don't worry. Let him get it out of his system."

"But Daddy will kill him. You know how he gets."

"Kill who? James Bond? Myself, I wouldn't worry too much. Frankly, it'd do your father good to get his own ass kicked for a change."

"You fucking creep. . . ."

What Lesko saw, what had made him snap, was the man who had to be Paul Bannerman standing over Susan, her body exposed from rib cage downward, his hand deep between her thighs, probing, massaging, as her body arched and trembled.

Bannerman saw Lesko but he didn't stop. He probed deeper. Even when Lesko seized him by the hair and bent his head backward he kept his grip. Lesko's right fist drove into his kidney. Bannerman went rigid, he gasped, but still he blindly groped.

"No, Lesko," Elena shouted. "Leave him."

Another blow to the kidneys. The hand came free. Elena saw it, encased in a plastic glove that gleamed with moisture. She saw the hand clawing at the sheet between Susan's legs, finding and grasping an object that resembled a dirty piece of chalk.

Lesko tore Bannerman from the bed and sent him tumbling over a metal chair. He lunged after him. The hand with the plastic glove was balled into a tight fist but Bannerman made no move to strike with it. He used his feet. He whipped one leg at the side of Lesko's knee and again at Lesko's head as, off balance, the bigger man fell. He landed on Bannerman's legs, pinning them, then clawed toward Bannerman's neck.

Too late, Lesko saw the fingers of Paul's free hand go rigid. Like the strike of a coiled snake they darted first at Lesko's throat and then his eyes. Choking, blinded, he turned his head away and, attacking by feel, cocked his right fist to hammer Bannerman's face.

"Stop it." Elena was at his ear. "It is not what you think."

Her shoe was off and in her hand. She hooked his drawn-back arm with one hand and with the other brought the shoe down hard against his temple. Lesko saw a burst of colored light and he heard himself roar. She hit him again, this time with all her strength. Through the flashing lights, Lesko saw Bannerman's hated face rising up toward his own, then nothing.

"It is the girl's father." Elena spoke in rapid German to the nurse and two orderlies who rushed to the sound of the violence. "He was overcome. He went mad for a moment." In his emotional state, she explained, he lashed out at a man who did nothing more than bring his daughter on a holiday to Switzerland. Certainly not a matter for the police. Is there a room perhaps, where she might take him and calm him?

The nurse looked doubtfully at Lesko, who was trying drunkenly to sit upright, and then at Paul, who assured her in German that there was no damage that would not quickly pass.

Molly appeared at the glass partition. Behind her, Billy McHugh. Bannerman waved them in.

"Did they get past you?" he asked quietly.

"They didn't come out the front," she whispered, "but the only other exit's the Emergency Room. Carla and Gary are covering it."

Paul grimaced. Carla tends to leave bodies all over the street. And he wasn't sure how much help Russo would be. "Give me your keys. Billy, you come with me. Molly, you stay with Lesko." He flicked his eyes toward the woman talking to the nurse. "I take it that's Elena."

Molly nodded, surveying the wreckage. "And I take

it there wasn't love at first sight between you and
Lesko."

"She'll explain." He peeled the plastic glove over its
contents and slipped it into his pocket.

The girl at the message desk flagged Bannerman as
he passed. A call from Mr. Zivic in America. Very urgent. Paul hesitated, then took it, first handing the keys
to Billy and waving him on.

"Anton?"

"How is she?"

"Better, but I can't talk."

"Paul. Listen. Are those Americans from the train
still with you?"

"Yes." There was no time to elaborate.

"I have definite confirmation that the Basses of Lumberton, Mississippi, are at this moment in Brussels. Your
instincts were correct. There are several possibilities
concerning the identity of your two Americans. The
most likely is that they are the team of Harold and
Lurene Carmody."

"They've already tried and missed, Anton. I'll get
back to you."

"And call Roger Clew. He's most anxious. Molly has
arrived?"

"They're all here. Anton. . . ."

"She told you I sent her to Chevy Chase yesterday?"

"There hasn't been time. Anton, I must hang up
now."

"Call when you can." Anton broke the connection.

The girl at the desk gestured toward the largest of
several floral arrangements that were awaiting distribu-
tion to patients.

"That is for your lady," she said.

"Who from?" He paused at the door.

"The card says, 'Prayerfully, Palmer Reid.' "

"I'd say we got company, darlin'." Harold Carmody
had his wife's arm as they climbed the steep, narrow
street that led from Davos Hospital to the Promenade,
where they'd left their car.

Lurene nodded that she'd seen him. "It's real sloppy
company if you ask me." He was probably the only man

in Davos wearing a chesterfield and he walked with
both hands in his pockets like Peter Lorre. "You don't
suppose Elena sent him after us?"

"Weren't time. Anyhow, he sure ain't Swiss." He
could have come over with the father, Harold guessed.
He could be almost anyone. The question wasn't worth
trying to sort out. The point was he was watching them
and Harold Carmody did not want anyone getting a
look at their car, even though he'd stripped off that
dumb pod, which they turned out not to need.

"Well," Lurene shrugged. "we said we were going
out for a breath of air. Let's do just that until we get a
chance to lose him or gut him."

"Darlin'," Harold shook his head. "I don't know how
casual we can afford to be right now. All that bangin'
and smashin' back there by Susan might mean that suppository wasn't as slow releasin' as you think."

"The suppository was just fine, Harold." She made a
face at the implied doubt of her expertise. "More likely,
that big ugly Lesko just tripped over a chair on his way
in."

"Well," Harold let out a sigh, "unless you're willin' to
bet your life on that, I say we leave this other feller in a
doorway or an unlocked car and get on away from
here."

"Fine by me. How do you want to do it?"

The street they were on angled upward toward the
Promenade in a series of dog-legs, past old stone and
stucco buildings that had once been private homes but
had long since been converted to warehouses. No pedestrian traffic down this way. No commercial vehicles
in motion this early. No people lived here and no tourist
was likely to come up or down this way. It was a good
place. Some fifty feet ahead of them the street veered
sharply left. Harold knew that it veered right again
another hundred feet beyond.

"I'll wait 'round that corner up ahead. You go on to
the next corner and let him see a little piece of you
turnin' out of sight."

"All right, but don't dawdle with him," Lurene said
sternly. "Never mind asking any questions. You just kill
him and be done with it."

"I wasn't of a mind to socialize, darlin'."

* * *

Carla Benedict, who said "I'll be damned" when she saw them slip out the Emergency Room, was tempted to take them then and there. She felt sure that she could handle the man and that Gary Russo could at least keep the woman occupied. But an ambulance or police car might appear at any moment. Better to let them move on a bit.

The big question: Where was their car? It might be out front, where Billy and Molly were waiting, and they might be abandoning it. They were climbing the hill up toward the Promenade. Maybe the car's up top. Maybe they're going for a taxi. She could see no likely vehicle parked on the street they were taking.

"I'm going to try to get above them," she told Russo. It would take a sprint up another way but she could do it. "You follow. For God's sake, don't lose them."

Russo looked up the narrow street and frowned. "They'll spot me in the first block."

"You worry about keeping *them* in sight. But keep your distance. And walk in the roadway, Gary, not on the sidewalk." She patted the shoulder of his chesterfield and took off down a side street at a measured run.

Lesko was a mess. He held a towel dipped in ice water against the side of his head, where Elena's shoe had reopened the cut made by Loftus's gun four days earlier. His eyes were red where Bannerman's fingers had jabbed them, and his throat felt as if a hole had been poked through it.

Elena was explaining, trying to explain, what he'd seen when he parted the curtains around Susan's bed. Lesko heard the words but their meaning came slowly to him. His mind held the picture of Bannerman's fingers, those same fingers, digging deep into his daughter as her wired up body writhed in response. It was a scene from a sick porn movie.

"He was saving her life, Lesko." These words came from Molly Farrell.

Lesko was beginning to accept that. It was the way Bannerman had behaved that convinced him more than anything being said. There was no fear in his expression, no embarrassment, no sense of being caught in the act. He just went on with what he was doing even after Lesko threw a punch that must have half-paralyzed him. And those jabs at Lesko's eyes and throat. The guy was hurting bad but he was cool, precise. He'd also pulled those jabs. Lesko knew that. Bannerman could have split his eyeballs like grapes if he'd wanted to.

"Where is he now?" Lesko looked at Molly.

"He and Billy went after the man and woman."

"He's going to kill them?"

"Not if he can help it. Not right away."

"I want them."

"I know you do. We'll see."

"I want them," Lesko showed his teeth. "And then I want a nice, private talk with Bannerman because before I crush his face I want him to explain why he gave those two another crack at my daughter just so he could nail them."

Elena explained again about the suppository. An insurance device. That it would melt, depending on its coating, in anywhere from twenty minutes to four hours and would have brought on irreversible cardiac arrest before any trauma team could find its cause.

"He still took a goddamned big chance. What if they gave her an injection instead? Or stuck an ice pick in her ear?"

"They couldn't, Lesko," Molly explained patiently. "It's an Intensive Care Unit. The way Susan's wired, any direct assault would have set off an alarm the instant her system reacted to it. It was you, charging in here, that put Susan at risk. Paul knew what he was doing."

"Is that so?"

"As a matter of fact, it is."

"Well, I'm getting very fucking tired of Paul Bannerman knowing exactly what he's doing. I'm getting fucking tired of all of you." He threw his ice towel on the floor and stomped off in the direction of Susan's bed.

The curtains had been drawn again. The nurse parted them to let two doctors enter. She saw him approaching and held up a hand that said he should wait. Now she showed ten fingers. Ten minutes. And now an upraised thumb and a nod of encouragement. Lesko felt his eyes go moist.

He looked toward the room where Elena and Molly waited. Then toward the front entrance. Then at his watch.

Ten minutes is ten minutes.

He walked quickly down the corridor.

Billy, in the rented BMW, was exiting the hospital parking lot when Paul emerged. Paul took an extra thirty seconds to find another unlocked car, push it into the narrow curb cut of the lot, lock it and leave it blocking the exit on the chance that the Basses—or whoever they were—had indeed left their car there and would double back for it. Failing that, Paul could see only two other directions they might have taken. One was toward the station. Too easily trapped down there. Up toward the town was more likely. Billy agreed. He dropped the BMW into its lowest gear and started up the hill.

"Carla and the Doc aren't armed," Billy said as he passed Paul a Belgian automatic and laid his own silenced Ruger across his lap. "Molly wouldn't give them any 'cause they been made. Swiss cops'd put 'em away."

"She was smart." He peered ahead. "Billy, if Carla spotted them going up this way, what would she do?"

"She'd split off from the Doc and try to get ahead of them. The Doc isn't real good at this, so, I was her, I'd tell him to stay back and be a decoy. Slow 'em down, get them looking over their shoulders."

"Good call, Billy." Paul pointed up ahead and to the left. "There he is."

"Not what I had in mind," Billy shook his head ruefully. "Hugging along that wall's a good way to get his throat cut."

Had Billy looked in his rearview mirror, he would have seen Susan's father, on foot, chugging up the hill behind them.

Gary Russo was damned if he was going to walk like a dummy up the middle of the street where they could see every move he made. He might not be all that expert in surveillance techniques, which he was tired of hearing, but he knew common sense. Out in the street like that, he might as well be shouting and waving his arms.

As he approached the corner at which the man and woman had turned, he could see that it angled off about forty-five degrees to the left. If it was the same as the last stretch, it would soon zigzag the other way, which means they would be out of sight if he didn't hurry. He stopped at the corner and peeked around it. They were gone already. Damn. Lose them and he could look forward to about a month's worth of crap from Carla.

Rounding the corner, he lengthened his stride. As he passed a recessed doorway, his eyes locked upon the corner ahead: his inner brain told him that something was wrong. There was a shape there and now he sensed movement. His head turned to glance over his left shoulder, but a hand seized it before he could focus. A gloved hand. Clamped across his face, jerking him backward. Another arm, he felt it, coiled around his waist. At its end a sharp, stinging point had punctured his chest. He felt it gouging at his ribs as it probed for a path to his heart. Russo choked on his own scream.

"Car-mo-dyyy." A distant call. Heard through a red veil of pain. Carla's voice. Then the squeal of a car's brakes. "This way, Carmody. Up here." Who was Carmody? a part of Russo's brain wondered dimly.

The gloved hand came down from his eyes but seized him across his burning chest. He could see, through welling tears, but he could barely breathe. He looked down past the arm and saw, to his horror, the long, thin knife, blood running down its blade, that had entered his body. He could not tell how far except that he saw no tapering at all, only parallel edges of steel.

"Just ease it back out." A voice to his right. Billy's voice. Oh . . . Billy. Oh, good . . . good. His head shuddered in the direction of the voice. There was Billy, his face dipped low over the barrel of a silenced pistol aimed at a point just behind him. And Paul, in the seat next to Billy, climbing out now. And Carla. Here comes Carla. She's walking with the woman, half-dragging her. The woman's face is smeared with blood.

"Well, I'll be . . ." Russo heard the voice at his ear. There was no fear in it. More a sense of wonder. "Hello there, Carla honey. Little rough on an old friend, aren't you?" Russo felt himself being dragged backward. He wanted to shriek from the pain, but he could only gag.

"Paul?" Billy's voice. "I got no shot."

Carla was close now. With the woman. He saw a knife in Carla's hand pressed against the woman's temple.

"Lurene?" The voice again. "Lurene, darlin', are you all right?"

"I'll mend," she said thickly. "Just don't you let go of that hole card."

"Paul, my friend," the man who'd been Ray Bass pressed his back against the padlocked door, "I'd say we got ourselves a standoff here."

Paul rounded the BMW. Carla caught his eye and motioned down the hill. There was Lesko, slowing, breathing heavily, trying to assess the scene he'd come upon.

Paul's expression didn't change. His eyes locked back upon those of Harold Carmody.

"Billy," Paul held out a hand toward the Ruger, "give me that and get the trunk open."

"Darn it," Carmody clucked his tongue. "I just knew there was somethin' about you." He shrugged and sighed. "Anyhow, Paul, put that thing up. Shoot me and you as good as kill your friend here."

"You stick him any more, Harold," Carla warned, "and you'll watch me core old Lurene's eye like a fucking apple."

"Paul?" Carmody's voice went higher as Bannerman shifted the Ruger into his left hand and approached. "Paul, it weren't personal. Fact is, me and Lurene liked you two real. . . ."

Paul grasped Russo's right hand, which was hovering feebly over the hilt of the knife. He lifted it, then fired three times through Russo's armpit.

Lesko was the first to return to the hospital. He came alone. The look in his eyes, thought Elena, who was waiting for him, was strangely distant.

"Did you find them?" she asked.

Lesko nodded. "I want to see Susan." He walked past her into Intensive Care, and through the curtain surrounding Susan's bed. Elena followed.

"The news from the doctor is good," she said to his shoulder. "She's responding. He says the coma has become sleep. Her lips have been moving."

"Her face," he said. That was all. He had barely glimpsed it when he first came in. He hadn't realized they had done that to her.

"Being knocked unconscious," Elena said gently, "helped save her life. The doctor said so. Because of it she swallowed less. Even being left in the snow helped to slow the absorption of. . . ."

"Yeah, look . . ." he said without turning. "Leave us alone, will you?"

Elena backed out. She closed the curtain. Behind her, a tapping on the glass partition. Molly was there, her expression anxious.

Elena listened as Molly told her the events of the past fifteen minutes. The two who did this have been taken. One of Bannerman's people has been hurt. Flesh wounds and powder burns under his armpit, a knife wound low in his chest. The injured man is himself a doctor. He insists that his injuries are not immediately life threatening. It is his own wish that he not compromise the rest of them by seeking treatment here at this hospital. Does Elena know of a reliable doctor?

"Yes," she answered, "but in Zürich. Can he last so long?"

"He expected Zürich. He says he will make it. He's now in a warehouse just up the hill. We broke in to give him shelter. It's a lot to ask, but can you go there with me now in your car?"

"My cousins will help. Two moments. I'll tell Mr. Lesko I'm leaving."

She stepped through the curtain surrounding the bed. "I must go. One of their men needs help."

"Yeah. Go ahead," he said hoarsely. He still did not turn.

She brushed against him, reaching to touch Susan, to remove a strand of hair from her face.

"Look," he snapped. "I asked you. Leave us alone."

Elena stepped back from the bed. She paused, hugging herself as if she did not know what to do with her hands, benumbed by the unexpected brutality of his dismissal. There seemed nothing to say to it.

"Good-bye, Lesko."
She turned and walked away.

The three cars, by turns, headed north from Davos.
Billy drove one BMW. Bannerman rode in the front,
Carla in the rear seat with her feet upon the back of a
bound and gagged Lurene Carmody. The corpse of
Harold Carmody rode in the trunk. Bannerman di-
rected Billy to his Klosters apartment.

Elena, with Molly, swung by the Davos railroad station in her Mercedes and signaled her two cousins to
follow in the second BMW. They found Gary Russo
where, profoundly humiliated, he'd insisted upon being
left. He was pale, still badly shaken, but not yet in shock.
His right arm and left hand were clamped over com-
presses that Molly and Paul had hastily fashioned out of
articles of clothing. Elena's cousins helped him into the
Mercedes which, Elena in the rear seat and her cousin
Josef driving, departed at once for Zürich. The other
cousin, who, with a bow to Molly, introduced himself as
Willem Brugg and offered to see her safely to Klosters in
the BMW. As Willem bowed, his topcoat fell open and
she could see an Uzi slung outside his suit.

Arriving at the garage beneath his building, Bannerman left the car while the others waited. He checked
the garage for any other presence, then took the elevator to his apartment two floors up. He unlocked his door,
then rapped sharply on the elevator's metal wall and
sent it back down to the garage level. Billy pulled
Lurene from the car and was about to lift her onto his
shoulder when Lurene mumbled urgently to Carla,
communicating with her eyes that it would be more
decorous if she walked and that if she hadn't screamed
thus far she was not about to start now. Carla nodded to
Billy to let her stand but to leave the gag in place.

Quickly, they walked her into Paul's apartment and
sat her in the middle of his living room floor. Paul had
drawn the drapes. Carla walked into the bedroom,
where she gathered all pillows and blankets while Billy
moved all the upholstered furniture as close to Lurene
as possible.

She understood what they were doing. Soundproof-

ing. For an interrogation that could last the day and the
night. Now came Carla with the bathroom shower curtain which, Lurene cooperating, she spread on the floor
beneath her. Lurene mumbled again, this time shaking
her head irritably. Her eyes, aimed at Carla, said all this
is dumb. Take off the gag.

The buzzer sounded. Molly was let in. With barely a
glance at Lurene, she began making coffee and setting
out mugs while reporting on the status of Gary Russo.
Lurene rolled her eyes, then crossed them, all the while
nodding furiously at Carla.

"You mind?" Carla said to Paul.

He shook his head. She bent over Lurene and unfas-
tened the gag.

Lurene sat silently for a long moment, breathing
deeply, waiting for the moisture to return to her mouth.

"Don't suppose you have any bourbon around here,"
she said to Carla, finally.

Carla looked at Paul, who gestured toward the three
bottles of wine that had sat on the counter since he
came back from his marketing and found Susan gone.
Carla chose a Chablis and uncorked it. She poured a
glass and held it to Lurene's lips. Lurene nodded grate-
fully.

"How long's it been, Carla?" she asked.

"About ten years."

"I heard you retired. Settled down somewhere."

Carla glanced again at Paul but said nothing.

Lurene scanned the other faces. "Old Billy McHugh,
I'd know anywhere. And I heard you call the one Harold
stuck Doc. That'd be Doc Russo. Who's the pretty
lady?"

"That's Molly Farrell."

"Heard of you, too," she nodded respectfully, ruefully. "Professional courtesy's reached a sorry state
when the likes of us start killin' each other off." Then to
Carla, "Did you have to bust up my face, by the way?
You had me cold once I turned that corner not lookin'."

"You might have been armed," Carla shrugged. "I
wasn't."

That, Lurene thought, was like sayin' Dracula was
unarmed, but the point wasn't worth arguin'. Harold
was dead. She'd be with him soon enough. The only

question now was how easy or how hard they were
going to make it. Be grateful old Doc Russo got put out
of action. The way they tell it, he could make a stump
talk once he started stickin' and carvin'. The hard part
might be convincing these folks that she and Harold
knew as little as they did.

"Paul," she said, not looking at him, "are you who I
think you are?"

He didn't answer.

"You're Mama's Boy, aren't you?"

Still nothing.

"Is there a way in the world I can convince you that
Harold and me never once made that connection until I
saw Carla and Billy here?"

"Would it have made a difference?"

"Sure as heck would," she raised her eyebrows. "For
one thing we would never have let you see us. For
another, even if we took this job, which I'm not real sure
we would have, we would have charged triple our going
rate and we wouldn't have fooled with drugs. Harold
and me don't like 'em anyhow."

"Who hired you?"

"I truly want to answer that, Paul. Me and Harold
got an awful careless briefin' so I'm not feelin' real loyal
to the son of a bitch who left out all those details. I got a
suggestion."

Paul waited.

"Let me go home after this and I'll let out his air
myself. My word on it."

"Carla?"

"She'd keep her word. But no."

"Billy?"

"That's games. Don't play games."

"Molly?"

"Let's end this, Paul."

"I agree." He reached into his pocket and pulled out
the plastic glove containing the suppository. He tossed
it to Carla.

Lurene made a face. She knew what it meant. He
was making her an offer. There sure were worse ways to
die although she was gettin' damned tired of symbol-
ism. Still, given the choice, she'd take easy.

"The man I'd have got for you," she said, "is Oscar

Ortirez. He's a general down in La Paz. I swear they got more generals than bathtubs."

"He's connected with Elena?"

"Was. They go 'way back."

"And after Susan, you were to kill Lesko and Elena, in that order?"

"Yep. For half a million." Would have earned it, too. If they hadn't had to go back for a second shot at Susan. And they wouldn't have had to do that if Harold hadn't jammed the zipper on Susan's pants tryin' to get at her with that plug of cocaine. Poor Harold. Got a touch of arthritis, and he's just not used to workin' this kind of climate. Fingers aren't as nimble as they used to be.

"How am I involved?"

"You tell me."

"How is Palmer Reid involved?"

The eyebrows went up again. "If he is, Paul, we didn't know it. Me and Harold got out standards."

Molly touched his arm. "We've been busy back home. I haven't had a chance to bring you up to date. Whenever you're ready, you can call Reid's home number and ask him yourself."

Paul held her eyes. Anton had started to tell him. Now he knew why she went down to Chevy Chase.

"For now," Molly said, "why don't you get back to the hospital. We'll clean up here." She caught Billy's eye and, with a motion of her head, asked him to stay with Paul.

"I don't know. There's not much point. . . ."

"Paul," she tugged him toward the door, "get down to the damned hospital."

"Open wide now." Using a napkin, Carla held the suppository to Lurene Carmody's lips.

"Oh, Carla honey," she screwed her face in disgust. "You do know where that's been, don't you? At least bring over that jug so I can wash it down."

Carla obliged. Lurene pinched her nose and swallowed. She drained a tumbler of white wine and took a slab of cheese Carla found in the refrigerator. Not so bad, she thought. But damnationally unhygienic.

"Well," Carla, poured a glass for herself, Molly de-

clining, and sat down cross-legged with Lurene,
"what'll we talk about?"

"How 'bout last requests? Any chance you'd do me a
favor?"

"If I can."

"I don't guess my body or poor old Harold's will ever
turn up."

"Fair to say. Unless we send a piece of each down to
your friend, Ortirez."

"I could have done without hearin' that."

"Don't worry. Paul would think it's in bad taste.
What's your favor?"

"We have a lawyer in Lubbock, Texas. Name's
Wormwood, if you can believe it. Harold and me had kin
and the lawyer has a will plus instructions on what to do
if we turn up dead or missing. I wonder if you'd give
him a call to that effect."

"To say I killed you? You've got to be kidding."

"More like to say he won't be far behind if skimmin'
comes to gougin'. This ain't no no trick, Carla. That lawyer's apt to rob my grandchildren blind without someone around to put the fear of God to him."

Carla studied her, deciding the request was genuine.
"Wormwood, Lubbock. My pleasure, Lurene."

"That out of the way, you mind tellin' me how Paul
caught on it was me and Harold? I'd hate to think we
got set up."

"I don't know. Molly?"

Molly's back was to them. She was pouring coffee.
"You just had some bad luck," she said.

Carla brought the wine glass back to Lurene's lips.
"If you want to know the truth, I was afraid Paul would
think I did it. I didn't like him getting involved with an
outsider who . . . Lurene?"

Lurene had stiffened, her eyes wide and blinking.
"Ooo-eee," she sang. "I think I just had what they call a
rush." She waited for it to settle, then, "I know what you
mean, though. Common interests is what brought me
and Harold together and kept us together. Lord knows
in our line of work it's drainin' enough to keep a front
without having to do it in the bedroom as well."

"And to stay on your toes."

"For a fact," Lurene nodded. She was rocking now,

having trouble focusing. "Who else is still runnin' with Paul? Anyone I'd know?"

"Janet Herzog, John Waldo, seven or eight more. We all more or less settled down together."

"Hard to imagine Janet or John bein' housebroke, let alone settlin' down. But then of course there's Billy. First time I ever heard him talk, by the way." Lurene leaned back as she said this. Her eyes were batting. Carla watched her in silence for several minutes. Her breathing became shallow. Carla reached to pinch her leg. Lurene did not seem to feel it.

"She's on her way. Convulsions will start soon."

Molly sipped her coffee.

Carla looked toward the silence. "Anything wrong, Molly?"

"Not especially."

Carla turned back to Lurene, thoughtfully. "You know what's funny? Look at all the fluky little things that can end up killing you. If I hadn't been stopped when I followed that girl to Davos, Lurene and Harold would have spotted me for sure and they would have aborted. They'd still be alive, Gary wouldn't have been cut, and Paul and that girl would be up skiing right now."

" 'That girl' has a name. It's Susan."

"So it's Susan. What's bothering you?"

"Whether you like it or not, they could have been good for each other."

"For how long? You heard Lurene."

"It's none of your damned business for how long. Six months. Six years. I'd take it."

"The Carmody's had more like forty years. How does good-for-each-other get any better than that? They were two professionals who. . . ."

"Bullshit, Carla."

"Now what did I say?"

"They were shits, Carla. Two pieces of shit who would kill anyone at all for money."

"We were talking about their relationship. Personal standards are another subject."

"You were also saying how professional they were. I told Lurene she just had some bad luck. I lied, Carla. They made every possible mistake."

"Name one, besides not making sure she was dead and getting out fast."

Molly ticked them off. "They had no plan; they improvised. They go to lunch with Susan, they not only let her pay on a credit card, they left the receipt in her purse. They let Paul see them and get to know them on the train, so when he started wondering who Susan knew well enough to take to lunch over here, theirs were the first names he thought of. They didn't make sure she was dead. They let Paul sucker them into trying again. Then someone sounding like old Harold called to ask about her condition before he was even supposed to know she was there."

"They weren't so stupid," Carla said stubbornly. "Paul was just smarter."

Molly knew better. It was Lesko who was smarter. Paul had admitted it. He'd been pretty much in a fog just like anyone normal. She shook her head. "Too many years, Carla. Too many easy killings. Never able to talk from the heart to anyone except another killer. Look at you and Lurene. You're killing her, but she's chatting away with you like this is a pajama party."

Lurene's leg kicked out, convulsing. Carla reached to feel her throat. The arterial pulse was erratic. An eye was twitching but her face was otherwise composed. Content. "I'd settle for that many years," Carla said, putting down Lurene's wine glass. "Especially if at the end I could just go to sleep with a smile."

"That's all you want?"

"I could do with getting laid more often."

"And that's your idea of being happy."

"Okay, throw in a red Porsche."

Also an occasional Stanley Gelman, Carla thought, but she knew better than to say it. And maybe an occasional all-night fuck with Paul, now that he's worked up an appetite but, hopefully, lost his little Polish bonbon. Carla chose not to say that, either.

CHAPTER 26

The doctor with the Swiss-British accent stepped around Lesko and leaned across Susan. He held a pen-light over her eyes, moving it from side to side over each of them, then up and down.

"The nurse says you heard her speak?"

"I think so." Lesko wrung his hands helplessly. "I don't know. Maybe I imagined it."

"What words? Did she say your name?"

"No, it was . . ." he stopped himself. He was already feeling foolish for jumping up and yelling for the nurse.

"What words, Mr. Lesko?"

"Oh, shit," he answered. "I thought she said, 'Oh, shit.' "

The doctor smiled, more out of compassion than amusement. "Possibly only an expulsion of breath. With a dry mouth it could sound like this."

"She's not waking up?"

"She is," he said. "She might have already, then slept again. This is also possible. Waking up will be sporadic, as in the case of general anesthesia. However, I would not expect her first words to be an assessment of her situation."

"What's with the flashlight? How does she look?"

"Pupillary reaction is quite good. So is corneal reflex. Response to touch is also encouraging. From this I would say that catastrophic brain damage is unlikely. Beyond that, it is difficult to say."

"But you're saying there could still be aftereffects. Is she going to be normal or not?"

"I am hopeful, Mr. Lesko. We must both wait and see."

"Oh, shit."

Susan hated it when this happened.

It was like falling asleep with the TV on and not being able to wake up enough to turn it off.

It was worse.

It was like going to bed after eating Chinese food loaded with soy sauce and by four in the morning you're so thirsty you could die but you can't wake up enough to get a glass of water.

Her mouth, her nose, felt as if they were stuffed with cotton. She tried to remember where she'd been. What she'd eaten.

So many dreams. Skiing dreams. Sexy dreams. Tacky, but still sexy. Getting-murdered dreams. By Caroline and Ray, of all people. Fight dreams. Dreams with Uncle David. And he's dead. Isn't he? Wait a second.

Yes, he is. That must have been like one of daddy's dreams. Without the morning bagels.

Daddy?

You're here, aren't you? Little bright lights in my eyes. I can't see. But I hear you.

Wait a second. Where are we? I was in Switzerland with Paul. The skiing wasn't a dream. Daddy, what are you doing here? Did I get hurt?"

". . . I get hurt?"

"What?" Lesko's head jerked up. "What?"

"Daddy?"

"I'm here, sweetheart."

She felt his weight against the bed but he was hidden in a thick gray cloud.

"Daddy, how come. . . ? What happened?"

"It's okay, baby. Talk to me."

"Daddy, where's Paul?"

The BMW, its rear end still weighted with Harold Carmody's body, began its descent down the mountain road into Davos. Paul had the wheel. He'd barely spoken since they started.

"I'll be glad when we're home," Billy said, staring ahead.

Paul didn't answer. He took a slow, deep breath.

"We get to the hospital," Billy read his mind, part of it, "you let me handle her father. He comes at you again, I'll take him. It's not dignified, you rolling around the floor like that."

"It's my problem, Billy." He held up a hand to stay any objection. "Let's just try to get home without any more damage."

Billy thought that he meant the Doc. "You handled that real good, by the way."

Another breath. No answer.

"I know it was hard, shooting through your own guy. But we didn't have all day to stand around there. It's what me or Molly would have done. Lesko got there soon enough, he would have done it, too."

"I guess."

"You see his face? He would have done it, but he gets all shook when he sees someone else do it."

"He didn't just see that, Billy. He was seeing me with his daughter. He wants it to be over. It is. I can't expose her to anything like this again."

Not that she'd want to see him, either, he thought. Especially after her father tells her a few things.

"Maybe she won't care. Women marry cops. And soldiers. Even mob guys. Which brings up something I been meaning to tell you. Know what I'm going to do when I get home, it's okay with you?"

"What, Billy?"

"I'm going to see if Mrs. DiBiasi maybe wants to get married."

The BMW swerved.

"What do you think? You'd be best man."

"I, um . . . I don't know, Billy. Does she know anything about this?"

"She likes me enough, I think."

"Billy . . . even if you both . . ." Paul groped for the right words. Nothing came that was not a cliché. "It's an awfully big step. There's a lot more to marriage than. . . ."

"You mean sex? I know about sex."

"You do," Paul answered blankly.

"It's from hookers, mostly. But there was this one up in Hamburg who taught me what women like."

Paul was afraid to ask.

"She said I was too rough and not considerate. First I figured, what would a German know about considerate? But then I tried it on this Italian hooker and she liked me so much she fixed me dinner after."

"But not . . . nothing with Mrs. DiBiasi?"

"If I did, I don't think I'm supposed to say."

"You're absolutely right."

"Anyway, we didn't. Couple of times, though, she looked at me like the other Italian. And sometimes she puts her head on my lap when we're watching television."

"Billy," Paul tried not to smile, "you're living under the same roof now. Don't you think it might be a good idea to keep on the way you are and see how the relationship develops? Molly can give you any advice you need on. . . ."

"I don't want to talk to Molly about it."

"Why not? I thought you were very close."

"Yeah, but she thinks me and Mrs. DiBiasi are cute. I don't want to be cute."

Susan's vision still hadn't cleared. She was seeing everything through a milky film. And she was still dropping off to sleep every two minutes.

"Daddy?"

"Right here, sweetheart."

"You and Paul were fighting, weren't you. It wasn't a dream."

"He slipped. I helped him up. They use too much wax here."

"You were fighting. We saw you."

"Yeah, well . . . it was more of an accident. A misunderstanding."

"Did he win?" she asked drowsily. Then she abruptly smiled. "Uncle David said it would do you good to get your ass kicked for a change."

Lesko's head came up. The *we* in *we saw you* suddenly registered. "What are you talking about?"

"He said don't worry. You were just feeling parental."

"You saw Katz?" His voice dropped to a whisper. "What was he wearing?"

"What was he wearing?" Susan raised her head. "Daddy, it was just a dream."

"Yeah," he nodded slowly. "Yeah, I know."

Susan frowned as another memory came back to her. She pushed herself up on her elbows, her arms tugging at the IV tubes. Lesko reached to quiet her. "Caroline and Ray," she said, squinting at him. "That wasn't a dream. They grabbed me and. . . ."

"It's okay now, sweetheart." He eased her back to her pillow.

"Daddy, why? Was this. . . ?" She remembered Paul and that bread knife. "Was this about Paul?"

"Don't you worry. It's all okay."

"Why isn't he here? Did they hurt him, too?"

"Paul's fine. He went out looking for them. It's all under control."

"They were so . . . they must have been crazy," she said distantly.

"You just get better. We'll take care of them."

"Daddy, you shouldn't have let Paul go alone. You should have gone. Paul doesn't know about people like that. . . . Or does he?"

"I don't know, I. . . ." He saw movement at the glass partition. Bannerman. And the bartender. But now a woman from down the hall was running up to them waving a little piece of paper. They stopped and listened. They went back with her. "He's here now, Susan. I don't think he can stay long, but he's here."

Lesko stepped into the corridor outside Intensive Care and waited for them. He held up a hand as they approached. When Bannerman stopped, Lesko placed his fingertips against his chest.

"You don't want to do that," Billy moved toward him.

"It's all right, Billy," Paul said softly. "I heard she's conscious. How does she seem?"

"Mostly okay, no thanks to you," Lesko answered, though the Katz thing made him wonder. "What's with the woman? Caroline . . . Lurene, whatever?"

"You won't see her again. That's over."

"I want to know what she told you. And if she's dead I want to see the body."

"If that will please you. Right now I want to see Susan."

"Five minutes, Bannerman. That's long enough to say good-bye. I don't want you near her after today."

Billy leaned forward again. Bannerman eased him back. "As it happens, Lesko, I agree with you." He stepped around him.

"You know you're a jerk?" Billy glared at him. "You ought to learn who your friends are."

Lesko ignored him. He was watching through the partition. Bannerman leaning over her. Hugging her. Now touching her cheek. Come on. Get on with it.

"Helping you, we lost the Doc. He's dead now, too."

The Doc? Oh, yeah. The guy who got cut and his armpit chewed up. Elena took him to Zürich. He didn't look that badly hurt. Elena. Maybe he shouldn't have talked to her the way he did. She tried to help. She did help. It was just that he didn't want any of this shit, none of it, near Susan anymore. Maybe she'll come back down, he'll apologize. Maybe he'll write her a letter.

"Helping you," Billy stuck a hand on Lesko's chest as he'd seen Lesko do to Bannerman, "even your own friends got shot. You don't care about that, either?"

Lesko considered breaking his fingers. Except another fight would get him thrown out of here for good. . . . "Wait a minute. What?"

"The lady who drove you. When she drove back."

Lesko brushed the hand away. "What the hell are you talking about?" He suddenly felt ill. In his mind, he saw the woman who'd run after them in the corridor. She had a message. He saw how Bannerman looked, dead eyes like Billy's, when he came back up.

"The car they were in," Billy told him. "It got ambushed."

"Today?" Susan reached for the hem of his ski jacket, gripping it. "You have to go today?"

"There's a . . . whole set of problems back home. I have to, yes."

"Paul, what's going on?" she asked wearily, sadly. "What's happening here?"

"Well," he looked away, "your father and I are trying

to sort that out. By tomorrow, maybe, by the time you're a little stronger, he'll be able to tell you about it."

"Is he going to tell me who you are?"

Paul didn't answer.

"I keep trying to tell you I'm not stupid. You're saying good-bye, aren't you?"

"You weren't stupid. I was."

"Answer me. Are you saying good-bye?"

"I'm saying," he pried her hand free, gently, "that I will never expose you to anything like this again."

"You told me you loved me. Do you?"

"That was . . . selfish. It was a need."

"Do you or don't you?"

"Susan," he shifted uncomfortably, "if I say yes, you're going to tell me we can work the other things out, but there are some things. . . ."

"I was going to say that? Oh."

"I'm sorry. What were you. . . ? Oh, heck."

She took a long, deep breath, then let it out. "You haven't done this sort of thing very often, have you?"

"Um, no. I haven't."

"When you want to break off with a woman, you're supposed to come on like a rat. You don't say 'Oh, heck.' You say things like 'It's been a great ride, kid, but I'm getting off in Chicago.' Or something Yuppie like 'We're just not in sync, long-haul-wise.' That way I could decide you're an asshole and be glad to get rid of you."

He didn't want to smile. He turned away so she couldn't see it.

"Now that I think of it, though," she told him, "your line about it being a selfish need was pretty schmucky, too."

"I'm . . . ah . . . I'm glad you're starting to feel like your old self again."

"Paul? Who are you? There's no way you're a criminal. Was Caroline right? Are you a spy? Is that what all this is about?"

"Susan . . . I have to go." He backed away.

"Good-bye won't end this," she warned. "You're going to tell me."

"Talk to your father."

He closed the curtain partway so she couldn't watch him leave.

"Hold it." Lesko fell in step with Paul as he strode down the corridor. "What about Elena?"

"She's been shot. I don't know how badly." He kept walking. Billy had gone ahead for the car.

"Look, talk to me." He grabbed Bannerman's arm. "Where is she now?"

Paul turned to face him, his eyes inches away from Lesko's. "There are two dead," he hissed. "One was a friend of mine. The other was Elena's cousin, the one who came here to protect Susan. Mr. Lesko, I really don't have time for you right now."

"You're going to her? I'm going with you."

"You're staying with Susan. The killing isn't finished." He pulled the Belgian automatic from his hip and jammed it into Lesko's belt. "I'm sending Molly Farrell down here to spell you."

"I don't need any of your damned women. And don't you tell me what I'm going to. . . ." He didn't finish. Paul seized his lapels and slammed him backward against the corridor wall. Then he stepped back, eyes blazing, and waited.

Lesko made no move. His fists went into balls and he dropped to a crouch, but that much was reflex. Slowly, he straightened. Paul turned for the door.

"Bannerman," Lesko said huskily. "Wait. Wait a second."

"Now what?" Paul slowed.

"Okay. Sometimes I can be a jerk where my daughter is concerned. Not just with you. Always."

Paul waited.

"On top of that, I was a shit to Elena. I don't even know why, because I know inside she's a good lady. I'm ready to break your back for putting Susan in danger and a minute later I'm ready to leave here while I run to Elena. I don't know. I. . . ."

Paul's expression softened a shade. Still, he waited.

"It's okay to send Molly. I appreciate the thought. I'd appreciate also if you'd call me when you know something."

"You have a place to stay?"

Lesko shook his head.

"Use my place. Molly will give you the key and a car."

Lesko nodded thanks. "You see Elena, if you talk to her, tell her for me. . . ."

"Tell her yourself, Lesko." Paul walked briskly toward the street at the sound of Billy's horn.

The phone message, marked *Extremely Urgent*, had been left by Urs Brugg, who identified himself as Elena's uncle when Bannerman hastened to return the call. The introduction was unnecessary.

It had happened near the town of Lachen, forty kilometers south of Zürich. A van had overtaken the Mercedes driven by his nephew, Josef. Two men in the back of the van fired automatic weapons as it drew past. Josef was killed outright. Bannerman's man, Russo, seated behind the driver, was also killed outright. His niece, Elena, was hit twice and is now in surgery. One bullet pierced her left arm, which had been holding Russo. Another struck her high in the chest after passing through Russo. The van was then driven off, after an exchange of fire with another nephew, Willem, who had been following only two kilometers behind.

"My niece remained conscious throughout," Urs Brugg told him, "insisting that Mr. Bannerman at Davos Hospital be notified immediately. It is her impression, and that of my surviving nephew, that she was the primary target. Both gunmen concentrated their fire in her direction after hitting the driver."

"I see."

"She is alive because she was shielded by the body of the injured man, Russo. She asks me to assure you that such use of him was inadvertent."

"I understand," he said. "Mr. Brugg, can I help you in any way?"

"Can Mama's Boy find the men who did this?"

Bannerman remembered his words to Anton about Urs Brugg, deeply regretting them. "I'll do better than that, sir. You have my promise."

"Elena suggests that you do it from outside Switzerland. The police have identified Russo and will soon connect him with the rest of your people. They are likely to detain all of you regardless of my wishes. The Swiss police have little tolerance for assassins of any stripe."

"I have a flight in four hours. Can you steer them away from the airport?"

"I will do my best."

"Mr. Brugg, I did not get a chance to meet your niece. I regret that because she sounds like a very considerable woman."

"Yes. Yes, she is."

"I will be in touch, sir."

Paul and Billy returned directly to Klosters, where Paul told Molly and Carla about the ambush. He gave Carla no chance to brood about the death of Gary Russo. The trick was to move fast and keep moving. He sent her out to rent another car and to purchase an axe and keyhole saw at the local hardware store.

By the time she returned he had packed his bags and Susan's, including their skis, and wrapped Lurene Carmody's body in a mattress cover. With Carla waiting at the garage elevator, Billy carried Lurene to the trunk of the BMW, where she joined her husband Harold. The axe and saw were put in with them. The luggage was stacked on the rear seat and the ski bags on top.

Carla was instructed to take the first southbound train, carrying no luggage lest she be observed by the police, then make her way to Milan and book the first available flight home. Molly was to take the rented car to Davos and make sure that she or Lesko was with Susan at all times, and stay until she was told it was safe to leave.

Paul and Billy were on the road shortly before sunset. Billy insisted upon riding with the luggage, his window open and his silenced pistol ready in the event of a second ambush. Paul said it was a waste of heated air. Billy said it couldn't hurt.

An hour out of Klosters, by the shore of the Wallensee, Paul pulled off the autoroute and made his way to the lake's frozen surface. Leaving Billy on shore near a stand of pines, he walked fifty feet onto the ice, carrying the axe and saw. He hacked out a hole six inches in diameter, then cut out a two-foot disk with the saw. Fifty feet downstream, he hacked a smaller hole. He dropped the tools through it.

He returned to the BMW, where Billy had finished

stripping Harold's body of all identification. Paul took these, plus Lurene's effects and jewelry, to the smaller hole, and tamped them through. He turned to see Billy dragging Harold and Lurene across the ice to the larger hole. Harold went in headfirst. Lurene followed. Billy threw his gun after them.

Paul took the two-foot disk, inverted so it would freeze shut more quickly, and plugged the hole with it. Next he used his car key to scratch *kein verdammen fischen* in the ice, hopeful that it would induce the next morning's icefishermen to try another part of the lake. It all took twenty minutes.

They reached Zürich Airport with only thirty minutes to spare. Leaving Billy and their baggage at curbside, Paul drove the BMW to the parking lot where, after carefully wiping all surfaces, he locked and abandoned it.

He joined Billy, who was checking their baggage and securing boarding passes. Billy watched the clerk's face for any sign that she'd been alerted to watch for them. There was none. Just two more men with skis. Best way to remain inconspicuous at a Swiss airport in January. Their only remaining obstacle was passport control. The official at the glass Immigration booth examined their passports, then stared at each of them with what Paul took to be interest but not alarm. Nor did he bother checking their names against his stop list print-out or bulletins. The official's eyes flicked past his shoulder. Paul turned, his stomach tightening. But standing there, arms folded, touching a finger to his hat, was Willem Brugg.

From the departure lounge as final boarding was being called, Paul telephoned Anton Zivic, to alert him that they were coming. Zivic knew already.

"Molly called from Davos," Anton told him. "Urs Brugg called as well. I'll have security and transportation waiting. Have you spoken to Roger Clew? He's most anxious."

"I'll call him when I get there. Everything quiet otherwise?"

"Calm before the storm, I think."

"Anton, I had no business asking Molly to stay. Will

you call back and tell her to get out? I have to run for the plane."

"Urs Brugg has seen to that as well."

As the Swissair flight left the runway, a profound sadness, born partly of exhaustion, settled upon Paul. He tried not to think of Susan. And he berated himself for leaving Molly with her. He'd told himself he'd done it for Susan's protection, even that of her father. But that wasn't the reason. Carla would have been the better choice as an attack dog and Molly would be needed in Westport. He left her because he knew that she, unlike Carla, would talk to Susan. Tell her about him. In a way that would ease the hurt. And Susan would talk to her.

Mama's Boy. Always calm, cool, in control. Always the professional. Some professional.

He was asleep before the clouds blurred out the lights of Zürich.

At Kennedy Airport, passing through Customs without incident, he spotted John Waldo among the limo drivers and waiting relatives. Janet Herzog and her knitting bag were by the door. He did not acknowledge them. Billy hauled most of the bags to a stretch limousine waiting at the curb while Paul carried the others to a telephone. He had two calls to make.

"Mr. Brugg, it's Paul Bannerman. How is she?"

"Out of danger," Elena's uncle answered. "One bullet shattered her collarbone but missed the lung. She seems more concerned about the scar and how it will effect her choice of wardrobe."

"That's the best possible news, sir."

"Easy for you to say. You don't wear low-cut gowns."

Paul smiled, both at the joke and at the relief that it implied. "Sir, I made you a promise. Will you stay close to your phone this week?"

"I am in a wheelchair, Paul. I am always here."

"Sir, is Molly Farrell. . . ?"

"She is en route by way of Munich. The girl and the father are well guarded."

"Thank you. And for your help at the airport."

"I am confident that you will return the favor."

"I'm going to ask just one more. Can you arrange for the return of Doctor Russo's body? He ought to be buried where his friends are."

"Give me an address."

His next call was to Lesko. It was two in the morning there. He tried the Klosters apartment. Lesko answered on the fifth ring. Paul waited for Lesko's head to clear before he repeated the news of Elena's condition. Lesko was silent for a long moment. He asked where she was. Bannerman had neglected to ask the name of the hospital but he provided the number of her uncle.

"You're back in New York?"

"Yes."

"Don't you ever sleep?"

"I slept during the flight. How is . . . how is your daughter?"

"She's sleeping, too."

"Come on, Lesko. You know what I'm asking."

A long pause. "Yeah, Bannerman. I told her about you. But I laundered it a little."

"Why?"

A longer pause. "I don't know. I could still change my mind. Listen, you had two calls. One was from that Palmer Reid a few hours ago. I picked up, he thought he was talking to you. He starts off saying he just heard about the try on Elena, who he says he warned you about, and how it's a case of the chickens coming home to roost. He also warned you about me because I'm a crook, too, and he says by tomorrow he's going to have his hands on the guy who's behind all this so you should know who your friends are. You people say that a lot, don't you. Anyway, I couldn't get a word in edgewise."

Paul winced. "What did you say to him?"

"Go fuck yourself is what crossed my mind. But I said thank you and hung up. Guy's nice enough to call, what's not to be polite?"

"He had no idea?"

"I don't think so." Lesko's voice dropped. "It's him, isn't it? The bartender was right."

"We'll see. Who else called?"

"Guy named Roger Clew. From the airport."

"He's there? In Switzerland?"

"Yeah. I didn't tell him you weren't so he's on his way down. What's with him?"

"He's a good man. State Department. In fact, it's good he's coming. He'll be able to save you both any inconvenience with the Swiss authorities. Tell him I asked him to do that."

"What inconvenience? I didn't do any damage here. You didn't give me the chance."

"Is your name Dumbrowski?"

"Oh, yeah."

"When will the hospital release Susan?"

"They want her for a week. She wants out tomorrow."

Bannerman bit his lip. "Lesko, I'm about to do some damage over here as well. It's against people who have long arms. If Susan can travel, I'd like to have her where I can guarantee her safety. She can convalesce at the clinic. I promise I won't see her."

"This damage. I get a piece of it?"

"You might even get to push the button."

Lesko replaced the phone and returned to the couch where he'd been sleeping. He wouldn't use the bed. They'd used it.

Yeah, he'd told Susan about Bannerman. Some of it. Parts of it hurt her. Not so much because of what he was, but because he didn't tell her himself. And because his only interest in her, at least in the beginning, was to keep her from snooping around Westport.

He had to tell her they were killers. Probably all of them. Even this Molly, although Susan wouldn't buy it. Maybe they weren't criminals in the normal sense. Maybe you could even agree with some of what they've done and figure maybe the country needs people like them now and then. But, he told her, whatever face you wanted to put on them, it still came down to this. Paul and the rest of them can't live in a world with regular people and regular people can't live in their world, either.

So what does she say? She asks, "How is he different from you, daddy?" He says, "There's a difference, believe me. I told him to stay away from you and I'm telling you to stay away from him."

"Daddy?" She gives that look of hers. "You know I love you, right?"

"Yeah, so?"

"You and Paul Bannerman. You can both fuck off."

Lesko stretched out on the couch. He wanted to sleep because he wanted to dream. Which was a first. But the dreams weren't coming. Jet lag, maybe. Throws everything else out of whack. Why not dreams?

He didn't want to think about Bannerman anymore. Bannerman was still a prick, even if he was starting to show signs of being Lesko's kind of prick. What he wanted to do was talk to Katz. No matter how stupid it felt, he wanted to ask Katz flat out, was Katz a dumb dream or was he a ghost, after all. If he was just a dream, how come Susan saw him, too?

Probably a waste of time, though. Katz says "I don't know" to any question harder than where's the nearest toilet. So if he's a ghost he's the world's dumbest ghost, on top of being the worst dressed.

But he isn't. All it was, Susan for half her life was used to seeing him and Katz together. And he'd told her about his own dreams. Katz coming with the bagels. That's all it was.

The other dream Lesko wanted to have, although he'd hardly admit it even to himself, was that one with Elena. The one with her in his bed. He wanted that dream back, except without Loftus, Donovan and Katz hanging around. She didn't have to do anything or say anything. All she had to do was be there. Maybe they'd talk a little.

Thursday. Noon in Westport. A corner table at Mario's.

Paul and Anton had just returned from a two-hour visit with Robert Loftus. Filling in the pieces.

Loftus, his wife and children were being moved that day to Gary Russo's house. For the present, Doug Poole would move in with John Waldo who said, "He asks for an autograph, he's out on his ass."

"Loftus's face is a mess," said Paul, sitting. "Can it be restored?"

"Except for a few scars, he'll be more or less normal

within three months. Gary Russo would barely have left a mark. Too bad."

"We need our own doctor. We'll find someone else. How's his family doing?"

"The wife is terrified. Loftus told her more about us than is probably good for her. But she's even more afraid of Palmer Reid."

"We'll see if we can ease her mind." Paul opened his menu, then put it down. He raised a hand and began counting off with his fingers. "Seven . . . eight people dead so far. Plus two near-misses. All in one week. All for a mistake."

Anton nodded agreement. "One man's paranoia."

Paul looked at him. "I didn't mean Reid. The mistake was mine."

"If you're about to say that because you underestimated Palmer Reid. . . ."

"I didn't underestimate him, Anton. The man's capable of anything. I know you've wondered why I didn't finish him three years ago."

"I didn't wonder. I knew the reasons."

Paul sat back. "I don't think so."

"I knew because I know you," Anton told him. "The first is that you kill when you must, not when you like. That's what sets you apart from a Carla Benedict, for example."

"That's not it." He glanced at Billy who was back at the bar greeting customers. "I played games with him."

"Yes, you did," Anton leaned forward. "But it was a very good game."

Paul stared at him. "How long have you known?"

"That you allowed Reid to live, to keep probing us, in order to give us a common enemy? That you saw the need to focus the homicidal tendencies of a dozen violent people upon a distant bogeyman? So that they would behave as an interdependent unit and be less apt to randomly depopulate Westport? Is that your question?"

"My question was how long?"

"From the first day."

Paul kept staring. "You're a very wise man, Anton." Zivic shrugged.

"Very perceptive. Very smart. But happily there's a little corner left that still has some dumb in it."

"How so?"

"You just talked yourself into a full-time job."

Wednesday afternoon. Zürich. Misericordia Hospital.

Elena's eyes were closed. She had a sense that she was not alone. Another nurse. Another needle. Or worse, another policeman.

"Please go away," she said to the figure that filled the doorway to her room. She said it in German.

"Yeah, well . . ." Lesko got the meaning. "I just wanted to drop this off. I wasn't going to stay or anything."

"Lesko?" She blinked to clear her vision. He was holding a very large poinsettia plant in both hands.

"I wanted red roses," he said uncomfortably. He looked around the room for a place to put it. Her bedside table was too small, the window sill too narrow. "The guy at the florist said you don't give red roses here except to. . . ." He didn't finish.

Fiancés. Lovers. Lesko would not have known that. "Please come in. The plant is lovely."

Lesko approached the bed. He still had no idea what to do with the pot. He shifted it under his left arm. The petals tickled his face.

"I would have come sooner. . . ." He stopped. His face fell at the sight of the cast that covered her left arm from the shoulder. There was a metal contraption that looked like a carpentry clamp. At each end was a long screw that must have been drilled into the bone. Her right shoulder was heavily padded. Some kind of strap held both shoulders in an unnaturally backward arch. "I mean . . . I would have been here waiting. But you know I had to wait for Susan."

"I know," she said gently. "I hear Susan is much better."

"Much better. Yeah."

"There may be hallucinations. Some nightmares. Some memory loss. But it will soon pass."

"Yeah," he nodded. "It's what the doctor said." He gestured feebly toward her injuries. "If I knew, last time

I saw you . . . if I could have taken the bullets myself . . ." again he stopped. Dumb things to say.

"I know. Come sit by me, Lesko. And please put
down that plant."

"Where?"

"On the floor. They'll bring a stand for it."

He put it in the corner, dropping to one knee as he
straightened the foil wrapping that he'd crushed. He
was stalling. All the way up he'd thought about what
he'd say. He could remember none of it.

"You probably got friends coming. Relatives. Why
don't I just. . . ?" He edged toward the door.

"They were here. They've left."

"Oh."

"When are you going back home?"

"I think tomorrow."

"Will you ever come back?"

"What, like to Switzerland? I don't know. I don't
travel that much."

"Would you consider coming here as my guest? Under happier circumstances, it is quite a beautiful country."

"Well, yeah . . . I mean . . . that would be nice."

"But would you come?"

"Look, you had a lot of painkillers and things. I want
you to just take it easy and get better."

Her chest heaved in a sigh. It made her wince. She
looked away. "I see."

"Wait a minute. You see what?"

"I am foolish to think that you can forget."

"Bullsh . . . oh, Christ." Lesko felt his throat getting thick and his eyes becoming moist. He turned away
from her. "Excuse me."

She said nothing.

"I know . . . you saved Susan's life. Except for you,
Bannerman wouldn't have known to check for that . . .
thing. We're square. That wipes it clean."

"Fair enough," she whispered.

"I come over here, I'd just embarrass you."

"Embarrass me?" She looked up.

"You're so pretty and I'm. . . ." He was still looking
at the wall. "You ever come to New York, though,
there's this place I go. Gallagher's."

"I know Gallagher's. Fifty-Second Street. Big beef-steaks."

"No kidding?"

"But I cannot go. I cannot go to the United States."

"Oh. Yeah." Federal warrants. "Listen," he said, "not that I can promise anything, but what if I could square that, too?"

"Lesko," she patted the edge of her bed. "Come sit with me. Sit here."

He obeyed, but slowly. She shifted to make room. Still, he would do little more than lean against it for fear that he might jar her.

She took his hand. "Such a rough man," she said. "Such a tender man. I know that you like me. You say it in every possible way except, 'I like you, Elena.'"

Her fingers were cool. The touch made him shiver. "Look. What I said to you in Davos. The way I acted. . . ."

"I understood. Not at that moment, but later."

"I'm really sorry."

They sat for a while, not speaking.

"Come to Switzerland, Lesko," she said at last. "Leave the ghosts behind."

"What do you mean? Move here?"

"An indefinite visit, if you prefer."

It's the painkillers, he thought. This is crazy. She's rich, she's got so much class, and he's just a nasty ex-cop who scares most of the people he meets. Katz'll have a field day with this one. "Listen," he kept his voice soft, "What I'll do . . . a couple of weeks and I'll call you. Let's see how you feel then."

"I suppose that is wise. As long as you promise."

"We'll talk. See how you're making out. One way or the other, if you still want, maybe we'll at least have dinner."

"Here? In Zürich?"

"We'll see what happens." Lesko glanced at his watch, taking care not to dislodge her hand. "Listen . . . you better get some sleep."

"You'll stay a while? Sit with me?"

"I'll sit with you."

CHAPTER 27

Westport. Late afternoon, the next day.

Roger Clew pushed through the door of Luxury Travel Limited, glared exasperatedly at Paul, then scanned the office layout for a place where they could talk. He saw the conference room, walked to it past desks and consoles, sat down in it and waited. Paul followed, closing the door behind him.

"You realize I've been to Europe and back looking for you? I haven't showered in two days?"

"Ships in the night," he shrugged. "Where did you put the Leskos?" They had, he knew, come back with Roger, who smuggled them to Frankfurt and then aboard an Air Force plane complete with armed airmen and an Air Force neurologist.

"I just delivered them to Greenfield Hill. The girl's shaky but okay. Lesko says he going to call some New York cops he knows to come up and guard her. His message to you is, 'Nothing personal, he won't tell them much, don't try to prevent it.'"

Paul felt a headache coming on.

"The Swiss have a message for you, too. Theirs is, 'You even think about going back after who ever hit Russo and the Lesko girl and they'll lock you up for ten years.'"

"I'm not going after anyone. Not in Europe."

"You already got them?"

"Come spring," he said, "the ones who attacked Susan might turn up. Or they might not. The Russo ambush was by two other men and a driver. I'm not interested in them. They're just shooters. Europe's full of them."

"You figure it's Reid? Behind all this, I mean?"

"There is that chance."

Clew moved his chair closer, "That's what I want to talk to you about. We're about to force Reid out. He's nuts. If the secretary had his way we'd haul him off to a rubber room at St. Elizabeth's, but the man's got all those files. We don't want you doing anything until we have our hands on them."

"For that you chased me to Europe?"

"There's more. Him out of the way, we want you to come back to work."

"No chance, Roger."

"I'm not talking like before. Not exactly."

"Then what, exactly?"

"You have a hell of a team here, Paul. It's an awful lot of talent not to be put to good use."

"What do you consider good use?"

Clew brushed aside the question. "And I don't have to tell you there are lots of shitty people in the world. The worst of them always seem to be just out of reach. Just the other day I heard the attorney general telling the secretary how frustrating that is."

"And you want us to start killing them off."

Clew raised his brow. "I didn't say that. Barton Fuller certainly didn't say that."

"I'll try to pay closer attention. What did you say?"

"That *sometimes . . . occasionally . . .* we could use specialized help that is not answerable to any civil hierarchy. That maybe sometimes your people could use a little exercise."

"When that happens I'll take them jogging." Paul pushed back from the table, disappointment plain on his face. "Someone probably said that to Palmer Reid once. Haven't you learned anything from it? Anyway, I'm not interested."

"Whatever you say, Paul." Roger folded his arms.

Bannerman looked at him suspiciously. Nothing's that easy.

"As long as I'm here," Clew asked innocently, "and we're through talking, you mind if I just think out loud for a couple of minutes?"

"Be my guest."

"The room isn't bugged, is it?"

"*Now* you're asking?"

"You see why I need professional help. Quiet now. Let me think." Roger Clew leaned back in his chair and began talking to the ashtray. "In addition to his own group, Mama's Boy is now wired into the Brugg family of Zürich, which incidentally has a lot of juice over there, and to the Betancourt family of La Paz which— who knows?—could also be useful. He's also wired into Raymond the Terrible Lesko, who reminds me of Billy McHugh except he knows more words. This is the basis of a considerable network."

"I barely know Lesko. I hardly know the Bruggs at all."

"I'm not talking to you." He focused again on the ashtray. "Now, Bannerman doesn't want to be back on the payroll, for which I don't blame him because he's retired and besides he's independently wealthy having ripped off a few million of federal funds and a few prime pieces of Westport real estate. But we're not even going to mention that. No hard feelings."

"Roger. . . ."

"We're going to stay friends. We're going to stay in touch. And if I ever have anything bothering me, I'm going to come see him, cry on his shoulder, maybe just mail him a newspaper clipping. And likewise, any time Paul Bannerman needs a favor, boy, I'm going to be right there."

"I'm glad to hear that."

"The trouble is, Lesko reminds me that it's hard to have a network with the Bruggs as long as there's a federal Jane Doe out on Urs Brugg's niece and another one from New York as a material witness to some old shooting. So by Monday, there won't be."

"That's very thoughtful of you, Roger."

"What are friends for?"

"Maybe I owe you one."

"I'll try to think of something."

"One, Roger. Just one."

Late Friday afternoon. Westport.

Raymond Lesko had not been in Westport thirty-six

hours before his patience began to wear thin. Four New York policemen with assorted weaponry had joined him at Greenfield Hills. They fell to discussing tactics, agreeing with Lesko that it made no sense to let an enemy pick the time and place for an assault.

In the halls and washrooms of Greenfield Hills, Lesko had also picked up two rumors. One was that Palmer Reid had holed up in his Maryland home, where he had established an elaborate command center. The house was heavily guarded, the streets patrolled. The second was that the same long-distance shooter who was such a show-off on Lesko's street in Queens had been dispatched to a street in Chevy Chase, Maryland.

With these rumors in tow, he confronted Paul Bannerman at Luxury Travel Limited.

"Your guy's down there to hit him, right? You promised me a piece of it."

"He's just there to observe," Paul raised a calming hand. "As for Reid holing up in his house, he often does that when he's nervous. It's good that he's nervous."

"So? What happens now?"

Until Roger Clew's visit, the answer to that had been clear. Roger's friendship was valuable. That of the Secretary of State even more so. Still. . . . "I haven't decided," Paul told him.

"What's to decide? You know he's behind what happened to Susan and Elena."

"I don't know it. I think it."

"But you got no question about Donovan."

"None at all."

"What more do you want?" Lesko threw up his hands. "We just sit until he drops a bomb on Westport with a signed confession taped to it?"

Paul shook his head. "He won't move yet. Not until he's sure where you are and where Loftus is. He's probably not even sure where I am."

"Bannerman," Lesko slid into a chair. "I want this guy. I'll work with you or I'll do it alone. But I want him dead."

Paul said nothing. He seemed to sigh.

"Hey, look," Lesko leaned toward him. "The last few days I heard a lot about Mama's Boy. All of a sudden you're not acting much like the guy I heard about. Does

Susan, by chance, have anything to do with the change?"

A small shrug.

"I hear you're thinking about hanging them up, is that true?"

"More or less."

"Well, if you think backing off is suddenly going to make you better son-in-law material. . . ."

"I don't."

"Then what do you say you get off your ass?"

"You're a smooth talker, Lesko." Bannerman reached for a pad and scribbled an address. "That's where Reid lives. You want to go after him, be my guest."

"You don't think I will?"

"I think you might. You won't last a day."

Lesko reddened. He stood up, paced the office, struggling to control his temper. "You got a better idea, let's hear it."

Bannerman looked at him coldly. "I don't need you, Lesko. Try to understand that. If my problem was in some New York back alley, you'd be the first one I'd call. You're tough and straight-ahead. Reid is devious, cowardly and probably crazy. But he'll dance rings around you."

Lesko knew he was right.

This wasn't his element. That's what angered him as much as anything. Even Katz knew it. He said so this morning. Somehow he knew about New York cops. *What do you think this is, Lesko? Fort Apache? You think a bunch of Feds are going to come in here blasting? Hoping the locals won't notice the bodies all over their lawns? That's your trouble, Lesko. For ten years I try to teach you finesse but all you know is blasting.*

Lesko bit his lip. His expression softened. "I have to be in on this," he said earnestly. "Are you going to make me say please?"

Bannerman studied him for a long moment. Then he reached for his phone.

"Who are you calling?"

"I'm going to find out what Reid is up to."

"How do you do that?"

"I'm going to ask him." He motioned Lesko to the extension at one end of his office sofa.

"Paul . . . is that you? . . . Where are you calling from?"

Bannerman could almost see, in the pauses, Reid urgently gesturing for someone on his end to listen in. Probably Whitlow. Reid had already tried to call him twice.

"I'm in Westport, Palmer." Paul kept his voice downcast and preoccupied. "I'm sorry I didn't get back to you. I've been spending most of my time at Susan's bedside."

"How is she, Paul?"

"Somewhat better, but she's sleeping a great deal. She has no memory of what happened to her. I'm concerned about brain damage." He saw Lesko's eyebrows go up and he touched a finger to his lips. "Thank you for the flowers, by the way. That was very thoughtful."

"The least I could do." A long pause. Bannerman thought he heard whispering. "Paul, I called your Klosters apartment two days ago. Did I talk to you or someone pretending to be you?"

"It was probably Lesko, his daughter gave him a key so he could collect her things. Do you know where he is, by the way?"

"He's not with you?"

"Hardly. He blames me for what happened to the girl. He's threatened to kill me for it. At the moment, he's probably in Switzerland with Elena. You were right about him, Palmer. He's a bad one."

Another silence. Paul knew that Reid would be trying to remember what he said to Lesko. And now his mind would be sorting out all manner of promising new equations.

"Paul," he asked finally, "did you find the people who assaulted Susan?"

"They sank right out of sight."

"Probably shot your man Russo as well, don't you think?"

"It wouldn't surprise me. But they're only hired hands. I want who sent them. Tell me who that is."

"Paul, I've just about pieced it together. But I'm

reluctant to tell you until I have evidence that will stand up in a court of law. Moral certainty is not enough."

"Tell me, Palmer."

"You don't go off half-cocked? It's vital that we work together, because I'm afraid we have a conspiracy that reaches to a very high level."

"We need each other. I won't make a move without you."

"I'm pleased, Paul. Very pleased. We never should have been adversaries, you and I. We should have been. . . ."

"Palmer . . . who?"

"It shames me to admit that I've been fooled. Betrayed. By two of my own people. One is Robert Loftus. The other is Douglas Poole. Both have vanished. Loftus's family has vanished as well. It wouldn't surprise me if they've all been murdered, possibly by Lesko, more likely by the man behind all this."

"I want his name."

"I hope you're sitting down, Paul." Reid dropped his voice. "Because the ringleader is none other than our Secretary of State. Your friend, Roger Clew, is involved as well, though I'm trying to believe that he's an unwitting dupe."

"Barton Fuller?" Paul hushed. "And Roger?"

"I'm sorry, Paul."

"Palmer, I just can't believe it."

"You will when you see the evidence. Not enough for a jury, perhaps, but. . . ."

"The bastards."

"We'll have to move quickly, Paul. And well coordinated. Your people and mine."

"Palmer, I'm going to call an immediate council meeting here. Then in, say, two hours, let's have a conference call. Will you be there?"

"Depend on it."

"The bastards."

Lesko put down his extension. He stared disbelievingly at Paul Bannerman. "What the hell was all that?" he asked.

"I think he wants me to kill the Secretary of State."

"I heard. You believe any of that shit?"

"No."

"Why'd you tell him you and me are on the outs?"

"Because now Palmer will look for you, show you evidence that I ordered the attacks on Susan and Elena to frame him, and recruit you to kill me. You wanted a way to get at Reid, there's your opening. All you have to do is go home and wait for your doorbell to ring."

Lesko pondered this. "Let me ask you something."

"Shoot."

"You two do this all the time? In that whole conversation, neither one of you said a word that was true."

"Except that I know when I'm lying and when I'm not. I'm not sure Reid knows the difference."

"You don't get tired of that?"

"Yes, I do."

"You made up your mind?"

"Yes. If Anton agrees."

"I'm in, right?"

"If you do it my way. And you do as you're told."

"You get first shot. You miss, it's my turn."

"Fair enough. Be here in two hours."

"What happens then?"

"Happy hour."

General Oscar Ortirez glowered darkly from a leather wing chair in the study of Palmer Reid's Maryland home. The unaccustomed collar beneath his pinstriped suit was too tight and Reid's overheated house was making him perspire heavily.

"I would like something to drink," he said to Charles Whitlow, who sat in a chair at the other end of Reid's memento-covered desk and who never seemed to perspire at all.

"The bar is there, sir," Whitlow pointed. "I'm afraid we'll have to do our own fetching today." The household staff had been furloughed for the duration.

"It is too much to ask of an assistant?" Ortirez said the word drippingly. "It would at least be a task you can manage."

Whitlow rolled his eyes. The man hadn't stopped carping about the failed attempt on Elena since he arrived. What's more, he hadn't showered. And the man stank of garlic.

It was hardly Whitlow's fault, as he'd explained to Palmer Reid. Who would have expected a person like Russo to have shielded her with his body? And Ortirez is a fine one to talk. The Carmody's are the very best, he says. They never miss because they never quit, he says. Well, why is the girl still alive, then? And where are they, then?

"Enough bickering." Palmer Reid rapped smartly on his desk. He glanced at his watch. Ten more minutes. He was supremely please with himself. Justifiably so. What a masterstroke. Before this weekend is out, Barton Fuller may well be a dead man and Paul Bannerman will be either dead or hunted by every government in the western world. Hunted by Lesko as well if it comes to that. And Bannerman's people will be in the field. Scattered. Vulnerable. Bannerman will want proof, of course, and he'll get it. Whitlow has already accessed over twelve hours of Barton Fuller's speeches. Give one good editor half a day and he'll produce tapes proving that Fuller is anything from a KGB mole to a child molester.

"Mr. Brugg? This is Paul Bannerman speaking."

"How are you, Paul?"

"I'm well, sir. How is Elena?"

"Recovering nicely. A visit by your Mr. Lesko has greatly lifted her spirits. He must be a man of great charm."

"Um . . . yes, sir." Paul looked at the ceiling. "Mr. Brugg, I'm about to place a call to the man who caused your niece to be shot. Please stay on the line but say nothing at all. Just listen."

"Am I to hear a confession?"

"It will be more in the nature of a repentance, sir."

"I will listen."

Reid's only regret was that Fuller would never actually know who gave him his comeuppance. Strange, the way things work out. Whitlow's plan seems to have worked out in spite of all the bungling. The idea of the attack on the girl was not only to break the linkage if it existed or to keep it from connecting if it didn't. It was also designed to distract Bannerman, shatter his concentration, make him vulnerable, perhaps even give him cause to sue for peace. And, yes, to punish him.

The death of Elena was to shatter that linkage once and for all. If that attempt succeeded it would have been a simple matter to point the finger of guilt at Bannerman. He saw the cocaine in Susan Lesko's mouth, presumed Elena to be its source, and in a rage ordered her execution. Then the Bruggs would be hunting him as well. No corner of Europe could hide him.

But this, in its way, was even better.

Reid glared at Ortirez, who was was now at the bar, petulantly pouring his own drink while offering none to himself or Whitlow. Disgusting person. He'll never know how close he came to being sacrificed to Bannerman had not Bannerman called practically begging for help. He'll be sacrificed in any case. It's merely a question of to whom and for what.

Paul's outer office, which he'd closed for the day, was filled. Lesko entered to see what he presumed to be Bannerman's entire group except for the shooter in Maryland. He recognized fewer than half. Nearly all were wearing headphones. Molly Farrell was seated at a call director. In one hand she held an instrument that had switches and meters on it with bright LED readouts. It looked homemade.

Billy McHugh was at another cleared-off desk, setting out champagne bottles and a row of plastic glasses. Paul was at the desk nearest Molly Farrell and sitting next to him was Robert Loftus, his jaw wired, the rest of his face a wreck. Loftus waved when he saw him. Bannerman looked up from his phone and motioned Lesko over.

"I told you," Bannerman said, "that I might let you push the button but the vote was to give Loftus the honor. You've been bumped."

Lesko looked at him blankly. "What the hell is all this?"

"I told you. Happy hour."

"Happy hour," he repeated. "

"Go find a chair."

Ask a silly question. . . .

*　*　*

Reid stared at his watch. The minute hand moved slowly toward six and then past it. Twenty seconds. Thirty seconds. Thirty. Stay composed, he told himself. You're in control. Act the part.

It rang.

Reid forced a smile. He motioned Charles Whitlow to the other extension. Whitlow scurried to the chair nearest it, a notepad on his lap, knees close together.

Four rings.

On a signal from Reid, they picked up their receivers together.

At the call director in Paul's office, Molly peered at a meter on the instrument she held as Reid answered. The drop in amperage was twice what it should have been. She held up two fingers for Bannerman to see.

"Palmer? It's Paul. Is your phone secure?"

"It is. I had it swept an hour ago."

Molly looked toward her audience, her expression smug. Most of them broke into mimed applause. Lesko scratched his head.

"Are we alone, Palmer?"

Reid considered telling the truth. After all, it was Bannerman who had proposed a conference call. But the lie came out by reflex. "We're alone at this end."

"At this end," Paul told him, "we have Molly Farrell monitoring for any cut-ins by listening devices. We also have Anton Zivic, who shares our outrage at all that has happened. You don't object, do you?"

Reid was less than comfortable but he could not object. He did not like working with women, even if they were only technicians, and was appalled to discover that the communist Zivic appeared to have risen to a position of high trust. "Not at all," he said.

As Reid spoke he saw Whitlow waving vigorously and pointing toward Ortirez. Ortirez had found a third extension and was quietly lifting the receiver. Reid gestured angrily. Ortirez ignored him.

Molly's hand waved. Her meter showed a sudden drop of 15 milliamperes. The two fingers she'd been holding aloft changed to three.

Paul looked at her questioningly. He'd presumed the second person to be Charles Whitlow, but who was the third? Molly shrugged. He hesitated for a beat, then shrugged in return.

"Palmer, our whole group is assembled here." He looked to his left where every available chair and desk top held one or more of his agents. All were seated except Billy, who'd begun pouring champagne. Janet Herzog had brought her knitting. Carla Benedict used the time to balance her checkbook, but her eyes were shining. All the rest were eagerly attentive except John Waldo, who'd had a sour expression since he arrived and was idly leafing through a Bermuda brochure. "Everyone wanted to be part of this," Bannerman told Reid.

"I understand . . . of course. . . ." Reid's voice trailed off. Paul could almost read his thoughts. Reid was envisioning them, all together, trapped in one place, lightly armed at best. However, he would be thinking, his day would come. Bannerman would soon divide his forces, send them out, and they would be caught in the act of murdering the Secretary of State. After that, there would be a slaughter. Even if some stayed behind, no one would hide them, protect them. Public outrage would be such that. . . .

"Palmer," Paul interrupted his reverie, "As long as we're being truthful with each other . . ."

"At long last, Paul."

". . . I should tell you that Anton was pretty sure you were behind all this a few days ago. That was before we knew it's been Barton Fuller working with the cocaine traffickers all along. So he sent Molly Farrell down to your house."

A long silence. "To what purpose, Paul?"

"You'll see in a minute. I'm afraid I wasn't entirely truthful about Lesko, either. He's here listening in."

"Paul. . . ."

"Bear with me, please." Bannerman could hear an exchange of frantic whispers. "Palmer, I have one more person here who especially wants to say something to you. I believe it's in the nature of a resignation."

He waved Molly forward. Watching her meter, she kept three fingers aloft to show that all three were still listening. She placed the instrument before Loftus, guiding his hand to a plastic switch. Now Paul raised his arm. The arms of all the others, except a confused Raymond Lesko and a sulking John Waldo, rose up in unison. Loftus took the phone.

"Hello, Mr. Reid," he slurred through wired teeth.

A gasp through the line. "Robert?"

"I won't tie up the phone. I just wanted to say good-bye."

"Robert! What are you. . . ?"

"Good-bye, Mr. Reid."

Paul's arm came down. The others fell in unison. Loftus hit the switch.

A sharp snapping sound. Then, instantly, a duller *thukk*, like an archer's arrow hitting a target pad. A chorus of bird-like squawks, each at a different pitch. A telephone clattered against a desk top. A glass smashed against a hard surface. Now there were the sounds of furniture toppling over and of bodies thumping against a thickly carpeted floor.

Silence now. No sound at all. Loftus stared at the machine grimly. Lesko, his eyes wide and disbelieving, clung to his earpiece. Molly listened for a few seconds more, then broke the connection.

In the silence, Anton rose to his feet.

He walked over to the waiting champagne and picked up two glasses. Billy passed out others. Anton handed one to Molly Farrell and raised the other.

"To Molly," he said. To Molly who had once demonstrated to him, in a wooden phone booth in Rome, that she was a woman to be taken seriously.

"To Molly," they answered.

Lesko, his headphone still at his ear, his mouth open, said, "What the hell . . . was that what I think it was?"

"I believe," came the voice of Urs Brugg, "it was a promise being kept. Paul?"

"Yes, Mr. Brugg."

"You will come visit me one day?"

"I'd like that, sir. First chance I get."

"Mr. Lesko?"

"Yeah. Yes, Mr. Brugg."

"You especially. I think we should talk."

"Well, you see, I hardly ever get over to. . . ."

"I gather your horizons have broadened considerably in recent days. Come see me, Mr. Lesko."

"I have some things to work out. But maybe. Yeah."
Molly broke that connection as well.

John Waldo, who in his mind saw Palmer Reid's life-less body, eyes wide, blood from both ears, and two more like him—whoever they were—darts in their brains, messing up the rug, would rather have seen a simple hole in his forehead. That's the trouble with the world, he thought. All this high-tech shit. You lose the personal touch.

"And you," he jabbed at Billy's arm. "You keep saying you don't like games."

"Who said that?"

"You do. As long as I've known you."

"Yeah, well," Billy refilled Waldo's glass, "you gotta grow with the times."

EPILOGUE

Palmer Reid's obituary appeared in Sunday's edition of *The New York Times.* An outstanding career. One of the original Cold War warriors. Served his nation under seven presidents. Died suddenly. Cerebral hemorrhage. Alone at home. Working at his desk.

The funeral service was held three days later. Roger Clew witnessed the lowering of his casket, then was immediately flown to Connecticut. He appeared at Paul's office. Paul led him to the soundproofed conference room.

The Secretary, Clew told him, was furious. The act was insane. It could well cost Paul every friend he had in Washington. What would happen if the wrong person got his hands on Palmer Reid's files?

"How do you know I don't have them?" Paul asked.

He didn't. Nor did he much care who did, if they existed at all. The question was for the benefit of the wire that his old friend might just possibly be wearing. Wire or no, it had its effect. Roger gazed longingly in the direction of Paul's liquor cabinet. Paul opened it and poured two scotches.

"Okay," Clew appeared to surrender. "What's done is done. I won't say we're not relieved in some ways. Still. . . ."

"The paper said he died alone." Paul handed him his glass.

"If he didn't," Clew curled his lip, "would you mind telling me how you managed to get Whitlow and a Bolivian general in the same room with Reid and then

get all three to pick up separate booby-trapped telephones? That was neatly done, Paul. Even for you."

Bannerman said nothing. He had assumed one of the
eavesdroppers to be Whitlow, but had not dared hope
that the other might be the man who, according to
Lesko and Elena, had sent the Carmodys after Susan.
Both bodies, obviously, had been quietly removed along
with all physical evidence that they'd ever been there.
They would, he imagined, be kept in cold storage until
more convenient and unrelated deaths could be arranged for each of them. In any case, Paul was not
inclined to correct Clew's assumption that no part of
the massacre had been left to chance.

"Roger," he asked, "why did you come here?"

Clew sipped his scotch. "To chew you out. And then
to tell you we covered for you." He leveled his eyes on
Paul. "And to say that you now owe us one hell of a
favor."

"Roger . . ." Bannerman stared at him thoughtfully.

"Yo."

"All this we and us business. Palmer used to talk like
that, too. Whatever went wrong with him, you want to
try very hard not to catch it."

Roger Clew started to speak, but he saw the look in
his old friend's eyes.

"Cheers," said Paul. He lifted his glass.

On the following day, Anton met with Robert Loftus
and Doug Poole. Poole had asked to stay permanently.
Anton, gently but firmly, said no. Roger Clew would see
that Poole could return to his job without prejudice.
Loftus, however, could remain until reconstructive surgery, already arranged by Anton, could be completed.
His wife and children, however, would have to return to
their lives. Roger Clew had also guaranteed their safety.

Lesko stayed in Westport those four days, waiting for
the fallout that never came, watching over Susan as the
predicted aftereffects of her cocaine overdose faded
into nothing worse than lightheadedness and nightmares. On the fourth day he sent his cop friends homes
with thanks. He spent the fifth day teaching Billy Mc-

Hugh to shoot pool and helping him paint his landlady's kitchen.

On the sixth day, Susan, her own face nearly healed, announced that she was going home. Lesko, carrying her suitcase and ski bag, took her to New York City by train and saw her safely to her Manhattan apartment. He asked if he might stay the night. She said she needed time alone. Lesko took a cab to his Queens apartment.

Susan, on the morning of that sixth day, had considered calling Allie Gregory. She needed a friend. Someone she could talk to. But there was so little she could tell Allie. A part of her was afraid that if she began talking at all, she wouldn't stop. Worse, still another part was afraid that if she did, Allie would not be surprised. That Allie, or more likely her husband Tom, was also a part of this . . . thing . . . in Westport. So far, she hadn't met anyone here who wasn't. She went home.

But three days later she was back. She took the train to Westport, crossed the tracks to Mario's sat down and ordered lunch. She came again the next day. And the next. And the next.

It was early afternoon during the third and final week of her vacation time. The lunch crowd at Mario's had thinned. Susan entered, waved hello to Billy McHugh, and took a small table by the front window. Billy caught Molly Farrell's eye and gestured with his head. Molly picked up a menu and walked to Susan's table. She pulled out a chair and sat.

"Susan. This is getting a little dumb," Molly said, not unkindly.

"I know it is," she nodded.

"Why don't you just go over to his office and get it over with?"

"He knows I'm here, doesn't he?"

"Except for today, yes."

"I keep hoping he'll come and have this out. If I go over there I'll get mad, or say something stupid, or God forbid I'll start crying in front of his travel agents. I do better in restaurants."

"Speaking of which, what can I get you?"

"Just a salad, I guess." She took a bread stick from the basket and bit off an end. "Can I ask you something personal, Molly?"

"Sure."

"How do you stay like you are? I mean, with everything you've done."

Molly looked into her eyes. She did not see a reporter there. Only a hurt young girl trying to understand people like them. "You grew up with policemen," she answered. "Some get better, some get worse. We're not all that different."

"And like policemen, you're only comfortable with your own kind?"

"As a rule, that's true. Sad, sometimes. But true."

"And you've never seen an exception?"

"A few. But I've seen some real disasters."

"Molly," Susan touched her hand, "I would just love to be able to turn off what I feel and walk away from this. My father's trying to do the same thing. I don't know if you noticed, but he's in love with a woman who, two years ago, he'd have happily sent to prison."

"I could see it," Molly nodded. "He's struggling with it, just as you are."

"And like Paul is?"

"I think so."

"Then why doesn't he have the guts to come and talk it through? Damn it, I'm going to keep coming here until he does or until I lose so much respect for him that I don't care whether he comes or not."

Molly rose to her feet. "What kind of salad?"

"Hello, Susan."

She'd seen him come in. He stopped first for a few words with Billy. She kept her eyes on her plate, which she'd barely touched. Now that he was here, standing over her table, all the words that she had imagined saying to him were gone. There was nothing. Except that she was getting mad.

"You're a real pain in the ass, you know that, Bannerman?"

"Um. . . ." He placed a tentative hand on the empty chair. "That's basically what Molly said." Also that if he didn't come over of his own accord, she'd get Billy to drag him over. "May I sit down?"

"If you like."

"Have you had lunch?" He looked at the salad.

"No, and I don't want to dance, either. Sit down."

Paul obeyed. He, too, on his way over, had thought about what he'd say. And what she'd say. So far, Susan was not following the script. "Susan," he said carefully, "can we start by trying to be friends?"

"I hate that word." Bannerman glanced toward Billy as if for help. Billy turned his back.

"I have an idea," he said. "Why don't you start? The way this is going, I'll never get any of the good lines."

"Okay," she folded her arms and sat back. "I'm writing an exposé for the *New York Post*. All about you and Westport."

"Come on, now."

"That's a good line? I'm talking a can't-miss Pulitzer and you give me dialog like that?"

Billy approached the table, to Paul's considerable relief. He set down two glasses of wine. "That's the good stuff," he said to Susan. "Yours is on the house. His isn't."

"Thank you, Billy."

"Also I'm bringing two bacon cheeseburgers, medium rare. A salad's no kind of lunch in the winter." He raised a finger to Susan. "Don't argue."

"That's very sweet, Billy," she smiled.

Paul gave him an I'll-get-you-for-this look, then stared at his place mat until Billy left. "Susan," he spread his hands, "I know that you're not going to write about us. Why are you even talking about that?"

"I'm a woman scorned. I'm allowed to get nasty."

"I didn't scorn you. Didn't your father explain why. . . ?"

"Listen," she said evenly. "I've been explained to up, down and sideways. My father says a nice girl like me doesn't belong with killers, but he couldn't explain why I belong with him. Molly likes us together but she's afraid I think you're Robin Hood. Carla says a candy-ass like me would only be a distraction who would mope and moan every time you're ten minutes late for dinner, and I'm probably not even a good lay."

"Carla said that?"

"I read between the lines."

Molly had replaced Billy at the bar while he went to grill the cheeseburgers. She was leaning on her elbows, watching, enjoying Paul's discomfort. He glowered at her. Glad you're having a nice time.

But this was only making it harder. They'd have their cheeseburgers, the meal would end and, as empty and aching as it made him feel, he would have to make Susan understand. Maybe if he told her how he'd tapped her phone for four months. Or that he'd used her as bait in Davos. Her father was supposed to have told her these things but he hadn't.

Or maybe if he went into detail about the little office party they'd held two weeks ago. Would she still think Molly was such a good egg if she'd seen her kill three people with the flip of a switch? And then see all of them drinking champagne afterward?

Not that he'd wanted to do it quite that way. The cheering section was Carla's idea. The champagne, surprisingly, Billy's. They all had a right, he supposed, to be in on handing the final bill to a man who'd done his best to kill most of them at one time or another. Her own father would have happily thrown the switch. But toying with Reid, prolonging it, was essentially childish, not to say unprofessional. Susan would have been sickened.

Now Susan has convinced herself that he and her father are the same. She knows, at some level, about the things her father has done but there was always a distance between herself and those acts. Between them, Susan and Paul, there would not be that distance. True, he was backing away, handing it over to Anton. But he was still Mama's Boy. He could back away just so far. Roger Clew knew that. He seemed to be betting on it.

"I hear," Susan glanced toward Molly, "that Uncle Billy's going to marry his landlady."

"That's . . . a long way off. They have what I'd call an understanding."

"Do I go see her and tell her to run for her life? I mean, Billy may not be a walking disaster like Calamity Carla, but I bet he can get rough when he has to."

"Billy is, um, different." Paul wished he hadn't even touched that one.

"Anyway, I've made a decision."

"Am I going to hate hearing this?"

"I'm going to shoot somebody tonight."

Paul closed one eye.

"Then one more every week until I get used to it."

"Every week," he repeated blankly.

"Until you say, 'Hey, maybe this kid's my kind of woman.' And then you'll take me on the ski trip that you still owe me, don't forget; and after that I'll dump you and let you sit outside my building five nights straight before *maybe* I let you come crawling back, you creep."

Paul looked skyward. "It must be in the genes."

"And don't you forget it."

"You're really going to shoot someone tonight?"

"Someone with six kids and a sick wife."

"Maybe I should stop you. Maybe I shouldn't let you out of my sight tonight."

"There's always tomorrow."

"Maybe before then we can take a walk. Down along the beach. We'll talk."

"About how it can't work?"

"About how to keep your father from beating up on me when he hears we're even thinking about it."

"Thinking about it can't hurt."

"No, maybe it can't."

"Maybe. . . ." She saw Billy coming with two platters. "Maybe we can reach what you call an understanding."

"A day at a time?"

"I want my damned ski trip."

"After that, I mean."

Four in the morning. Lesko didn't even have to open his eyes. He heard Katz in the kitchen. He heard the paper bag with bagels or Danish. And he heard Elena, snoring softly beside him. He'd been waiting for this. Lesko eased his face off the pillow as Katz entered the room.

"Where the hell you been?" he hissed.

Katz jerked a thumb toward the kitchen. *"Looking for a clean cup,"* he said innocently.

Katz had not come since on the airplane to Switzerland. He had thought about Katz, argued with him, even been insulted by him like about the cops in Westport. But that was all daytime. All in his head. *"Last time I saw you was on the plane, you got all out of joint about Elena. Then next thing I know you're bothering*

Susan when she's in that hospital. Anyway, where you been?"

"I don't know. I forget."

"I could have figured."

"They why'd you ask?".

Lesko jabbed a finger at him. *"You know why you don't know? It's because you're not real. If someone's not dreaming about you, there isn't any you."*

Katz looked down at his hands and body. He lifted one shoe and looked at that. *"I'm real,"* he said, his voice small.

"You're not real because you're dead."

"You really get your jollies out of saying that, don't you, Lesko? Anyway, so what? I'm here, right?"

"The point is I don't want you here. I don't want you talking to Susan anymore and I sure as hell don't want you walking in on me and Elena." Lesko gestured toward her sleeping body. Katz followed his eyes.

"What are you talking about?" Katz asked.

Lesko looked again at Elena's form. Something was wrong. It was too small, even for her. He reached to touch her. She was gone. Only some bunched-up blankets.

"You were dreaming it, weren't you?" Katz's expression was smug.

Lesko didn't answer. Absently, sadly, he stroked the bedding smooth.

"I got news for you, Lesko. Dreaming is about the only way you'll ever get her in the sack because you're such a nasty son of a bitch."

Lesko tried to think. Yeah. Katz was right. She was still in that hospital. Starting therapy. He had called once but he hung up before they put him through.

She'd asked him to call. Even to come over. Maybe she meant it. Except she was all drugged up at the time. She probably doesn't even remember.

"And let me ask you something else," Katz said gleefully. *"How come you dream about her and she's real but when you dream about me I'm not real?"*

"Because when I get up to punch your face in, you're going to be gone, that's why."

"You think that doesn't come in handy?"

Lesko let his body sag. *"Look, David. . . ."*

"You missed me, didn't you?" Katz said more softly.

"No."

"Because I'm all you got."

"Bullshit."

"You know sooner or later Susan's going back with Bannerman. And you know nothing's ever going to happen with Elena, because you're such a schmuck with women. I'm all you got."

"I'd kill myself."

"Hey, yeah," Katz brightened. *"Then you and me could. . . ."*

"I changed my mind."

"Lesko?"

"What?"

"What's so bad about this?" The voice became small again. *"Talking to yourself is better?"*

"What's bad is it's crazy, David. It makes me worry if I'm crazy, too."

"For a while there you were talking to me like always. Asking me what I thought about things."

"See what I mean?" Lesko drew up his knees. *"David, I'm getting up now."*

"I . . . I got prune Danish today." The voice was more distant. *"You like them, right?"*

"Now I'm pulling back the covers."

"I'm not mad at Elena anymore." It was fading.

"Good."

Good.

Lesko sat on the edge of his bed in the dark. And the chill. And the quiet. No sound but the hum of trucks on Queens Boulevard. A loneliness settled over him like a wet fog.

Maybe Katz was right. Maybe he was better than nothing. And he was probably right about Susan and Bannerman. And Elena. Goddamned David. If he's going to hang around he could at least be a little encouraging sometimes.

Elena.

Yeah. Sure he's right.

The closest he'll ever come to being in bed with her already came. In her hospital room. Sitting on the edge. All the while holding this dumb Christmas plant. Which he gives her in January. Very suave, Lesko.

"Such a rough man," she said then. *"Such a tender man. Come to Switzerland, Lesko. There are no ghosts here."*

He didn't make that up. She said it. Even if she forgot, he could always call her up and say, listen, I was in the neighborhood because your uncle asked me to visit and I wondered maybe we could. . . .

Who's he kidding?

"Lesko." Katz's voice. Yelling from the kitchen. *"For Christ's sake. Go for it, already. Pick up the damned phone and call her."*

"Yeah. She'd love that, you jerk. Hearing my voice at four o'clock in the morning."

"Schmuck! What time is it there?"

"Oh yeah." Lesko looked at the clock. Ten after four here. Ten after ten there. Maybe four in the morning has its. . . .

"Go on. I have to dial it for you?"

"Hey. What's with you all of a sudden?"

"I hate it when you mope. It's boring. Besides, this I gotta hear."

No ghosts there, she said.

Who says she's wrong?

Lesko reached for the phone.

DON'T MISS
THESE CURRENT
Bantam Bestsellers

☐ 27597	**THE BONFIRE OF THE VANITIES** Tom Wolfe	$5.95
☐ 27456	**TIME AND TIDE** Thomas Fleming	$4.95
☐ 27510	**THE BUTCHER'S THEATER** Jonathan Kellerman	$4.95
☐ 27800	**THE ICARUS AGENDA** Robert Ludlum	$5.95
☐ 27891	**PEOPLE LIKE US** Dominick Dunne	$4.95
☐ 27953	**TO BE THE BEST** Barbara Taylor Bradford	$5.95
☐ 26807	**THE BEET QUEEN** Louise Edrich	$4.50
☐ 26808	**LOVE MEDICINE** Louise Edrich	$4.50
☐ 26554	**HOLD THE DREAM** Barbara Taylor Bradford	$4.95
☐ 26253	**VOICE OF THE HEART** Barbara Taylor Bradford	$4.95
☐ 26322	**THE BOURNE SUPREMACY** Robert Ludlum	$4.95
☐ 26888	**THE PRINCE OF TIDES** Pat Conroy	$4.95
☐ 26892	**THE GREAT SANTINI** Pat Conroy	$4.95
☐ 26574	**SACRED SINS** Nora Roberts	$3.95
☐ 27018	**DESTINY** Sally Beauman	$4.95
☐ 27032	**FIRST BORN** Doris Mortman	$4.95
☐ 27458	**NEW MEXICO—WAGONS WEST #22** Dana Fuller Ross	$4.50
☐ 27248	**'TIL THE REAL THING COMES ALONG** Iris Rainer Dart	$4.50

Prices and availability subject to change without notice.

Buy them at your local bookstore or use this page to order.

- -